OPERATION SHADOW BOX

JENNIFER HAYNIE

To those who mourn the loss of a loved one or their fallen state.

Blessed are those who mourn, for they will be comforted.
—Matthew 5:4 (NIV)

A Word from the Author

As *Operation Shadow Box* went into production, my cousin, Whitney Ball, lost her battle to metastatic breast cancer on August 17, 2015. Whitney was much more than a cousin to me. She was my mentor, my friend, a woman who loved God and followed hard after Him. I also have her to thank for introducing me to my husband.

When I received the news, I wept. Now, as I sit here the night after her memorial service with tears streaming down my face, I've come to realize one thing. I'm broken. I am at the ends of myself. I am at a place where God will take me and rebuild me based upon the hope of eternal life found in Christ.

As you read this novel, you will find themes of brokenness in it. Sometimes God puts us in those hard places to call us back to Him. Other times, He breaks us because He wants to build us into an instrument that will continue His kingdom-building activities.

As you read this, I don't know where you are. Maybe you're at a place where you think you're on top of the world with everything before you. If so, count your blessings for each day you have. Maybe you're struggling just a little. Not enough to trust God with your concerns but enough to think that no problem is too big for you. I plead with you to lay your worries at the foot of the cross. Or maybe you're like me, feeling that brokenness deep within you that the only way to handle it is by fixing your gaze upon the cross of Jesus. If you're in that last situation, don't lose hope. God has heard those strangled cries, those pleas. He will lift up your head. That, I can promise.

Whitney, thank you for all that you taught me not only by the way that you lived but by the way that you passed from this life into eternal life with Christ Jesus. This one's for you, my dear cousin.

Jennifer Haynie
August 30, 2015

SHADOW BOX TEAM

Victor Chavez — Former Secret Service agent, commander of Shadow Box

Suleiman al-Ibrahim — former Hezbollah, sniper and observer of Shadow Box

Fiona Mercedes — Former Army and private contractor pilot, now pilot of Shadow Box

Sana Jain — Former Olympic gymnast, ninja, and reformed cat burglar, breaking-and-entering specialist of Shadow Box

Shelly Wise — Computer scientist, computer-and-security-system specialist of Shadow Box

Butch "Cajun Man" Addison — Ex-Special Forces sergeant, escape-and-evasion specialist, ordnance specialist, and mechanic for Shadow Box

Diana Kasem — Former Army, cardiothoracic surgeon, doctor for Shadow Box

Skylar James — Former CIA agent, procurement officer for Shadow Box

Her glance worried Victor since the angle of Rachel's face told him she checked her cell phone.

Again.

From his position at the back of the stage close to the First Daughter, the subtle motion from the front corner stage right caught his eye like the light of a laser pointer. Annoyance flashed through him. Work took precedence over family concerns. He'd told her that, had told everyone as they'd laid out the plan for protecting Maggie McCall, daughter of the president. He bit back his concerns and focused on the crowd of educators sitting in the ballroom of the downtown Raleigh hotel.

No worries there.

The Secret Service had screened everyone.

No potential threats existed.

Maggie's words rang clearly and confidently through the ballroom. "Thank you again for recognizing my continued desire to see to it that every girl in the Middle East can read and write. The *mullahs* and others may disagree and issue *fatwas*, but knowing my colleagues have faith in me boosts my courage and helps me to continue this fight. Thank you again, and good night."

She turned and winked at Victor.

He ignored it as he murmured into his wrist microphone, "The Professor is on the move."

Now he could get her off the stage, into the hallway, and safely into the SUV. Then they could all go home after calling it a good night's work.

He touched her back.

They stepped through the black curtains and descended the short flight of stairs.

Mike and Dex, the two Secret Service agents who had stood stage left, joined them, as did Rachel.

"Form up." Victor moved to the left of Maggie.

Rachel took point as they created a tight diamond around her.

He nodded at the two agents from the Raleigh Secret Service office who stood in the hallway. "Professor on egress. Have the SUV standing by."

"Roger that. SUV waiting," Charlie, the agent on driving duty, replied through Victor's wire worm.

Victor glanced at Rachel.

The cold glow of her cell phone's screen flickered and died.

Annoyance flared to anger.

He shifted to the point of the diamond, forcing her to the right as he clutched her arm. Victor drew her so close that his lips almost touched her ear as he murmured, "When we get back to the house, we're going to have a little talk about your distraction."

His fiancée smiled weakly at him. "I'm sorry."

"Don't be sorry. Do your job." He released her as they turned left into the corridor that would take them to the egress at the southern side of the building. Their steps echoed on concrete floors and walls painted a glossy white. Only his sunglasses kept the glare from blinding him. From somewhere overhead, a flickering fluorescent light hummed.

"Almost to the egress," Victor reported.

"I'm waiting." Charlie's voice filled his ear.

Ahead of them, only the metal door with a crash bar remained as their final obstacle between them and the safety of the SUV.

Victor shoved it open. He stepped into chilly night air clammy with a settling fog.

Mike and Dex followed with Maggie.

No Chevy Suburban awaited them.

Confused, Victor stopped and demanded, "Charlie, where are you?"

"I'm at the northeastern side of the building like you said."

"What?" Shock rooted him to the spot. He glanced at Rachel, who held the door.

"Rachel said you needed a new egress point." Charlie infuriated him with his calm reporting.

"I didn't tell…" Victor's gaze swung to the blonde.

She refused to meet his gaze.

He grimaced. "Never mind. We'll sort it out later. We need you at the original egress point as planned."

"It might be a few. We're kind of stuck with people coming out."

"Get unstuck. We'll be waiting inside the doors. Shout when you're close."

Victor turned.

Rachel let go of it.

"The door!"

She lunged for it. Her fingers barely brushed the handle.

It thumped closed.

Victor grabbed it and yanked.

Locked.

Like he'd ordered when they'd put together the security plan for that night.

Dampness coated his cheeks. He shivered as the early April chill penetrated his suit. "Something doesn't feel right. Tighten up, everyone."

His breath quickened. He checked the empty parking lot across the street.

No one stood beside any of the cars.

Victor glanced at Dex. The agent's eyes scanned the roofline of the convention center across the street. They widened. He opened his mouth to shout.

A hole appeared on his forehead. He collapsed as a gunshot split the stillness.

Maggie cried out.

Another shot echoed.

The bullet slammed into Mike's chest. He gasped. A second one ripped through his throat. His scream turned into a gurgle. He tumbled to the concrete and lay still.

"Go!" Victor shoved Rachel and Maggie away from the door.

They ran west down the street toward the corner. Another bullet chipped concrete near Victor's feet. The window of a Toyota Camry shattered.

Victor skidded to a stop and drew his Sig Sauer. He focused on the roof of the convention center.

Did he see two forms lurking there?

He fired toward them.

As if to punish him, a bullet whistled past his left ear and punctured the lamppost.

Rachel touched him on the small of his back near where his comms unit rested. "Someone's coming."

She jerked her head in the direction of the convention center.

Heart hammering, Victor took Maggie's hand and ran. "Professor under fire. Professor under fire. Need immediate assist. Southwest corner of the hotel."

Nothing.

No reassuring reply that someone had heard him and was on the way.

Then came the sound.

Footsteps.

He looked over his shoulder and sucked in a breath. Six human forms cleared the low fence surrounding the parking lot with ease. They moved at a slow, graceful trot, like a wolf pack on the hunt.

A metallic taste filled Victor's mouth. His hand tightened around Maggie's. "This way. Let's go!"

The trio ran across the street and along the southern side of the convention center.

Thanks to the cold, misty Tuesday evening, no one milled about, no one to call the cops, no one to help.

His pulse skittered upward. His jaw tightened. "Go! Cross the street."

The cadence of footsteps behind them increased.

A bullet pinged off the hood of the car next to them. Maggie flinched and yelped. Another one blew out a newspaper stand.

He steered them away from the shots.

"There!" Beside him, Rachel drew in a noisy breath. "The amphitheater. Maybe we can lose them."

"What?"

"What choice do we have?"

"We could go—"

Bullets chipped the sidewalk next to the turn that would have taken them toward others and safety. Concrete fragments stung Victor's cheek.

Maggie whimpered.

"Maggie?" Victor didn't relinquish his grip.

"I'm okay." Her words trembled. "She's right."

"It's our only choice." Rachel's voice shook.

Victor fought the panic that threatened to engulf him. "If the gate's open."

They bolted across the asphalt, narrowly avoiding getting hit by a car.

Victor desperately called in their position. Again, no one responded. "Rach, see if you can't reach HQ."

"I can't."

"Try again." He grabbed one of the gates and rattled it.

Locked.

"Nothing." Rachel's voice pitched upward. "They must have gotten comms at the source."

Victor risked a glance toward the street.

The human wolf pack loped across.

"Down farther." Once again, Victor grabbed Maggie and darted to the next gate. "Try that one."

Rachel grabbed it. On soundless hinges, it swung open.

"Go!"

They ducked inside, and he slammed the gate. Victor pointed to the open lawn. "This way."

"What?" Rachel's question barely registered.

Jennifer Haynie

"To another gate. Get our six." At a run, he led them down the central aisle and toward the stage.

Metal rattling on metal told him their pursuers had scaled the fence with ease. A chuckle reached them.

He stared over his shoulder. One stayed behind, and the rest re-engaged their targets.

"This way." He pulled Maggie to the left where there was a break in the seats. Soft snuffling told him Rachel kept pace with them.

He swallowed hard as he turned. Four of the men split into two pairs and slipped into the darkness surrounding the outbuildings. The fifth melted into the shadows.

Victor raised his gun. His hands shook. His breath came in short gasps.

Before them, the tunnel used by the bands that played at the theater yawned deep and dark. An idea struck him. "Maggie, do you have your cell on you?"

"Y—yeah."

"Call this number." He rattled it off. "Rob should answer. Tell him to meet us at the amphitheater tunnel entrance to the convention center."

"Vic…" Rachel hesitated as Maggie punched in the number and began speaking.

"It's our only option." He herded them to the entrance.

Concrete loomed overhead, blocking them from any ambient light.

Victor shoved Maggie behind him so the glow from her phone wouldn't reveal their position. "Rach, take the left."

She obeyed.

The scraping of boots grew louder.

One pair of pursuers approached from the right, the other from the left.

They slowed as if uncertain where their prey had gone.

Victor stilled. He aimed at the sounds to the right. His finger tightened on the trigger.

He hesitated.

To fire would reveal their position, which would entrap them.

Uncertainty made the muzzle shake.

"They said they'll be there in two minutes." Maggie's whisper sounded almost like a gunshot to his ears.

Two minutes would be too late.

The click of someone pulling back the hammer on a gun reached him.

His grip on the Sig Sauer tightened.

Then it dawned on him. The pairs approached from different directions. But the fifth man? Had he—

Pain exploded in Victor's shoulder.

His gun fell from his paralyzed hand. He sank to his knees, his other hand clutching his shoulder.

"No!" Rachel's cry reached him.

"Maggie…" he wheezed. He winced.

His good hand came away bloody.

Oh, no.

He moaned.

"Well, well, well, if it isn't the great Maggie McCall."

Victor froze at the statement in a finely accented deep voice. Instant recognition flashed through his mind. He blurted, "Mak…Makmoud Hidari. *Q—Quds.*"

"So sorry about the wound, Agent Chavez."

Victor started.

"Why so surprised?" The man stepped into the sickly yellow glow emanating from a streetlight near the tunnel's entrance. "Of course I know you. Just as it seems that you know me. And you, Agent Marina, your gun on the ground, please. Hands on your head. Don't move, Dr. McCall. Drop the phone. Now."

The women laid gun and phone on the ground.

"Perfect. Just where I want you. Now step away." The man gestured to Rachel.

"No!" Rachel shook her head.

Victor got one foot underneath himself and tried to rise.

"You stay where you are, Agent Chavez. I'll ask you one more time, Agent Marina. Step away from Dr. McCall."

"I—I—I won't." Rachel's body and voice trembled.

"Rach, don't do it," Victor pleaded.

"Now, Agent Marina."

Suddenly, Rachel squared her shoulders. Her chin lifted. The tremors ceased. "No. I won't."

The man locked gazes with her for a long moment. He shouted an order in another language.

A gun report, louder than any pistol, echoed across the steel and concrete of downtown Raleigh.

Rachel collapsed onto her side. She moaned and rolled onto her back.

Victor began crawling toward her. "Rachel!"

The stain on her shirt, at first the size of a marigold bloom, quickly blossomed to that of a sunflower. Her chest heaved. She reached toward him.

"No, no!" He grasped her hand.

Her mouth worked. Pink foam trickled down her cheek.

So did the tears.

Lungs hit. Victor's short-circuiting mind made that connection. *Bleeding out. Probably heart.*

A deep red puddle began spreading across the ground from underneath her.

"No, Rachel, no! No!"

"I—I'm…" Her grip on him tightened. "I'm…sorry."

She stilled, her eyes open. Her limp hand slid from his.

New agony tore at his spirit. "Rachel! No!"

"Oh, yes, Agent Chavez." Makmoud had stepped a little closer. "She died gallantly, did she not? In the line of duty is what they'll say. A fitting ending to a good life."

"I'm going to…" Now it felt like an elephant stood on Victor's chest. He wheezed. "I'm going to…"

He crumpled to the ground.

"To what? Find me? Kill me? Pity you won't live long enough to do so." Makmoud smiled and turned his attention to the shadows. "Dr. McCall, it is time for you to come with us."

He took another step closer.

Victor suddenly felt the hard outline of Rachel's gun pressing against his side.

From somewhere in the darkness of the tunnel, a small sob from Maggie reached him.

"You have nothing to fear, Dr. McCall. We'll take good care of you." Makmoud laughed. "You'll even make the news."

Victor's fingers gripped the Sig Sauer. He shifted, the slight movement burning a hot line of agony to his brain.

From somewhere far away, sirens wailed, growing louder with each passing.

"You're going to come with us. You've always wanted to lead by example, and now you will." Another stride brought the *Quds* agent to within twenty feet.

Without hesitation, Victor brought the gun up and fired.

The shot, meant to kill, made contact.

Makmoud cried out and gripped his neck. He didn't collapse, only shouted something in a language that didn't register in Victor's faltering mind. He turned and fled.

Now fire consumed Victor's entire body. The gun clattered to the ground.

"Vic, don't you dare pass out." Maggie's voice echoed in his ears. Her hand gripped his. "Don't you pass out on me."

"Rach…"

The rattle of metal on metal reached him. Light flooded across the tunnel's entrance. A male voice shouted, "Vic!"

He forced open his eyes. "Rob?"

"In the flesh. We've got you. Just hang on."

Footsteps rushed toward him.

Then Maggie and her reassuring hold were gone. He heard her voice and her weeping from somewhere nearby.

"Rachel. She's…she's…"

"She's gone. I'm sorry." Rob now leaned over him. "You hold on, you hear? Don't you die on me."

"I'm…too stubborn to quit." Suddenly, Victor couldn't breathe. His vision tunneled.

He passed out.

1

August 2013

Victor couldn't find Staci. Not in the midst of the craziness of the Hollywood nightclub. Like some sort of sea monster, the dance floor pulsed and writhed with people. Lasers and flashing lights nearly drove him mad as the music pounded through the earplugs he wore. The smoke emanating from the machines next to the lights made him hack. He sucked down a sip of Coke and climbed onto one of the chairs lining the wall.

Great. No Staci Logan, washed-up movie starlet. What was it with him? He'd gone from protecting the First Daughter to guarding…her. He scowled.

A movement caught his eye. A blonde with hot pink highlights slipped through a beaded curtain into a hallway.

He hopped from the chair and pushed his way onto the dance floor.

It reminded him of what it might feel like to be in a crowd of raucous zombies going to an all-you-can-eat human buffet. The music penetrated his skull and increased to a frenetic pace. A guy slammed into him. Victor staggered and nudged him away. As a woman threw her arms in the air, her hand slapped him across the face. Her pal laughed and turned. Her stiletto heel almost drilled through his hiking boot.

"Sorry." She giggled and lifted a glass of bright green cocktail to her lips.

Victor winced and limped as the pain faded. Once in the hallway, his breath quickened. Where had Staci's friend gone?

He crept onward. Only black lights lit the way before him. More bead curtains separated private rooms. He lifted one. The male half of a couple making out on a couch raised his head.

"Wrong room ," Victor muttered as he let the curtain drop.

Then he smelled it.

Hookah smoke.

Victor grimaced. He hated hookah smoke with a passion.

As he progressed down the hallway, it grew stronger until his eyes began watering, then his nose. He shoved the beaded curtain aside and stepped into the room.

A group of several people sat on the floor around a hookah that bubbled with water. He instantly recognized most of them. A minor Saudi prince and known playboy. A young man who'd had one big movie before succumbing to drugs. Staci's pink-highlighted friend who'd spent a stint in rehab by the age of sixteen. And others, most of them with stars rapidly fading as they over-indulged in the life money could buy.

Then he saw Staci.

She sucked on the pipe and sighed as a blissful smile tipped her lips upward. As if she noticed him for the first time, she grinned. "Vic! Hey. Come and try some."

"Pass, thanks." His eyes narrowed. "Stace, it's two and time to go."

"No, it's not."

"Your curfew is three."

The group began giggling as if he'd said the funniest thing in the world.

Anger nipped at Victor. He stepped to his client and hauled her to her feet.

"Hey!"

"Sorry, Stace. Time to pack your toys and come with me. Say goodbye."

"I'll see everyone tomorrow." She waggled her fingers at the group.

Victor gripped her arm and led her down the hall, along the perimeter of the dance floor, and into the hot, airless night. Even outside, the music reached him. His gaze swept the long line of people huddled behind the velvet ropes as they waited to get in.

No threats.

At least none he could see.

His eyes never ceasing their scan, he stopped at the valet's stand and handed the young man his ticket.

Staci leaned against him and coughed.

"Hookah smoke's bad for you, you know."

"Says who?" She reeked.

"Me. And it stinks to high heaven." Victor sneezed.

"What are you, my mother?"

"Just a concerned bodyguard."

A silver Cadillac Escalade pulled up.

He handed the valet a fifty from Staci's money and helped her into the front seat.

As they pulled onto the street and headed toward The Ten, she turned on the satellite radio and hit a button. Another throbbing dance tune filled the interior.

The headache that had begun in the nightclub increased. "Can we have something different?"

He pressed another one.

A soothing Garth Brooks ballad reached him, and he lowered the volume so he didn't have to scream to talk.

"Yuck!"

"What?"

"That song. It's awful."

"Country music's some of the best stuff out there. At least the older tunes are." He got up to speed on the interstate that would take them to the Pacific Coast Highway and Staci's home in Malibu. "You know, three months ago, the judge was very generous with your parole terms. I had to pull you out so you don't violate them."

"No one would know."

"Says who?" He nodded toward her left leg where a small unit had been attached around her ankle. "Four more months, okay? I'm trying to protect you from yourself so you won't wind up behind bars."

"I'll never go to jail."

"You keep thumbing your nose at the judge, and you will."

"Whatever."

He bit back a retort and let the rest of the ride pass in silence.

They turned through a pair of gates and down a winding drive guarded by trees. Spotlights highlighted the way they swayed in the breeze. Victor drew in a breath of tangy salt air through the open window. Almost instantly, his headache receded a little.

He helped her from the SUV and led her to the front door.

As he turned to leave, Staci stopped him. "I want to go shopping tomorrow afternoon."

"What?"

"Shopping. Be here at one, okay?"

Victor blinked. "Tomorrow and Monday are my days off. Jeremy can take you."

"No, I want you to take me."

"Stace…" He rolled his eyes. "I haven't had a day off in two weeks. I need some downtime."

"Why?"

Take a deep breath. Hold. Don't scream at her. "Because I'm exhausted. And I've got chores to do. Like cleaning and doing laundry."

"So get someone to do those for you."

Take another deep breath. Hold longer. Don't tell her what you really think. Slowly, Victor released it. "No can do on my salary."

Staci stepped closer, bringing her hookah stink with her. "I'm going to go shopping tomorrow." She slowly enunciated her words. "You're going to go with me. Then I'm going clubbing again. Say anything else, and I'll have Stuart call Benny to have you fired."

Victor held her gaze for a long moment. Then he huffed out a sigh. "Whatever."

A saccharine smile crossed her face. "I'm glad we have an understanding."

With that, she turned and flounced into the house.

Victor climbed into his white Jeep Commander and sat there as he stared at the front room of the house. Two forms stood in the dim light and appeared to argue. The light switched out.

"Why couldn't you stand up to her?" he muttered into the still air. He banged the headrest with the back of his head and started the motor.

As he sped down the highway toward West Los Angeles, his answer came clear. He had no fire, no drive.

And Staci knew it.

"Dumb, dumb, and dumber." He turned into the parking lot of the three-story apartment complex. He stopped under the only functioning streetlight, secured a club on his steering wheel, and slid from the SUV as he began his self-flagellation. "You knew this wasn't a good idea. Yet you jumped at it."

Victor climbed the open staircase. Even at this late hour, a television blared from one of the second story units. A sickeningly sweet odor seeped from underneath another where his neighbor got high on a regular basis. He turned a one-eighty and headed up the last set of stairs.

"Why did you think this could help you start over?" He continued his one-sided conversation as he unlocked his apartment.

He sniffed his jacket. It reeked of hookah smoke, which made the headache return full force. After shoving open the sliding glass door, he left his jacket on the plastic lawn chair he'd bought for his balcony. Now fresh air and the sounds of the nearby freeway penetrated the small living room.

Victor snagged a bottle of water from the refrigerator and sank onto the recliner. He lowered his head and rubbed the back of his neck. Several deep breaths relaxed his muscles. He leaned back and stared at the dark night toward where pinpricks of red and white raced by on the freeway. The tautness in his shoulders finally dissipated.

"Hey, silly, it's time to go to bed."

Victor opened his eyes to see Rachel crouching next to his recliner.

"Sorry. I guess I fell asleep." He stared.

She still wore her navy pin-striped suit from that fateful night sixteen months before. Her honey blonde hair tumbled around her face.

She brushed his cheek with her fingers. "You're so focused on making sure nothing goes wrong."

"Huh?"

"This." She nodded toward the pile of papers that sat on the arm of the recliner.

With a start, Victor noticed the words Makmoud Hidari in bold, black type across the top, along with the man's face. When had he gotten that? He blinked and gazed around the room. Walls in a warm camel color surrounded him instead of the dull contractor's beige of his apartment. How was he back at his house in Raleigh?

"I promise you're worrying over nothing. It'll go off without a hitch."

"I hope," he murmured.

"Come to bed." With that, she leaned forward and brushed her lips across his.

"Rachel," he sighed.

Victor's eyes flew open.

Contractor beige surrounded him now.

He'd been dreaming.

"I hate this," he muttered as he pushed himself to his feet. After draining the remainder of the water, he tossed the bottle into the recycling bin that sat in a corner of the dining area. He crossed the living room and shut the door.

As Victor turned toward the hallway, the bookcase from the study of his old house caught his attention. He'd placed books on the two lowest glass shelves. He touched the deep blue sweater on the middle shelf. How many times had Rachel worn that?

"Our first kiss," she'd always murmured to him since he'd given it to her the night he'd kissed her.

His eyes filled as he stared at the velvet jewelry case that held the diamond ring he'd used to propose.

"You should be over this," he muttered.

As per habit, his gaze shifted to the top two shelves. Pictures crowded there. Pictures of Rachel on her own, of her with her family, with friends, with him. The pearl necklace he'd given her snaked through the frames on the top shelf. Had Staci seen that display, she would have suggested that he light candles and worship his dead fiancée.

One particular picture caught his eye. A much younger Rachel crouched next to the family golden retriever and hugged him. The rose arbor from her parents' house arched overhead. Victor picked it up and ran his finger across her face.

"I miss you so much, Rachel." He set the frame on the glass.

Part of it caught on the necklace. Off balance, it tipped over, tumbled from the glass, and hit the tile floor. It shattered, sending shards of ceramic frame and glass front all over the living room floor.

Grumbling, Victor made his way to the kitchen closet and grabbed a dust plan and broom. He turned on the overhead light, which only increased the intensity of his headache. He stooped and tossed the larger pieces into the dust pan.

A golden gleam caught his eye.

Victor picked up the necklace that must have been between the photo and the backing. He stared at it. The writing wasn't English or any other western alphabet. It seemed Semitic but not Hebrew. Arabic, maybe?

He couldn't be sure.

Victor remained in his crouch as he turned the necklace over and over in his hand. Finally, he set it aside and finished cleaning up his mess.

After dumping the remains of the frame in the trash, he shut off the lights and retreated to the bedroom.

He eased onto the edge of the bed and examined the necklace again. Why would Rachel have hidden it in a frame? Was it from a long-lost boyfriend? A family heirloom? He doubted the second hypothesis. Victor laid it on the nightstand in front of another photo of Rachel and switched off the lamp.

Its mystery would have to wait until later, when he could focus.

"Rachel." Victor sighed her name in his sleep as he shook her head from side to side. As he dreamed, images from the past couple of years swirled and melded together like two different colors of paint.

"I love you," Rachel whispered. The soft touch of her lips on his forehead calmed his frazzled nerves as he huddled at the kitchen table of his old house.

Another, more strident voice of the Secret Service agent interrogating him broke into his peace. "Did you know that your comms unit was off?"

"No." Victor gripped the edge of the table so hard that the edge bit into his palms. Suddenly, he realized that the light wood of Maggie McCall's table spread before him rather than the dark one of his own kitchen table.

"Why did you order her to change the egress point?"

"What?" Shock rooted Victor to the spot. "I didn't!"

"Agent Cooper says Agent Marina called him, per your directive, to change the egress point." The agent tapped his pen on the notepad.

Suddenly, Victor realized what he insinuated. "You think Agent Marina had something to do with the ambush?"

"I'm not thinking anything. I'm simply gathering facts, Agent Chavez." He offered a tight-lipped smile as he doodled on the pad. The red lines began coagulating and spreading.

Like blood.

The liar.

A phone started ringing.

"I need to get that." Victor couldn't rip his gaze from the growing puddle.

"You'll do no such thing."

Victor leapt to his feet and dove for the phone.

His eyes flew open. He lay in bed, the sheets kicked down and wrapped around his feet.

He'd been dreaming.

His cell phone buzzed incessantly from its place on the nightstand. He snatched it before it rolled over to voice mail. "Victor Chavez."

"Vic, hey!" A chipper baritone echoed across the airwaves.

"Gary?" Victor pushed himself upright and slouched over.

"You got it." His best friend laughed. "I figured since you're such an early bird that I'd catch you up already."

Victor muffled his groan as he stared at the clock. Six in the morning. Already, the anemic light of another LA day pushed around the edges of his venetian blinds. On the other side of the thin wall of his bedroom, a radio played, even though it was Sunday. "I didn't get in bed until four."

"Uh, oh. I'm sorry. I didn't realize that." Gary cleared his throat. "I'm flying out to LA for a conference, like leaving in a few minutes, and I wanted to see if you'd be up for grabbing some supper tonight."

Victor ran through his calendar in his head. Then he grinned since time with Gary meant he could truly tell Staci he had plans for that night. "That'd be great."

"Name the time and place."

"Six at Sunset Pier? It's in Santa Barbara, has the best hamburgers around, and has a great view."

"That works. I'll be there. Get some rest, bro." Gary hung up.

Victor remained hunched on the edge of the bed. His eyes slid to the necklace, and the headache returned with a fierceness that turned his stomach. As he rubbed his temples, he stumbled into the bathroom and threw back some aspirin. He braced himself against the counter and hung his head as the accusations from the attempted kidnapping that left three dead faded. Finally, Victor shut off the lights and retreated to the bedroom.

His gaze slid to the picture of Rachel. "They accused you of treason, said you colluded with Makmoud Hidari. How dare they?"

As he climbed back into bed, the beautiful but undefinable writing of the necklace haunted him.

He needed answers.

Fast.

2

"C'mon! Can't you work with me on this?" Gary put his hands on the bar.

"Special Agent Walton, the Sunset Pier is known for one thing. Its sunsets." The owner's knife sliced through a lemon. "Got it?"

She pointed the blade at him.

A seed flew through the air and landed on his arm.

She resumed her cutting. "If people can't go out onto the deck to watch them, they're going to get ticked and not come back."

Gary flicked the seed away. "Look. If I don't get this done, the president told me to pack a parka because he'll have me transferred to Nome."

"Your problem, not mine."

"It's a matter of national security."

"And I'm Bill Clinton." She shoved the slices into a container and dropped it into a cooler. Then she attacked the crate of clean wineglasses. They clanked together as she slid them onto the overhead rack.

"You're better looking." Gary smiled at the seething owner.

She tried to keep that straight face, but her lips twitched upward.

"Look." Gary put his foot on the low rail and rested his elbows on the teak wood. "I know that sounded trite. I take it you're a veteran." He nodded toward the battalion insignias gracing the walls of the bar area.

"My husband and I both are. We served in Afghanistan until three years ago." Pride echoed in her voice.

"Then you know that while we're officially winding down, things still aren't secure. What I'm going to be doing out on that deck..." He jerked his chin toward the french doors that opened onto a spacious covered deck overlooking the ocean. "It requires privacy. My other agents will sweep it for bugs, but I need it to be empty and the doors closed."

The woman pulled the crate off the bar and wiped it down. She ran her hands along her ponytail, then cocked her head and studied him. "I want compensation."

"Name it."

"We can seat a hundred out there. On average, people spend thirty dollars a meal. And in the two-hour time frame you're requesting..." Her fingers danced across a calculator. "Everything would turn over twice. That would be $6,000 total."

"Fair enough." Gary pulled out a credit card. "Half now, and half when I'm done. And one more thing."

"Don't push your luck."

"I need two agents at the window. Can you arrange for that at six?"

"So long as they pay."

"Growing girls and boys have to eat." Gary grinned. "Thanks."

He joined his three agents, who waited at a nearby bar table, and led them onto the deserted deck. "Chris and Annie, you two are on for a table for two by the window. Matt, you take the parking lot. I want all of you to start out somewhere different and follow him. If he doesn't spot you, you pass. He does? We start over. Now let's check for listening devices."

They nodded. Chris and Matt fanned out and began a visual inspection of the deck while Annie scanned everything with a hand-held device. Gary picked his table and settled on a chair where he could watch the ocean, restaurant interior, and parking lot, all at the same time.

"Clear," Annie reported.

"Matt? Chris?"

"The same."

"Then get going." Gary called his wife and checked his e-mail. The waitress brought him both a Corona and a basket of chips and salsa.

As six neared, sweat gathered on his palms. He had to seal this deal because he'd heard housing prices in Alaska were as expensive as Arlington where he lived.

The sound of a door opening made him turn his head.

A few seconds later, the blonde hostess in short shorts and a tank top stepped through, followed by Vic.

Gary rose. "Vic, hey, bro."

"Hey, man." His best friend smiled and hugged him with three slaps on the back. "I was wondering if you'd get a seat, seeing how crowded it is."

"I have my ways. I take it the burgers are good?"

Vic pulled out his chair and settled onto it. "The best. And reasonable. I'm not eating on Ms. Logan's tab, you know."

"How is life with her highness?"

"Don't get me started." Vic scowled. He studied the menu. Once he'd ordered a Dos Equis and Gary another Corona, he continued, "I hate it, to be honest. Last night, she went clubbing until I had to take her home to meet curfew at three."

Gary grinned. "Curfew?"

"Ordered by a judge."

"I see."

"I haven't had a day off in two weeks, and she insisted that I take her tonight. I told her I had plans, so thanks for getting me off the hook."

Gary smirked and drawled in his Nashville accent, "You're very welcome."

Vic laughed. Then he sobered. "You know what she asked me when I went over there today? She asked if I was gay because I turned down her setting me up with someone. Then she had the audacity to snatch my wallet and look at the picture I have of Rach. After I told her what happened, she didn't say anything. Not even 'I'm sorry.'"

Vic seemed as miserable as Gary had thought. He stashed that tidbit in his mind for later. "Sounds like a real winner."

"I'm calling my boss tomorrow to ask him for a transfer."

"I don't blame you."

Vic stared at the ocean before he dipped a chip in the salsa and popped it into his mouth. "Do you remember how, right after Rachel died, I saw her everywhere?"

"Yeah. You were imbibing a bit too much at the time. It was a tough time for everyone, especially you."

The animation vanished from Vic's face as quickly as it had come. "Almost every night, I dream about her. They seem so real to me."

"How so?"

"It's like I can feel her touch." Vic rested his elbows on the table as he studied the glass top. He raised his gaze, and the sadness in them shook Gary. "I miss her."

"I know. You loved her. That's natural."

"Something else happened." Vic reached into his pocket and extracted an object. He laid it on the table. "Last night, I accidentally knocked one of her pictures off a shelf. I found this hidden in it."

"A necklace?" Gary stared at the writing carved from gold. He picked it up. "It's beautiful. Like it's custom-made."

"Why would she hide it? It's like she didn't want anyone to find it."

Gary shrugged. "You got me. You never saw it before?"

"Nope."

"Looks like you've got a mystery on your hands."

The waitress approached and asked for their orders in a chipper tone that reminded Gary of his daughter.

Her cheerfulness helped to erase the sadness creasing Vic's brow and hooding his eyes.

Once she'd gone, Vic asked, "How's the family?"

"Doing well. They miss seeing you a couple of times a year. David keeps asking when Uncle Vic's moving back to the East Coast. Mary said to say hi. She said to stop being a stranger and to come visit a little more often." Mentioning his wife made Gary cast a glance at the soft-sided briefcase that held the information he needed.

It wasn't time.

Not quite yet.

"And Morgan?" Vic set his bottle on the table.

"She's discovered boys. This is new territory for me." Gary shook his head and laughed.

Their talk shifted to family and their time in the Army together. As they chatted, Gary noted the way Matt paced near the Ford Edge they'd driven from LAX to the restaurant. Though he wore earbuds and bobbed his head to something, his whole countenance screamed, "Surveillance!" The same thing with Annie and Chris now at their table in the windows. No lovebird action for them. More like a couple headed for a breakup. He had much to teach them.

"Tell me something." Vic leaned forward.

"What's that?"

"Do you really have a conference out here?"

"Huh? What makes you say that?" He fought to keep the smile from breaking through his poker face.

"This deck is normally packed at this time of day. You must be paying the restaurant a small fortune to keep it clear. And even a dumb criminal would realize they're under surveillance." Vic nodded toward the table in the window. "They've been watching me ever since I arrived. The same with the guy in the parking lot listening to music. You need to send your spooks back to remedial spook school."

Gary chuckled and slouched against the chair's back. "You got me. There's no conference. I came to see you specifically, and surprise, surprise, it's not just for business. I'm genuinely concerned about you. It's not like you to drop off the radar for sixteen months with only two phone calls to me during that time."

He glanced up as the waitress brought their steaming hamburgers. Once she left them alone, he took a deep breath. Time to rock and roll. "I have something I'd like to discuss with you that requires the utmost privacy."

His dark gaze never leaving his friend, Vic unfurled his napkin.

Gary did the same. He placed his silverware exactly parallel to each other by his plate. "How much do you know about what I do?"

"I know you've worked for the FBI in Counterterrorism for eight years."

"Exactly." Gary popped the top on the ketchup bottle and squeezed. A red glob dropped onto his plate. "Last year, the whole kidnapping incident with Maggie McCall gave the president a scare."

Vic winced.

Don't dwell on that. Move on. Under the table, Gary rubbed his hands together.

"He got the FBI and DHS together, told them to give him names and résumés of three people each who could put together a quick-reaction team that could carry out special missions for him." He popped a fry into his mouth.

"Huh?" Vic blinked. "I'm not sure—"

"Bear with me here. The director of the FBI handed over my name and two other names. DHS did the same. The next thing I knew, I got a call from the White House telling me to get my rear there for a meeting. The president seemed to like my experience. He said it was both my FBI work and my work in Special Ops, and because I've got, well, rather unique experience as a former POW."

Gary tamped down his flinch.

A low buzzing filled his head as it always did when he ventured toward that topic.

Vic straightened. "What is this team supposed to do?"

The buzzing receded as they steered away from it.

"It'll function like a special ops team but with some additions like a pilot and breaking-and-entering specialist. It's supposed to be flexible enough to go anywhere and bring in people for justice." Gary bit into his hamburger. "You were right, bro. This is most excellent."

"Told you so." Vic chewed for a moment and swallowed.

Gary's pulse picked up a little. He wiped his hands on his napkin, reached into his briefcase, and set a manila envelope in front of his friend. "That was in January. I've spent the past seven months pulling together the team. Meet Operation Shadow Box."

"Operation Shadow Box?" Vic grinned. "Is that like Operation Diorama?"

"Hah. Good one. I didn't pick the name. The computer did. But believe me, this team is going to operate so deeply in the shadows that no one will see them coming. Check out the one-page profiles I pulled together. More detailed info about everything is on that DVD in there."

Vic popped the clasp, lifted the flap, and pulled out the stack. His eyes widened. "Former Hezbollah? Are you nuts?"

"Emphasis on former."

Suleiman al-Ibrahim's voice from the week before rang clearly in Gary's ears. "I'm not a Hidari. No more. I am nothing like my brothers. Don't ever call me Ibrahim Hidari again. And I don't want that name to show up anywhere."

Gary twirled a fry in the ketchup. "Do you remember when that Special Ops team nearly bagged Makmoud last year?"

"Yeah."

"Suleiman handed over some information to the CIA that helped us. Unfortunately, we missed. Suleiman's payment? WITSEC gave him a new life here in the States. He's the sniper for the team."

"He's young."

"Young but gifted. I've seen the kid shoot. Check out the next one."

"Fiona Mercedes?"

"You know her?"

"No, but...wow. Over 10,000 hours in all types of aircraft."

"She's our pilot. Sass and attitude with a capital A, but she's got the touch. Keep looking." Gary leaned forward, his eyes on Vic's face to gauge his reaction.

"Sana Jain. Wait. She's a civilian." His friend frowned. "More than that, she's on parole."

"Not anymore." Gary grinned when he remembered how Sana had firmly held her ground on that particular issue. "Former gymnast turned ninja-gone-bad, all in a failed bid to please her daddy. I guess being a cat burglar didn't pay off."

"She's mended her ways?"

"Yep. She said two years in the slammer taught her a lot."

Vic turned around a picture of a young woman with frizzy, curly, dark-blonde hair and thick glasses. "And where did you find her? A laboratory?"

"Almost. That's Shelly Wise. Doctor Shelly Wise, mind you. She lives in Maryland right now. Man, you talk about a brainiac. Reading at a ninth grade level by age three. Built a computer at ten. Graduated high school at twelve. Then college at sixteen. A doctorate by twenty-one."

"I'm impressed."

"Yeah. An experiment went wrong and embarrassed the CEO of the R&D company where she worked. He fired her. I've got her on board as our security, comms, and computer specialist."

Vic flipped to the next picture. "Hey! That's Cajun Man. I haven't seen him in years. Like since I left the battalion."

"I thought you'd remember Butch Addison." Gary chuckled. It hadn't taken much convincing for Butch to sign on. Only a night at a restaurant and a few beers. "I think everyone in our battalion wanted him on their team. The man can fix anything mechanical, like a one-man A-team. Too bad someone falsely accused him of running guns. He'd be our ordnance guy and mechanic." Gary polished off his hamburger.

"Diana Kasem, cardiothoracic surgeon. I see the theme now." Vic set the paper on the table. "Down on her luck because she was a surgeon in a CSH in Afghanistan. Tried to save a kid and got raped by the locals for her efforts."

"You got it." Gary's mind flicked back to that night when he'd convinced the doctor to join Shadow Box. Her questions and his answers echoed in his ears until finally, she'd agreed. "I got her as our doctor. There's one more."

"Skylar James." Vic studied the profile, then laid it down. "Former CIA."

"Yup. A spook's spook. Skilled more than most in the arts of spookology. He spent a lot of time operating with the CIA in Afghanistan and Pakistan as well as other places in the Near East. At least until CIA busted him for running a little side operation. I think the only reason why he wasn't arrested and thrown into prison is because the CIA wished they'd been in on it. Instead, they burned him and dumped him in Richmond.

He's been working in the restaurant business ever since. Running scams, too. He'd be our procurement specialist."

Vic picked up his hamburger and took a bite. As he chewed, he kept his gaze on his friend.

Gary's nerves kicked into high gear. Now was the time. Do or die. Keep his place in Counterterrorism or call Mary and tell her to start packing for Nome.

Vic finally finished his burger. "Our. You keep saying that. And I noticed you don't have a commander for the team."

"That's right." Gary leaned forward. In a low voice, he said, "That's because I want you to lead it."

"Me?"

"Right. Look." Gary rearranged his fork next to his spoon, then speared his friend with his gaze. "I remember how well you led people when we were in SF. You inspired them. People looked up to you, and they wanted to be on your team. You did the same in the Service too. In my opinion, you got handed a raw deal when they asked you to resign."

Vic looked away. "It is what it is."

"Regardless, when I got charged with pulling together Shadow Box, I immediately knew who I wanted to lead the team." Gary pointed at him. "You."

"I'm happy here."

"Liar." Gary allowed himself a brief smile and rested his forearms against the edge of the table. "You hate it here. You've got no life. Your client is a ditz, and it's not helped you get past Rachel. I think this would."

Vic remained still, as if his friend had stunned him. He toyed with his bottle. "How would it work?"

At least he'd begun asking questions.

"You'd be the one dealing directly with the team. I'd be like your handler. Anything you need, I'd get for you. I'd also handle the money, since it'll be complicated to camouflage everything. C'mon." Gary opened his arms. "You know you're interested. I can see it in your eyes."

"Gary…"

"Ask me any question you want."

"Here's one."

"Shoot."

"If I took this, I'd want compartmentalization. You know. Not read you in on everything so that if something goes south, you wouldn't take the fall, just me, the washed-up Secret Service agent."

Inwardly, Gary rejoiced. Vic had taken the bait. Now he had to reel him in. "Anything you want. I'm there with you on that. I've got full rein to accommodate almost any of your needs."

"I'm still not sure."

Gary knew he was. Vic had seen the team, had expressed interest. All he needed was a push over the edge.

"Open this." Gary tossed another manila envelope onto the table, this one containing a ticket from LAX to Dulles. First class all the way. And a hotel reservation.

Vic's eyes widened ever so slightly. He was playing it cool, but the curiosity burned in those dark depths. "Gary?"

"I've set up a meeting with the team Wednesday morning in DC. Get to know them in person, and then, if you're not interested, you can say no."

Good. Offer him an out.

"But what if I can't get off?"

Gary wanted to smack him over the head and shout, *You'd turn down something like this to guard Staci Logan?* Instead, he simply replied, "Oh, I think you'll find a way, because this has you written all over it. You've got a chance to get back into the game, to lead a team that's well trained and on a solid mission."

Gary glanced up and saw the owner standing in the glass door and staring daggers at him. He nodded.

She strode onto the deck and placed the bill before him. Without even looking, he handed her the credit card.

She ran it on the spot. Seconds later, people began filtering onto the deck.

"That's all I've got." He tucked the slip into his wallet and rose. "Let me take young Obi Wan and the Bobbsey Twins and head to LAX. We're on the red-eye back to DC. I'll see you then?"

"Maybe." Vic had already pulled the stack of profiles from the envelope.

Gotcha.

Gary grinned. "Nah, you'll be there. It was good seeing you."

"Huh? Oh." Vic rose and shook his hand. "See you soon."

Had he even realized he said that? Gary wanted to do the happy dance. He settled for escorting his young charges to the Edge.

"Guys, he fingered you within ten minutes," Gary told the trio as he unlocked the vehicle. "Looks like we've got some more work to do."

"It's hard," Matt said.

"Yeah, it's hard." Gary was about to say more when his phone chimed with a text.

The name and number?

Restricted.

The message?

The desert is nice this time of year.

That buzzing hummed low in the back of his mind.

Gary inhaled sharply as normally inaccessible information began filtering into his mind.

"Are you okay?" Annie asked.

He deleted the message. "Uh, yeah." His mind darted in all directions. "When we get to the airport, I need to call the wife. Then…then I'll be fine."

With that, he swallowed hard and put the car into gear.

3

Wind whispered through the leaves of the four oak trees surrounding the farmhouse in the Piedmont of North Carolina. It stirred the scents of the gardenias in the shrub beds along the brick foundation. The delightful aroma swirled in the air and slipped through the screen of the window that was barely open.

Deborah drew in a breath and released a sigh. That warm North Carolina night, darkness wrapped around her like a cloak. A refrigerator-blue glow filled the study of the old farmhouse. On her laptop, the response from the personals website dared her to answer.

Hamid, you want a one-night stand? One with a bang? Tell me more, and maybe I can deliver.

The sender?

A guy named Murdock.

She sucked in her breath. "Finally!"

That one word exploded across the small room.

Deborah turned on the lamp next to her and scribbled her contact in the composition book that had sat dormant for six weeks. She opened another message and began typing her find. She stopped. This was too good to e-mail to TL and Nasser.

She had to call TL.

Now.

Her fingers trembling from excitement, she dialed her handler's number. It rang three times, then rolled to an answering service.

"Counterterrorism, may I help you?" The woman's smooth voice ramped up her impatience.

"I need to speak to TL Jones."

"And you are?"

"Deborah Fields. Code five-eight-two-four-five." The numbers validated her as a civilian contractor working as a web hunter.

"Special Agent Jones is on leave this week. I'll connect you with Special Agent al-Saad."

A click and more ringing followed.

"Nasser al-Saad."

"It's Deborah."

"Hey, Deb, how's it going?" His Texas drawl filled her ears.

"Awesome."

"Oh? Did Anna win a horse show? Or did DJ get a merit badge?"

"Neither." Deborah giggled with the giddiness of her find. "The kids are out of town this week at my in-laws in Georgia. I got a hit on Murdock."

A sharp intake of breath rewarded her.

"Surprised you, didn't I?"

"You did." Nasser cleared his throat. "Read it to me."

Deborah recited the post she'd placed by posing as Hamid on the personals site, then did the same with Murdock's response.

"What do you think?" she asked.

"I'm thinking this has the potential to be big. We need to discuss this in person. Can you meet me in Raleigh tomorrow at noon?"

"Say 2:30, and I can do that." Deborah smiled as she thought about an afternoon out of town. "Where?"

"Let's meet at our usual Starbucks in Cary. We'll go from there."

She made a note on her calendar before hanging up. It took her another hour to pull together the summaries she'd written after each contact with the elusive Murdock. Once she collated everything into a folder, she turned to place it at the end of the desk.

Her gaze landed on a picture.

A lump swelled in her throat as she picked it up.

Derek, her husband, offered a devil-may-care smile from a rappelling position when he'd just stepped over a cliff. Her eyes filled as she noticed how his hazel ones crinkled at the corners.

"You'd be so proud of me." Her whisper broke the stillness of the room. "We're going to bag this guy, make him pay for the way he's killed those who serve our country."

She set it down and blinked several times.

Deborah rose. She took a deep breath, let it out, and took another one.

The threat of tears receded.

Her eyes shot to the clock. They widened.

Ten already, and the horses remained in the pasture.

"Edgar, Colonel!" she called to her dogs.

The Doberman Pinscher and Belgian Malinois skittered across the tile in the kitchen and charged toward her.

"Let's go outside and get the horses in."

Edgar yipped as if he couldn't agree more.

"Come on, silly." She tousled his ears and let them into the night.

As she stepped onto the screened-in porch, the humid night air surrounded her in a suffocating embrace. Why hadn't she noticed it when she'd cracked the window?

Deborah headed toward the barn, her Tevas barely making a sound on the thick grass.

A breeze whispered across her bare arms and stiffened into a wind that made the leaves of the two nearest oaks rustle. A smell wafted up from down slope where a wetland had formed below the pond. Rotting vegetation and maybe even something else. Had an animal fallen in and gotten stuck? She cringed and shivered as the elation from her find that evening faded, leaving in its wake a bit of fear.

The FBI had promised her that her anonymity was her safety.

She was safe, right?

Deborah set that one aside as she snagged the leads for two of the horses from the barn. Soft clucks brought them to the fence, and she walked the first two inside and secured them in their stalls. As she brought the remaining six inside, she glanced around the barn in search of her dogs.

They nosed around the entrance.

Deborah lowered the bar across the last stall and shut off the lights. She put a foot forward to return to the house.

Something rattled in the feed room.

Deborah froze. Her breath remained locked in her throat.

"Who's there?" she softly called, hating the way her voice shook.

Nothing answered.

"Maybe I'm hearing things," she muttered. She padded toward the double doors.

This time, she clearly heard the scrape of metal on concrete.

The Colonel growled low in his throat.

Deborah reached for the pitchfork resting against the wall near the doors. Her feet carried her forward before she realized it. She gripped it in both hands.

Another growl emanated, this one from Edgar. Both dogs stood rigidly at attention.

Murdock.

Had he found out who she was and come to kill her?

She wanted to laugh at the absurdity, at least until she realized how vulnerable she was.

In the dark, her eyes began adjusting. She noted the long, cylindrical shape of a flashlight clipped to the wall. She grabbed it. With the pitchfork in one hand and light in the other, she tensed. Deborah raised the pitchfork like she was a farm jouster. Her finger depressed the button on the flashlight. With a war cry, she charged toward the feed room.

The raccoon caught in the glare shrieked.

Deborah screamed. She staggered backward. The pitchfork clattered to the concrete, and she grabbed the nearby stall door to keep from falling.

The dogs charged.

More squeals and barking ensued.

Suddenly, she began giggling, then laughing. "Out, you two. Enough."

The dogs backed away and sat. The raccoon fled from the grain room, down the aisle, and from the barn.

"That was too much." One last guffaw escaped her as she slipped into the night and secured the barn door. Only after she returned to the house, locked all of the doors, and lowered all of the blinds did her good humor fade.

What if it hadn't been a raccoon sneaking cat food from the barn cats' bowl? What if there really had been an intruder, like an escaped con or someone looking to rob her? Or what if Murdock really had shown up to verify Hamid's identity?

The thoughts drove her upstairs and into the bedroom. She fully armed the alarm the FBI had installed when she'd become a web hunter three years before. As she crawled under the covers, the vulnerability that had occasionally crept over her since Derek's death visited again like a deadly shadow.

She stared at the picture of the two of them at the Grand Canyon when they'd hiked it. That had been BC, or before children, as they'd joked. Before God had taken Derek so suddenly.

"I wish I didn't feel this way sometimes," she murmured as she ran her fingers down the glass. "Usually, I feel so capable. I have you to thank for that, since you made me stand on my own two feet."

Sadness replaced the worry, and she found it better to turn out the light and pull the sheet and blanket up to her chin.

Something made her open her eyes later that night.

Deborah raised her head and listened. The Colonel sighed in his sleep from his bed in the corner. Beside him, Edgar snuffled in slumber.

Then she saw it.

Lightning.

A storm approached.

She cringed since she loathed thunderstorms.

The wind intensified, once more making the leaves clatter. Lightning flickered through her filmy curtains, followed by the low grumble of thunder.

Deborah clutched the blanket closer to her.

With a loud crack, the storm began in earnest.

She trembled.

The rain poured onto the tin roof. Lightning strobed across the room with hardly a break. Thunder exploded around her.

She began praying and clamped the pillow over her head.

A bright flash nearly blinded her, followed by a huge explosion.

She yelped.

The house shook.

That wasn't simply lightning striking the house.

Deborah flung back the covers and turned on the lamp.

Nothing.

Fear uncurled within her. She found another flashlight in her nightstand.

With its beam shooting ahead of her, she stumbled into the hallway. The doors to DJ's and Anna's rooms stood open. Had she shut the one to Gracie's and Marie's?

She shivered.

Her hand reached for the knob.

She pulled back.

Maybe she should call the police.

With one last, deep breath, she pushed open the door.

Deborah cried out and gaped at the leaves, branches, and wet that greeted her.

One of the old oaks out front had hit the house and come clean into the bedroom of her two youngest children. Somewhere underneath the mess lay their beds.

She began trembling as the overwhelmed feeling slammed into her again.

Staggering down the hall to the master bedroom, she fumbled for the cell phone she kept on her nightstand.

Not tonight.

In her haste to escape upstairs, she'd left it on the kitchen counter.

By the weak beam of her flashlight, she stumbled down the stairs and into the kitchen. Her fingers trembled as she dialed the number.

When her best friend's sleepy voice answered, Deborah sagged against the granite. "Wanda? It's me. I need yours and Jeff's help. Fast."

"I'm not sure I can keep doing this." Deborah scrubbed her burning eyes as she stared at the stack of messages she'd printed the night before.

"Are you worried?" Nasser's question broke into the thoughts rampaging through her skull like spooked cattle.

She blinked. "I'm sorry?"

He gazed at her, his head cocked. "You said you weren't sure you could keep doing this. We're so close with Murdock, but if you want—"

A dull flush filled her cheeks. "I must have been thinking aloud." She closed her eyes and rubbed her temples. "I'm sorry. Thanks to everything that happened last night, I've barely had four hours of sleep. I meant this being a single-mom-of-four thing."

"Allah must have smiled on you." The young FBI agent sat back in his chair. "He kept you safe."

She took a deep breath.

Outside, chainsaws buzzed as the guys from the Delta Force, or the "Delta Family" as she called them, continued chopping the oak tree into smaller and smaller bits.

"From what I see, you're doing a fine job with raising your children."

A wan smile crossed her face. "Sometimes I wonder."

She cleared her throat and straightened. Much as she enjoyed speaking with him, she wanted to head upstairs and curl up in bed for a nap. "So what do you want me to do?"

"Write him a message. The key is to not sound overly eager. I'm afraid that if we jump on it, reply that you'd like to meet right away or something, we'll tip our hand."

Deborah folded her arms across her chest. "So maybe a little hesitant? Play hard to get?"

"Spoken like a woman."

A genuine smile finally forced its way loose. "We do have our ways. How about I write back that I'm not sure about his sincerity and that I want to see more of a sign of that? It might push his buttons."

Nasser fell silent. Slowly, he nodded. "Do it. We'll see what he says. That'll also give TL time to get back from vacation."

Deborah went to the personals site and typed her reply. Nasser read through it, and he nodded. "I think that's perfect."

She hit Send, then blew out a big sigh. "We've done some tough ones together, but I think this takes the cake. Who do you think he is?"

He rested his chin on his hand and gazed at her, obviously considering his answer and how much he should reveal to a civilian. "I think he's someone who's highly placed. In the agency or DHS, I'm not sure since we tend to share informants and information from our undercover operatives. Personally, I think he's able to get his hands on both. Let's just say he's set us back several years, and we're out for blood, since we've lost a dozen or so to him, including five deep cover agents."

They fell silent.

Nasser rose. "I'd better head to Raleigh. I've got a late shuttle back to DC."

"Thanks for understanding and coming down."

A quirky smile crossed his lips. "I think you had your hands a bit too full today to come to Raleigh."

"Yeah, of leaves."

He laughed. "Keep that sense of humor, and you'll be fine."

Deborah saw him to his car. Once he pulled down the driveway and into the stand of woods separating the house from the highway, she retreated upstairs.

Though she yearned for her bed, she found herself stopping at the doorway leading to Gracie and Marie's room. The late afternoon sun shining through the blue tarp over the gaping hole cast an eerie glow across the space. Leaves and twigs littered the carpet.

Her gaze slid to her daughters' twin beds.

Both frames lay shattered; the sheets, blankets, and mattresses were ruined.

That slightly panicky feeling returned in the form of exhaustion and short, shallow breaths.

Deborah leaned against the inside wall and slid down until her knees rested against her chest. *God, why did this have to happen? Why, when I don't have a helpmate to lean on? Why?*

"There you are." Wanda Dalton's voice reached her.

Deborah's eyes snapped open. "I must have fallen asleep."

"It's been a long day." Her best friend settled beside her.

That earned a brief smile. "I'll say." She stared at the mess before them. "I keep looking at this. What if the kids had been here? They...they would have..."

She broke off.

"They aren't."

"I know, but what if they—"

"Deb—"

"I could never forgive myself if—"

"But it didn't happen." Wanda carefully enunciated the words. "God knew this would happen. It might have surprised you, but it didn't surprise Him at all. Keep that in mind."

"You're right." Deborah sighed and rested her head against her friend's shoulder. "I'm feeling so overwhelmed right now. So alone."

"What are we? Chopped liver?" The playfulness in Wanda's tone gently reprimanded her.

"No, no. It's just that..." Deborah fell silent.

Outside, the chainsaw ceased. One of the guys hooted. Then came the easy laugh of another. Zach Maynard. How many times had he been over to help her when she needed a strong back or something done beyond her basic tool skills? It seemed like whenever she called.

"Times like this are when I badly miss Derek. Somehow, when he was alive, it made these types of incidents easier to bear, even if he was deployed."

"You want a man."

"Not just any man..."

41

"A husband." Wanda chuckled. "But to get a husband, you need to let people know you're available, so to speak."

Deborah shifted so she faced her friend. "I'm not sure what you mean."

"I think you know."

"Huh?"

"You haven't noticed the way Zach's sweet on you?"

"Zach Maynard?"

"Is there anyone else? Zach, as in the guy who's spent since sunrise calming you down and then cutting up a hundred-year-old oak tree for you. He's had a thing for you for close to a year now."

"Really?"

Wanda rolled her eyes. "You haven't seen that?"

"Uh, no."

"Zach respects wedding bands, even on the fingers of widows." Wanda tapped the diamond solitaire and gold band resting on the ring finger of Deborah's left hand. "I understand what you're saying, and I understand why you're wearing that. But if you want a guy to take a risk on you, to ask you out, then he's got to know you're ready to see someone. Do you get what I'm saying?"

"Yeah," Deborah whispered.

"Perfect." Wanda squeezed her arm. "I came to tell you I've ordered some pizza. It should arrive about the time they finish cutting your tree into enough firewood to last you a couple of years. So freshen up and come on down. And think about what I said."

Deborah climbed to her feet and helped her friend up. "I'll do that. Thanks," she softly added. "It's given me something to think about."

Much later that night, Deborah's gaze slid to the picture of Derek. She uncurled from her tuck on the bed and lifted it. Her fingers skittered across the glass. "I miss you, Derek. I do. But I also know you wouldn't want me to stay single simply to honor your memory. I'd never have expected you to do that either. Would it be okay if I saw someone else? Maybe married someone?"

She closed her eyes. They filled, but she pushed the tears down. Somehow, she knew what he'd say.

I love you and said I would until death did us part. I'm gone now to the Father. You're free.

Deborah returned the picture to its place. Then she rose. Slowly, she stepped to the dresser and gazed into the mirror. Her slate blue eyes held a solemnity about them. Most likely they always would, thanks to the events that had unfolded in her life.

Now they glimmered with something different. A yearning, maybe? A wish to be seen as more than a mother and a widow? A desire to be known as a woman who could give love? And a need for a sincere kiss? How could she show that?

Her gaze slid to her left hand as Wanda's words echoed in her ears.

"Derek, I love you. Thank you for the twenty-one years we had together."

With that, she slid the rings from her finger and stashed them in the drawer.

She closed it and turned away to begin a new phase of her life.

4

Music from steel drums, horns, and guitars filled the warm, silky air whispering across the patio of the White Sands Resort. The notes as well as the smoke from the flaming torches spiraled upward into a Costa Rican night sky studded with stars. Laughter peppered the murmur of conversation. On the tile dance floor, salsa dancers crowded against each other, yet moved in time with the lively rhythm.

Makmoud Hidari took a deep breath. The tangy air filled his nostrils. With a sigh, he released it before stretching his long limbs in a catlike motion and settling on the high bar chair. The mojito tasted sweet and cool, with a bit of zing from the rum. Perfect after a day of lounging on the beach and playing with his nieces in the warm sea. Now all that remained before retreating to the bedroom in the spacious villa the Hidari clan had rented was drinks with his two brothers. Once sprawled in bed, he'd read until he fell asleep. He'd repeat the same process the next day and the next, until he finished his badly needed ten-day vacation.

Silvery laughter interrupted his thoughts.

The salsa tune had ended, and a woman in a red pantsuit with a silver belt and silver flats retreated to the bar table between his and the dance floor. Her glance met his and stayed.

Makmoud traced her bare arms with his gaze and smiled at her.

Oh, you pretty thing.

A delicate flush tinted her cheeks. She tucked some black hair that had fallen across her face behind the ear that didn't hold the scarlet hibiscus.

He sipped his drink and began considering ways to flirt with her.

"There you are." The bass voice in Farsi made him glance up.

Makmoud smiled as his younger brother joined him.

Jibril held up his beer mug. "The imams wouldn't approve."

Makmoud shrugged. "Would they ever? Why should they care when we do their bidding?"

"They don't want anyone to be happy, no?"

"Perhaps. Even *Quds* agents need a vacation at some point."

"I won't disagree with you."

"Where is Ahmad?"

"Tending to the children. Mira didn't want to go to sleep. She wants another story read to her by Uncle Makmoud."

"Uncle Jibril wasn't good enough?" Makmoud grinned. Once more, he noticed the way the woman glanced at him.

She twirled the end of one of her dark locks around her finger. Again, she shifted her gaze away.

Jibril rubbed a hand through his short hair. "She says I'm good for scary stories."

Makmoud chuckled. "Uncle Jibril. The scary one."

"I'm not scary. I just have a deep voice."

That made Makmoud laugh, drawing another appreciative look from his lady in red.

"So sorry I'm late," Ahmad said in their native tongue as he set his margarita on the table. "Mira wanted to go swimming in the ocean tonight. I told her we had to wait until morning. I promise that girl is a mermaid."

"She'll be a very pretty one when she grows up." Makmoud smiled at the woman again.

She ignored him and messed with a silver earring of intricate design as she studied her phone.

Why the sudden change? Makmoud tried to shove his unease aside.

"She's my jewel, but when she gets to be a teenager?" Ahmad shook his head. "I shudder to think what will happen."

"Which is why she should wear a headscarf." Jibril set his beer mug on the table with a thunk. "Right, Makmoud?"

Makmoud ripped his attention away from the woman. "I'm sorry?"

"Mira should wear a headscarf when she becomes a young woman."

"Maybe not. In America, she would be better served not to wear one."

"But purity—"

"Does not have be shown by a headscarf. Purity comes from within, not from without." Once more, Makmoud's attention and gaze slid to the woman.

Now she had eyes only for her phone.

Why?

Jibril cocked his head. A smile played about his lips. "Yes, the imams would disagree with you at every turn. Like the way you gaze at the lady next to our table."

"Shhh." Makmoud shook his head ever so slightly. He pasted a smile on his face as if he didn't have a care in the world. "You will not talk of such things. You must understand that while I love my country, I do not like the rules our current leaders have."

"Then I will talk of something else." Ahmad leaned close. He cast a glance around the patio, and too low to be heard above the hubbub of voices said, "Murdock called."

"Oh?"

"Yes. Hamid replied. He is interested in working with Murdock."

Out of the corner of his eye, Makmoud noticed a small motion.

The woman put her hand to her ear. He would have assumed she absentmindedly played with her earring except for the deliberate way it moved. Her phone too. It shifted in small increments.

The back of his neck tingled.

He kept her in his peripheral vision as he said, "I triggered him to make the contact with Hamid. I wanted him to feel this person out, to see what kind of reaction he could provoke."

"Could Hezbollah attempt to run him without your permission?"

"No. It's not possible. Even if it was, they would be fools to do so since he is our man."

"What are your thoughts?"

Makmoud divided his attention between his brother and the woman. "What was the tone of the e-mail?"

"He said Hamid is acting like a woman."

"Maybe he is."

Jibril shook his head. "You confuse me."

Makmoud rested both elbows on the bar table and leaned forward. In a low voice, he added, "Perhaps Hamid is really someone who does not have Murdock's best interests at heart. Tell him to continue that charade, that he will consider meeting Hamid on US soil. In Charleston, since it is most convenient for you. Murdock should ask for a down payment of one hundred thousand as proof of interest. And the meeting will happen when we say. How he phrases that is up to him, but that's the way it must be. Understood?"

"Perfectly."

"Good."

Something snapped into place for Makmoud. He leaned back, smiled, and picked up his drink. He raised it, all the while keeping a discreet eye on the woman.

"To brothers!" he announced in English.

"To brothers," the other two chorused. They clinked glasses.

Makmoud turned to the woman.

She'd leapt to her feet. Her hands fumbled with her phone as she slid it into the small silver purse attached to her belt.

"Miss, would you mind taking our picture?"

"Are you crazy?" Jibril softly demanded in Farsi.

"I'm, um, so very sorry. I was leaving," she replied in English with a light accent. She turned and fled into the night.

"Jibril, come with me. Ahmad, return to the villa and wait for me."

"But—"

"Go." Makmoud made sure his youngest brother rose before heading in the direction the woman had gone.

"What are you thinking?" Jibril followed.

"She was spying on us. Let's see what she has to say." Makmoud quickened his steps.

Ahead of them, no sound came from the woman's flats. The buildings faded into jungle as she ventured into the natural part of the resort's property. Concrete turned to crushed shells lit by lights bordering the path.

She broke into a run.

"She wants to lose us!" Jibril caught up with him.

"And she'll do no such thing." Makmoud upped his walk to an easy jog. "You know these trails, yes? She thinks she can hide. All she's doing is isolating herself."

The lights disappeared, leaving them with only the silvery glow of the full moon.

Makmoud had to keep her on the move, keep her running so she had no time to make contact with anyone.

A rattle and a low cry told him she'd connected with a branch.

Makmoud increased his pace, as did Jibril.

She did the same to a sprint.

What did she do? Run track in her spare time?

They burst onto the playground where Makmoud had taken his nieces the day before.

The woman bolted toward the other side where he knew more paths would allow her to lose them.

His lungs began burning.

Then Allah, if he believed in him, smiled.

The woman cried out. She tumbled to the ground.

As she staggered to her feet, Makmoud slammed into her.

The hibiscus blossom went flying.

She kicked him, catching him on the chest and knocking the breath from him.

Makmoud collapsed and wheezed as he tried to suck in air.

She staggered upright and stumbled toward the jungle gym that held the slide, monkey bars, and miniature zip line.

Jibril dropped onto her from the platform above. He grunted as her punch made contact.

Makmoud flung himself at the woman, this time catching her around the knees.

She kicked him. One of her feet caught him in the neck, right at the scar from two years before.

Pain blazed in his brain. Gripping his neck, he pushed himself to his knees.

An arm snaked around her. She cried out as Jibril wrapped his other one around her neck and squeezed.

With a moan, she slumped to the ground.

Jibril knelt beside her. Using a penlight turned to red, he searched the small purse. "Cell phone."

"Give it to me." Makmoud toggled it on. It had a biometric scanner. He recalled the way her right hand had toyed with her earring. "She's right-handed. Most likely she uses her index finger to activate it."

He grabbed her limp hand and swiped her finger across the screen.

Success.

The home screen popped up. Without wasting time, he accessed the Settings menu and sent the phone into airplane mode to disengage the GPS. Then he reset the security lock to a code of his choosing. "Does she have a passport?"

Jibril flipped it open. "Panamanian. I rather doubt that."

Makmoud recalled the map he'd studied upon his arrival a couple of days before. "The parking lot is adjacent to the playground. Let's get her to the car. We need to take her to the safe house in San Jose."

Jibril swung her unconscious form over his shoulder like a sack of laundry.

Makmoud swept the area with his gaze. Thanks to their isolated location, no one had witnessed their takedown. He was about to follow his brother when he noticed the hibiscus blossom on the ground at the site of their scuffle. He grabbed it and caught up with Jibril. As he walked point, they made their way to the car they'd rented.

Jibril popped the trunk and dumped her inside. That elicited a moan.

"We need a gag," Makmoud muttered.

"We'll use my undershirt and belt. Give me yours to bind her." Jibril secured a gag over her mouth and tied her hands behind her back.

By that point, the woman had awakened. Her eyes widened. Muted bleats reached Makmoud through the fabric.

He smiled. "I'll take those from you."

After he undid the earrings, Jibril slammed the lid.

Makmoud said, "Swing by the villa in ten minutes and pick me up. Be sure to blast some music to cover any sound she might make."

"And our vacation?"

"Only interrupted. We'll continue once the señorita tells us all she knows."

Five hours later, Makmoud sat on the edge of the couch in the San Jose safe house's living room. His shin ached where she'd kicked him as they'd dragged her from the car to the house. He rubbed his arm where her fist had caught him as he'd helped secure her to a chair from the dining room. Her screams as they'd transitioned from the gag to tape over her mouth still echoed in his ears. She'd stilled only when Jibril had wrapped rope around her chest and pulled a burlap bag over her head.

Makmoud knew that wouldn't last long.

She sagged against her bonds. In the harsh light of the construction lamps they'd set up in the living room, her silver belt still gleamed, as did the bracelet and watch on her wrists.

He lowered his gaze to the coffee table in front of him. Her earrings sat on it, one of them disassembled to reveal a tiny microphone synced to her phone. That told him all he needed to know.

Now he wanted answers from her.

Quickly.

Car doors slammed.

The woman raised her head. Her hands gripped the arms of the chair.

Jibril shifted from where he slouched in an easy chair. He withdrew his pistol from underneath a pillow.

Makmoud tensed and did the same.

His brother approached the door and muttered something.

Their guests must have replied to the pass phrase in the affirmative because Jibril undid the locks.

Makmoud rose and stepped into the foyer to meet their fellow Quds agents.

"So sorry we're late," the team leader said in Farsi. "It was a long drive from Managua."

"We have a situation." Makmoud jerked his head toward the living room.

"That would be?"

"CIA, I suspect." Makmoud briefed him on what had transpired at the resort.

"Show me."

Makmoud led the way into the living room.

The woman once more struggled against her bonds.

In one swift motion, Makmoud reached up and yanked the bag from her head. He ripped away the tape.

She cried out. In the glare of the construction light, she blinked and squinted. Her eyes watered slightly.

"Welcome to Casa Linda," Makmoud said in English.

She clamped her jaw shut.

"I can understand why you aren't chatty." He pulled her passport from his shirt pocket and flipped it open. "Adriana Cortez, eh? Of Panama? You were vacationing at the White Sands Resort?"

"I—I don't understand why I'm here." Her tremulous voice held the slightest trace of the accent he'd heard earlier. "I was there for work—"

Makmoud slapped her across the face.

She yelped.

A red mark appeared.

"Adriana, if that is indeed your real name, why were you were so interested in the conversation I was having with my brothers tonight?"

"I don't understand what you—"

He backhanded her.

Blood oozed from her cut lip. It trickled down her chin in a scarlet line that matched her pantsuit.

He began pacing around her. "I believe you understand very well. You see, I know how vital this is to you and your mission." He stopped and held up her cell phone. "While you were unconscious, I had the great fortune of using your finger to get behind its security. Meaning, I now have total access to your phone, and no one knows where you are."

He examined her face for a reaction.

The faintest twitch in her jaw rewarded him.

Makmoud recalled the pictures she'd taken. He selected one of him. He leaned over her and shoved it in her face. "Perhaps you think I'm handsome. You certainly took enough pictures of my brothers and me."

He pulled up another one of the three brothers. "Show and tell, eh?"

Adriana briefly met his gaze, then looked away.

"Look at me, Adriana." He lifted her chin with his finger.

She spat in his face.

Anger flashed through him. He slammed his fist into her cheek.

The chair toppled over. She crashed onto the hard tile and lay there moaning.

Chest heaving, Makmoud glared at her. He lightly kicked her. "You are a fool, Señorita Cortez. Jibril, right her."

His brother hauled her upright.

"I—"

"Who do you work for?"

"No one! I'm a travel writer. Part of my work is to review the White Sands Resort for a travel magazine specializing in the tropics."

"You lie." Makmoud turned away and muttered something. He whipped around. "If you are a writer, did you want to write about us? About what we do?"

"I don't—"

He slapped her again. "Wrong answer, Señorita. I found our conversation to be rather scintillating. That microphone we found in your earring recorded us perfectly."

In one swoop, he grabbed the pieces of earring and hurled them at her.

They hit her face and toppled onto her lap.

He hit the Play button on her phone's recorder. His voice along with those of Ahmad and Jibril in Farsi filled the air. With perfect clarity, he heard everything, including their discussion about Murdock.

Makmoud examined Adriana's face.

A fine sheen of moisture had broken out along her brow. It glistened in the bright light.

"I do find it quite interesting that a simple writer would have something so intricate hidden away in her earring. Don't you find that telling, Jibril?"

His brother crossed his arms and nodded.

Adriana stared at him. Her jaw flexed. Her fingers clawed at the arms of the chair.

"I might believe everything you say except for something else. You see, your phone was rather sophisticated for a writer." Makmoud studied her.

Now her chest rose and fell in small, rapid breaths.

"I can tell that I am on to something with you. The *coup de grace* for me was the telephone number you called earlier today. You see, we called it a good distance from here. And who should answer?"

Adriana met his gaze with a stony expression of her own. Despite her bravado, she trembled slightly. A line of sweat trickled from her hairline.

"Yes, that's right, Señorita. Listen to this." Makmoud pulled out his phone and recalled the recorder.

"This is Neil. Is that you, Adriana? Adriana?"

He cut off the recording. "Neil. Who is Neil, Adriana?"

"My boyfriend," she whispered. Her hands clenched into fists.

"At a 703 number? That is the United States, is it not? Northern Virginia? Perhaps Langley?" Makmoud glanced at his comrades from Iran's Nicaraguan embassy. He resumed his circling before stopping behind her.

He bent, rested his hands on her forearms, and murmured into her ear, "You say you live in Panama, yet your 'boyfriend' speaks rather formally to you and lives in northern Virginia. That tells me there is more to you than meets the eye. Hatim."

The older of the team from Managua stepped forward and opened a case. He pulled out a needle and syringe and drew some fluid from a vial.

Her whole body quivered under Makmoud's fingers. "I don't know what you're talking about. I promise. I'm sorry if I recorded you. I was testing a device I wanted to use on interview subjects that wouldn't make it obvious I was recording, and—"

Makmoud grabbed her hair.

"Please—" A gasp choked her voice.

He tightened his grip until she moaned. "Enough, Adriana. Enough of your lies. You're going to tell us who you are. If you are who you claim to be, that is, a foolish travel writer, then all is well and good, and you'll wake up in your bed at the resort. If not?"

He let the implied threat hang in the air like a toxic mist.

Hatim approached with the loaded needle.

"No!" Adriana bucked.

Makmoud wrapped his arms around her chest and held her to the chair. Even then, it took Jibril immobilizing her forearm before Hatim could inject the drug.

She moaned as he pressed the plunger.

Her chest heaved against Makmoud's hold.

He stroked her damp hair away from her forehead. "You see, was that so bad? Was it? You'll feel sleepy. And then you'll tell us all you know."

He released her and walked over to the coffee table where his comrades had set a recorder.

Adriana's head tilted forward. He tipped her chin and studied her face in the bright light. A drunken gleam had appeared in her eyes.

It was time.

Makmoud seated himself on the couch and turned on the recorder. "Now, Adriana Cortez, we'll start from the beginning again. Why were you so interested in us?"

Two hours later, he leaned over and cut off the device. Adriana had fallen silent, her head drooping, her eyes closed as she finally sank into sleep.

Makmoud surveyed her.

Her hair hung in limp strands wet with sweat and tears. Mascara streaked her cheeks in dark smudges. The blood that had dribbled down her chin had dried.

It'd taken minutes to break her and only slightly longer to discover all she knew. Even now, her sobs and moans echoed in his ears as she'd begged for mercy.

"CIA suspects Ahmad is neck deep in working for *Quds*." Jibril ran a hand across his face and muttered under his breath. The way he scrubbed his hands through his hair conveyed his concern.

"Present tense is correct. They sent the señorita to confirm it. My suspicion is that they weren't quite certain since Ahmad publicly claims he has nothing to do with us. I imagine they wanted to see the three of us together for confirmation. Had we not followed her, she would have sent the pictures plus the recordings to CIA headquarters, and Ahmad might have had a greeting party waiting for him upon his return to Charleston."

"Is there a risk to him?" Hatim asked from where he leaned against the tile counter of the kitchen.

"No. I saw no communications on her phone. We ambushed her before she had the chance to call anyone. And now?" Makmoud rose and tossed the phone onto the tile. He brought his heel down onto it, destroying it. "She never will. Ahmad is safe."

"And what about her?"

"She is too junior to risk sending to Tehran for further interrogation. It is quite clear to me that she is a new field agent. Maybe they thought this was a safe assignment for her." Makmoud shrugged.

He leaned over and retrieved the scarlet hibiscus from the table. As he rolled the stem between his fingers, his gaze met Jibril's.

A slight nod from his brother answered his question.

Makmoud tucked the hibiscus behind Adriana's ear. He smoothed her hair as Jibril pulled out his pistol, loaded a bullet into the chamber, and pulled back the slide with a *schnick*.

"There is only one solution." Makmoud met the team leader's gaze. "She must die."

5

"I've almost got everything wrapped up," Gary said as he hurried down the Washington, DC hotel's hallway toward Vic's room.

"You've been telling me that for two weeks!" The president's frustration rang in his ear.

Gary blew out a small sigh. "I know, sir. These things take time and are delicate."

"I know they take time. But I'm done with waiting. You've got until tonight. Understand?"

"Tonight?" Gary's voice rose a bit. "But I thought Friday was—"

"Tonight. If you don't have this locked down by midnight, then I suggest you and your wife put your house on the market and pack your parkas. I've heard Nome starts getting cold in August."

A click sounded.

Gary smacked the heel of his hand against his forehead. He needed to close the deal.

Today.

With a deep breath, he raised his hand and tapped on the door. "Vic? Hey, Vic!"

It flew open.

His friend stood there, resplendent in his charcoal gray suit with its dark red tie slightly askew. "Sorry, man. Come on in."

Gary studied him with a practiced eye. "You're looking good, bro. Here. Let me adjust that knot for you."

Victor scowled. "I can't help that I haven't worn a suit for sixteen months."

"You haven't needed to." Gary made the adjustment and patted the silk. "Much better. C'mon. Let's go meet the team. I figured we'd do introductions. Then you can do whatever spiel you want before we complete the reams of paperwork that comes with launching a covert team. After that? Lunch."

Gary led the way to the elevators. He stabbed the button, and the doors opened. "How does that sound?"

"How about if we do the introductions first, then you do your HR thing, then you go and get us lunch while I talk with the team?" Vic flashed a grin. The doors opened onto the third-floor mezzanine. "You know, get the pain over with as quickly as possible."

Gary glowered. "Even super-secret agents need to have a 401k."

He led his friend over the street via a sky walk and into the convention center.

"You're right. We do." Vic followed.

"Have you called her highness and quit?"

"I haven't made up my mind yet."

"And when will that be?" Gary ground his teeth. "The president now wants an answer by tonight."

"I'll give it to you after I meet the team." Vic matched him stride for stride as they strolled along a wide walkway. They stepped onto an escalator that lowered them into a cacophony of noise, people, and light. He gaped at the displays of vendors showing all sorts of pumps, valves, and electronics. "What's all of this?"

"Water infrastructure national conference." Gary grinned and shoved his way through the crowd spilling from various ballrooms into the reception area. He almost had to shout as he added, "You should see the exhibit hall. I figured no one would find us in this mess."

"Or we might not see tails," Vic muttered.

"Oh, ye of little faith. What better way to spot a tail than an escalator going up five stories?" Gary stepped onto another massive escalator. The crowd receded below, and he nodded when no one paid them any mind. They turned down a hallway, and the noise faded, especially when Gary opened a door. He stepped aside with a mock bow. "After you, kind sir."

The room housed a conference table with nine seats, four on each side and one at the end with a screen at the other end where the hotel's logo glowed. Seven people lined dark wood topped by glass. LED lighting around the edges of the room provided background lighting, and recessed bulbs spotlighted the table.

Gary gestured to the black leather chair at the head of the table. "Have a seat, bro."

With the barest of hesitations, Vic took a seat.

Gary let the door shut behind him. "Welcome, everyone, to the inaugural meeting of Operation Shadow Box. I take it no one had a problem finding the conference room?"

Silence reigned.

"Good. All right. I'd figure we'll do introductions first. Just your name, where you're currently living, and what your role in Shadow Box is. Vic, you want to start?" Gary took his seat to the left of his friend.

He nodded, steepled his fingers, and said, "I'm Victor Chavez, currently residing in Los Angeles. Gary tapped me to be your commander."

"You guys should know me. I'm Special Agent Gary Walton, FBI Counterterrorism and living here in the DC area. I'm to be your handler." Gary nudged the young man to his left.

"Suleiman al-Ibrahim," the young man said in softly accented English. Wisps of a beard lined the edge of his jaw, and he kept his eyes on the glass of the table. "Living in Myrtle Beach, South Carolina. Your sniper."

"I'm Sana Jain." The young woman beside him had skin the color of tea with milk in it. Her dark gaze flicked upward. "I'm living in Austin, Texas, and will be the cat burglar of the group."

"Me-ow." The blond man sitting across from her leered.

Sana scowled at him.

Gary could already sense the tension radiating from the former gymnast. He shifted. "Moving on."

"Shelly Wise," the woman with frizzy, sandy-blonde curls stated. She adjusted her glasses. "Currently in Bethesda, Maryland. Gary told me I'm your computer geek."

"Meaning?" Vic smiled.

This was good. He'd already developed some rapport.

"Meaning that I'm responsible for your comms, computer, and security system needs." Shelly gestured to the big guy across from her. "Okay, Butch, your turn."

"Yeah, man. Butch Addison, otherwise known as Cajun Man from my SF days. Living in Hope Mills, North Carolina. I'm your mechanic and ordnance guy. Escape-and-evasion specialist as well."

The woman to his left had her curls tamed in a bun. Only one had escaped and teased her cheek. Gary easily saw how, if he hadn't been married and been so in love with his wife, he could have asked her on a date. "Diana Kasem. I'm currently living in Portland, Oregon, and am your doctor."

The blond man shifted and offered an easygoing smile. "Skylar James, currently surrounded by two beautiful women."

Diana smiled. "You flatter me. Tell us where you live, and don't say heaven."

"Naw. Residing in Richmond, Virginia, with a huge desire to get out. Gary says I'm to be your procurement guy and resident spook."

"And you are?" Vic shifted his focus to the woman who sat to his right.

"I'm Fiona Mercedes, living in Smithfield, North Carolina. My specialty? Your pilot."

Vic's eyes widened slightly.

Gary bit back his smile as he imagined his friend reading the tough-girl vibes oozing from Fiona like sludge.

"Come again?" his team leader said.

"I'm Fiona Mercedes, living in Smithfield, North Carolina. My specialty? Your pilot." Now she almost growled each word.

"Roger that." Victor offered a smile to smooth over the awkward moment.

"Okay, guys." Gary rose and pulled out stacks of forms from his briefcase. "Sorry to have to do this, but we have paperwork aplenty to complete. First, take a lunch form. Fill it out, and while Victor talks, I'll go and get us something to eat. Then, each take a 401k, non-disclosure, health insurance, and well, all of the HR forms you need to complete. When we finish, make a stack and clip everything together." He tossed some clips onto the table.

He had to admit the next couple of hours would have driven the most sober-minded teetotaler to drink as they endured seven levels of HR hell, from 401k forms to non-disclosure forms to health insurance forms. Even Vic's eyes glazed over. From the way Fiona fidgeted, Gary thought she would throw down her pen and run screaming from the room. Finally, he collected everyone's thick stacks and turned to his new team commander—hopefully. "Vic, you've got this?"

"I do." His friend nodded. "Gary, thanks for the introduction."

"No problem. I'll be back in an hour." Gary strolled from the conference room. On the way back to his office, he swung by the deli and dropped off the lunch forms. An hour and long discussion with HR later, the FBI agent paid a copious amount for the nine lunches. He returned to the hotel and once again rode the escalator to the fifth floor.

He shoved open the door. "Okay, everyone, I've got sandwiches and..."

The room was empty.

"Vic? Sana?"

Nothing.

Everyone had split.

Anger began low in his gut. Visions of igloos flashed through his mind.

The bag of lunches crashed to his floor.

He whipped out his cell phone. "Matt? Gary here. I want you, Chris, and Annie to get to the hotel where Victor Chavez and his team are staying. If he pokes his head out, follow him. Same with the others. Got it? Get over there ASAP."

He dialed another number. As it rang, he kicked the table. "Vic, you'd better answer me. Now!"

6

"Are you crazy or something?" Gary's voice blasted through the cell phone and slammed into Victor's eardrum.

"Hi, Gary."

His friend spluttered for a moment. "What do you think you're doing? I go to the deli, pick up sandwiches, pay for them, and show up, only to find an empty conference room. You left me holding the bag. Of sandwiches, that is!"

Victor clamped the cell between his cheek and shoulder as he slid the last of the papers he'd printed in the hotel's business center into a manila envelope. "I told you I needed compartmentalization."

"I at least thought I'd be in on it at the beginning." Gary's voice hadn't lowered a bit. "Thanks for nothing, bro."

The tiniest bit of guilt pulled at Victor, but he shoved it away. "I know. Trust me on this, okay?"

"I guess I've got no choice. Where are you meeting?"

"Gary." Victor rolled his eyes.

"Give me an update when you get back."

"That, I can do. Thanks, man. I appreciate your putting this kind of trust in me."

"Whatever." A loud click made Victor flinch.

He blew out a sigh and carefully set the phone on the worktable. For a moment, he remained still as he contemplated the annoyance emanating from his friend. Gary would have to understand his need to speak with the team in confidence and without any listening devices.

Along with his portfolio, he took all eight envelopes and slid them into a knapsack with his laptop. He slung it over his shoulders. Once in the hallway, he tore off a small strip of paper from the notepad of hotel stationery. After folding it, he slipped the altered end under the edge of the door with the edge barely showing. If the door opened, the far edge would catch and shift it inward.

Victor picked up a tail as soon as he stepped onto the busy sidewalk in front of the hotel.

He hissed as he drew in a sharp breath. His pulse skittered upward.

As if he'd seen nothing, Victor strolled down the sidewalk. He paused in front of a storefront as if enthralled for the moment by the food advertisements in the window of the takeout Chinese deli. Hidden by sunglasses, his gaze slid to the right.

The blonde from the restaurant in Santa Barbara stopped.

He noted her jeans, white sleeveless blouse, and hair up in a twist.

Turning, Victor strolled past the Mt. Vernon Square Metro Station.

The rising rush hour crowd carried him along.

He stopped at a street corner and knelt as if to tighten the lace on his hiking boot. He watched the blonde, who waited close to the back of the cluster of people. His attention flicked to the pedestrian signal.

It began its countdown. Ten...nine...eight...seven...six...five... four...

Victor bolted to his feet and trotted across the intersection with the stragglers.

Caught off guard, the woman remained stuck, her face a storm cloud as she stared at him. Her lips formed a silent cuss word. She snatched a cell phone from her belt.

He continued his walk.

The young man from the parking lot fell in behind him.

Victor noted his black T-shirt, spiked belt, and jeans.

He needed to shake him.

Now.

Victor headed toward the escalator at the Gallery Place Metro Station. Once he got his ticket, he shoved his sunglasses on top of his head and played with his phone while he waited for the train.

He noted his tail's location.

The train heading south arrived, and he stepped onto it.

The young man boarded the car behind him.

Two stops later, the train pulled into L'Enfant Plaza, one of the busiest Metro stations where four lines converged. Hoards of people waited on the platform. When the doors swished open, the people on the train surged outward. Victor let them pass, then stepped off when the flow slowed to a trickle.

The young man did the same and moved onto the platform.

A mass rushed inward.

Victor stood still, slightly to the side as the crowd buffeted him. He raised his gaze.

The young man froze as they locked stares.

The bells dinged, signaling that the doors were about to close.

Victor grinned and saluted him. He jumped back on just as the doors closed.

The young man flipped him the bird.

Victor spent the next hour or so riding the Yellow Line south all the way to King Street in Alexandria, where he switched to the Blue Line. As he leaned against the pole and pretended to mess with his phone, he kept an eye out for the other man who'd been with the woman in Santa Barbara.

Nothing.

Only then did he switch to the Orange Line to East Falls Church before backtracking by taking the Silver Line to the Balston station. A short bus ride brought him to his destination.

Victor pushed through the doors of a combination gas station and convenience store.

A man, two days' worth of beard on his chin, scowled at him. He glanced at the paper spread on the counter in front of him, then at Victor.

Victor approached him. "Is Kamal Akram in?"

"Victor Chavez! I would recognize your voice anywhere." The big voice preceded the diminutive man who stepped from the hallway to the right of the counter. He smiled broadly. "Welcome. Wasim, please see to it that we're not disturbed."

The clerk nodded.

"Please, come to my office." Kamal led the way into an office crowded with a desk, chair, and bookcase. Stacks of books and papers piled on the shelves and almost any other horizontal surface.

"*As-salaam,*" Victor told him in Arabic.

"*Wa 'alaykum salaam.*" Kamal smiled, embraced him, and kissed him lightly on both cheeks. "It has been too long." He lifted a stack of papers from a chair and nodded. "Sit. Please."

"Still as disorganized as ever." Victor grinned.

"So says Yana." Kamal scowled and added in English, "We've been married for nearly twenty-five years, yet she does not seem to understand that I'm truly very organized."

Victor laughed. "Spoken like a true genius."

"May I interest you in tea?"

"Please."

"Are you well, my friend? It has been much too long since I've seen you. Perhaps almost two years?"

"It was…the summer of 2011." He swallowed hard as his temporary good spirits vanished.

Kamal added water to an electric teapot. "I was sorry to hear about your Rachel."

Victor's head snapped up. "You heard?"

"From Gary Walton. He lives not too far from here and comes by a lot to visit. Tea?" Kamal held out a small box of dark wood.

Victor lifted the lid and chose some chai. He placed it in a delicate china cup. "I should apologize for not keeping in better touch. It…I lost everything. Rachel. My career. My friends since I had to resign. I wound up moving to Los Angeles to work in private security."

Kamal studied him as the water rumbled to a boil. When the pot clicked off, he carefully poured water into the two cups. Once he returned it to its stand, he picked up his cup. "And did it help?"

Victor started. "How did you know?"

"Your unhappiness. It was written on your face the moment I laid eyes on you. Not even your smile hid it, my friend." Kamal took a sip, closed his eyes, and sighed. "You still mourn her."

"I do." Victor rested his elbows on his knees, cradled his cup between his hands, and savored its warmth. "We'd planned on spending the rest of our lives together. Sometimes I wonder if I'll ever get over her."

Kamal set his cup aside and reached out to touch him on the arm. "It is all right to grieve for her, yes?"

"But sixteen months later?"

Kamal fell silent for a moment as he sipped his tea. He set his cup on a stack of books at the corner of his desk. "In Iraq, many families lost loved ones, be they sons, fathers, even daughters or mothers. Especially those of us who were translators for your Army. And if you didn't lose someone in your immediate family, you lost a relative. Me? I lost my brother. He was kidnapped, as you know, and murdered as retribution for my work. That was eight years ago. I miss him every day, Victor. *Every day.*"

For a moment, Kamal remained quiet as if thinking hard. When he met his friend's gaze, tears had pooled in his eyes. "I think what matters is what you choose. Do you choose to remain paralyzed with grief or acknowledge its presence yet move forward?"

Victor nodded. He knew he was stuck, not only in his job but also in his life. If only he could find new purpose that would push him beyond his paralysis. Maybe the offer Gary dangled before him would be a start. His sadness receded, if only a little. He cleared his throat. "How is your family?"

They chatted through another cup of tea, this time about Kamal, his wife, and two daughters. Their conversation helped chase the sadness into the dark recesses of his mind.

Finally, Kamal set his empty cup on a small tray and took Victor's as well. "While it has been good to catch up, I know you have something you wish to discuss with me."

Victor reached into an inner pocket of his backpack and pulled out the necklace. "I wanted you to take a look at this."

"This is beautiful!" Kamal pulled his desk lamp closer and examined it with a practiced eye. "Handmade. From…" He turned it over. "It appears to be 1998. A long time ago. This was Rachel's?"

"I think so. It was hidden in a frame behind a picture of her."

"Interesting." Kamal picked up a small scale from a cluttered bookcase. He removed the charm from its chain and set it on top. "Let me do some calculations."

He scribbled something onto a sheet of paper before examining it again. His fingers danced across a calculator.

Victor clasped his hands between his knees. "What can you tell me?"

"I think this is eighteen-carat gold. Very intricately made. It's clear that it is a custom job."

"Spoken like the goldsmith you are." Victor's voice tightened.

"You flatter me. From its weight, I gather that the cost of the gold alone might have been close to 900 dollars back then. Add to that the workmanship, and I would have probably charged double that amount."

Victor whistled low. "Wow. That's a lot of money."

"Someone must have loved your Rachel."

"I know." Victor swallowed hard. "What does it say?"

"My beloved."

"Arabic, right?"

"No, no, my friend. This is Farsi."

Victor's stomach clenched. "Come again?"

"Farsi. Remember that I grew up near the border with Iran and am fluent in both. It's a very elegantly written language." Kamal handed it back. "This person loved her. To me it's clear since he took the time to write out the Farsi for a goldsmith and was willing to pay a large sum of money to have it made. I'm sorry, but that is all I can tell you."

"It's enough." Victor glanced at his watch. It was getting on toward five. "I guess I'd better get going. Kamal, it was good to see you."

His friend and former translator him saw to the door. "As was you. Allah go with you, Victor Chavez."

Victor wandered into the late afternoon, this time barely remembering to check for a tail. He began walking toward the bus stop.

His head spun. Farsi? Why would Rachel have an expensive, custom-made necklace of gold with lettering in Farsi? Had this come from an ex-boyfriend?

As he waited for the bus, he closed his eyes.

Rachel's voice from the night he'd shared about his divorce teased his memory. "I understand about wanting to get rid of everything about Olivia. That's what I did with my ex-husband, and I've done the same with every guy I've ever dated."

Doubt nibbled at the walls of his trust in her.

How could he figure out if she'd told him the truth?

Her journals.

Slowly, Victor nodded as if he'd figured out a mystery. Had the Secret Service taken them during their investigation of the attempted kidnapping?

He couldn't remember.

Victor dialed a number on his phone.

"Miles Norton."

His shoulders tensed at the voice of the Secret Service agent now heading Maggie McCall's detail. "Miles, this is Victor Chavez."

"Hi." He remained guarded.

"Um, I was wondering if there was any chance I could get a copy of the investigation into the kidnapping attempt last year."

"No can do, Vic. I'm sorry, but you're not cleared."

"But—"

"I can't do that if you don't have the proper clearance. Understand?"

"I do. I'm getting ready to get on with the FBI and will be undergoing all of the proper checks for that."

"I'll take that under advisement. Good day." The phone clicked in his ear.

Another idea hit him.

When the Service had searched Victor's house and carried away certain items like Rachel's financial records, Maggie McCall had demanded that they provide both her and Victor a copy of the inventory. His resided at the family home in Flagstaff, Arizona.

But he needed his answer.

Quickly.

His breath hitched as he called up her number. "Maggie?"

"Why Victor Chavez, what a surprise!" Her southern drawl filled his ear and made him smile. "How are you?"

He made small talk as he let a bus pass. After a glance at his watch, he asked, "Did you ever get the inventory of what the Service took out of my house last year?"

"Oh, yes. Do you need it?"

"Can you e-mail it to me?"

"That, I can do. I'll send it right now since I'm at home."

"Thanks. I really do appreciate it." Victor hopped aboard the next bus and slouched on the hard plastic seat. His phone pinged, signaling an e-mail message.

Maggie had delivered.

He accessed the inventory. Financial records for both him and Rachel. Both of their computers. Her scrapbooks.

But no journals.

Huh?

He scanned the list again.

He let his head hang forward as he closed his eyes.

A memory from the cold March night a month before Rachel died flashed through his mind. Rachel had huddled in bed, her eyes red, her right eye black from being struck by a falling flour canister. "I destroyed my journals while you were away."

Victor stared at her. "What?"

"I destroyed them. They can't comfort me. Not after losing Susanna." With that, she buried her face in her knees and cried.

He pulled her close and held her. "Let me do that."

70

The hiss of air brakes made his eyes snap open.

Had she really destroyed them? He wanted to believe that.

But if she'd lied about the necklace, had she kept the journals?

No. She'd always been honest with him. With that matter settled in his mind, he turned his attention toward the remainder of the evening.

"Do you think we're safe?" Ahmad asked in Farsi.

"We are." Makmoud leaned against one of the screened-in veranda's posts. "That, I can promise."

For a moment, the wind whispering through the fronds of the surrounding palms filled the night air and carried on it the tangy aroma of salt.

The youngest Hidari brother lifted his drink to his lips. The pale yellow liquid of the margarita trembled in the dim light emanating from the lanterns.

Annoyance sizzled through Makmoud. "Ahmad, my brother, I understand your concerns. I know you don't want to walk off the plane and into a trap. I promise you won't."

"But if they come looking for her?" Ahmad paced and swept a hand through his hair.

"I hacked into the system." Jibril's low rumble penetrated the gloom from where he sat on a chair next to the windows. "Señorita Cortez checked into the resort yesterday, which was the day we saw her. She isn't due to check out until Sunday. I added her name to the tour manifest of the group that went to San Jose today. Then it will seem as if she wandered away and got herself mugged and murdered."

"You killed her?" Ahmad stared.

Now the annoyance returned full force.

"What did you want us to do? Let her report to her handlers all she recorded?" Makmoud set his icy mojito glass on the railing. "Then you would most certainly walk into a trap."

"You're right." Ahmad sighed and shook his head.

Makmoud studied him as he picked it up and took another sip. "What does your wife know?"

Ahmad shrugged. "Nothing. Only that you both work at the Iranian embassy in Caracas, Venezuela, in the economic relations section. If the authorities question her, all Monica could say is that we had a falling out and only recently patched things up enough to vacation together. Nothing else in my life would reveal any contact with you."

Makmoud smiled. "It is perfect. Ahmad Hidari. Family practice physician. US citizen. Family man." The smile turned to a smirk. "*Quds* agent running Murdock."

A little girl burst onto the front porch, followed by her sister, who toddled after her. A tall brunette in yoga pants and a T-shirt followed.

Mira, the little girl, scrambled onto Jibril's lap. "Tell me a story, Uncle Jibril."

"You want me to tell you a story? What about Uncle Makmoud?"

Makmoud smiled as her sister wrapped her arms around his leg.

"I want a scary story," Mira announced.

Makmoud couldn't help it. He laughed and winked at Jibril.

Monica, Ahmad's wife, settled on the love seat beside her husband.

Makmoud's cell phone began chiming. His breath caught when he noted the number. One of his informants from northern Virginia.

"Let me get this. Then you can start." Makmoud handed off the toddler to her mother and stepped into the silky night air.

"How are you doing, my friend?" he asked in English to avoid tipping off the spies at the National Security Agency.

"I am well. And you?"

"Very well. Has anything interesting happened?"

"One of your old friends visited. He said he knew your girlfriend." Eagerness pushed at Wasim's voice.

Makmoud rested his foot on the edge of the fire pit. His pulse jumped. "Oh?"

Seeming to gain momentum, his informant continued, "Yes. He did. He was speaking with my boss and mentioned a gold necklace. It sounded handmade and really expensive."

"Tell me more." Makmoud glanced at the villa.

Monica's silvery laughter floated to him and reminded him of when he and Rachel had dated.

"They talked for a long time. It sounded like his girlfriend died."

"Did this man have a name, or did he never mention it?"

"He said Victor Chavez."

Makmoud's mind began whirling. How had Victor come across the necklace he'd given to Rachel so long ago?

"Are you there?"

"So sorry." Makmoud eased onto an Adirondack chair. "I was thinking. Thank you for letting me know. I'll send you a present."

Makmoud tapped his phone against his hand as he considered the implications of his informant's words. Victor Chavez had discovered a potential link between Rachel and him. What impact did it have? He thought back to the last face-to-face conversation he'd had with Rachel.

"You'll take those journals of yours," he'd told her as he'd tossed all of the composition books he'd found in her nightstand onto the bed. "And you'll destroy them. You see, I know you've written all about me in them. If you don't want to go down with me, then you'll do what I say."

Rachel, her blonde hair hanging in tangled strands that partially hid her face, huddled on the bed. The black eye from his ambush had caused her right eye to swell almost shut. A tear slid down her cheek. She whispered, "Okay."

Now, he wondered if she really had.

Did it endanger him?

Makmoud considered that one.

No.

At least not now.

If Victor Chavez found those journals, he wouldn't stop until he had answers.

And that would be when Makmoud would finish what he'd started over two years before.

7

With a cheerful ding, the elevator doors slid open. Darkness pressed against the floor-to-ceiling windows at both ends of the hall. Only recessed sconces provided a dim glow. The carpet muffled his footsteps as Gary strode to Room 1234, where Victor stayed for the duration of his visit in DC.

He knocked on the door. Not that he expected a response since his best friend had vanished to parts unknown.

With another furtive glance up and down the hall, Gary pulled out the key card that would grant him access. He slid it into the lock and slowly removed it. With a flash of green lights and a beep, the lock clicked.

Gary stepped inside. Only the lamp on the worktable glowed. Perfect for what he had to do. He glanced downward. A smirk curled his lips as he found the small slip of paper with the end folded upward. He crumpled it in his hand and threw it toward the trashcan next to the dresser.

Nothing but net.

After draping his suit jacket over the back of the worktable's chair, he tossed his phone onto the table's smooth surface and paced around the room as he searched it. He turned out the pockets of Vic's suit. Not even a stray thread. Nothing in the safe either, indicating his friend had taken his computer to wherever he'd gone. Gary turned to the suitcase and lifted the bundles of clothing. His friend hadn't tucked anything between the folds.

He muttered under his breath.

Hadn't Vic understood that Shadow Box was his baby, that he wanted to be in on the planning?

Gary scowled. He eased onto the chair and rested his elbow on the arm, his chin in his hand as he picked up the phone.

It chirped, indicating a text. It was from Mary.

I've started researching Hawaii. Let's do a resort.

He tapped out a reply.

That's ten months away. LOL.

One can dream. Two weeks away with you?

He chuckled as his thumbs worked again. *Dream on. I'll see you in about an hour or so.*

I've got a plate of spaghetti for you. Love you.

His lips twitched upward as he thought about his wife. Next year, they'd celebrate twenty years of marriage. When talking about their milestone, he'd suggested going big, especially because their tenth anniversary celebration hadn't existed. That's what happened when the husband wound up as a POW for six months.

The smile dimmed, then disappeared. He wouldn't think about that. Not right now.

The bird tweet signaled another text.

Mary again? He toggled on the screen.

The desert is beautiful this time of year.

No name. Blocked number.

Gary swallowed hard as the buzzing began in his head, at first sounding like one bee but increasing in intensity. He leaned over and braced his head between his hands. He clenched his jaw, and his chest heaved.

His phone started ringing.

As if warned, the buzzing retreated to a murmur before disappearing.

"Let me guess, you're in my room," Vic said when he answered.

"Right here and waiting on you, bro."

The lock clicked again, and Vic, clad in a black T-shirt, jeans, and hiking boots, stepped into the room. His short black hair stood up in odd spikes, indicating he'd run his fingers through it as he always had when thinking hard. "Why am I not surprised?"

Gary's cheeks heated. "What'd you expect? For me to go home and have spaghetti while you outwitted my tails—again?"

"Uh, yeah."

"Vic."

"Sorry, man. I told you I wanted to keep it compartmentalized."

Gary jumped up and planted both hands on the table. "And I wanted to be in the on the planning. Don't you trust me?"

"You know I do. You're my best friend." Vic tossed his knapsack onto the king-sized bed and followed it. "The question is, do *you* trust *me*?"

"Huh?" Confused, Gary eased onto the chair.

Vic lay back. "Do you trust me to act without your supervision, to get this team trained up and mission ready?"

"That's why I chose you."

"Then remember that because you trust me and I trust you, I want to protect you. All I ask is for the latitude to do that, okay?"

"What do I tell the president?"

"That you chose a leader who is working hard to get a team up and running in six months. He gave us a tall order, you know."

"I know. But what if he wants to know where you're based? Or the details?"

"Do you really think he'd want to know the details? And wouldn't you want to shield him as much as possible? C'mon, Gary. Why this angst all of the sudden?"

"Because this is just as much my baby as it is yours." His voice had risen, but he didn't care.

"Well, if it matters any, you did a great job in choosing a team."

Gary blinked. "Thanks, I think." Suddenly, it clicked. "Wait. You're taking the job?"

"Yep."

Inwardly, Gary rejoiced. No igloos in Nome for him!

Vic raised his head and smiled. "You were right. And seriously, you chose a great team. Sure, they've got different personalities and varying levels of experience, but it's enough to work with. Look. I'll give you weekly updates and be in constant contact. Will that help?"

"Whatever."

"Gary."

"Sorry. Not feeling my best," Gary muttered as the buzzing began humming again, this time almost low in the depths of his soul. Now came the headache that had always accompanied the buzzing ever since his release from captivity almost nine years before. It pulsed low and dull somewhere near the base of his skull. He needed to leave and make a call for both to go away. He rubbed his temples.

A long silence followed, so long that he thought his friend had fallen asleep.

"I went and saw Kamal Akram. He said you visit him regularly." Vic's words made him open his eyes and raise his head.

"What?"

"I saw Kamal Akram about the necklace I found behind the photo."

"What did he say about it?"

"It says 'Beloved.' In Farsi."

"Farsi? Wow. That's unusual."

"Yeah. Tell me about it." Vic finally sat up. He sighed as he began undoing the laces of his boots. One by one, they clunked to the floor. "I mean, I don't understand. Rach made a point to state how she always tossed photos, gifts, and other mementos of her exes, including her ex-husband. Why did she hide this?"

"Maybe she loved him deeply and couldn't let go of that. Maybe that embarrassed her. Or maybe she stuck it in there and forgot about it."

"It was made in 1998. At least that's what he could tell. And it probably cost the guy close to a couple of thousand dollars."

"That's impressive."

Vic muttered under his breath. He rested his elbows on his knees and stared at the light gray carpeting.

"Look." Gary leaned forward. "You've got to let it go for now. Can you do that?"

His best friend met his gaze for a moment. Then he sighed. "I guess I've got no choice."

"You've got a team to prepare and I'm sure a lot of logistics to take care of as you move to where?"

A muscle twitched in Vic's jaw at his latest jab. "Where we're going. Don't worry. I know what I need to do. Here's a list for you."

He dragged his backpack to him and extracted a notepad. He ripped off a sheet and handed it over. "Your shopping list."

Gary glanced at, folded it, and slid it into his shirt pocket. "I'll get started on this."

He rose, added his phone to the clip on his belt, and picked up his jacket. "Sorry to have to run, but Mary's waiting on me. You keep in touch with me. Understand?"

"Absolutely."

Gary crossed the room and opened the door. He turned. "And Vic."

Vic now leaned against the wall next to the bathroom door. "Yeah?"

"I hope your secrecy doesn't come back to bite you on the butt."

With that last warning, he turned his back on him and retreated to the elevators.

8

Victor hefted the last box onto the worktable of the design studio behind the Chavez family home outside of Flagstaff, Arizona. The growling in his stomach signaled it was lunchtime. Just this one more box. Then he'd be ready to eat and would greet the first members of the Shadow Box team when Butch, Sana, and Suleiman arrived later that afternoon.

He lifted out a set of folders and slid them into one of the file drawers under the worktable. He reached inside and took a bigger stack.

Too big.

They slipped. He grabbed at them, but they tumbled from his hands. Papers spilled everywhere until they covered the slate floor around him.

Grumbling, Victor stooped and began gathering them to himself.

Several yellowing newspaper articles caught his eye. His breath hitched as he realized what they were.

A history of the attempted kidnapping and Rachel's death.

With trembling hands, he gathered them into a neat stack. He added them to the appropriate folder and stashed them in the drawer without another look. A sigh shuddered through him as he collected some more papers.

The tremors worsened when he realized he held Rachel's last will and testament that had given him all of her possessions. He bit down hard on his lip until the sadness receded slightly.

The will went into another folder, and he reached for the last sheet.

He held in his hands the inventory of what the Secret Service had removed from his house.

Victor remained in his crouch as Gary's words slammed into him.

"You've got to let it go for now. Can you do that?"

Maybe it was like Gary had said. For the past ten days, Victor had convinced himself it was true.

Rachel might have been too embarrassed to admit her past relationship.

But what about the journals?

Had she really destroyed them like she'd said?

Like yeast slowly diffusing in dough, the doubt spread into his trust in her honesty.

He needed to put his worries to rest.

How?

In a flash it came to him.

He had to search for the journals.

After rising, Victor turned on his heel and strode through the warm September air toward the house of glass, wood, and stone that had been his childhood home and now belonged to the Chavez clan since his parents had passed away several years before.

He crossed the slate terrace with its wrought iron furniture and headed inside through the mudroom and past the archway that opened onto the eat-in kitchen. The great room loomed before him, its ceiling soaring two stories. Thanks to the warm fall weather, the massive stone fireplace between the kitchen and great room lay dormant. Sunlight splashed through the large windows and lit several paintings by local artists as well as Navajo pottery. He passed over the hardwoods and climbed the stairs on the other side of the half-wall from the foyer. Once on the walkway, he returned to the back of the house and took a second set to the master suite on the third floor.

Victor pushed the door open.

Inside sat the furniture he'd bought for the master bedroom of his house in Raleigh. In their search, had the Secret Service missed checking his mattress?

He pulled off the comforter, sheets, and mattress pad. A careful study of the seams showed no tampering.

Where else? Victor remade the bed and eased onto the edge. Then he nodded. He had the remainder of Rachel's furniture in one of the outbuildings so he could sell it at a later date. She could have hidden something there.

Two hours later, he leaned against her jewelry table and contemplated what he'd learned.

No journals.

Meaning she must have destroyed them like she'd said.

Victor nodded. That had to be it.

Relief surged through him. Satisfied, he shut and locked the door before heading to the studio to finish decorating.

While his two new Blue Heeler dogs lolled in the sun outside the door, he unloaded some boxes of books and stashed them on the shelving beneath the worktable's surface. More pictures, these of landscapes and friends, went onto the sills. He turned to the conversation area made up of the furniture that had been in the living room of his house.

Victor settled onto the drafting chair and contemplated the layout. After making some adjustments, he considered the hibachi pots that had been Rachel's. They fit perfectly with the Oriental décor of the room and could flank the fireplace.

Right now, they sat side by side next to the door where the movers had left them.

He crouched. Victor groaned when he tried to move one.

"I've forgotten how heavy these things are," he muttered as he strained against the iron.

Rachel's words shortly after they'd gotten engaged echoed in his ears. He'd helped her move her furniture into his house. "Silly, I know they're heavy. Why don't you take off the lids to lighten the load a little?"

"You never learn, do you?" he now muttered to himself. He grasped the handle on the lid and pulled.

It didn't move.

"What on…"

He tried again.

Nothing.

Victor bent and peered at the underside.

Along the lip of the pot where the lid rested, the paint seemed too black.

He grabbed a penlight from one of the worktable's drawers and returned to the pots.

Fresh black paint gleamed at him in a small line. The paint on the rest of the pots appeared worn, the metal showing in some places. Patina was what the experts called it.

Victor used his pocket knife to scrape the area covered with fresh paint. Gradually, metal emerged, the sheen and luster incongruent with the rest of the iron. He got the same result on the other one.

Victor sat back and scratched his head. Why would Rachel weld the lids onto the pots?

He massaged his temples. "Think. Think. Think. Why would she do something like that? When did she do it?"

With his wrists resting on his knees, he considered this new twist. He closed his eyes. Those last few weeks before Rachel's death nipped at him.

Her tears when he told her he had to go out of town with the detail when Maggie and Rod took a vacation. Her brave smile and assurances she'd be okay. The shiner on her eye and her listlessness when he returned. After that, they'd worked the same shifts, and Victor had stayed near her to offer his support. They'd hardly been apart until that fateful night.

Meaning…

Victor leaped to his feet. He located his welding equipment in the large tool shed and dragged it into the studio. It took him only minutes to cut through the lid of the one on the right. He lifted it and set it aside. Wadded up newspapers, dated from March 2012 on the day he'd returned from his trip, sat on top. He pulled those out.

"Rocks! Huh?" That didn't compute. Why weigh down something that was already heavy?

The idea struck him, almost like a blow to the head.

To make it weigh the same as the other one.

Wielding the torch, he cut into the other pot and removed the lid.

More newspapers, again with the same date.

Those went flying through the air.

"Eureka!" Victor drew in a sharp breath as he stared at the composition book. Rachel had scrawled "2012" in her messy handwriting on the cover.

He stilled.

Almost like he handled fine china, he extracted twenty notebooks, each three hundred sheets thick.

A sick feeling started in his gut as he realized how wrong he'd been in his assumption about Rachel.

Before him lay the innermost thoughts of the woman he'd loved and now mourned.

"Rach…" His word barely penetrated the noise of the breeze murmuring through the ponderosa pines. "You…you lied to me. Why?"

He ran his thumb along the smooth cover of the one on top.

Did he dare open them? Penetrate her privacy? Did it matter?

She was dead.

Hands suddenly trembling, he lifted the one for 2012.

Then he laid it down, closed his eyes, and began shaking his head. "I can't. Or maybe I don't want to."

Victor stretched his neck and rubbed the back of it. Rachel's emphatic "Yes!" when he'd proposed and her silvery laughter echoed in his mind. Then came the sleepy smile when she woke up in his arms the following morning. At that moment, he'd considered life perfect.

No more. The past sixteen months had wounded his soul in more ways than he could count.

"Who were you way back when, Rach?" His words surprised him because he suddenly realized their truth.

The necklace proved he hadn't known her as well as he thought he had. Questions hammered at him.

When had she met the man who'd given her the necklace? How involved were they? Why hadn't she told him? What other information had she withheld from him? He hadn't known, since he'd never broken her trust by reading her journals without her knowledge.

Victor reached for the one he'd set on top. He traced the 1991 she'd written in silver marker. "I need to know the truth."

He opened the cover and began reading the first entry that talked about her therapist's suggestion to journal as a way to recover from the rape after her freshman year of college.

He hesitated.

Finally, curiosity got the better of him. Grabbing 1991 through 1997, Victor rose and wandered to the couch. He set the journal from 1991 on his lap. His fingers brushed its cover. For a moment, he remained frozen. Did he dare delve into the very private thoughts of the woman he loved?

She's gone. She's not here to get upset with me.

Victor drew in a breath, held it, and slowly released it as he opened the notebook to that first entry.

As he read, he learned one thing.

Rachel had a great eye for detail, so much so that he began realizing his knowledge of her, even after a year of friendship and two years of dating her, fell far short of what he'd expected. Now he knew how much the rape had impacted her. It nearly tore apart her family. She had difficulty in forming friendships with girls, let alone dating boys. To her, they wanted not friendship but to sleep with her. She couldn't and wouldn't do that.

Getting commissioned as an officer in the Army healed her. During her posting in Japan, she thrived in her work as an analyst in Army Intelligence. Then came a change in duty station to the University of Arizona. While there, she sought a Master's Degree in Psychology and taught ROTC.

Victor finished the one for 1996, which ended as she completed her first semester. After breaking to fix himself some coffee, he reached for the one for 1997. He fanned the pages. Two photos fell out and fluttered to the Navajo rug underneath the coffee table.

"What's this?" he muttered as he scooped them up.

His heart nearly seized as he stared at the first one.

Rachel, with her shoulders almost bare save for the straps of a black dress and her blond hair in a sleek chignon, stood next to a twenty-something Makmoud Hidari, who held up a velvet case holding some sort of medallion.

"What the…" The words dribbled away as he flipped the photo to note what Rachel had scrawled on the back.

Fall 1996 Psychology Department Awards banquet.

He studied it again.

So they were in the same department at U of A. Big whoop.

Like he believed that.

Victor turned to the other one.

Clad in a white shirt and khakis, Makmoud held Rachel close. The red sheath fit her perfectly. A sensual smile played about her lips. And that look in her eyes? Victor knew it all too well, because that was the way she'd gazed at him once they'd begun dating.

Rachel had loved Makmoud.

"I don't…" The lump in his throat choked off his words. Victor sipped his coffee and set the mug on the glass top table. The ceramic rattled against the glass, a small indication of the way the revelation shook him to his core.

He set the pictures beside him and stared at the notebook. Could he read any further? Rachel's journal from 1997 sat on top of the stack, almost taunting him to look inside. Did he dare delve into Rachel's relationship with Makmoud?

"Boss? Hey, boss? Where are you?"

Victor jumped when Butch Addison's Louisiana twang rocketed into the studio and bounced off the glass and stone walls. Where could he hide the journals? He grabbed an afghan and threw it over the ones he'd been reading before jumping to his feet. With one scoop, he shoved the others onto a shelf underneath the worktable.

"There you are." Butch, his bald head and small silver hoops gleaming in the late afternoon light, grinned. "Wow. Nice digs. Is this your lair?"

"Something like that." Victor's stomach growled, making him realize how he'd spent lunch as well as the entire afternoon digging into someone's very private thoughts. His cheeks began flushing. In an effort to distract his deputy, he asked, "Have you heard from Sana and Suleiman?"

"Yep. They're about an hour behind me. So tell me where to dump my junk." Butch gestured to the small rental moving van with a silver Ford F-250 trailered on the back.

"Right this way." Victor stepped into the early evening air that already chilled as the sun receded toward the horizon. As he shut the door behind him, he deliberately locked away thoughts of Rachel into the dingy depths of his mind. Right now, he'd fulfill Gary's request. He'd put his mind, heart, and soul into training the team, even if it nearly killed him to avoid reading the journals.

"You didn't have to do that." Nerves pricked Deborah as she returned to the kitchen and found Zach placing the last of the supper dishes in the dishwasher that mid-September Friday evening.

He grinned at her. "No worries on this end. I knew you had to get Gracie and Marie to bed. Are they asleep?"

"Finally."

"Anna and DJ are coming home when?"

"Late, late tonight. It's bowling night for the junior high youth group. Wine?"

"I'll take a glass."

Deborah pulled a bottle of chardonnay from the refrigerator and found the wine opener in the drawer amidst spatulas, slotted spoons, and other serving paraphernalia.

The night air, laden with the luscious smell of gardenias, whispered through the open windows, lulling her, tempting her with the promise of romance.

He placed his hands on her shoulders.

She started as their warmth soaked through the fabric of her T-shirt and into her skin. "Gracie didn't want to go to sleep."

"Oh?" Amusement danced in his voice. His fingers, rubbing muscles weary from an afternoon of yard work, sent tremors of delight down her spine. "Why's that?"

"She likes to be in the middle of the action." Nerves made her jab the screw into the cork. She twisted it down.

"I was thinking she harbored a crush on me."

"You're silly." She pulled the cork out.

"Not so silly that I can't admit to crushing on her mama." Zach ran his hands down her arms and took her hands.

Deborah stilled as he kissed her on neck. "You flatter me."

"No flattery needed. That's the truth." He reached around her and pulled two glasses off the rack. With her almost in his arms, he poured the wine.

She turned. "Seriously, Gracie always wants to be involved in everything."

He was so close that her nose quivered from his aftershave. "But some things…"

"Are not meant for consumption by under-aged children."

He rewarded her cleverness by drawing her close. His lips brushed her forehead.

Deborah shivered. Her heart hammered.

He touched his lips to hers.

Oh, my…

His arms tightened around her. He deepened the kiss.

Derek.

Deborah stiffened as she thought of her husband, now dead almost four years. She hated herself for her reaction.

"Deb…"

She pulled back. "Zach, I—I…I'm sorry."

He completed the chasm. "It's okay."

"No, it's not." Deborah took an unsteady sip of wine. She swallowed hard. "I thought I'd be ready. I led you on, and—"

"No leading needed." He leaned against the counter and folded his arms across his chest.

"I thought that when I took off my engagement and wedding band, that I was ready. I guess I was wrong." She closed her eyes and fought the tears of frustration pushing against them.

"Look at me."

She shook her head.

He took her hands, and her fingers curled around his.

"Deb, please."

She opened her eyes.

He smiled gently. "I know it takes time. I'm not going to pressure you, okay?"

Deborah nodded.

"When you're ready, give me a call."

"That might be forever." Her attempt at a joke fell flat.

"Let's hope not." Tenderness filled his gaze. He brought her hands to his mouth and kissed her fingers. "I'll see you around."

With that, he stepped through the door and out of her life.

"I hate this," Deborah muttered. A tear finally worked its way loose. Feeling like a loser, she slapped it away and gulped some of the golden liquid. She coughed as it burned its way down her throat.

Her cell phone began chiming.

"Deb, it's me, TL." Her handler's voice did nothing to lift her spirits.

"TL, what a surprise." She earnestly hoped her voice didn't sound hoarse from emotion. "You're working mighty late on a Friday."

"Had a case going on. We brought down another bad guy. How about you?"

"I've learned I stink at this dating thing." She swallowed hard. "What can I do for you?"

"You heard from Murdock lately?"

"Not since Nasser read through the message I sent last month." She pushed away from the counter and padded into the study. "Let me check." It took only a moment to log in to my e-mail. "Wait..." Her breath caught. "I've got something."

Deborah deciphered the rambling message about looking for a quick hookup at a deserted spot in Charleston. "I think we got a hit. He…he wants to meet in Charleston at a place of our choosing."

"When?" Steel came into TL's voice.

"Nineteenth of December. We're to let him know where and what time. Should I respond?"

"No. Not yet. We wait. We wait until the middle of October. Let him sweat a little bit since he did that to us. That'll give us time to set up a location we can manage."

"All right."

"Good going, Deb. We've made him take the next step." They talked for a few minutes before hanging up.

As she tiptoed upstairs, a smile pushed its way to her face. She'd accomplished something by taking a crucial step toward bagging Murdock.

Now if only she could take that next step in her personal life.

9

October 2013

Deborah knew she should have been happy, should have been laughing at the way four-year-old Marie flounced up to one of the fathers of her friends and held out her bag for trick-or-treat candy. Instead, her head began hurting, thanks to the din of noise that had risen with each hour of the Halloween harvest festival. The overly sweet smell of caramel candy apples added to the headache.

Automatically, her gaze sought out six-year-old Gracie, who ran toward her sister, the angel wings of her costume staying only half on. Marie, the light catching the fake jewels of her princess tiara, opened her bag to show her the haul she'd already made.

Where was DJ? There he was, elaborate as ever in a shirt, vest, pants, and boots. A fake sword hung at his side and an eye patch covered one eye as he guided youngsters toward the line that had formed for the fun house. This year was the first year as a twelve-year-old where he could help rather than participate, and he'd planned his costume for weeks.

And Anna? Deborah spotted the green martian as her fourteen-year-old manned the Whack-a-Mole table. She laughed as one of the children hefted the hammer and tried to hit a mole.

"Is the noise getting to you?" Wanda Dalton's teasing voice made Deborah cease rubbing her temples.

"Something like that." Deborah clasped her hands between her knees and stared at the dirty linoleum, now coated a faint orange where someone had spilled punch. "You're going to have quite a cleanup in the morning."

"Nah. It's a small price to pay for offering kids a safe alternative to wandering dark country roads."

"I hear ya."

"So how are things going with Zach?"

Forget her headache receding. If anything, it increased. "I told him yesterday when he came over that I couldn't do it."

"What?" Wanda stared.

Deborah began twisting her purse strap. "I couldn't do it."

"But...but why? I thought you two would be perfect for each other."

"I'm just now...I—oh, I don't know." Hot tears filled Deborah's eyes. Tears of what? Sadness? Frustration? "I guess I thought I was ready to date. Turns out I wasn't. I told him so in September, but he kept coming around."

"He's like that. He loves to help people."

"Oh, I know." Deborah swallowed hard. "And that's what kills me. He's a good guy. Solid. Dependable. Loves the Lord like Derek did."

"There you go." Wanda leaned against the vinyl of the chair with a small smirk on her face.

"There I go, what?"

"You're comparing him to Derek." With that, she folded her arms across her chest and lifted her chin as if she'd figured out all of world's problems.

Faint irritation flashed through Deborah at her mentor's truth. "I can't help it, okay?"

"I get that, but it puts him—or any guy—at a disadvantage before they even get to the starting line with you."

"I know, but..." Deborah bit her lip as she once more searched for Gracie and Marie. They stood in the line for the fun house. She sighed. "Anna's not fooled. You know what she told me last night?"

A smile played at Wanda's lips. "What?"

"I need a man in my life."

At that, Wanda laughed. "From the mouths of babes. Or at least a young lady who's growing up very fast."

"Don't mention it. I get what she's saying. I want someone to teach Gracie and Marie how to throw a baseball and how to fish. I want a man who could share in DJ's budding interest in cars. But I want a loving husband-wife relationship too. Not just for myself, but to teach Anna how a husband should love a wife. I don't want to…don't want to settle, I guess."

Wanda nodded. "I know what you're saying. You've got good instincts. Maybe I've pushed you too hard on Zach. All I ask is that you keep an open mind."

Deborah opened her mouth to respond, but she jumped when the phone in her pocket began vibrating. She pulled it out and glanced at the number.

TL.

Her breath hitched a little. "I've got to get this." After rising, she wandered toward the double doors leading to the outside. "TL, hey."

"Deb, how's it going? What's that noise? I thought you'd be trick-or-treating with your kids."

"We're at a harvest festival." Deborah bit her lip. "What's up?"

"Have you heard from Murdock?"

"Not since I sent that message a couple of weeks ago."

"Right. When you get home, can you check? My boss is getting antsy."

"I can check right now and call you back." Deborah noticed how Wanda had risen and drifted toward the Whack-A-Mole table. "Wanda."

The older woman looked her way.

"Could you keep an eye on the kids? I've got to make a call outside."

Wanda nodded.

Deborah stepped into the chilly night air. Dead leaves crackled beneath her feet. The smell of others burning mingled with the spicy sweetness of the hot apple cider drifting from the inside. She kept to the lit area near the doors as she checked her e-mail on her smartphone. Her breath caught.

A hit.

Her pulse skittered upward as she opened the message from Murdock.

Immediately, Deborah punched in TL's number. "TL, it's me again."

"You got something?"

"It's a go."

His exclamation confirmed his excitement. "Great! Deb, good work. We'll get to work on planning the op. And with any luck, we'll nail the bastard by the end of the year."

Victor popped the top on a bottle of Dos Equis and joined Sana and Suleiman in the great room of the Big House, which was what the team had nicknamed the main house. After stoking the fire, he settled on the hearth. Warmth spread across his back as the flames regenerated themselves. "How are you two doing?"

"Tired but happy." Sana Jain, the petite gymnast-turned-reformed-cat-burglar, smiled and wrapped her fingers around the ceramic of the mug of tea she held. "How'd we do?"

Victor traced the rough stone of the hearth. "That's confidential until everyone gets here."

He glanced toward the wide hallway of the mudroom just as the door banged open. "Speaking of which…"

"Sorry we're late, boss." Butch led the way with Diana Kasem, Fiona Mercedes, and Skylar James following. The newly formed dog pack of Victor's dogs plus two Golden Retrievers followed.

"Make yourselves at home. Where's Shelly?" Victor glanced around for the computer specialist.

"Something about she didn't want her hair to freeze." Diana smiled and stepped into the kitchen. "Wine, Fi?"

Shadow Box's pilot nodded. "Merlot if it's there."

"Suleiman, catch." Butch tossed several pieces of mini Reese's Peanut Butter Cups toward Shadow Box's sniper. "Your first bits of Halloween candy, right?"

"Chocolate?" Suleiman grinned and began undoing the foil.

"Sorry I'm late!" Shelly's voice carried down the length of the mudroom.

Hair more frizzed than ever yet still hanging in scraggly lengths, she joined them. "I gave up on drying it."

"Everyone, have a seat." Victor gestured toward the remaining couches and chairs and picked up the clipboard he'd set on the stone.

"Okay, guys, before we set aside work for the weekend, let's talk about the fitness test today."

"I, like, so failed." Shelly groaned. She stood and gave a mock bow. "It was nice knowing everyone. I'll be leaving in the morning."

"I hate to disappoint, Shelly, but you passed."

Her eyes widened. "What? Did I hear you correctly?"

"You passed. You know I was tough on grading, but even at my toughest, everyone passed."

The team cheered, then laughed. The sound filled the room like rich, dark chocolate. Butch and Skylar slapped hands, and Fiona actually beamed at the news.

Victor set aside his clipboard. "More than that, I noticed the teamwork and encouragement going on. When Shelly couldn't squeak out another push-up, Butch was right there shouting at her to pull out one more. When Fi almost fell off the ropes course, Suleiman helped her across. When Sana couldn't get enough height to make it over the obstacle course's wall, Skylar was there to boost her up. That's what I've wanted to see, and I appreciate everyone making the effort. Having each other's backs will save your lives when we go down range on a mission."

"Hooah," Butch softly said.

"Amen to that," Diana murmured at the same time.

"Tell me something, gang." Victor leaned forward and fixed his team in his gaze. "What produced that change?"

"Butch." Skylar mock-punched his friend. "After our disastrous start that culminated with Shelly nearly dying, he pretty much told us what he thought of us."

"That was?" Victor turned his attention to his mechanic.

Butch scratched his goatee. "I forget, boss."

"No, it was something like we were acting like second-rate, no-good whiners." Sana toyed with the string on her teabag. "And that we'd all voluntarily signed up, which meant we'd made the choice to be there. And that we should respect you because Gary placed you in the position of leadership over us."

"What she said." Butch mussed her hair.

She giggled and ducked away.

"I'm thankful for that because I didn't want anyone to leave." Victor nodded at his deputy. "Now." He cleared his throat and picked up the ornate copper box where he'd stashed the proposed names for the ranch. "It's time to choose the new name for the ranch. I've got seven names here. Let's see what we have."

He opened the first one and nearly laughed. "Geeks and Grunts Ranch. Shelly, right?"

"That's me." She grinned.

"Eh, we'll keep that one for a vote. All right. The next one is…Shadow Box Canyon Ranch. Whose was this?"

"Mine," Sana replied.

"I like it, but since we're classified, we can't use it. I'm sorry."

"I tried."

"Mountain View Ranch."

"That is mine." Suleiman sipped from the stout mug he cradled in his hands.

"I like it. We'll put it into the hopper for a vote."

"Boys with a 'z' and Babes Ranch." Victor chuckled. "Very funny. Who wants to claim this one?"

"That's me, baby!" Butch stuck both of his fists in the air in a victory pose.

Everyone laughed.

"Okay." Victor took the fifth one. "We'll hold that one in for consideration. Mysterious Members Ranch."

"That's mine, I confess." Diana offered a rueful smile. "I'm not very creative when it comes to naming things."

"Except for your dogs," Sana told her as she ruffled the fur of one of the Golden Retrievers.

"Vic's Vixens." Victor shook his head. "Skylar, that has to be you because I can't imagine Fi doing that."

"I confess." Skylar grinned and leaned back against Fiona's chair.

"With great reluctance, we'll consider it. And last but not least, Last Chance Ranch, submitted by none other than Fiona."

"Wow. I like that," Diana said. "Why did you choose that?"

Fiona looked at Victor for a moment, her sherry eyes serious. "Because Vic was right."

He raised an eyebrow.

Fiona held his gaze for a moment longer before lowering her wineglass. "In September, he called me down for my role in what happened to Shelly. That's when he told me I had one last chance to get my crap together and fly straight. When I got back to my room, I saw he was right. This truly is my last chance."

No one dared break the silence with a sarcastic remark.

Victor blinked hard and tried to pretend the tears stinging his eyes were due to smoke from the fire. "Okay. The names we have are as follows: Mountain View Ranch by Suleiman. Geeks and Grunts Ranch by Shelly. Vic's Vixens by Skylar. Mysterious Members Ranch by Diana, Boys with a 'z' and Babes Ranch by Butch, and Last Chance Ranch by Fiona."

Last Chance Ranch won hands down.

"Last Chance Ranch it is. I'll work on coming up with a design and then place the order for the ironwork by next week. Since you all have worked so hard and given me more than a hundred percent on training, we'll take a long weekend. All I ask is that you exercise tomorrow and Saturday by doing something. We'll start with the new training on Monday. Dismissed."

Butch rose. With dramatic flourish, he slapped a box of Uno cards onto the table. With a grand gesture and Italian accent, he announced, "Uno! I challenge everyone to a game. Or games."

"Huh?" Skylar frowned.

Victor laughed. "Uno is Butch's favorite card game. Has been since I've known him. But beware. His tournaments are infamous. Forewarned is forearmed."

"Yeah, baby!" Butch picked up the pack. "Who's in?"

Everyone began gathering around the coffee table. Butch set aside the small copper sculpture of a wild bucking bronco and began dealing cards.

Victor stepped into the kitchen and snagged another Dos Equis from the refrigerator. As the group arranged themselves around the large table, he wandered into the cold night and shivered as the wind cut through his fleece pullover. At a trot, he headed to the studio, eager to delve further into Rachel's journals.

After getting a fire going in the studio's fireplace and turning the lamps on low save for the reading lamp, he picked up the journals for 1997 and 1998, both of which covered Rachel's years in her master's program.

Victor settled onto the couch. He ran his fingers down the faceless blue cover marked 1997 in black permanent marker in the messy handwriting that screamed Rachel to him.

For a moment, he sat there as weariness flooded over him. He slid into a slouch and closed his eyes as his mind rushed into the past.

"This is nice," Rachel murmured. She leaned her head against his shoulder.

"Isn't it?" Victor nuzzled her hair as he soaked in the warmth of the fire.

For a few minutes, they listened to the low sound of jazz. Victor lost himself in the scent of her shampoo and softness of her hair.

"Can I ask you something?" Rachel had lifted her head from where she curled up against him on the couch in front of the fire.

"Sure."

"Were there any other women in your life besides Olivia?"

"Anyone serious?" Victor shook his head. "No. What about you?"

Her shoulders rose and fell in a shrug. "Besides my ex-husband, who was more a mistake than anything else, not really. Oh, I dated a guy for a bit in grad school, but it wasn't anything serious. It was almost like a summer romance."

He tightened his arm around her. "You're my main squeeze now."

She giggled and rewarded him with a kiss.

A spark popped.

Victor's eyes flew open. He sat in the studio, his aching neck the only indication he'd dozed. After gazing at the smooth cover of the notebook, he slowly began reading about Rachel's life in 1997.

She didn't mention Makmoud until that fall when she presented a draft of her thesis. He questioned her and later offered her guidance. Things happened from there.

A disastrous first date. A second date to make up for the first. They took an hour to say good night.

Chest heaving, he set the book down. He took a deep breath. *Okay. So they were hot and heavy. Who isn't in their twenties?*

Then came the night of an awards banquet when Makmoud received a prestigious award for his research. He took her to bed, and they became firmly a couple.

Heat surged upward in Victor's neck and face as she described that night in detail.

"No! Why, Rachel?" Victor clamped his head between his hands as pain seared his heart. His jaw ached from clenching it. His fingers knotted his hair until his scalp burned. "Why did you lie to me? He wasn't some sort of dopey boyfriend not worth a mention by name. You *loved* him!"

Victor muttered under his breath and willed his heart to settle from its rocket pace. Finally, with shaking fingers, he opened the journal for 1998. "It can't get worse, right? I mean, you obviously weren't with him when we met."

It did. Far from a simple night or two spent between the sheets, Rachel and Makmoud got serious quickly. He gave her the necklace Valentine's weekend. She wrote about their time together in morbid detail.

Victor slapped the notebook shut. Head and heart aching, cheeks flaming, he again stared at the fire as tears of something filled his eyes. What? Embarrassment at the way she'd described their relationship? Anger that she'd lied to him? Jealousy that she'd loved Makmoud first? He didn't know.

The agony formed a hot ball in his stomach. Wrapping his arms around his middle did nothing to assuage the feeling.

He needed to talk with someone about the tangle of emotions within him.

Who?

His gaze wandered toward the Big House. Thankfully, the Laundry Building blocked the view so his team couldn't witness the meltdown of their leader. Would they understand? He'd never trust Skylar and Fiona with this kind of information. Sana and Suleiman were too young to understand. Shelly too. Maybe Diana. Or Butch.

No.

He had to work closely with them, and based on what Rachel had described, he was afraid they'd judge him since he knew they went to church with Sana and Shelly.

He couldn't go to anyone in town since the Chavez name was so understood and respected. And counseling? Forget it. His pride nixed any thought of sharing his problems with a complete stranger.

Loneliness hit him so hard that he flinched. *If only...if only I could have an empathetic ear. One who wouldn't judge me and could maybe help me look past what Rachel did.*

Burning the journals could free him of the desire he had to find the truth, to finish what he'd started by cutting open the lids on the hibachi pots.

He moved to throw it into the fire, then stopped.

He lied.

Burning the journals would do nothing.

He had to finish them.

Only later.

Like after he had his team completely trained.

10

December 2013

Deborah hunched on the desk chair in the study, one knee tucked to her chest, her chin resting on her knee. Her eyes drooped closed. The sweet scent of the cookies she'd baked with the children earlier that night tempted her to wander into the kitchen where they cooled on the counter to nibble on one, then another, until she was too wired on sugar to sleep. The peaceful melody of a Celtic version of "Silent Night" wrapped itself around her and wooed her toward slumber.

She'd sleep in heavenly peace once she finished paying bills and checking her e-mail.

A soft ping reached her.

Deborah raised her head and blinked. In front of her on the computer screen, the bills she'd intended to pay before drifting toward la-la land glowed at her. She hit the appropriate button, then closed the program

"Finally," she murmured under her breath as she checked her e-mail for the source of the ping. It'd come from the account she used for her FBI work. Her gaze devoured the e-mail's text.

No. No, it can't be!

In the semidarkness, she fumbled for her cell phone and dialed TL's number with fingers that shook so much she misdialed twice. When his sleepy voice answered, she blurted, "TL, we have a problem."

"What? Deb?"

"We have a problem."

"I don't understand. We're headed to Charleston tomorrow at first light for final setup. I've already got a team down there setting up surveillance."

"Murdock changed locations."

"What?"

"He changed locations." Deborah again reviewed the e-mail. "Not on Bay Street in Charleston but Pier 4 in North Charleston."

TL muttered something. "When did he send it?"

"Earlier tonight."

"Listen. I'm calling Nasser. We've got to change gears here. We need to discuss this in person, so look for us at eight."

"Okay," she drawled.

"Get some rest. We'll handle this when we get there."

Deborah swallowed hard.

"Mommy!" A child's plaintive voice reached her.

Marie.

"I'm sorry, TL. I've got to go. Marie needs me."

After hanging up, she jumped to her feet, scurried across cold hardwood floors of the den, and ran up the stairs to the bedroom of her two youngest. She sat on Marie's bed and touched her forehead. The fever, passed to her by Gracie, had broken. "What is it, sweet pea?"

"I'm thirsty."

"Do you want some fizzies?"

Marie nodded and tugged the blanket closer to her chin.

"Let me go and get something." Deborah padded downstairs. She shivered as her feet hit cold tile. Now she remembered kicking off her slippers while at the desk.

When she returned with a glass of ginger ale, Marie took a few sips before Deborah set the cup on the nightstand between the two beds. "Does that help?"

Marie nodded and blinked in the dim light coming from the hallway.

"Do you want me to pray for you?"

Her youngest daughter nodded.

Deborah slid off the bed and enfolded Marie's tiny hands in hers. "Dear Jesus, thank You for my sweet daughter, Marie. Thank You that she's feeling better. Please help her to sleep through the night. Amen."

"I love you, Mommy." Marie threw her arms around her neck.

Grateful for this little reminder of Derek, Deborah's eyes filled. "I love you too."

She tucked the covers around her and finished locking up for the night.

Deborah curled up under the comforter. Though her body warmed the sheets, her mind refused to rest. For a while, she stared at the clock. Then she dreamed. While all of her children slept, images of Nasser fighting with Murdock haunted her. Then came those of Derek locked in battle alongside TL against Murdock and other unknown forces. When she finally awakened at 6:30, she couldn't make sense of any of them.

Then she didn't have time since she realized she'd overslept.

The great Fields Morning Routine stood a very good chance of crashing and burning thanks to that.

Deborah bolted upright as that overwhelmed feeling ambushed her. She stumbled to her feet and onto the landing.

"Anna, DJ, time to get up! Gracie, you too." Deborah roused her brood. "C'mon. Mrs. Davis is coming to pick everyone up to go to the bus stop, and she's going to be here by 7:20. Up. Up!"

Grumbling greeted her as she pulled a sweatshirt over the long-sleeved T-shirt and pajama pants she'd worn to bed. She got the coffee going, then the hot water for everyone's oatmeal.

"Get out of the bathroom!" Anna's hollering reached her in the kitchen. Banging followed. "DJ! I've got to get my shower."

Deborah hustled up the steps. "What's the problem?"

"DJ's hogging the bathroom."

"Go use mine for your shower. DJ, the sooner you get out of there, the better."

Deborah checked on Gracie. Her second youngest had begun dressing in the jeans and sweatshirt Deborah had laid out the night before.

She ran back downstairs to begin making lunches. One by one, her children burst into the kitchen, Anna being the last. They huddled around the kitchen table and shoveled breakfast into their mouths between gulps of orange juice.

"Everyone, go brush your teeth. Hurry!" Deborah shooed them upstairs.

The chime of the alarm and a honk a few seconds later signaled the arrival of her friend to take the kids to the bus stop.

"Anna! DJ! Gracie! Let's go."

Footsteps thundered on the stairs. Her children ran into the kitchen. They snagged their coats from the pegs to the right of the door and backpacks from the bench beneath.

Deborah kissed each one. "'Bye."

As quickly as the noise had risen, it ceased.

Deborah heaved a sigh. She slumped at the kitchen table and finished her own breakfast before loading the dishwasher and starting it. She didn't know how she did it, only that God multiplied her time when she most needed it. Her gaze wandered to the barn where the horses waited to be let out for the day. She hesitated, worrying about leaving Marie alone in the house, even for the ten minutes it would take to put the horses in the pasture.

Sometimes, her time simply didn't stretch far enough.

She put her head in her hands. "How do I keep doing this alone?"

Deborah snagged her work jacket from its hook and pulled it on over her T-shirt before adding the boots she wore to the barn. With her dogs in tow, she rushed outside into the drizzle. She threw the hay bales into the shelter next to the barn and snagged the pitchfork. Using a utility knife, she cut the string holding them together and spread them out. As she finished filling the water trough, the Colonel started barking. He stood between the driveway and her, his ears and tail erect.

Deborah froze. Her heart pounded when she realized how vulnerable she was. Then she recognized the standard white Dodge Charger with its government plates as it slowed to a stop next to her Suburban. Her pulse eased from its rocket pace. She put one hand on her hip. "You're a bit early."

"Are we?" TL Jones asked as he climbed from behind the wheel.

"And what time is it?"

"Almost eight," Nasser reported. He grinned. "I told TL to slow down so the cops didn't bust us."

That did it.

A smile forced its way loose. "Come on in."

She led the way inside, where she deposited her jacket and boots on the peg and under the bench by the back door. "Do you mind if I go and change into something decent? You caught me in my pajamas."

TL chuckled. "Sorry about that. I guess we should have called. Show me what you have first."

Deborah led them to her study and handed them the folder and notebook containing her work. "You have to read the tea leaves to decipher it. There's coffee in the pot. Milk's in the fridge, sugar in the bowl there. And…"

She hesitated as she noticed the way Edgar and the Colonel waited patiently by their bowls. "I'll have to feed the indoor animals later. Nasser knows where the facilities are."

"Are you in mommy mode?" Nasser asked. His dark eyes twinkled.

"Something like that." She fled up the stairs and threw on a white blouse, a pair of jeans, and a black vest. Makeup would have to wait until the FBI agents left.

As she stepped into the hall, Marie called, "Mommy!"

"Here, sweet pea." Deborah sat on the edge of her bed and brushed her hand across her youngest daughter's forehead. "Your fever's gone. Do you feel better?"

"Uh-huh. I'm hungry."

"Let's go get some breakfast." Deborah scooped her up, Lambkins and all.

Marie wrapped her arms around her neck.

"Well, look who you brought down. Hi, there." TL offered a smile to Marie.

"Marie, this is Mr. TL and Mr. Nasser. Can you say hi?" Deborah held on to her.

Marie buried her face in her hair.

"She's just gotten over a fever, so she couldn't go to daycare today. Sorry she's a bit shy." Suddenly, Deborah noticed the way the dogs munched on the food in their bowls and the cats crunched theirs in bowls on the den's cat tree.

"We, uh, couldn't find the guinea pig food." TL shrugged.

Deborah laughed. "Thank you for completing my chores for me." She dumped another round of grounds into the coffeemaker, then pulled out a box of cereal and the milk carton for Marie's breakfast. "What have you decided?"

"I need to make a couple of calls. We'll talk after that."

What could she do? Argue with them? Again, Deborah pointed them in the direction of the study. As she supervised Marie, her gaze kept wandering to the open door.

TL had his phone to his ear and paced, his free hand gesturing as he talked with someone, most likely his boss. Nasser leaned against the desk, his hands braced on the edge in such a way that he'd pushed back his suit jacket to reveal the dull black of the gun at his waist.

She shivered.

Deborah rose and poured a small glass of juice for her daughter before rinsing the empty cereal bowl. When she returned to her seat, she cast another glance at the study.

Nasser and TL murmured in voices too low to overhear. She did catch the words "gun" and "body armor," which made her thoughts swing to the impending takedown. Her hands knotted into fists on her lap.

Deborah bit back a sigh and focused on Marie. "Would you like me to read you a story?"

"Can you?"

Deborah tucked a curl behind her ear. "Of course I can. How about *The Lion, the Witch, and the Wardrobe?*"

"Can we?" Excitement lit her daughter's face.

"Of course."

"Then can I go outside?"

"Maybe. If it stops raining. Are you finished?"

Marie nodded.

"Why don't you play quietly for a bit while I talk with Mr. Nasser and Mr. TL?" Deborah carried her up the stairs and made sure Marie was ensconced on the area rug at the foot of her bed with her favorite toys nearby.

When she returned, she found TL and Nasser in the kitchen, both with mugs of coffee in their hands.

"What's the verdict?" she asked as she poured herself another cup.

"We're going in." TL dumped his drink into a travel mug.

Her gaze darted between Nasser and TL. "Are you sure that's a good idea?"

"Deb, look." TL rested his back against the granite, his dark eyes focused on her. "We've got one shot at nailing this guy. I'm not going to let it go."

"But—"

"Besides, if we pull out now, you'll have to send a message passing on this opportunity. He'll get suspicious and go to ground."

"But what if he's already suspicious and that's why he changed the location?"

"We'll roll with it. I've already got my guys checking out the location in North Charleston." TL cast a look at Nasser.

"I'm worried that he doesn't have the best intentions for Nasser." She faced the junior agent. "I think we should pull back and cut our losses. Maybe regroup and try again."

"Look. If you're worried about not getting a bagging bonus—"

"I'm not." She rolled her eyes. "It's not that at all. I'm concerned that someone will get hurt, like Nasser or you."

"Deborah, please don't worry." Nasser's Texas twang calmed her only a little. "I'll be wearing a wire so they can hear everything. Body armor too. And backup will be right there. We'll secure the place so well that he won't be able to escape. We'll also have a tracking device in the duffel."

Biting the inside of her mouth until she tasted blood, she finally nodded. "Promise to call me when you're done."

"We will." TL smiled at her. "Nasser, time to rock 'n' roll."

Deborah followed them into the misty morning. That helpless feeling washed over her as she wrapped her arms around herself in a feeble attempt to ward off the chilly drizzle.

Maybe she wasn't totally helpless.

She knew what she had to do.

As the sound of the Charger's motor faded into the damp morning air, she wandered inside and picked up the phone. "Wanda, hey, it's Deb. Could you come over this morning and take care of Marie for a bit? I need to spend some time in prayer."

"Everyone out. Anna, I need you to get Nana and Papa's bedroom ready since they're coming on Sunday. Clean their bathroom, too. DJ, I want you to get the den picked up and vacuumed. Gracie, you dust the den and living room." Deborah shut off the Suburban's engine. "Be careful with the breakables. Marie, I know you can pick up the toys in your and your sister's room."

The kids piled out and rushed through the chilly drizzle toward the house.

"Can I go to Kelsey's tonight?" Anna asked as she hung her jacket on the peg by the door.

"Aunt Liza's coming at five, so maybe after supper."

"That means no." Anna turned her steps toward the bedroom that sat off the kitchen.

"That means I'll think about it." Deborah hurried upstairs, too distracted to argue. Her hand shot to the cell phone she wore at her waist.

Why hadn't TL called? He always did after they bagged one of the bad guys.

She couldn't let herself get wrapped up in it, not with Liza arriving at the house soon. She scrubbed down the kids' bathroom first, then turned her attention to the master bedroom.

Downstairs, the vacuum hummed. The Colonel yipped as if to shout how much he disliked the noise.

Deborah slipped into the hallway and peeked into Gracie and Marie's room. Marie picked up each toy and set it in the toy chest. She set their dolls on shelves. She placed Lambkins and Woolie, Gracie's favorite stuffed animal, on the beds and pulled the sheets up as if they were sleeping.

Deborah bit back her smile and carried the cleaning supplies to the master bathroom.

Once more, her fingers brushed her phone. Now she could barely focus on wiping down the sink and shower. She returned to the hallway and pulled out fresh towels for both Liza and her.

The phone began buzzing.

Deborah grabbed it. "TL, I was getting worried when I didn't hear from you. What—"

"Nasser's dead." TL's words tore into her question like an angry dog.

Deborah's knees began shaking. She leaned against the wall. "What?"

"He's dead. It was a trap, just like you predicted." Bitterness laced his words.

"I—I—I don't understand."

"Pier 4 was a pure container maze. We thought we had it nailed down. Turns out we didn't."

"I—"

"We couldn't get backup in close enough. All we heard Nasser say was, 'You!' Then a silenced gunshot and the sound of someone ripping the wire out. He left the tracking device a few feet away. He shot him in the head, Deb." His voice caught.

She slid along the tile wall until she rested with her knees tucked to her chest. Cries rose from somewhere within her. "I—I'm so sorry."

"No, *I'm* the one who who's sorry." TL blew out an angry sigh. "I'm pulling you off this for a bit to let things settle down."

"Am I safe?"

"I think so. Your safety is your anonymity. Murdock only knew Nasser as Hamid, not you. Stand down until I call you."

"I—I will." Her lower lip began quivering.

"I'm sorry, Deb."

"Me too." Her voice grew small as the sobs fought to loosen themselves from the cage of her self-control. "I—I don't know…"

What? What didn't she know?

She had no answer.

"And don't worry about any kind of report. It's pointless right now. I'll be in touch."

"Okay," she whispered.

Deborah kept the phone to her ear. Finally, she set it on the floor. She forgot about making the bed and putting the clothes in the basket away. She hunched, her forehead now resting on her knees, her chest heaving with pent-up sobs.

God, why? Why? Why did Nasser have to die?

Small cries escaped her. Her fingers clenched her hair. She bit down hard on her lip in a vain effort to fight the tears.

"God, why?" Anguish rent her voice. She began sobbing.

"Mom? Mom!" Anna's voice reached her. Suddenly, warm arms enfolded her. "What's wrong? Why are you crying?"

Deborah opened her eyes.

Blue eyes wide with worry, Anna crouched in front of her. "Did something happen to Aunt Liza, Nana, or Papa?"

"No, no." Deborah took a deep breath in a vain attempt to bring her grief under control. "No, they're fine. Do you…do you remember how I told you about what I'm doing with the FBI?"

"You're getting terrorists arrested."

"Something like that. Well, we were supposed to get another bad guy arrested last night. But…" Hot tears filled her eyes. Her voice hitched. "An agent died."

Anna didn't say a word, only let her cry. She rose, wet a washcloth, and handed it to her mother.

Deborah mouthed, "Thanks."

She pressed it over her face.

"About tonight," Anna said, suddenly all business. "I'll call Kelsey, Katie, and Keeley and see if they can't come over and make cookies. If that's all right with you."

Love for her oldest child filled Deborah. She nodded.

Anna hugged her close. "I love you, Mom."

"I love you back." Deborah climbed to her feet.

Somehow, she made it through the rest of the evening. Liza greeted her with a hug. Zach, who had graciously volunteered to pick up her sister when he met his brother and sister-in-law, talked with her for a few minutes. Her laughter sounded too bright to her ears. Her smile felt too brittle, like her face would shatter into a million pieces. If things hadn't been so somber, she would have smiled at the attention Zach paid to Liza.

Only when Anna and her friends made themselves at home in the den and kitchen did Deborah retreat to the living room with a glass of wine.

"Anna's got lovely friends," Liza said as she settled onto the couch with a sigh. "It's nice to finally be here. The Miami airport was a zoo."

"I'm sure." Deborah wiggled her socked feet in front of the fire.

A spark popped.

"What's going on? You look like you're about to burst into tears."

Deborah stared at the dark red liquid in her glass. She shuddered as she imagined Nasser's blood being shed. "The FBI lost an agent today."

"Huh?" Liza frowned as if trying to make the connection. "What does—Wait! One of the guys who helps you with the web hunting?"

Deborah nodded because the lump in her throat choked off her words.

"What happened?"

"He...he was shot trying to do a takedown."

"Oh, Deb." Liza set her glass on the coffee table and hugged her close.

Tears began spilling down Deborah's cheeks.

Her sister held on tighter.

Deborah cried for a few minutes. "I feel responsible."

"Don't. Please."

Deborah sniffled and took a deep breath. TL and Nasser had known what to do. She couldn't blame herself each time things went awry.

"Are you safe?" Liza asked after a moment.

Deborah's thoughts slid to the study closet where she kept the five suitcases full of clothes, as per the FBI's instructions. In case they had to leave suddenly, TL had told her.

Her mind wandered back to the day and her conversation with him. "I—I think so. TL told me my safety is in my anonymity. He said to stand down, that there's no true link between me and the agent."

"Maybe it's for the better right now."

Deborah nodded. She sniffled and grabbed a Kleenex from a nearby box. She blew her nose and dabbed at her tears. "I think you're right."

"And besides, Christmas is coming." A smile played about Liza's lips, and she wrapped several strands of her corkscrew curls around a finger. "Did I tell you I met a really cute guy who gave me a ride from the airport?"

Liza sure knew how to pull her out of a down mood. "Zach?"

"Yeah." Liza giggled. "He said you two had tried to make it work, but it didn't."

"I stink at dating." Deborah shook her head. "When he kissed me, I thought of Derek. Did he show interest?"

A little grin flitted across her sister's lips. "Maybe."

"You're so coy." Deborah couldn't help but smile. "Thanks for distracting me."

Though she and Liza talked for another hour or two, thoughts about TL, Nasser, and the ambush stuck with Deborah for the rest of the night. Once she'd tucked the children into bed, she retreated to the master bedroom with her sister.

While Liza got ready for bed in the bathroom, Deborah shoved back the curtains and stared out at the backyard and pasture beyond. In the silvery moonlight finally revealed by clear skies, she noticed how the trees tossed to and fro as a front moved in.

Anger as cold as the wind slamming into the house swept through her. She wanted to nail Murdock to the wall for taking Massoud's life.

Who cared if Murdock had found out where she lived?

As Deborah turned away and let the curtain drop, she knew one thing.

When she got that opportunity, she'd take it.

11

Gary shut off the engine of his car. His heart hammered in his ears. His hands clenched the steering wheel to the point that his fingers hurt. Only the occasional gust of wind and the sound of his breathing filled the interior. In his head, no silence reigned. Not at all. The buzzing filled it like a swarm of angry bees. A bead of sweat trickled down his temple in a cold line.

"The desert is beautiful this time of year."

"You!"

The words from the past couple of days exploded in his mind like the gunshot that had ended Nasser's life.

He drew in a breath and forced his death grip to loosen.

After cramming his fedora onto his head and turning up the collar of his leather bomber jacket, he shoved open the door.

The cold wind blasted across The Battery in Charleston and raked his cheeks. The bare limbs of the trees in Bay Point Garden clattered in time with it and made the Christmas lights strung on their boughs tremble.

With one last look around, Gary snatched the duffel from the trunk and strode toward the garden. As he walked, his hand touched the outside of the jacket where his pistol rested in its holster underneath. He paused near the Sergeant Gray monument.

Ahmad was late.

As always, whenever Ahmad triggered him, the headache joined the buzzing.

Gary rubbed the back of his neck with a gloved hand.

"It's a cold night, is it not?" Those words in lightly accented English sounded too familiar.

For a brief second, Makmoud's face from ten years ago blazed before his eyes.

Gary whipped around.

Makmoud's youngest brother stood on the pebble path, his face in shadow and dim lights thanks to the tossing limbs.

"It's about time you showed up. I was about to leave." Gary's hand tightened on the handles.

"Things went well, it seems." Ahmad nodded toward his prize.

"I knew the guy."

"Oh?"

"Yeah. Nasser al-Saad. I recruited him straight out of law school three years ago. The kid instantly recognized me."

Ahmad pressed closer, his eyes narrowing and his hand stroking his bearded chin. Abruptly the motion ceased, and he focused on his contact with a piercing dark gaze.

Once more, Gary found himself lying on the floor ten years before, his own filth coating him as Ahmad's brother loosened the ropes and chains that had held his hands to opposite walls.

"How do you think the FBI discovered you?"

"Huh?" Gary blinked. The image vanished.

"How did they discover you?" Ahmad cocked his head as he stopped mere feet from him.

"Web hunters." Gary scrubbed a hand across his jaw.

"Web what?"

"Web hunters. The FBI has a program where they contract with civilians who hunt people like me online. When they're ready to make the kill, they send in the FBI to do it. Don't you remember how I was reticent to make contact with this Hamid guy?"

"I do."

116

"My gut was right." Gary held out the duffel. "Here. I even brought you a present."

Ahmad stared at the bag as if it were a poisonous snake.

"Oh, c'mon. Don't you trust me? I followed your directions to the T. A hundred grand. All unmarked twenties. I left the tracking device they added in the container maze where I met Nasser."

Ahmad still hesitated. Eyes not leaving his mole, he knelt and undid the zipper.

"It's all there. Fifty packs. I even counted each and every pack."

"Excellent." Ahmad straightened and smiled. "You did well, Murdock. Very well. For your services, I want you to have a bonus."

He reached inside, collected five packs, and placed them in his hands. "For a job well done."

Gary swallowed hard. When he realized his handler's actions, the headache intensified another notch. If the money were tainted and traceable, then Gary would take the fall for the double-cross. He forced a smile to his face. "Thanks. This will come in handy for my little venture to Vegas in March."

"You'll receive your stipend as well. We appreciate doing business with you."

Gary's thoughts turned to Nasser and TL. "I'm glad I could be of service. I'd better run. The wife wasn't too happy when I told her work called me out of town on an emergency. At least I got out of a Christmas party."

"Safe travels." Without another word, Ahmad picked up the duffel, turned away, and strolled through the cold night.

Gary stood there, then shoved all of the packs into his jacket. The buzzing increased to a crescendo, just as it always did when Ahmad uttered his phrase. The last time? He'd killed a cop under deep cover in Minneapolis.

"Make it stop," he softly begged.

He braced his head in his hands.

With a pop, the buzzing disappeared, as did any recent memory triggered by the the phone call he'd received a couple of days earlier.

Gary blinked. For a moment, he remained frozen in place. Why was he in the middle of the park in the wee hours of the morning? All he remembered was that he'd come to Charleston on the pretext of FBI business. Then it hit him.

Makmoud.

It had something to do with him. What, he wasn't sure. The stiff outline of money packs under his jacket told him he'd received an extra bonus for his work.

Whatever it was. He couldn't remember.

The headache began throbbing in time with his pulse.

He needed to get out of there, to go to his hotel and pop a pill to make it go away.

A Charleston police cruiser turned onto one of the roads surrounding the park.

Gary froze and stepped into the shadows of a tree. He remained still as it continued down the street and turned onto Meeting Street without stopping.

Gary fled to his car. When he finally arrived at his hotel room, he slipped in the back way and used the fire stairs to retreat to his room.

By that point, nausea from the headache turned his stomach.

He staggered inside.

Without even undoing his jacket, he stumbled into the bathroom. His shaking fingers located the pill bottle. He popped one and collapsed onto the bed as he waited for it to take the edge off the pain.

At least now, he wouldn't have to worry about the web hunter coming after him.

12

March 2014

Deborah rested the laundry basket against her hip and opened the back door to the screened-in porch. "DJ, cut that television off and get the animals fed before I get back. Anna, if you could help Gracie finish dusting, I'd appreciate it. And keep an eye on Marie. She should be cleaning their room."

With that, she stepped into the chilly March air. At least the sun had come out and melted most of the snow from the last snowfall. Grass squished underneath her feet as she hustled to the clothesline and began pinning up the latest load. The Colonel had followed, and she scratched him behind the ears. "I wish you had opposable thumbs and could help me."

He wagged his tail as if agreeing.

She smiled and picked up a pair of Anna's jeans.

As her fingers worked, she realized how ordinary and routine her life had become. Wake up. Get the kids to school. See clients in her counseling practice. Pick up the kids and take them to their activities. Come home and get in bed at a decent hour. No web hunting or anything like that. No dating either.

It even seemed surreal at times.

The door to the porch banged shut.

Anna strolled across the greening lawn. "Do you need help?"

"Sure. Is your room straight?"

"All done."

"Bathroom done?"

"Check." Anna smiled and pinned up a pair of sweats.

"Where's DJ?"

"He's playing video games."

Deborah scowled. "I see."

"So you're okay with me going over to the Markhams to babysit?"

"Of course." Deborah smiled. "You know I'm okay with you doing that anytime on a weekend. Do you need supper beforehand?"

"Mrs. Markham says she has some for me."

"If you can finish this for me, I'll talk to DJ. Then we'll go." Deborah turned and strode toward the house. As she put her foot on the lower step, the phone clipped to her waist began buzzing.

She stilled when she saw the number on Caller ID.

"TL, hi." She glanced at Anna. Her daughter pulled out a sweatshirt and clipped it to the line.

"Hey, Deb. How's it going?"

"Same ol', same ol'. Just being a mom."

"Are you ready to add something else into the mix?"

"I'm back on?"

"You got it. I talked with my boss, and he thinks it's good to get back into the game."

"Really?" Deborah sank onto a chair.

"We've run a voice analysis on that last word Nasser said, and we're pretty sure he knew Murdock. Meaning that Murdock knew him. He also knew where to find the tracker in the bag because he pulled it out and left it behind in record time."

"You think he's in the FBI?"

"Probably. We're starting to take a look at possible suspects, but nothing's gelling."

"What do you want me to do?"

"How about you make it look like Nasser was actually a double agent for another organization that wanted Murdock's services? Send him an angry message from a guy who could have been Nasser's handler. You're ticked that he killed your man, your only contact you had within the FBI. Threaten to hunt him down and exact your revenge."

Slowly, Deborah nodded. Ideas began forming in her head. "I can do that. I'll take care of it tonight after I get DJ to a friend's house and Anna to babysitting."

"That'll do. Let me know when you send it, and if and when you hear back from him."

Deborah hung up, then headed inside. She found her only son lying on the floor, his thumbs and fingers flying across a console as Mario jumped from one level to another.

She crossed her arms. "DJ, rumor has it you haven't fed the animals."

"I will." His eyes remained focused on the screen. A small trumpet sound told her he'd reached the next level.

Annoyance nipped at her. She grabbed the remote from the coffee table and turned off the television.

"Mom!"

"No, or I'm not taking you to Robbie's for tonight."

"But I was winning!"

"The animals haven't been fed. Weren't you one of the ones who insisted that we have two dogs, two cats, guinea pigs, and fish?"

"Anna said she'd do it."

"It's not Anna's week. It's your week until tomorrow."

He harrumphed and climbed to his feet. Deborah watched as he dumped dog food into Edgar's and The Colonel's bowls and filled the water bowl before doing the same with Shadow and Bruiser, their cats. Then he poured some into the bowl in the guinea pig cage in the den.

"The fish, DJ."

He tossed a pinch into the tank.

"Two more pinches."

"Mom!"

"Two more pinches."

He threw them in there and slammed the lid on the tank so hard that the fish jumped.

Deborah cringed. "Go get your bag, and I'll take you."

She spent the remainder of the evening carting Anna to babysitting and DJ to his friend's house before going out for pizza with Gracie and Marie. Once at home, they watched a video before Deborah read them the opening chapter of *Black Beauty*. Only when she cut out their light and settled in front of her computer in the study did her mind swing to the e-mail TL had instructed her to write.

Deborah sat there, her fingers tapping the keyboard as she considered her words.

She'd thought it would be difficult to dredge up the anguish and anger that had overtaken her three months before.

Surprisingly, they flowed like rich chocolate through her veins.

Slowly, with gathering speed, she began drafting the message.

"Hi, honey, I'm here." Monday night, Gary clamped his cell phone between his cheek and shoulder as he opened the door to his hotel room at the Black Diamond Casino and Resort in Las Vegas. The metal edge bumped his shoulder as he dragged his suitcase and briefcase inside. "How are things there?"

"Oh, fine. Morgan's studying for her chemistry test. And David's excited about his first game tomorrow. I'm sorry you'll miss it." Mary's chipper voice floated to him from the East Coast.

"Me too." Longing to see his son's first baseball game of his final middle school season pulled at him. "I'll catch the next one."

"I know. I've also found some cool things we can do in Hawaii."

"Oh?" Gary grinned as he hefted his suitcase onto the rack and unzipped his briefcase. He lifted his laptop from it and set it on the desk. He powered it on. "What's that?"

"Let me see. Snorkeling is one. They also have a helicopter tour if you want, but that's expensive."

"How often are we going to go to Hawaii for a twentieth anniversary trip?" He located the hotel's instructions for logging in to the Internet.

"True. They have some pretty hikes on Maui. And apparently, the sunrise on Haleakala is a must-do."

"Then we'll do it. Remember that I want to laze on the beach some too." He checked his personal account.

Nothing there that couldn't keep.

Mary laughed. "I know, sweetie. We've got two weeks. Don't worry about that."

Gary chatted some more as he checked his work e-mail.

Vic had sent him a message. Shadow Box would move in to position Thursday morning as planned. The rest of the messages could wait until tomorrow.

He opened the account for Murdock.

A message from the personals site he used for his communications glowed on the screen. He clicked on the link. As Mary chattered on, Gary's eyes devoured the angry message about two-timing.

A chill wracked him.

He muttered a cuss word. His fingers curled around the chair's armrests.

"Gary!"

"Huh?"

"That's no way to answer." Annoyance added an edge to his wife's voice.

"Uh, what?"

"I asked what time you were planning on leaving next Tuesday."

Spring Break. That's right. Mary and the kids were leaving on Friday. The following Tuesday, he'd fly to Nashville and then ride back with them. "I'm not sure what time my flight is. After lunch, I think. I'm sorry for cussing, sweetie. I saw a roach run across the floor. Let me go and talk to the front desk about switching rooms."

"Okay. I love you bunches."

"Right back at you, baby." He blew her a kiss before tossing his phone onto the bed. Gary remained rooted to the chair. His elbows rested on his knees. His hands trembled slightly.

What had he done?

His mind raced through all he'd read.

According to the sender, some guy named Walid, Gary had killed his one inside man with the FBI.

Now, Walid wanted Gary's blood and would stop at nothing until he was dead.

Unless Gary wanted to work for him for free since he'd pocketed their one hundred grand.

Had he made a mistake?

Gary swore long and loud.

He dropped his head into his hands. Staring at the floor, he saw nothing. Sweat built along his hairline.

What should he do?

Was it real?

Or some farce to draw him into the open?

It wasn't like he could go and ask TL if he'd put his web hunter back into the game or anything. Gary wanted to laugh at the ridiculousness of the thought.

He jumped up and paced.

He knew of only one way to find out.

With shaking fingers, he dug the phone he used only for this one reason from a hidden compartment in his suitcase.

His handler answered. "Yes, Murdock."

Gary whipped around and stared at the darkening skyline. "We need to talk."

Laughter intermingled with the nighttime humming and clacking of the jungle that filtered through the the screens of the dining room. In the yellow glow of the propane lanterns, several of Makmoud's men played a card game. The medic slapped down a winning hand. Everyone guffawed while Jibril shuffled the deck. At another table in a far corner, a group of four discussed something with the man who served as the imam for the compound deep in the Venezuelan jungle.

Makmoud's gaze skated from them to another table where a lone woman sat. A headscarf of deep blue covered her hair, but a blond lock escaped and clung to her cheek in the humid night. She had a book on the table and rested her chin in her hand as she read, just as Rachel had done years before.

For a moment, the woman morphed into Rachel.

Desire filled Makmoud. He set his mug on the tray for the man on KP duty to pick up, hopped off the table where he'd been sitting, and strode to her. He skimmed his hand across her cheek.

The woman started. Her gaze met his. Those eyes, blue so deep they almost bordered on violet, reminded him of her sister.

With a glance to ensure no one was watching, he bent, brushed back her scarf, and kissed her on the neck. Into her ear, he murmured, "Meet me at my room in half an hour."

She smiled shyly and nodded.

Makmoud retreated to his quarters. Rather than turn on the fluorescent lantern, he lit some candles sitting on his dresser. As he reached to pull off his shirt, his phone began chiming.

Makmoud scowled when he checked the number. Ahmad.

In English, he asked, "What is it?"

"It seems as if our friend thinks he was being two-timed."

"As in?"

"Someone else was interested in the woman he broke up with. Now this person is very angry and demands an apology."

Makmoud's eyes narrowed as he sifted through his brother's code talk and cut to the heart of the matter. "I see. How is our friend taking this?"

"He's worried, like maybe there was a rival for his affections that he didn't know about. No, I take that back. He's terrified and not thinking clearly."

Makmoud easily deciphered Ahmad's concerns. Gary had received a very angry message from someone else who purported to be a member of Hezbollah or at least a rival organization. Now this person was out for blood, which had sent Gary into a panic. "What are your thoughts?"

"I tried to tell him it was probably a hoax, a lie people want him to believe, but he didn't agree."

"I see." Makmoud began pacing the length of his room. "This is what I want you to do. Start rumors. Most likely, that will draw out the people behind this hoax. They'll come and ask him if it's really true. When he gets that information, he's to let you know. Do you understand?"

Muttered words answered him. "I do."

"Good. Let me know what he says."

Makmoud wandered onto the screened-in balcony. He tapped his phone on his hand as he thought about his options.

Having Gary panic was not good. Meaning one thing.

He needed to go to the States.

He could do it only if he planned well. He and Jibril.

Without another thought for the romancing he'd planned, Makmoud returned to the dining room. The card game continued strong. When the hand ended, he approached. "Jibril."

His brother lifted an eyebrow, rose, and joined him.

"What is it, brother?"

Makmoud led him to a corner of the dining room. "We have a problem that requires our personal attention."

13

TL Jones wished it were Friday afternoon instead of Wednesday morning. Already, a host of voicemails and fifty e-mails waited for his response. With Nasser gone, he couldn't keep up with the workload of managing sixteen web hunters. Maybe Rich would send him someone, especially now that they'd reactivated Deborah.

He scrawled each message on his notepad. Six could wait. Three couldn't. He picked up the phone's receiver.

A tap on the edge of his cubicle made him pause. He turned.

"TL Jones?" A young man stood there with a sheaf of papers in his hands.

"That's me." TL eyed him.

White shirt. Dark tie. Khakis. Glasses. Young face that made him wonder if he were old enough to take a drink.

"I'm Raymond Thurmond, an analyst who liaises with the NSA."

"Pleased to meet you." TL tightened his grip on the receiver. "If that's it, I'm busy, and—"

"They sent over some intel that might interest you. Here." Raymond thrust the papers in his direction.

"You couldn't send that in an e-mail?"

"I did. But then my boss told me to run a hard copy to you."

Finally, TL set the phone on its cradle. "These are mine to keep?"

"Yes, sir." With that, Raymond hurried away.

TL skimmed the papers. The words "Murdock" and "FBI" told him one thing. He needed that e-mail. He found it buried under several other messages. After opening it, he scanned the text.

TL muttered under his breath and hit Print.

As his printer whirred to life, he jumped to his feet and grabbed each page as it hit the tray. He read as he walked toward his boss's office.

"This isn't good," he muttered. "Not good at all."

"What's that?" one of his coworkers asked as she passed him.

"Life."

She smiled and continued on her way.

Rich yammered into his phone, his Boston accent carrying into the common area. TL cringed and paced as he read through the whole thing again and formulated his plan of attack.

"Hey, buddy. Come on in. Sorry about that." Rich grinned and laced his fingers behind his head as he leaned back. "What's going on?"

TL shut the door. "We have an issue with one of our web hunters."

"Go on."

"You remember how Friday we reactivated Deborah Fields?"

"Of course."

"She fired off a really sharp message. I've got to give the woman credit. She knows how to do them up right. Then yesterday, NSA picked up some stuff."

"As in?"

TL dropped the printout on his desk. "As in it got them worried enough that they sent Junior to ensure it got my attention, stat."

"Nutshell," Rich said as he picked up the papers.

"Nutshell is chatter started up indicating that sources the NSA believes to be Hezbollah have discovered there's a web hunter behind Hamid and Deb's new alter ego, Walid. They know the hunter's location and are sending people to investigate and possibly eliminate this hunter."

The chair creaked as Rich leaned forward. "Wow. You got that right. Strange that they didn't specify the gender."

"Could it be a ploy?"

"Maybe. I couldn't tell you if this is an imminent threat or not." Rich scanned the message. He took off his glasses, rubbed his eyes, and sighed. "You know who you need to talk to is Walton."

"You think he could help?"

"He's dealt with these types longer than you and I have."

"True."

"Is he in? I haven't seen him all week."

"He's out in Vegas on R&R until today. Then he's got something going on."

"Send him that e-mail and give him a call. Get his take on it. If he thinks it's serious, do exactly what he tells you."

"Will do." TL returned to his desk. For a moment, he sat there, wanting to churn through the problem in his mind until he could confirm on his own that no danger existed.

The arrival of a dozen new messages told him he didn't have the time.

He picked up the phone and dialed.

"You're sure this will work?" Gary asked the young woman who secured a camera in the corner of the room next to where he stood.

"Yes, sir. Promise." She offered a smile and the tiniest of eye rolls.

Leave me alone and let me do my job. Please.

Gary pushed away from the thick steel door and sipped a paper cup full of a Kona coffee blend that made his taste buds want to sing. "And the wireless transmissions will go through the walls?"

"They will," a male tech assured him. "We've got this under control. How about if we meet you in the conference room in ten minutes?"

Gary got the hint. "Will do."

He turned and strode from the vault, down the hall, and toward the conference room where they'd monitor tomorrow's Shadow Box exercise.

Angelo Ballesteros, the owner of the Black Diamond Casino and the Love Diamonds, stepped off the elevators. "Special Agent Walton, a word with you, if I may."

Gary nodded. He turned and followed the wiry Italian-American down the hall. "How may I help you?"

"What's your progress?"

"Things are looking good. We've got a few more rooms to wire. Then we'll have everything ready so we can record the whole thing tomorrow night."

Ballesteros rubbed his chin, which already showed a fine coat of dark stubble. "And you're sure these cameras will capture all of the actions of this team of yours?"

"I am." Gary nodded and planted his feet shoulder width apart. "More than that, it'll help you figure out any flaws in security related to the Love Diamonds."

"I still have my doubts. But, if it's as you say and they do indeed steal the diamonds, then I'll be sure to forgive that gambling debt of yours. What is it? A hundred grand?"

Gary's gaze shot toward the conference room. His eyes narrowed. "Yes. And I thank you for that."

His phone began chiming. He checked the number.

TL Jones.

"I'm sorry. Work calls."

"When you're finished, come see me." Ballesteros turned away and continued toward his suite of offices at the other end of the building.

"Gary Walton," Gary said as he stepped into the conference room and surveyed the bustling activity.

The female tech now studied the screen of a laptop. She nodded and said something to her colleague, who chatted on his cell phone. Another tech plugged in a freestanding monitor while still another one attached wires to various laptops.

"Gary, it's TL. How's Vegas?"

"Fun earlier this week. Busy now. What's up?"

"Rich wanted me to call you. We may have a web hunter in trouble."

"I'm all ears." Gary's breath accelerated as he listened to TL explain the chatter the NSA had intercepted regarding a Web hunter.

"I sent you the e-mail they forwarded to me."

"Let me check." Gary stepped over a mess of wires and into the smaller glassed-in conference room he'd made his office for the duration. He pulled up his e-mail and skimmed the message.

That buzzing began again, this time like a low hum at the back of his mind as if confirming that this was related to Nasser's death. His handler's instructions from a few days before resurfaced. "Listen. It sounds like you're right. This is what you need to do."

He shut the door and turned the blinds to hide any inquiring glances. In a low voice he continued, "I guess you know I got tasked with developing a unit that's like a special ops team, only outside the purview of the Army."

"Yeah, I remember that."

"Only the president can activate it. Not me. You've got to get a meeting with him ASAP. I mean, this chatter is serious, right?"

"Yeah, and she's a widow. Her husband was Delta Force. She's pretty isolated. Four kids too. She'd not stand a chance against anyone coming after her."

She?

Gary blinked.

He poured himself another cup of coffee and sipped it as he wore a groove in the carpet behind the table. "Then even more so. I don't care if you step on a ton of toes, meet with him today. He's in town, right?"

"Yep."

Gary's eyes shot to the clock. Seven in the morning here in Vegas, meaning ten on the East Coast. "Do so. Tell his gatekeepers that Gary Walton urged the meeting. Then tell him I recommended Shadow Box. The team's been in isolation for the past six months, so there's no way any of them could have been involved in Nasser's murder." He swallowed hard at the thought. "If he agrees, he'll call me, and we'll go from there."

"How in the world do you think I can get a meeting with the most powerful man in the world?"

The headache joined the dance with the buzzing. He needed to convince TL it was possible—and fast. "The guy's a vet, TL. More than that, he was Special Ops in 'Nam. From what you said, this woman's dead husband was Spec Ops. That's a soft spot for him, as is taking care of the families of the dead. Get Rich to work on it as fast as he can. From the looks of it, time might be running out."

"You're sure?"

Gary gripped the back of one of the chairs. "You want to waste time arguing with me about this?"

"I'll see what I can do." Doubt filled TL's voice. "Thanks, man."

"Anytime." Gary pulled out the chair and sank onto it. The buzzing pulsed low in the back of his mind, almost like tinnitus. Now the headache would worsen to the point it overwhelmed him unless he did something about it. After popping some aspirin, he put his head in his arms.

I want it to stop, to go away.

Someone tapped on the door.

Gary raised his head. "What is it?"

"Sir, we're ready to talk," the male tech reported.

"I'll be right—" His cell chimed the theme from "Raiders of the Lost Ark."

Vic.

"I'll be right there." Gary poured himself a third cup of coffee. "Hey, bro. What's up?"

"We're all set to move out tomorrow at first light. Is there anything else I need to know?"

"Angelo's counting on you not getting the diamonds."

His friend chuckled. "I'm afraid he'll be sadly disappointed."

"I won't be." Gary smirked. *Not when my debt gets forgiven.* "That means Shadow Box will be ready to go. Is there anything else you need? Because I'm really busy trying to get things finished here so I can grab some sleep."

"Uh, no." Vic cleared his throat. "Is everything okay? You sound stressed out of your mind."

What if he confessed his involvement with Nasser's death and a whole host of others? He'd be free of the torment of the past ten years. He'd go to jail too. And Mary and the kids? They'd be devastated. "I'm fine. Just tired."

"Okay. We'll link up after we're done. Take care." Vic hung up.

Gary tapped his phone on his hand.

"Sir?" The male tech's voice yanked him back to the present.

"Oh, sorry. I'm coming." With one last, accusing look at the laptop that had delivered TL's e-mail, Gary rose and rejoined his crew.

Gary snagged a T-shirt from the dresser and unfurled it. As he was about to pull it on, he caught sight of the bullet hole scar on his right shoulder. He froze. As if summoned, the buzzing that had receded over the busy afternoon and evening showed up for a nightcap. He shook his head.

"What do you want me to do about it?" he muttered aloud as he yanked on the shirt and traded his trousers for sweats. The mediocre meal of takeout Chinese stirred in his gut. Maybe a beer would calm his nerves. He shoved his feet into a pair of moccasins and headed for the door. As he reached for the knob, his cell phone began ringing.

"Special Agent Walton, this is the White House switchboard," the woman announced. "The president is on the line for you."

"Thank you." Gary's heart pounded.

"Walton, Badin here." The president's voice boomed loud and clear. "I guess you know why I'm calling."

Gary stood ramrod straight. "Yes, sir. I recommended that Special Agent Jones meet with you."

"He finally did an hour ago. I'd like to get your opinion of this chatter he mentioned."

Gary began his carefully crafted speech. "It sounds to me like the threat is elevated but not imminent. They don't seem to know that the hunter is a woman, and it doesn't indicate to me that they're sure of her precise location."

"A widow. Widow of a Delta operator, I might add. With four children and living in a very isolated corner of Moore County in North Carolina."

"Right. I recommended Shadow Box to escort the woman and her children to a safe house."

"Yes. As we speak, Special Agent Jones is contacting the Marshals to arrange for one in Billings. How soon can they get them out?"

"It has to be Friday." Gary's mind raced. He couldn't let this opportunity to get one hundred grand of debt forgiven slip through his fingers. "They're not certified yet. That happens tomorrow night. They can be there by Friday evening."

"Why not earlier? Why not tomorrow?"

Gary stared at the blank television as his mind raced. "Sir, I need to read through that e-mail from the NSA more carefully."

"Why haven't you done that before?"

"Special Agent Jones sent it to me this afternoon," he lied. "This is the first chance I've been free enough to take a look at it in detail."

"Then do that. If that threat appears imminent, then I want you to forget about that little training exercise and get over there to get that woman and her family out. Understand?"

"Yes, sir. I'll also look for her file."

"On its way, thanks to Special Agent Jones. Keep me informed. And if anything happens, remember that there's midnight sun in Nome. Got it?"

"I do. I'll make sure Victor Chavez gets the file as soon as the certification exercise is complete."

"Good." The line went dead.

Gary released a shaky breath and opened his work e-mail. A smile crossed his face. TL had sent the file on this web hunter. Immediately, he pulled it up and took a look.

Deborah Fields. Forty-three years of age. Mother of four. A widow, her dead husband a highly decorated former Delta operator who had retired, only to die when a deer hit his car one cold November night over four years before. She and her children lived west of Fort Bragg near a town called West End.

Thanks to her, he'd murdered a comrade. His lip curled. He tamped down his anger as he dug out the cell phone he used to call his nameless handler. No code this time, only straight talk. "I have it."

"The package?" The man's lightly accented English sparked nothing in his memory.

"That, and a name."

"Good. Send it to me."

"This could expose me."

"Not if it's done right. This is the address." The man ticked it off to him. "I'll call you in a few minutes."

Gary did as he requested. He got his beer, then returned to his room and found a baseball game on the television. Dodgers and Padres with the Dodgers winning.

The chime of his phone made him jump. "It's about time, I was—"

"I have a plan for you." This voice was lightly accented as well, but a slightly deeper one that stirred up bad memories.

Makmoud stared at Gary where he lay in the bed ten years before. He lifted his dog tags from around his neck.

Gary blinked.

He now slouched on the couch in his hotel room.

"Tell me what you were told to do." Makmoud remained smooth, unflustered.

"He wants us to put her into hiding. We're going in Friday evening."

"I see. It will take us until Friday afternoon to have our team in place and take care of her. In case something happens, I want some insurance. This is what you must do." Makmoud outlined his plan. "You do that, and you will be safe from detection, yes? And remember. The desert is nice this time of year."

The buzzing flared as if flung fully into action. Suddenly, it all spilled back at him, including the name of his handler. Ahmad.

"I will be." Gary closed his eyes. "If you think that is sufficient."

Silence.

Gary stared at the phone.

Makmoud had already ended the call.

Gary wandered to the window and braced his hands against the glass. He hung his head and willed the buzzing to recede.

It did.

Finally, he raised his face but saw nothing outside.

Could he do it? Could he send a widow to her death? Leave her children as orphans?

Gary swallowed hard.

He had no choice.

14

The helicopter neared the sparkling lights of Las Vegas. Inside, Victor sat in the copilot's seat.

Fiona murmured something into her headset.

Victor scanned the myriad of sparkling lights below. He spotted it. The black diamond on top of one of the tall buildings with a white "H" in the middle.

Their target for that night.

Fiona turned her head. "We've been cleared to orbit for the next hour or so. Ten minutes to go. Time to get ready."

Victor undid his harness and slipped into the back of the Blackhawk. He plugged his helmet's comms unit into the chopper's system and turned to the intercom frequency.

Heavy metal music penetrated his ears. He winced, at least until he saw Butch bobbing his head. His ordnance man obviously psyched himself up for the mission.

Victor cast a glance at their two comrades for this journey. The eyes of both Sana and Suleiman had widened to the size of black onyxes. He couldn't tell because of the dark camo paint, but he was sure Sana wore that slightly green look she got every time she prepped for a jump—at least until she was in the air.

Victor nodded toward Butch.

The Def Leopard ceased.

"Okay, guys, listen up. We're ten minutes out. Let's get ready."

Victor checked Butch's and Suleiman's harnesses to ensure they were secure, then helped them clip together so they would jump in tandem. As a last check, he tugged on the carabiner securing the ruck they needed to Butch.

Butch did the same with him and Sana.

"Five minutes," Fiona reported.

Victor's eyes shot to the digital clock on the bulkhead near the ceiling. Sweat built on his hands. He pulled on aviator's gloves.

"Time to rock 'n' roll, baby!" Butch patted Suleiman on the helmet.

"I'm so not looking forward to this," Sana muttered.

"You'll do fine. This is why we train." Victor touched her on the shoulder.

"Two minutes." Fiona's calm voice soothed his nerves.

Victor disconnected his and Sana's intercoms and crab-walked with her toward the cargo door of the Blackhawk.

Butch slid it open, admitting the howling rotor wash.

Victor took several deep breaths as he positioned himself at the lip of the door. He gripped the frame. His pulse echoed in his ears.

Sana's feet dangled into empty space. She lightly kicked him in the shins.

Victor squeezed her arm.

She relaxed.

Inside the bay, the light turned from red to green.

He thrust them through the door.

Sana stretched out like she'd trained.

Silence descended upon them.

Victor pulled the ripcord. A millisecond later, the black parachute jerked them into a slow descent. He focused on the lights below and picked out the helipad for the Black Diamond Casino and Resort. It rushed toward them almost too fast. He pulled on the brakes.

As his feet touched down, Sana hit the button that released her from him. She tumbled forward with a graceful roll and came to a knee. She immediately brought up her gun to pull security as Butch and Suleiman landed.

Victor turned and gathered the billowing ball of silk to himself. He lifted the comms unit from underneath his jacket and adjusted the boom microphone so it hung in front of his mouth.

Beside him, Butch and Suleiman did a repeat of their landing. The ruck touched first, then the pair.

"Butch, time to make our guests very uncomfortable," Victor said once his friend had collapsed his parachute and stashed his helmet.

"Roger that." Butch stepped to the panel of the AC units where they huddled. He pulled out a set of lock picks. Within seconds, he had the door open. "Thirty seconds. Beat that, Sana."

A tight smile crossed her face. "We'll have a contest later."

"AC units going down." Butch pulled a lever. The massive blowers wound down, leaving them in near silence.

"Team, check in," Victor ordered. "One, up and running."

"Two here," Suleiman reported.

"Three in the air," Fiona added above the noise of the helicopter.

"Four on the roof," Sana said.

"Five's online." Shelly's voice filled his ear. "With Seven and Eight."

"Six here." Butch winked at Victor. He pulled on a black baseball cap with the bill facing backwards.

"Seven's here." Diana's voice reached him.

"And looking fine, I might add," Skylar said. "Eight's reporting in."

"The AC's down. Let's move." Victor unslung the paintball gun that would serve as a substitute for an MP-5 or tranq gun. He waited, his body flat against the side of the massive metal units.

Next to him, Sana unzipped the ruck and came up with two smaller backpacks. She handed one to Suleiman, who shrugged into it. She did the same with hers.

"Seven's in," Diana murmured a few minutes later.

Victor visualized the scene. The invitation, expertly forged by Skylar, would allow her access to the two-story ballroom on the forty-ninth floor that had sweeping views of the Las Vegas skyline. Only now, the majestic space became a hot house as air ceased circulating. A half hour passed.

"Five and Eight got the call to fix the AC. We're going in," Skylar announced.

Victor waited, his heart racing. He glanced at his watch. Angelo Ballesteros would premier the diamonds at 9:30, meaning that if they didn't get a move on it, he'd show up at the vault at 9:20 to find Sana dangling from the ceiling.

"We've got the feed going," Skylar reported.

"Seven, let's do it." Victor shifted position.

The next step began. Skylar had choreographed it well. Diana would pretend to feel faint from the heat. Once a guard escorted her to the bathroom, she'd take him down and tag him out. Then she'd use his ID card to allow Sana and Suleiman access.

Victor gestured with his head. Together, he and Butch approached the stairwell door.

Butch dropped into the shadows.

The lock clicked.

Victor pressed himself against the wall next to the door. The rough concrete scratched at his jacket.

"Guys, it's me." Diana's soft voice reached them.

"Go, you two." Victor patted Sana on the back.

Sana slipped through the door.

Suleiman followed.

The door thumped closed behind them.

The pair would access the vault where Ballesteros kept the diamonds via the ventilation shaft. Using a hoist, Suleiman would lower Sana until she dangled above the diamonds and the threat of the laser beams surrounding them. All she had to do was secure the diamonds in her satchel. The problem was, it took time, something Victor worried could turn on them.

"We've got a problem." Skylar's voice broke into his thoughts.

Victor jumped. "What kind of problem?"

"Company coming. Eight out."

"Talk to me."

Silence.

Victor froze. Uncertainty assaulted him. Should he call a Nine-One-One, the signal for abort? Warn off Sana and Suleiman? What?

He cast a glance at Butch. "We need to get them out of there."

"Let it run," Butch murmured, his eyes never ceasing their watch. "You've got no choice right now."

Victor nodded. Sana and Suleiman were in the bowels of the air vent or maybe on the descent to the diamonds, meaning they had no radio signal.

Diana waited near the vent's entrance, completely vulnerable.

Skylar and Shelly? They were pinned down by something—or someone.

To abort would mean a certain end for Shadow Box.

He cast a glance at his watch. Nine on the nose.

Sana had fifteen more minutes to do her thing and get out of there.

Where was she? Shouldn't she be back by now?

Victor raised his hand to give the abort.

"Wait one, boss," Butch whispered.

"Five and Eight in the clear," Skylar said.

The tension drained from Victor's shoulders.

"Two and Four coming out," Diana said. "Success."

Rustling accompanied Diana's report, followed by the whirring sound as Sana and Suleiman secured the screws around the vent.

"Get up here." Victor eased to one knee.

"On our way," Sana reported.

A moment later, the door clicked open. Sana and Suleiman scurried to join their comrades.

"Seven, time to go." Victor turned to Butch. "Get those units up and running."

"Roger that." Butch shifted the lever until the fans began winding up. He closed the panel and stashed his picks in the ruck.

"Five and Eight, get out of there."

"Wilco. We'll meet you at the rendezvous."

"Three, we're ready for our taxi."

"On my way." Fiona's voice echoed with confidence.

Victor and Butch slowly rose, both eyes and guns trained outward. Sana and Suleiman crouched behind them, both remaining still to avoid detection by the video cameras that were now active.

The deep *whump* of the Blackhawk made Victor want to sigh in relief.

He couldn't. Not until they were safely on the helicopter.

Only when Fiona's wheels touched down did he turn to the two youngest members of the team. "Go. Go. Go. Keep your heads down."

Suleiman and Sana scurried to the helicopter.

Victor tapped Butch on the back.

His comrade ran, ruck on his back, to the open bay.

Victor followed, and he jumped into the chopper. "Go, Fi!"

The stairwell door flew open.

They lifted off.

Victor and Butch high-fived.

The ride to the airport took a mere three minutes. As soon as they landed at a hangar, Fiona cut the engines and engaged the rotor brake.

Nearby, headlights flashed a code.

"There's our ride. Butch, you drive."

The team piled in. Victor, Skylar, and Sana crammed into the middle seat of the Suburban while Fiona, Suleiman, and Shelly squirmed into the back. Diana rode shotgun while Butch drove.

Everyone chattered to release the stress from the day.

"That was crazy!" Sana's voice filled the vehicle.

"You should have seen Sana. She looked like something from *Mission Impossible*." Suleiman talked more than he ever had since Victor had met him.

Diana giggled. "I can't believe they bought the story that I was a reporter."

"What happened in there?" Victor asked.

"In the control room?" Skylar asked.

"I was, like, so freaked out." Shelly's voice reached him from the back. "I mean, like, we were down there and had just gotten the video feed running when Angelo Ballesteros himself showed up."

"He was pissed," Skylar added.

"Yeah, and he, like, demanded to know when we'd have the AC repaired. Thank heavens I'd had the foresight to download some AC diagnostic programs so I at least looked like I knew what I was doing." Shelly giggled. It turned into a snort.

"Ew!" That came from Fiona.

"That's why I couldn't talk," Skylar added. "We finally told him we'd found the solution and were working at reprogramming the system. That got us the extra time we needed. Let's see those diamonds, little lady."

"Don't call me that, and maybe I'll show them to you." Sana undid the satchel she'd kept looped over her shoulders. She loosened the drawstrings on a pouch and slid the necklace from the black velvet bag.

Victor had never been one motivated by accumulating money, but even his eyes widened as he held them up. The jewel-encrusted necklace glittered in the passing streetlights.

A low whistle escaped Skylar, and his eyes began glimmering. "Wow. I wonder what these would go for on the black market?"

"I don't know, and we're not going to find out. Sana, put those in their bag before Mr. James gets other ideas." Victor handed the necklace to his breaking-and-entering specialist.

Once they reached the Black Diamond Casino and Resort, they piled out of the SUV.

Gary stood on the steps with a small contingent of FBI agents. He grinned. "Good job, guys. You did it, and we got it all on video. Mr. Ballesteros wants his diamonds back."

"And I want to give them back." Victor nodded at the team. "They all did great. I take it we're certified?"

"Oh, yeah." The grin shifted to a smirk. "They never saw anything coming. Come on. My guys will guard the Suburban."

Victor cast a glance at Gary as they strode into the lobby.

Big men in black suits joined the contingent. Victor wondered if they were there more to ensure the diamonds made it to their destination than protect them from the gawking crowd.

Elevator doors opened, and one of their black-suited escorts gestured for them to enter. They crammed toward the back. Victor found himself staring at the back of a guy twice his size. A sick feeling started in his gut. Maybe Gary had been wrong. Maybe they weren't meant to leave the building alive.

"When we get to the conference room, I'll do the talking." Gary glanced at his friend. "Speak only if spoken to. And Vic, you're the only one I'm going to introduce. Got it?"

"Clear." Victor suddenly wished for at least a knife.

Seconds later, the doors swooshed open, admitting them into a richly appointed lobby full of white marble and black furnishings. They marched across the shiny floor and into a conference room dominated by a table large enough to seat twenty comfortably. At the far end sat Angelo Ballesteros. Another, even slighter man sat to his right, and two more men, muscles bulging against their black suits, stood behind them.

"Mr. Ballesteros, this was the team that heisted the diamonds," Gary announced.

The casino owner's gaze swept then. "What a motley group."

Victor's jaw twitched at the implied insult.

"This is Victor Chavez, their commander." Gary nodded toward Victor. "He was in charge of planning the mission."

"I'd like to see the diamonds, if you would."

Victor gestured to Sana, who stepped forward. She removed the velvet bag from the pouch and laid the necklace on top of the fine material.

"Carlitos, check those for me and make sure they didn't swap any out."

The man to Ballesteros's right rose and pulled out a loupe. The gemologist spent the next ten minutes checking each diamond that made up the necklace. "All there."

"Excellent." Ballesteros sighed and shook his head. "I suppose I should commend you for exposing some security flaws. It seems as if I have some work to do with that."

"We'll go over the tapes in detail tomorrow morning," Gary told him. He turned to Victor. "Vic, thanks to you and your team. You're dismissed, and we'll be in touch in the morning."

Victor nodded. "Let's go, crew."

As they returned to the Suburban, a sense of accomplishment washed over him. They were a far cry from the ragtag band of very different people who'd arrived at Last Chance Ranch in September. Now, their physiques had hardened. They'd united as a team. While they each had very different personalities, they had all contributed to make the mission a success.

For Victor, the mission had exceeded in his wildest dreams.

They were now ready to go downrange.

15

"I won! I won! I won!" Butch jumped up and danced a jig around the great room of the Big House. He threw his head back and howled like a wolf.

The entire Shadow Box team laughed at his antics that wrapped up the late-night Uno game.

He settled at his place around the massive coffee table. "Anyone up for another?"

"I'm beat," Diana said. Now dressed in sweats and a sweatshirt rather than an elegant evening gown, she yawned. "Hey, Vic, do I get to keep that dress even though the Feds paid for it?"

"So far as I'm concerned, yeah." Victor grinned. "How many heads did you turn?"

"None." She giggled.

"Doubtful." Skylar winked and drawled, "Hot stuff."

She laughed. "I'll see you guys in the a.m."

"Gang, sleep in tomorrow," Victor urged. "We'll do our usual debrief in the morning at ten. Then we'll have a long weekend."

The game broke up, and the rest of the team cleared the coffee table of all bottles, cans, and cups.

Victor wandered into the cold night air. Spring had yet to make its way to Flagstaff, and though much of the snow on the ground had melted, patches of it remained in piles near the walkways. A breeze blew from mountain peaks still under mounds of snow and added its own version of refrigeration. Wishing he'd not been on such a high from the mission that he'd left his parka in the Men's Building, he shivered.

Once he had a fire going in the studio's fireplace, he sat down on the couch with Rachel's journal from 1998 in front of him. For a moment, he wondered if he should leave it be and catch some z's, but adrenaline still coursed through his system despite the fact that the clock ticked toward two in the morning. He couldn't procrastinate in reading them, not when he had no more excuses, like training up his team, to delay him.

He was about to open the notebook when Butch tapped on the doorframe.

Victor waved him inside. "Hey, man, what's up?"

"I was headed to bed and wanted to come by and say congrats and good job." Butch sprawled onto one of the chairs.

"Thanks."

"Everyone did well. Suleiman and Sana. Fi too. And Skylar and Shelly played it cool, as did Diana." Butch yawned and covered his mouth. "Sorry. It's getting late. Anyway, if there's only one criticism of you, it would be that you almost played the control freak."

"I know. I came close on that."

"But you let everyone think independently and solve the problems that popped up. That's crucial. So good job."

Victor smiled at his friend's praise. "Thanks, man. You don't know how much I needed to hear that."

"No problem." His deputy climbed to his feet.

"You did great too. I couldn't have planned that on my own."

"Hey, I was trained by the best. Grab some sleep." Butch winked, then rose and pushed through the door into the night.

The smile remained on Victor's face as he returned to the couch and took a sip of the Dos Equis he'd brought with him. It faded as he contemplated the notebook.

With a deep breath, he opened it to February. Rachel detailed every aspect of her relationship with Makmoud. Sometimes, Victor looked away. Other times, he found himself captivated. Makmoud had proposed to Rachel. They were planning their lives together, far from the way Rachel had presented him as a nameless, faceless ex-boyfriend. Pain seared Victor's heart.

"Rach, why did you lie to me like that?" he whispered.

Once more, he yearned to be able to share everything that raged through him with someone who would simply listen to him.

Victor put his head in his hands. The room spun, from lack of sleep, the letdown from the mission, or the discovery he'd made, he didn't know. He stretched out and contemplated the exposed wooden trusses of the ceiling. "I don't understand. Why?"

A spark popped.

His question remained unanswered.

Gary thrashed in his sleep. He shook his head and murmured, "No, no. Someone. Save me."

Like Charon ferrying the dead, his dreams took him back to the day that changed his life forever. Gunfire crackled around him, and the sharp smell of cordite penetrated his nose. His pulse thudded in his ears as panic frayed the edges of his calm. He ducked behind the charred remains of a car. "Pull back! Pull back!"

His ordnance man laid down covering fire.

Gary grabbed the lifeless body of his comms guy and dragged him toward the Humvee.

Pain seared his leg.

I'm shot. That registered in his mind. Adrenaline kept him going as he emptied the remaining clip of his rifle and took down two tangos.

They kept advancing.

Gary's good leg gave out.

Forget Gizmo. As injured as he was, he couldn't drag the dead.

Kelso collapsed.

Gary drew his pistol. A volley from him took down the shooter.

Another bullet pierced his shoulder.

Blood loss weakened him. He fumbled the pistol as he rammed home a new clip.

His vision began fading.

With the gun clutched in his useless hand, he used his good leg and arm to push himself toward the Hummer. His strength drained away.

Gary propped himself against the wheel and shifted the pistol.

Someone approached. The bright sun burned his image to a silhouette.

Gary's gun hand trembled. He tried to tighten his finger, but even that failed.

The man batted it from him.

Darkness descended.

Gary awakened with a shout. He shook from head to toe. His breath whistled in and out as his mind pulled him to the present. He put his hand down on the sheets. Damp, thanks to the sweat his nightmare had left behind. Fingers gripping the fabric, he lay back. The buzzing had returned, ebbing and flowing with his ragged breaths. It nearly drove him mad.

You're safe, not caught in some destitute village with people shooting you. You're safe.

His hand shot up and rubbed the puckered scar from his shoulder wound, then the one on his right quad. He glanced at the clock.

Almost four in the morning.

Seven on the East Coast.

Deborah would see the sun one last time, would kiss her children goodbye as she sent them away to school.

At least her older ones.

The littlest did preschool in the mornings but came home at one. She'd die alongside her mother.

Unless Gary did something.

He rose and opened his laptop. He knew what Makmoud had charged him to do. Hold off Shadow Box until evening.

He couldn't do that. He couldn't let Deborah die.

Gary opened her file. Her blue eyes from the FBI Contractor ID photo stared back at him.

Save me, they implored.

He skimmed the information. Parents dead. Husband dead. Four children, all under sixteen. Anna, the oldest, was his Morgan's age. DJ, the only son, David's. Deborah's siblings? Liza Murphy, a half-sister who was ten years younger.

Gary knew what Vic would do. He'd make sure all family was safe, not just the immediate family.

"You will be safe from detection." Makmoud's words echoed in his mind.

Gary hesitated.

The headache flared.

He groaned and rubbed his temples. Maybe he could save Deborah and her family, but he had to give Makmoud something.

Gary moved the cursor and highlighted Liza's name. He replaced it with the word "None." Now, in his little world, Deborah and her children were alone. He saved the altered document and opened a new file. It took him only a few minutes to bang out a synopsis of all that TL had told him, including the pass phrase that would let Deborah know she'd been compromised. He also included the estimated time of attack.

He prepared an e-mail message to Victor and attached both the altered file and the synopsis. After sending it, he popped some aspirin to take care of the headache.

With a last, deep breath, Gary picked up his cell phone and dialed.

16

"Bad to the Bone" brought Victor out of the heavy sleep into which he'd fallen.

His eyes burned from exhaustion.

What time was it? He raised his head and squinted at the decorative clock on the side table between the chairs across from him. A little before four.

Why was Gary calling?

He brought the phone to his ear. "Gary, hey. What's going on? Shouldn't you be asleep?"

"I would be except the president called." His friend and handler sounded too alert for so early.

Victor pushed himself upright. "What?"

"We've got our first op. Seems we have a web hunter in imminent danger, and he wants us to get her and her family out."

"Web hunter? What? *Her?* I'm not following."

"I sent you an e-mail."

"Hold on." Victor rose and stumbled to the worktable, where he turned on the laptop. "Spell it out to me while the computer warms up."

Gary did so.

Victor tucked the phone between his cheek and shoulder as he logged into the system. The e-mail from Gary glowed on the screen. "I see it."

"Click the attachment called Synopsis first."

Victor did so. He skimmed it. His blood chilled. "This isn't good. Not good at all."

"Now do you see why I called you?"

"I do." He did a mental calculation. Five in the morning meant eight on the East Coast. If they left in an hour, they could be there by one.

They might be too late.

"How did you get the time of the strike?"

"The chatter mentioned it."

"That doesn't give us much time. If we can get wheels up in two hours and if you throw in drive times, we'll get there right before two."

"Do what you can. Vic, the woman's a local hero, as was her husband."

"I'm on it."

"Anything you need, call me. I'll be available, and there's plane-to-ground comms on the plane. This is the real deal now, not some cutesy exercise."

"Will do." Victor hit Print and sprinted through the chilly early morning air to the Women's Building. He burst inside and banged on Diana's closed door. "Hey, Diana! I need you up."

"What's going on?" Her door flew open. She stood there in flannel pajamas, her curls standing on end and her eyes almost closed in sleep. "I thought we could sleep in this morning."

"We could if we weren't called. Get the rest of the ladies up and meet at the Big House in five." He roused Butch and the rest of the guys before throwing on some fresh clothing and running to the studio to grab the printouts.

In total, it took two hours for him to explain what had happened and issue terse orders. Shelly gathered the needed communications equipment. Suleiman collected the ammunition and guns they might need. Diana put together a medical kit, and Fiona and Butch headed to the airport to pre-flight the Gulfstream G450 Gary had procured for them. Victor and Skylar began discussing options.

By 6:03, they were airborne. Victor could only hope they had tailwinds to get them to their destination before 1:00. Otherwise, he didn't know if they'd make it on time.

His team settled in for some more sleep.

Victor scoured the information Gary had sent. It was scant, far too little to carry out a successful op. The two oldest children were in eighth and sixth grade at the same school. The third-born daughter attended elementary school. The youngest would be at home by the time they arrived. He noted that on his scratch pad.

He skimmed the profile and found no other living relatives. Good. At least the FBI wouldn't have to track down anyone else. Using his laptop connected to the plane's WiFi, he scanned the aerial photographs and mapped out their ingress and egress routes. Only when he'd ordered the needed supplies did he stretch out for a couple of hours of rest.

The plane eased downward.

Victor awoke and roused the rest of the crew. "Guys, listen up. This is the real thing. No exercise. Got that?"

Everyone nodded.

"It's hasty, it's thrown together, but it's what we have now. Shelly, I need you to go to the middle school to get Anna and DJ. I've got the address here. We'll get the pass phrase from Deborah. Here's a map with the route highlighted."

He thrust a sheet of paper into her hands. "Take a sidearm, and if anyone questions you, flash the badge I'll give you."

Shelly studied it. "Um, shouldn't we let the police take them into protective custody?"

"We need to keep this as quiet as possible, so no sheriff. Diana, you go to the elementary school to collect Gracie. Same thing. Here's a map. Take a sidearm. Fi will stay with the plane and get it refueled and preflighted. We're heading to Billings, Montana from here. Butch, Skylar, Sana, and Suleiman, you're with me. Skylar, you, Sana, and Suleiman will have the chase SUV. Butch and I will get the other and go as lead. We get in, get Deborah and Marie, and get out. Understand?"

"Roger that." Butch nodded as the plane touched down and taxied to a parking area. Once they stopped, he lowered the door.

Victor peered outside.

Four FBI agents waited for them.

He deplaned and met them. "Ed Dayton?"

"That's me." A man flashed his badge, which Victor inspected. "Gary said you'd be arriving about now. Here. The info you'll need." He thrust a large, thick manila envelope into his hands and nodded at the two Suburbans and two Ford Edges lined up and waiting. "You've got those four vehicles over there. Keys are in the ignition. Leave them inside when you go."

"Will do. Thanks." Victor opened the envelope, and a set of eight FBI cred packs, complete with photos of each team member, slid into his hands. He raced up the stairs and passed them out. "Be back by three sharp and call if you run into trouble."

Everyone nodded.

"Let's hit the road."

Deborah stacked her Bible on top of her study book. For a moment, she sat in her reading chair and treasured the quiet. That would change when Marie awoke from her nap. Once the older three kids came home from school, it would be nonstop as they finished their chores. She headed downstairs and prepared a snack for Marie.

"Mommy?" Marie wandered into the kitchen and rubbed her eyes.

"Hi, sweet pea. Did you have a good nap?" Deborah hugged her close. She ruffled her disheveled light brown curls.

"Uh-huh." Marie climbed onto one of the chairs at the kitchen table.

Deborah placed a plate of banana slices with peanut butter on them before her. "Let me get you some milk."

Deborah reached to open the refrigerator.

The alarm chimed.

She froze.

Anna, DJ, and Gracie shouldn't be home yet. Meaning…

Deborah stepped into the living room.

Her breath caught in her throat when she noticed the two black Suburbans breaking through the trees and rumbling up the driveway.

Her hands began trembling. She raced into the kitchen. "Marie, go into the bathroom and pull the door closed behind you."

"Mommy?"

"Do it now."

"Mommy?" Her daughter's eyes widened.

"Go!"

Marie scurried to the bathroom.

The door thumped shut.

Deborah grabbed the key to the gun cabinet from the back of the silverware drawer. Her fingers shook as she unlocked it and grabbed the shotgun. She raced into the study and snagged the shells from a shelf in the closet.

Edgar and the Colonel began barking.

She loaded shells into the double barrel. Her hands shook so hard that she doubted if she could hit anything.

The hinges on the door to the screened-in porch squeaked.

Someone rapped on the back doorframe.

Deborah jumped. Hands gripping the shotgun, she crouched. "Hush, you two."

The dogs ceased.

The Colonel growled low in his throat. His lips curled, revealing his fangs. The fur on his back stood up. He shifted so he stood in front of her.

"Who is it?" She hated the shake in her voice.

Through the filmy curtain, the silhouette of a man and two others blocked the early afternoon light.

In a pleasantly deep baritone muffled by the door, he replied, "FBI, ma'am. May we come in?"

Deborah leaned against the cabinet. "No. I want to see some ID."

The man pressed something against the glass. Carefully, she reached up with the shotgun's muzzle and pushed aside the curtain. She noted the photo. It matched the face of the tall man standing at the door wearing wraparound sunglasses.

"Victor Chavez with the FBI, ma'am," he said. "TL said the sun's setting and that it's time to close up shop."

Deborah froze at the pass phrase TL had given her three years before. It told her all she needed to know.

She'd been compromised.

Deborah straightened. She undid the deadbolt and the lower lock.

"Deborah Fields?" the man asked as he removed his sunglasses. What with his dark hair, dark eyes, and slender, muscular build, he looked almost like the double of Mark Dacascos.

"That's me. Who's Mr. Clean and Pretty Boy?" she added as she stared at the other two.

"Butch Addison, ma'am," replied the bald guy with the black goatee. The small hoops hanging from his ears shifted with his smile. The tattoo of something on his right arm peeked the snug sleeves of his white T-shirt as he shook her hand. "I like the analogy. Nice shotgun, by the way."

His smile softened, and his dark eyes twinkled as he crouched. "Well, hi there. Who are you?"

Deborah turned and found Marie peeking from the bathroom.

Her youngest froze and pulled back.

"Sweet pea, it's okay." At least her voice had steadied. "This is Marie."

Marie ran to her mother and clung to her leg. She buried her face in the denim.

"And I'm Skylar James," said the blond guy wearing khakis and a light blue button-down shirt. He held out his hand.

Deborah didn't know what to do but shake it.

Victor asked, "Is that all you've got?"

"What do you mean?"

"A shotgun's hardly protection."

"My protection was my anonymity."

"You've been blown. TL sent me to get you guys out and to someplace safe until this blows over."

Deborah swallowed hard. "My other children…"

"What's the pass phrase you've given them?"

"The same as what I got from TL. Their principals and teachers know about me. They know that if someone from the FBI or Marshals shows up with that phrase, it's a legitimate threat."

"Good. Do you have suitcases for everyone?"

"I do. Marie, sit at the table and don't move." She pointed to a chair and turned. "In the study."

Deborah led the way to the closet and opened the doors. The five suitcases sat neatly aligned on the floor.

"Butch, Skylar, get those into the SUVs." Victor raised his phone to his ear. "Diana, the pass phrase is 'The sun is setting and TL says it's time to close up shop.' Take your badge and show it to them. Call Shelly and pass that along. She's to call you when she gets Anna and DJ."

Deborah snagged five backpacks from the hooks above the suitcases.

"What are you doing?"

Deborah ignored him and charged up the stairs.

She stopped in Gracie's and Marie's room first. Lambkins, some toys, and *Charlotte's Web* went into Marie's bag. She filled Gracie's with Woolie, some books, and toys as well.

"We don't have time for this!" Victor's voice and footfalls thundered up the steps after her.

She whirled, making him take a step back. "I don't want my children to suffer any more than they already will. You said we had time."

"I didn't say that! We've got to go."

She glared at him. "And the animals are coming with us. Two dogs, two cats, and guinea pigs."

"What? Come *on*!"

"No problem, ma'am," Butch called from the landing. "I've got the dogs right here and one of the cats too."

"Cages are in the laundry room off the kitchen," she told him.

"I don't believe this. I truly don't believe this." Victor followed her to DJ's room.

"Believe it." Deborah dumped his Bible, some other books, and his favorite handheld video games into the sack.

She rushed into Anna's room. Deborah located a picture of Derek and threw it into a knapsack, followed by her Bible and the stack of books her oldest kept on her nightstand for reading. "You don't have children, do you?"

"What's that got to do with anything?"

"Then you wouldn't understand. If you want to help, the guinea pigs are in Gracie and Marie's room."

"Guinea pigs!"

"Marie adores them." She shoved past him and ran into her room. Same thing. Into a pack went her Bible, a picture of Derek, one of her and her parents, and one of Liza. She added some books before facing Victor.

He stared at her, eyes wide, jaw slack in disbelief.

"Now I'm ready." Then she tried a smile to smooth things over. "Thank you."

How could she? How dare she waste precious time? To take keepsakes and mementos? And animals? Victor fought the impulse to drag her bodily from the house. But if Butch and Skylar could roll with it, so could he. He grabbed the guinea pig cage from the floor by the dresser. "Get going."

Deborah rushed down the steps.

"Vic, we've got company," Sana suddenly reported from her lookout position at the beginning of the driveway.

"What kind?" Victor followed.

"Two vans. We got rid of that peacock mailbox. They slowed but missed the driveway and are trying to find a place to turn around."

"Get up here, stat. Take the corners of the house and stay low." Victor muttered under his breath. "Butch, Skylar, they're here."

Skylar grabbed the packs from Deborah.

"I've got that." Butch snatched the guinea pig cage from his hand and ran out the back door.

"Oh, no!" Sana's voice shook slightly.

Victor's pulse shot up several notches.

Gunfire popped. A loud report answered, followed by the crunch of metal and the roar of engine.

"We're at the house. I forced them to stop down the driveway," Suleiman reported. "We have eight tangos."

The chatter of weapons answered Suleiman.

Victor winced. "Butch! Skylar! To the front. Mrs. Fields, get Marie and get down."

She snatched her daughter from the chair and hugged her close.

Victor pushed her onto the floor. He crouched. His phone rang with "Walking on Sunshine" by Katrina and the Waves. "Diana?"

"I got Gracie. Shelly's got Anna and DJ. What's that noise?"

"We're a little tied up. Get to the airport. Now. Butch, what's the read?"

"We're toast." Through the archway, Victor noticed how Butch peeked over the window sill. "We're outnumbered big time. They've got—"

The bass chatter of a big gun cut off anything else he said. Glass shattered. China tinkled. Bullets penetrated the wall between the dining room and kitchen as Butch and Skylar threw themselves into the relative protection of the kitchen.

Victor swallowed hard. "Armor-piercing rounds. Where the heck did they get those?"

His phone belted out Bon Jovi's "Dead or Alive."

Fiona.

"What is it?" he snapped. He cringed.

Outside, Sana and Suleiman continued returning fire.

"I've got company here. Seems like our friends decided to park their plane next to us. What do you want me to do?"

"Take care of it."

"What?"

"I'm kind of tied up here." Victor flinched as more bullets tore through the walls and slammed into the glass-fronted cabinets above their heads. Glass rained downward. He turned his face away to avoid the shards.

Bullets shredded the drywall.

The fish tank shattered. Water poured onto him. "Take care of it."

"Vic—"

A guppy landed on his cheek. Victor tossed it off. He broke the call and stuffed his phone in his shirt pocket. "Butch, Skylar, get to the SUVs.

Start the engines on my count. Sana, Suleiman, cover for them. On my count, lots of smoke and lights. Throw them, and get to the SUVs."

Marie wailed as the staccato sound of gunfire ceased. Shouting echoed through the now-empty panes in the front windows. Deborah clutched her tighter, her eyes wide, her lips moving silently as if praying.

Butch and Skylar threw themselves onto the back porch.

"We're in, boss," Butch reported.

"On my count. Three. Two. One. Go!"

A combination of flash-bang grenades and smoke grenades landed out front, temporarily halting the death squad's advance.

"Come on!" Victor grabbed Deborah's arm.

Mother and child stumbled after him and through the door to the lead Suburban.

Sana and Suleiman raced to the second one.

"Back road. Go!" Victor shouted once he'd slammed the door behind Deborah and Marie in the back and jumped into the passenger's seat.

Butch gunned the motor, and they shot forward into the woods on the dirt road that Victor had noticed led to the back of the property.

"I can't believe—" Deborah sat up.

"Get down!" Victor reached back. He shoved her down.

"Hey!"

"We're not out of the woods yet. Literally." He peered in front of him and kept the rifle he'd left in the front seat at ready.

"Sana, Skylar, Suleiman, anyone behind us?"

"Negative," Skylar reported.

Marie's cries rose to a crescendo.

"It's okay, baby. It's okay." Deborah's soothing voice reached him from the floor of the backseat.

Butch jerked a left, and they skidded onto asphalt and sped up.

Victor continuously checked the side mirrors. Nothing. He flipped on the blue and white strobes that were part of the vehicle. They slipped around cars that pulled over.

"May I sit up now?" Deborah asked.

Tersely, he replied, "No."

"Jerk," she muttered.

"Almost there." Butch slowed as they arrived at the airport and skidded around the corner. He paused only long enough to punch the gate code.

Once they were inside, it closed behind them.

Victor slid from the SUV and gaped at the scene before him.

Fiona paced nearby, her hands on her belt, the gold badge of her cred pack gleaming on it and her sidearm exposed. Two men, their hands cuffed to the stairway of the plane adjacent to theirs, struggled.

"It's about time you showed up." Fiona's Ray-Bans masked her expression.

"We were a little busy," Butch said. He jumped from the Suburban and popped open the back door. "Deborah Fields, meet Fiona Mercedes."

The doors to the Ford Edges flew open.

"Mom!" The blond girl raced toward her mother and threw her arms around her. The boy and the littler girl followed. Deborah clung to them.

"Mommy!" Marie's cry reached Victor.

He turned. At the sight of that tear-streaked face and ringlets of brown hair, his heart softened. He forgot about the urgency to get into the air. "Here, baby. I've got you."

He lifted the still-crying Marie from the backseat. She clung to him, her tiny hands balling his sailcloth shirt.

"Get the suitcases and animals transferred." Victor's arms tightened around her.

Marie's heart hammered against his chest.

"Animals? What on—" A cuss word escaped Fiona as she opened the back door to the second Suburban, only to be nearly bowled over by a Belgian malinois. "Are you crazy?"

"You and Butch get started on preflight. Suleiman, get your sniper gun ready just in case." Only with reluctance did he hand Marie over to Deborah. "Get going, Mrs. Fields. Into the plane."

Victor helped Skylar heave the suitcases and backpacks into the cargo hold. They almost tossed the caged animals onto the plane. Diana and Shelly took care of leading the dogs up the narrow stairs.

As Victor put his foot on the lowest step, the jet's engines began spinning.

Tires screeched.

He whirled.

One of the vans had arrived, and several men piled out. The first one out raised a rifle.

A bullet snapped over his head and barely missed the fuselage.

"Fi!"

"Give me thirty more seconds."

"Suleiman, I need you." Victor crouched at the top of the stairway and returned fire.

Above him, the click of a bolt sliding back reached him. Suleiman dropped one. The rest dove for cover.

"I need those stairs closed," Fiona called.

"Roger that." Victor pulled back and locked the door into place.

Fiona hit the engines, and they leapt forward in a rapid taxi.

Moments later, they soared into the sky away from danger and toward safety.

"You did a good job." Victor knelt in front of Sana.

A faint trembling emanated across her body. In her hands, she crumpled a cocktail napkin over and over until pieces of it began separating.

"It takes time for the adrenaline to wear off."

"I—I guess." Sana shifted her gaze to stare out the window. She took a deep breath and opened her mouth as if she wanted to say something. She closed it.

Suddenly at a loss for words, Victor sat there. He rose and felt his head brush the ceiling. "Why don't you get some rest?"

She nodded.

Butch stepped from the cockpit, his bulk filling the narrow doorway, his frame stooped since the plane didn't accommodate his six-foot, four-inch height. "We're on our way."

"Good." Victor moved toward the galley. In a low voice, he murmured, "Could you talk to Sana? She's a little stressed right now."

"Sure, boss." Butch clapped him on the shoulder and slid by.

Victor continued to the cockpit and found Fiona punching some numbers into a control panel. She pressed a button, then took her hands off the controls. For a moment, the plane bobbled. It steadied as the autopilot took over. She raised her hands above her head and stretched before twisting her neck.

Victor slid into the copilot's seat. He gazed out the windows as they skimmed over clouds and mountains below that were just beginning to show signs of green. "Good job today. I still don't know how you took down two guys."

"You do what you have to do." She shrugged. "You told me to fix it, so I did."

He nodded as his mind roved over the earlier terror. "That was close. Too close."

"Who do you think blew her?"

"You mean released her identity?"

"Yeah. Someone had to do it. I don't think they stumbled onto it."

"No. Whoever did was trying to protect this Murdock guy."

"Murdock?"

"A man she was tracking who killed an FBI agent. From what Gary sent me, the agent who died knew Murdock. I think he's with the FBI or DHS."

Fiona stared at him for a moment, her eyes unreadable behind her sunglasses. She turned to face the controls. "You mean there's a leak somewhere, most likely in the FBI."

"It's the best I can come up with." Victor shivered. Something wasn't right. "We need to change course."

"Huh?"

"We need to change our destination."

"And that's because?"

"If they knew Deborah's identity, what's to say that the person who leaked the information doesn't know where we're taking her and her kids?"

"I'm not following."

"Who would know about the safe house in Billings?"

"The president. Gary. This TL guy who was her handler. Other Feds. Probably the Marshals too. Are you saying—"

"Too many people know about her and where she's headed." He came to a snap decision. "Change course to go to Flagstaff."

"What?" Fiona stared at him. "Are you nuts? Shouldn't we run this by Gary first?"

"No."

"What do you mean? He's our handler."

"Look. We've been in isolation for how long? Six months? No way could we be part of this Murdock leak. No one knows where we're based. She'd be safe there. We could protect her."

"We need to train up for other missions."

"No, we need to finish the one we have."

"Gary's going to kill us."

"No, he's not. I'll take the hit for it, okay? That's part of my job. Just...trust me on this one. I think it's the best thing to do and will keep Deborah safe until the FBI can hunt down this Murdock guy."

"If you say so." Fiona sighed and ran her fingers across a tablet. "Okay. I've got the coordinates. Let me do my magic, and I'll keep the flight plan on the down-low."

"Thanks, Fi." Victor briefly gripped her shoulder before heading aft.

After pouring himself a cup of coffee in the galley, he made his way down the aisle. Butch and Sana sat on the starboard side closest to the front. They talked in low voices. Her body had relaxed. No tremors either. A smile even crossed her face.

Suleiman sat across the aisle from Sana and kept his eyes closed. Skylar and Shelly sat halfway back on the starboard side, Shelly busy with a tablet and Skylar already sound asleep. The guinea pigs and cat cages sat on the couch across from them. The Doberman Pinscher stretched out in front of the couch. To the rear, the two oldest Fields children curled up in chairs across from each other. His chin resting on her knee, the big Belgian malinois gazed at his mistress. Her hand stroked his head in a rhythmic motion as if it soothed her. At the rear, the door to the small bedroom was shut.

It slid open, and Diana stepped through.

"How are they?" Victor asked in a low voice.

"Holding their own. I gave Marie and Gracie something to calm them down." Diana reached up and touched his cheek. Her fingers came away bloody. "You're cut."

Victor jumped at her gesture. "I know. A small cut from all of that glass that rained down on us."

"Let me check it. I'll do the same with Deborah when she comes out." Diana offered a smile, squeezed his arm, and slid past him to take a seat on the port side across from Sana and Butch.

"Mrs. Fields?" Victor stepped into the bedroom.

Deborah sat on the bed, her hand stroking Marie's brow.

The child sighed and curled into a tight ball.

"She's an angel," Victor murmured before he realized it.

"That, she is, at least when she's asleep." Deborah raised her gaze. Its clear, slate blue depths startled him. "Please, call me Deborah. Or Deb if you wish."

"And I'm Victor. Or Vic." He smiled. "I wanted to make sure they're okay."

She nodded. "They are." She fiddled with the edge of Marie's blanket. "I need to thank you."

He cocked an eyebrow.

"I was stupid for insisting that we take the animals and keepsakes. It almost got us killed."

"You were right, though. It's already hard on the kids." His gaze slid to the two little girls curled up with each other. "It's all done with, and everyone's okay. Listen."

He took her arm and led her into the main cabin. They stood against the wall, and he continued, "I'm worried there's a leak somewhere, either in the FBI or DHS."

"Obviously."

"It's more than what happened today. Too many people know you're headed to Billings."

"Do you think someone could be laying a trap?"

"It's possible." Victor noticed how the plane banked to the left. "I decided we're going to go to Flagstaff."

"Flagstaff!" Her exclamation drew a long glance from Anna.

Victor drew her down so they sat in the chairs against the back wall. In a low voice, he continued, "We're based there. Look, we've been in isolation for the past six months," he added when she opened her mouth to protest. "Because of that, we've not had any direct dealings with the FBI. No one knows where we're based, not even my handler. It's going to stay that way. Our base is a ranch outside of town. I promise it's secure. Like you, our best defense is that no one knows where we're located. We'll keep you there until the whole thing blows over."

Deborah opened her mouth as if she were going to protest. Then she sighed and swiped a hand across her face. "I guess I've got no choice."

"We could go to Billings and let you take your chances."

"No. You're right." Deborah stared out the window. "I've got to trust you on this."

"I promise we'll take good care of you."

The smile on her face caught his heart. "I know. You have already."

"Let Diana take a look at that cut."

"I will. Thanks." Deborah rose and touched Anna's hair.

Victor watched her go. His smile faded. They'd evaded one attempt on her life. The question remained as to whether or not they could keep her alive until they found Murdock.

17

"You ran into difficulties?" Makmoud leaned his head against the seat and clamped his phone to his ear.

"They were heavily armed. One of their shooters stopped us before we could breach the house's security."

"Who were they?"

"How should I know?" Exasperation rang through the voice of the death squad's leader. "We tried, but they were too organized and must have arrived shortly before we did because an infidel woman ambushed our pilot and copilot. Then they shot one of my men as they escaped."

Makmoud's eyes narrowed as he realized the implication of the man's words.

Gary.

"Again, I'm sorry. We barely made it out of the country, and—"

"Enough. It is enough that you are safe. We have insurance. I'll take care of things now."

The man hung up without asking how.

Makmoud's breath huffed out as he contemplated the turn of events. Anger boiled inside of him, then left abruptly.

He switched his attention to the house across the street from him. In so many ways, it reminded him of Rachel's house, what with its pansies, swing on the front porch, and picture window.

A minivan with its back hatch up sat in the driveway. The front door to the house opened, and a boy who appeared to be about twelve carried a sack with a bat sticking from the top. He heaved it into the back. Gary's son strolled to the house.

Makmoud reached for his camera and began snapping pictures.

A pretty woman with blonde hair caught in a ponytail stepped onto the porch, a watering can in hand. Mary Walton, Gary's wife of almost twenty years. Seeing her in person, Makmoud now understood how, ten years before, Gary had refused his offer of a woman for him.

Gary loved his wife, was faithful to her. If she died at Makmoud's hand, Gary would lose all reason for living. He'd turn on his handler. It was far better to use the threat of loss to keep his mole in line.

Mary tousled her son's hair as they retreated into the house.

Makmoud lowered the camera and took a sip from a water bottle. He attached the camera to a laptop and transferred all of the photos from that morning's surveillance to a jump drive.

He reached for the hard hat he'd bought as part of his cable company disguise. As he strolled down the street with a clipboard in hand, his gaze swept the Walton house again. Now the boy carried a suitcase. A teenaged girl with a backpack followed.

Ahead of him, a light blue Toyota Camry pulled over to the curb as if lost. The driver's side window hummed down.

Makmoud smiled when he noticed Iman's long, dark hair and fair features. Her pale green eyes gazed at him.

"Your drive," he murmured through his smile. He gestured as if giving her directions. The jump drive fell from his fingers onto her lap. "Your subjects' faces are on that. Keep tabs on their movements."

The *Quds* woman nodded before pulling on to the street as if Makmoud had shown her the way to go.

He pretended to check one of the cable junction boxes before retreating to the van. Once inside, he resumed his surveillance as he reached into a cardboard box and brought out another burner phone. He dialed a number. When Jibril answered, he simply stated, "We need our insurance."

"I'll call you when we have it." The dial tone echoed in Makmoud's ear.

The three Walton family members minus Gary climbed into the minivan. Its lights flashed as it backed onto the street, leaving the house unprotected save for an alarm system.

A smirk turned up the corners of Makmoud's mouth before fading.

Now he had all of the time in the world to deal with Gary.

Gravel crunched beneath her feet as Liza stepped from the bright lights of the restaurant into the gathering gloom of the parking lot. The breeze sweeping through Key Largo stiffened, sending chilly whispers across shoulders left bare by the tank top she wore. Her curls, herded into a ponytail, brushed the skin of her neck. Then came the damp, tangy smell of wetness from the nearby bay.

Rain would arrive shortly.

Liza hastened her footsteps.

Footfalls murmured along the ground.

Was someone following her? She stopped and whirled. No one else had come from the restaurant.

Clutching her purse to her side, she continued toward where she'd parked her Jeep Wrangler at the far end of the parking lot. Dimness shifted to blackness as she left the safety of the main parking lot. A drop of rain hit her on the arm. She shivered once more as if she sensed someone following her.

Liza whipped around again.

No one, only a couple of guys who stood slightly outside the restaurant and smoked. Faint orange pinpricks glowed from the tips of their cigarettes.

More drops hit her shoulders. If she didn't get a move on it, she'd be soaked. She darted to the Jeep. By the time she threw her purse onto the passenger's seat and climbed inside, the rain thickened.

"That was close," she murmured as she cranked the engine.

As Liza hung a right onto US 1, the drizzle increased into a heavy downpour. She turned her wipers onto High and slowed down. A left turn and one more right brought her to the driveway of her house.

"Oh, great," she muttered when she noticed the metal furniture she'd pulled into the carport and the driveway to repaint. She'd have to make a run for it from farther out than she liked.

The ten seconds it took to scurry to the carport left her soaked with her feet squishing in her sandals. She slammed the door to the kitchen and leaned against it. Water sluiced from her and puddled on the floor.

Her canaries chirped when they saw her. Her cat padded into the kitchen but refused to wind around her legs like she normally did.

She giggled. "I'm a mess, aren't I?"

A chill wracked her. She needed to get out of her wet clothes. A cup of tea would warm her as well. Liza dropped her purse on the desk in the dinette area. She ran water into the shiny silver teakettle and turned on the burner.

As she made her way through the house toward the bedroom, she opened the louvered glass windows and turned on the ceiling fans. The breeze brought the organic smells of wet vegetation and damp earth into the house.

Liza's shoulders relaxed. She was home, ready to finish her evening.

Once dressed in a pair of pajama pants and cami top, she wandered into the kitchen to sort through the mail she'd hastily dumped on the table earlier that night. Junk mail went into the recycling bin, bills onto the desk for payment later. As she waited for the water to boil, she reached for the Bible study she kept beside the laptop and opened it to that week's lesson.

Steam began seeping from the kettle's nozzle.

Liza pulled a mug from the cabinet and placed a teabag in it.

A small noise reached her.

She raised her head from her book. "Hello?"

Only the sound of rain hitting the leaves and fronds of the foliage outside answered her.

Liza listened for a moment longer. She shivered, then muttered, "It's nothing."

The rain on the roof intensified to a dull roar that overcame any other noise.

Her cat hopped onto the desk. Liza rubbed her ears and located a pen. Her gaze fell on the calendar that served as her blotter. She'd marked out Spring Break on several of the days. Now she remembered. Deborah and the kids were coming to visit in a couple of weeks. She'd make plans for their stay tomorrow.

Suddenly, the cat jumped down and, with a loud meow, ran from the room.

"Cassie, what on earth?" Liza moved to follow but shook her head. Sometimes, cats never made sense to her.

That cold feeling returned. She probably needed to close the windows. She'd do so after she poured her tea.

The kettle began hissing.

Near the windows opening to the carport, her canaries, who'd chirped happily ever since her arrival, fell silent.

Liza rubbed her bare arms.

The kettle shrieked.

She reached for it.

A hand clamped over her mouth.

Liza tried to shout.

An arm snaked around her chest.

"No!" Her cry came out as a bleat.

She struggled against the man's hold. With a thrust of her legs, she pushed against the cabinets.

The man grunted as he slammed into the counter. From somewhere distant, the mug shattered on the tile floor.

Her lungs emptied.

His arm tightened around her chest like a boa constrictor.

She couldn't breathe. Sparks popped before her eyes.

The kettle screamed for attention.

She struggled. Her mouth formed a silent plea. For what? To let her go? To tell him to turn off the burner?

Her vision began tunneling as if he dragged her down a subterranean corridor.

The man wrestled her to the floor.

The kettle's whistle pierced the air.

Then everything went black.

Liza slowly came to. She rested upright against something hard and cool. Her head hurt. It took so much work for her even to open her eyes.

She must not have been out for too long because the kettle on the stove across from her rumbled in an angry boil.

A blurry form crouched in front of her.

Liza blinked.

The image sharpened into that of a man. The day came rushing back at her. She knew the man from the dive trip that morning and only an hour earlier at the restaurant. Her mouth worked to form the words. "J—J—Jibril!"

He crouched in front of her. "It's good to see you're awake."

"What…what do you want?" Her breath came in soft pants. "How…how did you find me?"

"We followed you."

"We?" Liza's gaze slid to the archway between the family room and kitchen.

Daoud. He'd been Jibril's dive buddy and had been with him that night. Now, he leaned against the frame, his arms folded across his chest. His dark gaze bored into hers.

A faint trembling began deep within her. Liza drew in a shuddering breath. "If…if it's money you want, take my ATM card. It's there—"

"It's not money we want. It's you, Liza Murphy."

"Me? W—why?"

"Because we have need of your sister."

"What?"

"You obviously have animals." Jibril nodded toward where the canary cage sat in its corner. "Who cares for them when you leave town?"

"My neighbor, Marlene."

"Daoud, the phones." Jibril took two receivers from his comrade, one from the kitchen and its twin from her bedroom. "I want you to call this Marlene. Tell her your sister has an emergency and that you must leave suddenly. You're not sure when you'll return."

"No." Defiance crept into her voice.

"What?"

"No. I won't. I—"

The *schnick* of a switchblade silenced her. She flinched. Jibril cocked an eyebrow at her. "I suggest you follow my directions unless you want to die tonight."

Liza swallowed hard. She nodded and took the receiver.

"I'll be listening to make sure you are honest with me." Jibril raised the other receiver to his ear.

With shaking fingers, Liza dialed her neighbor. "Marlene? It's Liza."

"Liza, dear, are you all right?"

Liza stared at the switchblade looming inches from her nose. "I…"

The point of it pricked the skin of her neck. Wetness oozed down it. Slowly, she continued, "No, I'm not. Deborah called. I—I need to go up to North Carolina for several days to help her take care of the kids. Can you feed the animals for me?"

"Of course, dear. I can certainly do that. Is there anything else?"

Tears welled in her eyes. "Um, no. It's not been a good night. I'll call you when I'm back."

Liza hung up. She raised her gaze.

"Satisfied?" she asked when she'd lowered the phone.

"Very. Now do the same thing for work. You call your boss and leave a message."

Liza did so.

When she finished, Jibril grabbed her phone and tossed it onto the counter. He took her arm and hauled her to her feet. "Come with me."

"What? Where are we going?"

"We're leaving."

"Can't I change?" she demanded. Her heart caught. She'd blundered.

Daoud's voice surprised her. "No. I like you just the way you are."

Liza's gaze swung to him. He smirked as he devoured her with his eyes. He approached and slid the strap of her cami top off her shoulder.

Hot anger filled her. "No!"

She pushed Daoud. He stumbled against the refrigerator.

The front door.

Liza dashed into the living room.

Heat ringed her wrist as Jibril whirled her around and flung her against the counter.

The sharp edge bit into her back. Pain shot up her spine. She staggered.

Jibril twisted her arm behind her. Again, he used his weight to propel her to the floor.

Pain in her shoulder made her sag to her knees, then all the way down. "No, please, no!"

"You leave me with no choice."

Something stung her arm.

He released her.

Liza pushed herself to her hands and knees. She stumbled to her feet. The room tilted. She fell against the edge of the desk.

She moaned. Something ran down her face. Blood? She couldn't tell.

Then nothing mattered as blackness descended.

18

Deborah shut the door to her bedroom and leaned her head against the rough wood with a small thump. She closed her eyes and deeply inhaled the cold, crisp air filtering through her slightly open window. The sharp scent of the ponderosa pines surrounding the house at the mouth of the box canyon comforted her. Across the room, a deep sigh reached her as the Colonel took up residence on the area rug.

Slowly, she opened her eyes. The queen sheets she'd found in the linen closet shortly after her arrival remained in a neat stack on the bed since making sure the kids were comfortable had taken precedence. Deborah pushed away from the door and began making the bed.

As she did so, the muffled sound of three beeps reached her as Victor armed the security system on his way out. An unwilling smile crossed her face. He'd done his best to make his unexpected guests feel welcome, from showing them around the house and immediate surroundings to making a pancake supper for the kids.

And in terms of their security? The tension in her shoulders had gradually faded as he briefed her on their escape and evasion procedures. Butch would take care of their training starting the next day. Victor had also shown her their security measures, from the cameras Shelly had placed around the property all the way to the gun cabinet containing sleek, deadly MP-5 guns. He'd assured her that only he had the key.

Deborah closed the window and pulled the filmy curtains. Once she'd changed into a nightshirt, she snuggled on the cool sheets underneath the down comforter. As her body warmed the bed, her muscles finally relaxed. Her mind drifted as if unmoored from the terror of the day.

Victor reminded her of Derek in so many ways. How? His kindness, at least once they'd gotten through their tiff about taking keepsakes and animals. He'd shown compassion to the children, especially Marie. The child had barely left his side save for when he'd briefly disappeared to make contact with his handler. His easy-going manner had soothed nerves left raw from nearly dying only hours earlier. For that, she was thankful.

Drowsiness overcame her, and she nuzzled the pillow as she drifted.

Deborah's eyes snapped open at the sound of a coyote howl near the house. From somewhere in the distance, another howl reached her. She raised her head from the pillow and found the clock on the nightstand.

Three in the morning.

She must have fallen asleep. Now, the full moon filtered through the curtains and illuminated the Colonel as he slept on the area rug.

While the room remained chilly, her body was warm. Relaxed. She laid her head back onto the pillow as her mind strolled leisurely through the evening.

A question Anna had asked when Deborah had said good night to her echoed in her ears. Would they be home by Spring Break? She couldn't imagine not being so, especially since Liza was expecting them at the family home in Key Largo.

Liza.

Despite the warmth, Deborah shivered. How much danger was her sister in? Did whoever had come after her know about Liza? If so, she needed to get to safety as well.

Deborah sat up and pushed back the covers. As quickly as she could, she pulled a sweatshirt over her nightshirt and slid her feet into her cowboy boots. Then, with the Colonel trotting after her, she disarmed the alarm and tiptoed down the stairs.

Maybe Victor would know what to do. Once outside, she made her way down the path toward the Men's Building. She was about to step onto the front porch when she noticed lights on in the outbuilding beyond. Victor hunched on a couch.

Without missing a beat, she turned her steps in his direction.

Victor sat on the couch in the studio, his mind and heart numb as he closed Rachel's journal for 1999. Part of him ached at what he'd read. After graduation, Rachel had transferred to a new posting at Fort Bragg while Makmoud headed to Iran to be the executor for his father's estate. He never returned, leaving Rachel with a broken engagement and heart. Victor's hands balled into fists. He wanted to jump up and shout, "What'd you expect by dating a guy like Makmoud?"

He couldn't. Not when his divorce several years before reminded him of how painful a broken heart could be.

Confusion washed over him. Was the smugness he felt at what happened normal? How did that change his image of Rachel? Obviously, she'd held back on telling him, but why she had nagged at him.

I wish I had someone I could talk to about this, he thought as he carefully set the composition book on the coffee table. *Someone who could listen. Maybe not offer solutions, but listen to what I had to say and not judge me for what I'm thinking and feeling.*

He raked his hands through his hair as the weariness from the past few days surged over him. Suddenly, catching a few z's seemed to be the best thing.

Maybe then he'd feel like facing his questions about Rachel.

Tapping like that of a tiny bird reached him.

His head shot up.

Deborah stood on the stoop and shivered slightly in the cold night air.

He rose and let her in. "What are you doing up so late? It's three in the morning. Come in so you won't freeze to death."

"Shouldn't I be asking you the same thing?"

"I couldn't sleep. Too jazzed up on adrenaline, I guess."

"Me too. I mean, couldn't sleep, that is." Deborah gazed around her. "Nice place."

"Thanks. What brings you out here?"

"I'm worried."

"About the kids? If kids are anything, they're resilient, and—"

"My sister. Liza."

Victor blinked. "What? Sister? I'm not following."

"I'm not sure what you mean." Deborah stared at him. "Because of everything that happened, she could be in danger."

His mind finally clicked into gear. In a few strides, he crossed the studio to the worktable where he'd placed the file upon their return. "You don't have a sister."

"Of course I have one. What are you saying?"

"Here." He flipped open the manila folder and held out her profile. "It says 'None' where siblings should be listed."

Deborah snatched the paper from him. "I—I—I don't understand."

"You and me both."

"Why was this omitted? I'm worried they could go after her. The FBI needs to know." She shoved the paper to him.

"I couldn't agree more." He tossed the file onto the desk and picked up his cell phone. "What's her number?"

Deborah gave him both land line and cell number. He called the land line first. Nothing. Just a cheery message asking him to leave a name and number and they'd get right back to him. A call to her cell phone rolled straight to voicemail.

"This isn't good," he muttered as he set the phone on the worktable.

"What?"

"It's three here, meaning six on the East Coast. She should be in bed at that time on a Saturday morning, but no one's answering. I'm calling Gary. If anyone can get protection to her, it's him. Go on up to the Big House. I'll meet you inside."

He made his call. Gary, who'd just arrived at Dulles on the Red Eye from Vegas, immediately sprang into action and told Victor to stand by. The Shadow Box commander had no choice but to do so as he paced the length of the studio. Three clicked over to four, then to five.

Finally, dawn lit the area, and he headed to the Big House to inform Deborah that Gary was on it. They both paced, Deborah downstairs and Victor in the music studio on the second floor where his mother had once practiced on the grand piano.

Outside the room, the house gradually came awake. Anna cast him a long look before she made her way down the stairs across from the studio doors. He stayed still as Gracie and Marie charged past him without noticing. The sounds of the television reached him, and he stepped onto the walkway. The smells of bacon and eggs wafted from the kitchen.

His stomach rumbled, and he yearned for a cup of coffee.

"Bad to the Bone" boomed from his phone.

Gary.

"What do you have?" Victor demanded as he closed the studio's door so no one could hear.

"Bad news."

Victor closed his eyes. "Like?"

"Our Miami office sent a couple of agents down. On the way, they tried her cell and her land line. No dice on either. When they got there, they found her Jeep gone. Based on the info we provided, they had probable cause to enter. They found her purse, and her cell was on the counter."

"Figures."

"They were about to leave when one of them noticed a broken mug on the floor. Then a bloodstain on the corner of a desk and spatters on the floor."

Victor drew in a sharp breath. "Your take?"

Gary sighed. "I don't know what to say. All signs point toward a kidnapping. They have Forensics going over it now and doing interviews around town. We've got to give them time to work."

"I want to be in on that."

"Oh? Why should you be?"

"I'm not sure I follow."

Gary's voice hardened. "You blew me off, took Deborah and her family not to Billings but to wherever you are. All without telling me. And then you had the audacity to keep that information from me when the president was going ape wanting to know she's safe."

"He seemed satisfied that they were."

"I don't care! Why should I involve you in the investigation? You stay put and let me *do my job*. Got it?" Then he blew out a sigh. "Sorry. It's been a long night made even longer by this mess."

Victor stepped to the french doors overlooking the Juliet balcony and stared outside. "I understand. I'll wait."

Silence answered him.

Victor leaned his head against the frame with a small thump.

Gary was right.

They had no choice now but to sit tight.

Deborah placed the dishes into the dishwasher and turned her mind and hands to the big iron skillet where she'd fried some bacon. The chore of cleaning up from the breakfast she'd prepared for her children and the Shadow Box crew distracted her from the music studio, where Victor had sequestered himself as he waited on news from his handler.

For about the hundredth time, she wondered what took so long.

"Most excellent, Deb," Butch said as he raised his coffee mug in a mock toast. He drained the last of it and set it on the granite with a thunk. "I'm outta here. I need to organize the Tool Barn. Where's DJ?"

"Here, Mr. Addison," DJ called.

Deborah swallowed hard when she noticed her son already dressed in a pair of jeans, his hiking boots, and a fleece.

"Hey, little brother. You can call me Uncle Butch. I need your help outside in the Tool Barn."

"Can I, Mom?" DJ's excitement almost broke her heart.

"Go on." She stepped into the great room and noted Sana, Suleiman, and Shelly curled up in chairs and on the couch in the den as they watched Saturday morning television with Marie and Gracie. Anna had retreated upstairs. Diana was getting ready for a workout, and she had yet to see Skylar or Fiona.

"Deb." Victor's soft voice made her glance up.

He leaned against the archway leading from the kitchen to the great room. Stubble added shadow to his jaw, and his brow knitted. Since she'd last seen him, he'd rolled up the sleeves of his deep red shirt. He turned his phone over and over in his hands.

"Vic?"

"Let's go upstairs and talk." He grasped her arm and walked her toward the stairs.

Once inside the studio with the door closed so no one could overhear, she shook loose. "What happened? Did they find Liza?"

"Why don't you sit over there?" Victor nodded toward a love seat near the piano. Then he pulled over the bench and sat across from her, elbows resting on knees, his gaze on the floor. Finally, he raised it. Exhaustion turned his eyes red. The sadness in those depths shook her.

She knew.

Voice quavering, she asked, "What happened?"

"Gary called. The FBI got to Liza's house. She's been kidnapped."

Trembling started deep within. She clasped her hands on her lap. She bit down hard on her lip and began shaking her head.

"At first they thought she'd left on her own will because her Jeep was missing. But then they found a shattered tea mug in the kitchen and blood spatters on the floor."

Her fingers tightened around each other. "Nothing else?"

"Not yet. They're going over the house with a forensics unit and are doing interviews in town. We've got to give them time to work."

Her stomach knotted as her face went cold, then hot with frustration that made her jump up. "Why didn't you go after her?"

"I don't understand."

"Why didn't you go after her?"

"I didn't know. It caught Gary off guard too."

"I said when I filled out the form that I had a sister." Deborah's voice rose. She didn't care. "And now, some stupid clerical error may cause her to die? Why don't you go after her?"

"I was told to stand down, to let the FBI—"

"Oh, *can* the FBI. You don't care! And now…" Her vision blurred. Tears wet her cheeks. "And now, Liza could die."

Deborah burst onto the walkway.

"Mom?" Anna's door flew open.

Deborah ignored her. She charged down the stairs, out the back door, and past the Women's Building where Diana and Fiona stretched on the porch. She ignored their calls and kept running, this time beyond the studio and even the barn. Her feet shook the camouflaged grate Butch told her he'd laid out over a chasm he'd dug as part of their escape and evasion plan. Lungs burning and legs aching, she stumbled over an exposed root and almost fell. The walls of the box canyon narrowed and towered nearly fifty feet above her. Finally, she collapsed and huddled against the red rock near where the walls met and entrapped her. With her knees tucked to her chest, she wept into her arms.

Who cared that she shivered in the chilly morning air?

Thanks to her work, Liza had paid the price.

"There you are." Victor's voice penetrated her tears.

Something draped over her shoulders, something heavy. A blanket.

He sat down beside her, his shoulder touching hers.

"I'm sorry." Those words came out strangled.

"For what?"

"For yelling at you. It's not your fault."

"I'm strong. Promise. Here." He shoved a travel mug of something into her hands. The rich sweetness of hot chocolate tickled her nose. "This will help warm you up."

For a few minutes, they sat in silence, Deborah's sniffles in staccato rhythm to the melody of the breeze whispering through the pines near the house. Her head hurt, and she still trembled. Gradually, the drink and blanket warmed her.

"You scared Anna when you ran out like that."

"I'm sorry."

"No worries. Diana's taking care of her and the others." He fell silent and wrapped his arm around her shoulders. Finally, he spoke again. "Gary called back. They found Liza's Jeep off a dirt road near Everglades National Park. They found another set of tracks too, as if they transferred her. They also talked to a bunch of folks, like the bartender at a restaurant and Jack and Natalie Raymond, who own a dive shop. Liza went diving with them all last week, and it seems like she made friends with two guys, Jibril Kidari and Daoud Rahman from the Emirates who were on vacation. The bartender reported seeing Liza talking with them last night."

"Do you think they did it?"

Victor sighed. "I don't know. Forensics hasn't finished, but so far, the only prints they've pulled are Liza's. A neighbor, Marlene Stapleton, reported that Liza called her about ten or so last night in tears, saying that she had to go and help you. No one saw anything because it was raining so badly."

Deborah's fingers worked the blanket into wads. A new round of tears slid down her cheeks. She sniffled. "No ransom demand or anything?"

"None." His arm tightened around her shoulders. "I promise they're looking for her. If anything pops, we'll be the first to know."

She could only nod. Emptiness filled her, and a headache kicked up behind her eyes. She hung her head. "I'm so sad."

"I know." Victor fell silent. "Look. We've both gotten hardly any sleep in a long time. I think the best thing you can do is get some rest. Diana's left you some Ambien. Please take it. And don't worry about the kids, okay? Diana has it under control. All I want you to do is rest. I'm going to do the same thing."

"All right."

Slowly, not letting go of her, Victor rose. He kept his arm around her shoulders.

Deborah let him walk her toward the house.

Liza was in the hands of her enemy, and she couldn't do anything about it.

Except pray.

19

Gary parked his Jeep Cherokee in the driveway. For a moment, he sat there and rested his head against the seat. He needed sleep. Badly. He finally garnered enough strength to pull his briefcase from the back and wander to the front porch.

After disarming the alarm and changing to his house key, he fumbled key chain. It fell with a clink to the brick. Gary groaned and stooped. As he did so, his eyes landed on the flower pot holding the pansies. Water stood in the saucer, meaning Mary had watered everything before she'd left.

Mary.

Longing to see her and hold her filled him.

Gary straightened and put his key in the lock. The deadbolt slid back with a click, and the door opened on soundless hinges. He stepped into the total silence of an empty house.

Good.

If the kids had been around, he probably would have snapped at them out of total exhaustion and frustration.

He slammed the door.

Just who did Vic think he was?

A commander who did what was right with the circumstances he had, just as you would have done, he told himself as he tossed his change into the ceramic dish on the foyer's mahogany console table. He placed his briefcase on the floor of the coat closet and hung his overcoat on a hanger.

Gary grimaced as the exhaustion headache he'd had since arriving at Dulles introduced nausea. The sooner he popped some aspirin, the better. His shoes tapped on the shiny blond hardwood as he shambled to the master bedroom.

A note sat on the dresser. He picked it up, closed his eyes, and inhaled the delicate scent of Mary's perfume. She'd always sprayed some on her letters to him when he'd been deployed. He remembered how he'd lain in his rack in the middle of the Iraqi desert as he read the neat cursive on the pale purple of her stationery.

A smile finally crossed his face as he scanned her writing. They'd left a little late but planned to overnight in Roanoke before driving the rest of the way to Nashville. She looked forward to him joining them.

His assignment between now and then? To take a look at the brochures she'd left so they could figure out the activities they wanted to do in Hawaii on their anniversary trip in June.

His lip curled as his mind returned to the crisis at hand.

Yeah, right. He'd get no rest until they found Liza—if they found her.

Gary wanted to forget the whole thing had happened, that he'd had a distinct hand in a certain someone kidnapping her.

After exchanging his suit and tie for a pair of jeans and a sweatshirt, he wandered into the master bathroom and flipped on the light. It blazed overhead, revealing mussed blond hair going gray, five o'clock shadow lengthening even further, and deep lines on his brow. Exhaustion reddened his blue eyes, making them almost glow.

"You look terrible," he told his reflection before turning away.

Gary returned to the kitchen and pulled a beer from the refrigerator. Who cared if it was only one in the afternoon? Happy hour needed to start a bit earlier today. He popped the top, then washed down a couple of aspirin with a slug of the Heineken's amber liquid.

He wandered into the den and collapsed onto the leather couch. Soon, a basketball game played on the screen. Oh, yeah. It was March Madness. How could he have forgotten? He scanned the scores scrolling across the screen as he tried to pick out his team. Vanderbilt seemed to be neck and neck with Arizona at halftime. Front and center, UNC and Kentucky duked it out for the right to advance to the Sweet Sixteen.

Gary leaned his head against the soft cushion. A nap sounded great. Then maybe if daylight remained, he'd go for a short run. Nothing too elaborate, just enough to loosen up his muscles and get the blood flowing.

He took another swig and set the bottle on the end table. The roar of the crowd and the drone of the announcer entranced him. As his mind relaxed, he drifted toward the blessed cocoon of sleep.

"It is a close game, is it not?"

The voice came from behind him.

Gary jerked upright. Electricity flooded through him. His heart pounded. Every sense blazed with alertness.

The buzzing began thrumming as if it sensed its master close by.

Gary flinched but refused to turn. "Why are you here?"

Makmoud stepped around the couch, the Glock in his hand held close to his body and pointed straight at Gary's heart. "Why am I here? When I heard how a web hunter had been flushed from cover, I simply had to come and see for myself."

A smile curled his former captor's lips. "I jest, of course. Don't consultants, when they have clients, periodically send people to visit these clients to ensure their satisfaction? You Americans call that a quality call, I believe. I've decided to do a *reverse* quality call with you. You see, Gary, I as a 'client' am dissatisfied with your services. I had told you I would take care of this little problem of the web hunter. I specifically ordered you to delay in notifying the FBI of the need to get her to safety. Yet when my men arrived, you already had a team there. Now, Deborah Fields is gone, whisked to safety. You failed us, did you not?"

"You think I had a choice?" His face flushed. He glowered at him. "I have other bosses too, right?"

"And you had orders. From me, that is. Directly from me."

"Yeah, well, mine came from the president. If I'd stalled, if I made it look like poor judgment, then when she died, suspicion would fall on me. I hope you know I waited to send in my team as long as I could. I actually did you a favor there."

"Who is this team? According to my man, they were quite well trained. And armed, I might add."

Gary clinched his jaw shut.

"Come, now, Gary. We're friends of sorts, are we not?" Makmoud smirked, his perfect, white smile reminding Gary of a wolf.

His breath hitched. Suddenly, he remembered how he'd found himself naked and on his knees in the filthy cell with his hands chained to opposite walls. Makmoud stood there, hands in the pockets of his pants, a smile on his face when he saw how his prisoner had finally broken.

"Friends?" Now a short bark of laughter escaped Gary. "Friends don't torture friends. Friends don't hold friends captive for six months."

He made as if to rise.

"Stay where you are." Makmoud's eyes narrowed as he studied him. Then he clucked his tongue and sighed. "Yes, I suppose you're right. But keep in mind that I saved your life after that firefight."

"Only to nearly kill me again by torturing me."

"Perhaps. But after that? We got to know each other quite well." Makmoud's dark gaze bored into Gary's.

Gary couldn't break it.

Slowly, Makmoud repeated, "Now tell me. What is this team of yours?"

The buzzing flared.

Gary moaned and put his head in his hands.

"It is not a difficult question."

"I know." He'd do anything to make it recede. "Okay. Okay. I received orders from the president to form a team like a Special Ops team. Satisfied?"

"Do go on."

Gary winced. "Shadow Box. I started it in February of last year and had them recruited by August. When word came down that you were making a move on Deborah Fields, the president ordered me to send them into action. I had no choice, all right? You've got to understand that."

"Oh, I do. I know you serve two masters." Makmoud seated himself on the edge of a straight-back chair. The ugly muzzle of the gun remained focused on Gary's heart. "I'm quite aware of that. Where did this Shadow Box team take Mrs. Fields and her brood?"

"I don't know."

"You don't know. Hmmmm." Makmoud rubbed his chin. "Wrong answer. Tell me the truth."

"I. Don't. Know." Gary bit those words off.

"That would be, why?"

"Because Victor Chavez, the team commander, wanted to compartmentalize." Suddenly, Gary realized his blunder. He clamped his jaw shut.

A smile teased the corners of Makmoud's lips upward. He started chuckling. "Victor Chavez, eh? As in former Secret Service Agent Chavez? The man who tried to kill me?" His gloved hand shot up and rubbed the ugly scar along his neck. "I heard he ran away under a cloud of suspicion with his tail between his legs. Now, where did his team take Deborah Fields?"

"I told you I don't know. Truly, I don't. I have no idea where their base is because we're keeping things compartmentalized."

"Of course." Makmoud nodded. "That does make sense. Who else is on that team?"

Gary clenched his teeth. He knew all too well who else.

Suleiman al-Ibrahim.

Also known as Ibrahim Hidari, Makmoud's turncoat half-brother.

"You won't answer me?"

"No."

Makmoud sighed and shook his head. "So sorry. Pity that you won't, because I didn't want to show you these." He reached into his black leather jacket and brought out a manila envelope. He tossed it.

The envelope landed on the coffee table in front of Gary.

"Go on. Open it."

Gary did. His blood ran cold as he flipped through the photographs. They showed Mary and the kids packing the minivan, outside their hotel in Roanoke, and in a restaurant.

"You see, Gary, I have someone following your family. Iman has been behind them almost the entire time. One call from me, and she will take care of them. She may be a woman, but she is very proficient with a gun."

Gary's jaw began hurting.

Makmoud finally shook his head. "I can see I will get nowhere with you right now. This is what I want you to do. I want you to print out profiles of all members of your team. In full, glorious color. Do this by Tuesday. I'll notify you of when and where to meet. Then perhaps when this thing blows over, you'll be able to meet up with your family." His lips curled in a smile. "I did, after all, read that note your lovely wife wrote. I have taken quite a liking to her perfume. I'll take those."

Stunned, Gary remained sitting as his handler lifted the photos from his hand and secured them in the manila envelope.

"I'll be in touch." With another brief smile, Makmoud opened the door leading to the garage.

Only when it shut did Gary leap to his feet. He bolted to the garage and ripped open the door.

The door to the back thumped closed.

He rushed to the sliding glass door in the den.

Nothing.

No sign of Makmoud anywhere.

Gary cussed out loud and slammed the door so hard that the glass cracked, leaving a jagged line in it and one more chore for him to do.

Bile tasting of beer rose to his throat. The buzzing increased. As if punishing him, the headache returned with a vengeance. Nausea washed over him. He barely made it to the toilet before he threw up. Gary remained crumpled on the tile, his hands gripping the cold white porcelain. His stomach heaved again, but nothing came up.

Finally, he gripped the counter and hauled himself to his feet.

Forget running.

He barely had the strength to crawl onto the queen-sized bed.

He squeezed his eyes shut. A merciful sleep overcame him.

"I love you," Mary murmured to him, her breath whispering against his ear, her voice soft. She touched his face and kissed him.

He found he couldn't open his eyes.

Someone lifted his dog tags from around his neck. Makmoud's voice spoke, instructing his comrades nearby.

Angry shouts assaulted him. Rough hands grabbed him and dragged him from the safety of his bed and into a filthy cell smelling of blood and excrement. They chained his wrists to ropes on opposite walls.

Gary's sobs reached him. He now had no strength. Crying, he pleaded, "Let me die. Haven't you killed me already even though I breathe?"

"Ah, but your time with me has only begun." Makmoud released the chains. Hooking an arm around him, he rose. "Come with us."

Gary hobbled between Makmoud and Jibril, who helped him into a steaming tub of water. His festering sores stung, but the hot water felt so good, so cleansing.

"I love Mary." Gary sat on the floor of a room, a meal spread on the blanket between him and Makmoud. He met his gaze. "I'll never be unfaithful to her. I vowed that ten years ago."

Mary collapsed against him. Her sobs assaulted his ears. "You don't know how hard it was. This waiting. This having to deal with the media. With never knowing if the next body that turned up would be you."

"I love you," Gary whispered. He held her tightly.

Her blond curls tickled his chin.

"I love you so much." He closed his eyes, savoring her softness and lavender he'd grown to associate with her.

She cried out.

Someone ripped her from his grasp.

Gary came wide awake.

"Gary! Help me!" His wife's pleas echoed into the darkness.

Light flashed, revealing Makmoud's lips curled in a sneer for a brief instant. He held a gun to her head.

"Mary!" Gary had bolted upright. Sweat soaked his shirt. Tears poured down his cheeks. He blinked for a few seconds as he took in Mary's dresser with its lamp and the picture of their wedding day as well as his massive armoire. Suddenly, he realized he sat on their bed in Arlington.

I'm at home. I'm in the bedroom. Mary's safe and on her way to Nashville, at least for now. He slouched forward and rubbed his neck as the dream receded. The buzzing and headache did too, leaving him shaken and drained.

He raked his hands through his hair and wiped his cheeks with his sleeve.

He realized one thing.

Makmoud had entrapped him. He had no way out.

None.

20

Deborah slowly awakened. From downstairs, the sound of laughter filtered under the door and tickled her ears. The rich smell of spaghetti teased her nose and conjured memories of more innocent times. She closed her eyes and drifted once more.

Derek stood in the kitchen of their farmhouse with two-month-old Marie in his arms. On the stove, a vat of spaghetti sauce bubbled. He smiled. "Smells good."

"Want a taste?" Deborah brushed her fingers across her youngest child's forehead.

"Sure."

She got a spoon and dipped it into the rich sauce. She offered it to her husband.

"Hmmm. Wow. That's great! As always." With that, he bent and kissed her.

Marie's giggles drew her back to the present. The child's footsteps pattered outside her room.

Curious, Deborah sat up. Darkness enfolded the bedroom. Only a strip of light appeared under the door. She pushed her disheveled hair out of her eyes and glanced at the clock.

Seven.

She'd slept for eight hours.

Did she feel rested? Maybe not deeply so, but she realized that now she wouldn't have a meltdown. She shoved the covers aside and pulled on some jeans and her sweatshirt. As she arrived at the bottom of the stairs, the back door in the mudroom next to the kitchen thumped shut.

Again, the spaghetti sauce's aroma tickled her nose. Yawning, she followed the aroma.

Diana, clad in Crocs, leggings, and a sweatshirt, smiled at her from where she finished washing a large saucepan. "Look who's up. How are you?"

"Better, thanks. I'm sorry I missed supper."

"You needed the rest." Diana pulled a covered plate from the refrigerator. "We had spaghetti. Here. Let me nuke some for you."

"Thanks." Deborah located a glass and poured some milk into it. "Where is everyone?"

"Let me see. DJ went with Butch to the Tool Barn. Shelly's painting somewhere."

"I didn't know she painted."

"Neither did I until a few weeks ago. Sana said something about doing Bible study."

"Do y'all go to church around here?"

"Yeah, but we're sticking close until things get worked out. We're meeting for Bible study tomorrow if you're up for it."

"Will do."

"Anyway, I'm not sure where Skylar and Fi are. Or Suleiman for that matter. I promise you that boy's like the Cheshire Cat. He disappears until all that's left is that nice smile of his." She giggled, drawing a smile from Deborah.

"And I think Vic said something about heading to his studio. Oh, and Butch wants to play Uno later. You do play, right?"

"We do." Deborah seated herself at the table. "With Liza kidnapped, I don't see how I can—"

Diana gripped her hand. "Deb, look at me."

She did.

The doctor continued, "I know your sister's out there in the hands of her captors. I totally get that. But I also know that one of the worst things you can do is to worry this into the ground. The FBI's got their best on this case. They'll find her. Your job is to be there for your children. Can you do that? Can you be there for Marie when she begs to play Uno? When DJ's excited about someone who can show him how to fix an old truck?"

Her new friend was right. Her children picked up on her moods more than she realized. She needed to be strong. Slowly, she nodded. "Yeah."

"Good." Diana rose. "If you don't mind, I'm going to head out and shower. I barely had time to squeeze in a bike ride before Butch volunteered me to make supper."

Deborah watched her go. Once she'd loaded her dishes into the dishwasher and started it, she wandered into the deepening night in search of her children. She found DJ exactly where Diana had reported. He stood on a crate and stared at the innards of a dilapidated pickup truck as Butch explained things to him. They stopped for a few moments to chat, but she knew Butch's explanations intrigued her son more than small talk.

She wandered toward the studio. Beyond, she noticed how Gracie and Marie rode horses under the lights and Skylar's and Fiona's watchful gazes. Anna sat on the fence rail in a slouch that had become more and more common lately.

Satisfied, Deborah approached the studio's glass walls.

Victor sat on the couch, something in his hands making the furrows between his eyes and on his brow deepen. He flipped a page, seemed to mutter something, and shook his head.

Deborah could stand it no longer. She tapped on the door.

Victor glanced up, his gaze brightening as he smoothed over the anguish. He rose and opened it. "Deb, hey. Come on in. How are you feeling?"

"More rested." She offered a smile. "Thanks for insisting that I take something. Usually I don't, but I needed it this time."

"I hear you. I think I got six hours myself, and it felt good to do so."

"What are you reading?"

He crossed the room to the small coffeemaker sitting on the corner of the worktable. "Would you like some coffee or tea? Hot chocolate?"

"Vic."

"What?" He glanced at her with wide, almost innocent dark eyes.

"So what are you reading?" She picked up the notebook. "A journal? My, you have messy handwriting."

"It's, uh, not mine."

"Oh?"

Now red stained his neck and crept upwards. "It's, um, well, it belonged to my fiancée."

"Your fiancée? Belonged?" She cocked an eyebrow. "This is getting more interesting by the second. You're blushing."

"She died almost two years ago." His words came out terse, clipped.

Now her own cheeks flamed. "I'll take some hot tea, if you would. I'm sorry. I guess I'm teasing when I shouldn't."

"No, you're right. It does sound odd." Victor sighed as he poured water into the coffeemaker. "Do you remember when Maggie McCall was almost kidnapped two years ago?"

"I read about it in the paper."

"Rachel and I served on her Secret Service detail. Rach and two others died. I was shot."

Deborah shivered.

"There was an investigation as to how it happened. When it kicked off, I was still in the hospital. Then they started questioning me, mostly about Rachel."

"Why?"

He opened a box of tea. "Is full caf okay? That's all I've got here."

"That's fine."

He dropped a bag into a mug. "They thought she might have been involved. I couldn't believe they'd accuse someone with a spotless record who died by taking a bullet for Maggie."

"What did they conclude?"

"They didn't." Victor bit off the words. He shook his head. "I'm sorry. It still hurts. They had their suspicions, but what could they do? She died.

Thing is, they thought I might have been involved, but I guess they figured out I wasn't. I still had to resign. That took me to California."

He fell silent and ran his hand along the smooth wood of the worktable. "May I ask you a question?"

She nodded.

"Am I crazy still to mourn her? I…I can't seem to get past this."

"That's normal. For the first year after Derek died, I cried every day." Deborah winced as her grief jumped out of hiding and surprised her.

"But you were married for many years. I was only engaged."

"But your heart was wounded regardless. I can tell how much you loved her. It's okay to mourn her passing even two years later."

His slow nod told her she'd said the right thing. "We were so close. That's why the investigation was so hard on me. I fully believed that she had no involvement."

Deborah blinked. "Wait. You said 'believed.' Are you… what changed your mind?"

Victor opened a drawer in the worktable and extracted what appeared to be a necklace. "I found this hidden behind a picture of her."

He dropped it into her hand.

"This is beautiful." She ran her thumb across the writing. "Arabic?"

"Farsi." He turned away and dumped some hot chocolate powder into mug. "A friend of mine who was an interpreter for me in Iraq translated it for me. It says 'My Beloved' in Farsi."

"I'm not sure I follow."

"Rach and I met when we started working on Maggie's detail." Impatience pushed his words. "We were friends first before we started dating. She told me at one point that she'd not had any other serious boyfriend who warranted mention. She also said she always dumped her exes' things once they broke up. Except she didn't with this. Or these."

He reached into the drawer again and tossed a couple of photos onto the top of the table.

Deborah exchanged the necklace for the pictures. "Who's this guy?"

"Makmoud Hidari." Vic busied himself with pouring the hot water into mugs. "Sugar's in this container. Creamer's in the mini-fridge under the worktable if you need it."

Memories of the news reports two years before came flying back to her. "As in, the guy who tried to kill Maggie?"

"One and the same." He crossed to the couch again and picked up the journal. "She must have removed those from the scrapbooks she kept that corresponded to each year of her journal."

"When were they taken?"

He eased onto the cushions and pulled the composition book to him. "When she was in grad school in the late nineties."

Deborah joined him and settled on a chair with her legs tucked underneath her. She curled her hands around the mug. The ceramic warmed them. "You doubt her innocence?"

Vic didn't respond for a moment, only sipped his hot chocolate as he stared at the journal. His Adam's apple bobbed. "I don't know. It's weird. When the Service searched our house during their investigation, they did a really thorough job. I mean even to the point of knocking holes in my walls. They carried out everything they thought was pertinent, including Rach's scrapbooks and financial records. When they did and Maggie found out about it, she demanded a complete and honest list of what they'd taken. The journals were never on there."

"Like Rachel hid them?"

"Right. I found them in one of those hibachi pots." Her jerked his chin in the direction of the hearth where two large antique pots stood guard like sentries. A spark popped in the fireplace, and yellow flames licked the grate. "She'd recently welded the lids onto the pot and even put rocks in the other one to make them weigh the same. That got me to thinking. Why would she hide them? Why?"

Deborah remained silent because the way he'd stilled signaled more to come.

Victor set his mug onto the glass of the table and put his head in his hands. His fingers gripped his hair. "It's been so hard. I feel like I don't have anyone to talk this through with me. No one. And there are so many things running around in my head, so many questions about her, that I feel like I can't sort them out."

"You can talk to me."

His dark gaze shot up and met hers.

It shook her to the core.

Then he wagged his head. "I couldn't burden you with this."

"You forget something." A smile flitted across her lips. "I do this for a living. I think I can handle it. We counselors aren't wizards or soothsayers. What we are is a listening ear. I like to say I only guide you through what's going on."

Victor kneaded the worn cover of the book.

Lord, show me the right words, she whispered in her heart. Aloud, she said, "I don't know you well, but I think you're a man of integrity and a just person. Something tells me you won't stop until you know the truth about this."

Victor finally tossed the notebook onto the table. "I've read so much already. Rach journaled at first as a way to recover from a rape that happened after her freshman year in college. Then she kept at it. She got very good at capturing details. She wrote about everything, and I mean *everything.*"

His cheeks flushed, but he didn't volunteer the reason why. "Let's suffice it to say that during her last year in graduate school, Makmoud was much more than a mere ex-boyfriend. They were lovers to the nth degree. He even proposed to her."

Deborah kept quiet as he drew in a shaky breath. He bowed his head and rubbed the back of his neck for a moment.

When he continued, sadness choked his voice. "Then right after they both graduated, he had to go to Iran and tend to his father's estate, since he was the eldest son. He never returned."

"As in broke the engagement?"

"Something like that. It broke her heart. Messed her up too, because she essentially jumped into a marriage with her ex-husband, William Drake, right before Gulf II started. He was Army too, and I remember the only thing she said about them was that he was the wrong person at the wrong time. She mustered out in late 2004, and that's as far as I've gotten. I'm…so scared to read further. Like what if I'm right?"

"Then at least you'll know the truth. I think…I think you lack true closure to everything that happened two years ago. You yearn for it, which is normal and natural, even if it hurts. Maybe this is your opportunity to find it."

He closed his eyes and winced as if she'd hit a raw nerve.

Deborah pretended not to notice the tear that slid down his cheek.

She lowered her gaze and studied the steaming mug of tea.

"You're right." A shuddering sigh reached her ears. "Will you walk with me?"

"Of course."

The way his lips tipped upward jolted her.

She opened her mouth to say more, but footsteps thundered up the path. The door slammed open, and both Gracie and Marie dashed inside. Marie's voice echoed off the slate, stone, and glass of the room. "Mommy! Mr. Victor! Uncle Butch wants to start Uno."

"Does he?" Victor grinned and ruffled Marie's light brown curls. The sadness receded as his eyes lit up with delight.

"Come on!" She tugged him to his feet. "He says he can't start until we get back."

"Then let's go." He let her lead him from the studio.

"Mommy, can I sit beside you?" Gracie asked as Deborah shut off the lights and closed the door behind her.

"Of course, sweetie. Let's go. Sounds like we're going to have fun tonight." She winked at Victor.

He smiled and mouthed, "Thank you."

The gesture firmed her vow. She'd walk with him as he finished reading the journals. No matter what.

Even if he realized his deepest fear.

21

Laughter stirred Liza awake. Not close, like in the room, but far away. Where?

Sensation came next, the soft clean feeling of sheets against her arms. Cold air poured onto her face from above and clogged her nose. Her right ankle felt heavy for some reason.

Her eyes snapped open. She sat up, her head swimming from the motion. A few deep breaths steadied her. She whipped away the thin sheet covering her. A chain's shackle clung to her ankle, the links running to another shackle looped around the brass footboard. It clinked against the metal when she moved her foot.

"Oh, no." She shuddered.

Suddenly, voices reached her, this time from outside her door.

It slammed open.

A man's bulk filled the doorway. Jibril's companion from that fateful night. Daoud.

Liza shrank away as his eyes raked her up and down. She snatched up the sheet and clutched it in front of her. "What do you want?"

"To see if you're awake." He closed the door behind him, which sealed her from any form of safety.

Liza shivered.

He approached her. "And to see if you would like me to release you so you could use the bathroom."

At his mention, her bladder began pestering her. She nodded.

"Then do not try to escape. It is pointless." He undid the shackle around her ankle.

Liza swayed from the lingering aftereffects of whatever they'd given her.

Daoud steadied her. His hands began drifting down her arms.

She broke free and bolted into the bathroom. She locked the door and rushed to the lone window.

Her heart plummeted. Her prison, wherever that was, resided on the second floor of wherever she stayed. A townhouse, single family house, or apartment, she didn't know. Only a small stretch of grass and trees plus gray sky filled her view. She tugged on the window.

Nothing.

"No!" she quietly breathed as she jerked at it again. She examined the frame.

Nailed shut.

"God, please." Her desperate cry came out as a whisper as she clawed the glass.

Only after several deep breaths to stave off her panic did Liza press her ear to the door and listened. Nothing moved, no sound of feet shifting or even a man's breathing. She opened the door and stepped onto the tightly woven carpet.

Daoud grabbed her arm.

Adrenaline bolted through her. "No!"

His slap ripped the word from her mouth. He spun her around and shoved her hard.

Liza landed face first on the bed. She got to her hands and knees.

Daoud jumped onto her back, pinning her to the mattress. His hand groped her.

Panic fueled her shout. "Stop!"

The sheets muffled her words so they came out as a bleat.

His hot breath spilled across her neck. A chuckle reached her ears as he flipped her over.

Liza screamed.

He called her a foul name and clamped his hand over her mouth.

Trembling overtook her, as did desperate anger. She raked her nails across his cheeks.

Daoud yelped and grabbed his face.

Liza pushed him.

Off balance, he tumbled off of her.

She had one chance. Heart pounding, she scrambled off the bed.

Her feet hit carpet.

Pain seared her scalp as Daoud grabbed her hair and yanked her backwards.

The blow to her kidney sent sparks across her vision.

Agony blazed as he punched her in solar plexus. She curled into a ball and moaned. She couldn't breathe. She opened her mouth, but no sound came. Her world swam.

As it faded to black, she breathed out a frantic prayer. *God, please...*

The sound of fabric ripping reached her ears.

Then, nothing.

Rain speckled Makmoud's windshield as he sat behind the wheel of his rental car and soaked up the heat emanating from the vents. He surveyed the beige front of the townhouse with its standard navy blue shutters and low block of concrete that served as a sorry excuse for a front porch. His brother had done well. They had the end unit. For Rent signs stood in the windows of the adjacent unit and the one next to that.

Perfect for a safe house.

Makmoud climbed from the black Ford Fusion. Chilly mist clung to his cheeks and hair. He shivered, reached into the backseat, and slung his duffel over his shoulder along with his backpack.

His feet scraped the concrete as he climbed the stoop. In the picture window beside the front door, blinds twitched.

He knocked the code, twice fast, three times slow.

A deadbolt slid back, followed by the scraping of a chain lock and turn of the lock in the knob. The door opened a crack. Jibril peered at him. A grin relaxed his taut features. "Welcome, my brother."

Makmoud stepped inside and shut the door behind his brother. The two men briefly hugged and kissed each other on the cheeks. Makmoud eased his burdens to the floor as the scent of something delicious filled his nose. His stomach rumbled loudly.

Jibril chuckled. "You came at the right time. Saj made the perfect stew." He set the Beretta he'd drawn on the console table across from the door. "I just got here. Ahmad did well on this one."

"He did." Makmoud chuckled. "Typical American suburban home. What do they call it in Washington? I think someone called it Townhouse Hell."

Both men chuckled.

Jibril let the way through the small dining room toward the family room. "You should see the other safe house."

"Which is where?"

His brother smirked. "Historic Charleston. It seems as if one of our donors has a residence there and was more than willing to let us use it."

"How is our guest?"

"I don't know."

"Then I'll check." Makmoud stepped into the family room. Several of his men hopped up and called a greeting. As he answered, he noticed the way Daoud remained sitting on the couch.

"You're not going to stand for your commander?" he asked with a grin.

Daoud finally rose and mumbled something without making eye contact.

Makmoud's eyes narrowed. Something had happened. He took his bags upstairs and found two twin beds in the room reserved for Jibril and him. After depositing his gear, he stepped across the landing to the closed door where they held their guest. He put his hand on the knob and pushed it open.

He jumped at the woman's cry.

Liza stared at him. She snatched the sheet and turned away.

Makmoud inhaled. Scents hung in the air. The smell of blood. Of sweat. And of something else he couldn't place.

Until he refocused on Liza.

Her tight curls spilled in every direction. She'd wrapped the top sheet around her like a toga. Brown streaked the fabric.

Blood.

She shook, and soft whimpers emanated from her. She put her back to him.

"I won't hurt you. I promise." He closed the door and approached her.

She didn't move. Her mewling turned to quiet sobs.

Makmoud stepped around the foot of the bed. He reached out and drew down the sheet to expose the skin of her back to slightly below her shoulder blades.

Even at his gentle touch, she flinched.

Something tightened deep within his gut as he noticed the bruising and the cut that ran from her right shoulder blade across her spine. Blood had dried in it and smeared along skin purple from bruising.

"Face me, if you would."

She shook her head, her dark blond curls sliding across the ivory of her shoulder.

"I promise I will not lift a hand to you."

She partially turned. Her right eye was nearly swollen closed and also a deep purple, this one with tinges of green at the edges. She refused to meet his gaze, and her hands clutched the sheet so tightly that the tendons stood out.

Anger began simmering deep within him.

"Who did this do you?" Makmoud shifted so he faced her. He lifted her chin, then reached up and touched the cut across her cheekbone. His fingers came away with fresh blood.

She winced.

"I will not punish you. Tell me."

"D—D—Daoud." Her voice trembled. A tear trickled down her cheek.

"I see." The anger reached a boil. "Don't move."

He jumped to his feet, retreated to his room, and dug some clothing from his duffel. When he returned, Liza remained still.

"I promise you're safe, yes? No one will hurt you anymore. I want you to clean up. Take a shower. I'll leave this T-shirt and pair of sweatpants on the bed."

She stared at him, her eyes wide as if doubting his words.

"Go now." Makmoud turned away to give her privacy.

The soft whisper of fabric and hurried footfalls told him she'd jumped up and bolted into the bathroom. The lock clicked.

He stripped the bed and tossed the foul, dirtied sheets into the washer. He made it up with fresh linens, this time adding a light blanket he found in the closet.

A glimmer caught his eye. He bent and reached for it.

Makmoud muttered under his breath when he noted the iron links of a chain.

As he bent to tuck in the blanket, a strip of striped cloth poked from underneath the bed. Now, he swore long and loud as he pulled out a pair of pajama pants and a torn top. He tossed the ruined clothing into the trashcan and put it in the hallway. Makmoud stared at the door to the bathroom. Over the rush of the shower, he thought he heard Liza crying. Sobbing was more like it. After leaving the bundle of clothing on the bed, close to the bathroom door, he thundered down the steps.

All six guards plus Jibril focused on the soccer match unfolding on the television. Two slouched on the couch with their feet on the table. Smoke wafted from the cigarette one held. Saj, the stew maker, occupied the easy chair. Two others had taken seats on the bar chairs. Jibril pulled a bottle of water from the refrigerator. Daoud leaned against the archway between the dining room and the kitchen.

At the sight of Makmoud, his eyes widened. He straightened and backed up a step.

Anger turned to rage.

"You!" Makmoud shouted. He pointed at Daoud.

Daoud turned as if to run.

Makmoud grabbed him around the throat. With a growl, he slammed the man into the dining room wall so hard that the clock hanging next to them fell. It shattered on the tile.

Through the pounding of his pulse, Makmoud barely heard the gasps from his men.

"Brother—" Jibril began.

"Silence!" Makmoud drilled Daoud with his gaze.

"Why did you do it?" he shouted. His fingers tightened around the man's throat.

Daoud struggled, strangling noises emanating from him. His face began turning red.

Makmoud tightened his grip. "Why did you do it? Why did you chain her like an animal? Then rape her?"

His voice echoed off the ceiling. "She is our guest, not some toy. Did I not make myself clear when we trained?"

Daoud struggled. Red advanced to purple. His eyes rolled back in his head.

Makmoud released him.

Daoud collapsed to his knees. He crumpled to the floor, then began coughing. A noisy, wet gasp emanated from him.

Makmoud whipped around and glared at the rest of the guards.

Their eyes wide, they remained frozen in place. Even the soccer match had fallen silent.

"What happened?" Jibril demanded.

Makmoud whirled on him, causing his younger brother to take a step back. He shifted his gaze to the others. "What happened is that your comrade indulged himself by raping the guest. Something I strictly forbade."

He paced in front of the group.

"You all know better, yes?" He stopped near Daoud. "You are a fool, Daoud. Your stupidity has endangered our mission."

He kicked the man.

The sound of a rib snapping echoed across the room.

Makmoud whipped around again and pointed at the remainder of his team. "If I hear of anyone else doing such a thing, you will pay dearly, do you understand? She is to be treated with respect. And we will ensure that you accord her that respect."

Makmoud knelt and rooted around in Daoud's pockets. He came up with the key to the chain's locks and tossed it to Saj. "I want you to take Daoud upstairs. The chain he used on our guest is in the bedroom. You are to chain him to his bunk with that. Understand?"

"Y—Yes." Saj cast a look at the moaning Daoud.

Makmoud turned and stalked into the kitchen.

Jibril's voice followed him "Brother, if I had known, I would not have—"

"What is done is done." Makmoud braced his hands against the counter and took several deep, cleansing breaths. As quickly as it had come, the anger receded. Had Liza's mistreatment truly endangered the mission? Perhaps not. No, it didn't. A new calmness filled him. He could play the hero in Liza's eyes, maybe make her let her guard down enough to trust him.

He turned his head and found Jibril leaning with his hip against the counter in front of the sink. In a low voice, he said, "Daoud cannot be trusted now. Like a dog, he has tasted his version of human flesh. You will deal with him accordingly."

For a moment, Jibril opened his mouth as though he would argue.

This wouldn't do, especially coming from his brother. With the slightest hint of menace in his voice, he repeated, "You will deal with him accordingly."

Jibril nodded. "Shall I send for another?"

"Not yet. Take care of him when we transfer to the other safe house. Ensure he isn't found." Makmoud's mind shifted to the next phase of his plan. He located a bowl in the cabinet. "Our guest is hungry, I'm sure. Or she will be when she is clean and realizes she is safe. And that will be the way that we slip an arrow through her armor."

"How so?"

"My contact in Washington came through and left both a sedative and my requested package at our dead drop in Washington. We add a little spice to her stew." Makmoud reached into his pocket and came up with a vial that had been with the syringe in the package he'd retrieved from a newspaper stand. "She needs to sleep, does she not? This will ensure that she does so deeply. After that, we'll proceed."

He ladled some stew into a bowl, then added a few drops of the clear liquid. He placed the bowl onto the tray along with a pack of frozen vegetables and a glass of milk he tainted with the sedative. He carried it upstairs and tapped on the door.

Liza sat Indian style on the comforter. She now wore one of his long-sleeved T-shirts and a pair of his sweats with the cuffs rolled up. Her hair curled over one shoulder like small coils of brass wire.

Right then, she stared at where her hands twisted on her lap. She glanced up when he stepped inside before returning her gaze to her lap.

"Liza, I want you to eat." Makmoud set the tray on the dresser before leaning against the wall next to the bathroom.

"Why do you care so much? And how do you know my name?"

"I know your name because I've studied you and your sister. And I care because my man treated you disrespectfully. I can assure you he will no longer bother you."

"Jibril. He's your brother, right? You look like each other."

Makmoud smiled. "I'll take that as a compliment."

"He said you wanted my sister. Why?"

"She has something we want." Makmoud pushed away from the wall. "Now eat. I also left some frozen vegetables to put over your eye to reduce the swelling."

Makmoud put his hand on the knob to leave.

"Why do you care so much?"

Her question made him pause. He turned.

Liza had uncurled from her position. She now leaned on her hand as she faced him.

"Should I not?"

"I thought you would have applauded what Daoud did to me. That I would be amusement for your men."

Suddenly, Makmoud found himself at the age of ten. His father had struck him on the cheek when he failed to recite a *sura* from the Koran correctly. When tears rose to his eyes, he struggled not to give in. His father jeered him and raised his hand. His mother stepped in front of him, her shoulders back, her chin lifted as she protected him. His father struck her instead.

He blinked.

Liza sat before him, her slate blue eyes slightly red but clear.

Makmoud cleared his throat. "I love my mother very much. She endured much with my father, yet managed to raise us well."

She opened her mouth, must have thought about what she'd say, and closed it.

With that, he stepped into the hall and stood there for a moment.

In the adjacent room, Daoud moaned. It turned into a fit of coughing, followed by a plea to Saj to let him up. The chain clinked. Saj snapped back at him about how Daoud had shamed them all.

Had Daoud's actions endangered the mission? A mere meter from him in the master bedroom, the tray scraped across the dresser. The tiniest of sighs reached him as a spoon clinked against ceramic. A slow smile spread across Makmoud's face. No, not at all.

"Jibril," Makmoud softly called so as to not alert the rest of the men.

His younger brother joined him in the kitchen. "It is time?"

"Yes." Makmoud undid the zipper of the small satchel that had been in the dead drop with the sedative. In it rested the syringe with the tracking device. He added a small packet of alcohol wipes, some gauze, and some antibiotic ointment from the First Aid kit he'd found in the kitchen. "Come with me. We'll see how alert Liza is now."

Once on the landing, he tapped on Liza's closed door. "Liza. It's me."

No answer.

Makmoud opened the door a crack and peered inside.

Liza lay motionless on the bed, her damp curls now spilling onto the pale blue of the sheets. She lay in a tight ball with the blanket to her chin. The peas rested on a hand towel on her face. She'd set the empty soup bowl and glass of milk on the dresser.

"Liza," Makmoud called softly.

She didn't stir.

Makmoud nodded to Jibril, and both men approached the bed.

Jibril picked up the pack and tossed it onto the tray. After he lifted the towel from her face, he muttered under his breath when he noticed the massive bruising. "Daoud will pay for this."

He tossed it onto the tray.

"Yes, he will." Makmoud touched her on the forehead. She didn't move. His fingers skimmed down her cheek, then stopped at her neck.

Her pulse was slow, steady. Her breath whispered across his hand.

"She's out for a good twelve or so hours and sleeping very deeply."

Liza sighed and uncurled a little from her tuck.

Without hesitation, he drew the sheet down until her entire body was exposed. "The key is to insert the tracking device in a place that will not likely be x-rayed when she goes to the hospital. Though my contact promised me it wouldn't show up on traditional X-rays, I cannot take that chance. To me, her calf is the best place."

He slid the cuff of the sweatpants up to reveal the fair skin where the muscle began. He ran his fingers upward a few centimeters and nodded when he felt the muscle thicken. "Perfect. Give me the alcohol wipe."

Jibril opened the packet and handed it to him.

Makmoud cleaned the spot. "The syringe. And have that gauze ready."

"No wonder you wanted her knocked out for this. That needle is huge!"

"Precisely." Carefully, Makmoud inserted the needle, sending it deep enough that the tracker wouldn't be detected as a lump beneath the skin. All the while, he kept an eye on Liza.

She didn't stir.

He depressed the plunger and delivered its contents into her body. "Gauze."

He withdrew the needle and placed the gauze over it to staunch any blood. For a few minutes, he kept pressure on the wound.

"Ointment now." He lifted the square. Good. The wound had stopped bleeding. He took some of the ointment and applied it, rubbing it into the skin until the slick sheen had faded.

Makmoud rose and covered her with the sheet and blanket. His hand drifted across her hair. "You did well, my dear. Very well."

"She won't notice?" Jibril asked as they stepped onto the landing.

"She shouldn't. The wound will heal quickly." Makmoud stepped into their room and tossed the satchel into his duffel.

"And then?"

A smile curled Makmoud's lips. "We let her go."

22

Liza huddled by the cracked bedroom door and listened. Another day had passed, and she'd discerned their routine. Downstairs, silverware clinked on ceramic. Male voices reached her. She easily picked out Jibril's bass rumble and the baritone of his brother.

And Daoud? His moans reached her as did his begging for mercy. Only once had she heard Jibril's brother respond to him. A slap followed that. At least now she didn't live in fear of another attack. Thanks to the care of Jibril's brother, she felt stronger.

Chairs scraped back. Jibril's brother said something that sounded like a farewell.

Liza wrapped her arms around her legs as anxiety tightened her chest. If he left, what would happen? Would they release Daoud? Would Jibril suddenly take an unhealthy interest in her like his companion had?

She had to escape.

Tonight.

The front door opened and shut. Dishes clattered, and someone laughed. Voices drifted into the foyer, followed by the chatter of the television.

Liza scrambled onto the bed as footsteps thumped on the stairs. Gradually, the noises in the upstairs rooms faded. She waited another agonizing hour before crawling to the door again. After easing the knob to the right until the bolt slid all the way back, she opened it a crack and listened. She'd heard four voices to her left, then the bass voice of Jibril to the right. Now, she risked poking her head from the room.

Only darkness.

A snore emanated from Jibril's room.

The tightness that had gripped her chest released a little.

Downstairs, someone coughed and murmured something. His companion responded. The smell of coffee tickled her nose, meaning that most likely, two guards pulled the night shift.

Liza remained frozen. Could she do it?

She withdrew and resumed her tucked position next to the door. Her heart hammered. It wasn't a question of could.

She had to get out of there.

Now.

Liza gripped her knees. *Lord, let this work. Please!*

She swallowed the fear that threatened to overwhelm her. If they caught her, what would happen?

She'd probably die.

She almost laughed. At least then, she'd be with Jesus.

One last, deep breath shored up her waning courage. Liza opened her door and crawled onto the landing. She carefully tested each step. Even if they discovered her, she could at least tell them she'd wanted a bit more fresh air than what was in her room.

Liza listened.

Muted sounds reached her. Pale light flickering from the television into the foyer made ghostly shadows dance on the plain white walls.

She switched her gaze to the door.

Three locks. She mentally rehearsed her escape. Deadbolt first. Then the chain lock. Knob lock last. That order. Do it fast. Get the door open. And run.

Her fists clenched. Her heart raced.

Clutching the railing for stability, she rose. A deep breath calmed her.

Three...two...one...

Liza tiptoed the rest of the way down. She inched the deadbolt back. It didn't make a sound. She moved the chain lock, causing it to scrape.

Someone called something.

Adrenaline electrified her, focusing her.

She yanked the lock all the way off.

Someone shouted.

Her eyes widened as much as those of the guard who stood there. He pointed at her. "Stop!"

Liza bolted through the door and into the foggy night air.

More shouts reached her. The guard must have alerted his pals.

She ran as fast as she could toward where she thought the entrance to the complex was.

A light switched on in one of the townhouses.

Did she dare beg for safety?

No.

Too close.

Too dangerous.

She ran on.

Her bare big toe caught on the curb. Pain shot through her foot.

Liza stumbled. She moaned and collapsed onto the sidewalk, scraping her knees.

An SUV's engine roared. They were coming after her.

Panic threatened to destroy any semblance of hope.

Heart hammering in her ears, Liza pushed herself to her feet. She dashed toward the sign at the entrance and dove behind it as headlights swept toward her.

Liza curled into a tight ball. Whimpers tried to rise, but she locked them away in her chest. Her fingers clawed at her legs.

More voices called out. She clearly recognized the one of Jibril.

A door opened.

A flashlight's beam arced toward her.

Stay silent.

Nothing.

No noise.

She huddled there, scarcely breathing.

Jibril said something. Doors slammed. The sound of the engine faded.

All too aware of how she'd fallen for that before, Liza forced herself to stay still and listen. She peeked around the sign.

Nothing.

She ran down the street to the main road. To her right was a shopping center. To her left, a gas station. Maybe a bank.

All were closed for the night.

Her blood ran cold when she noticed a large, black SUV combing the shopping center. A bright beam of light shot from it and panned the storefronts.

Her captors.

Liza sprinted in the other direction. Pain seared her foot. Nausea assailed her and threatened to overwhelm her.

She had to get out of there, had to reach safety.

An engine raced.

"No!" The cry escaped her lips. They'd seen her.

Liza increased her speed.

Ahead, light spilled from a building onto a road. She gasped at her good fortune.

A fire station, meaning occupied twenty-four/seven.

Liza ran to the door. She banged on it. "Someone! Please! Help me! Help!"

The SUV neared.

A window whirred down. Jibril shouted at her.

Her heart hammered as fast as her fists.

"Please! They're chasing me!"

It flew open, and she gazed at the concerned face of a fireman. "Ma'am?"

The SUV sped down the street. Tires chirped, and the engine faded.

Liza fainted.

23

"Where are you?"

"What do you mean?"

"I'm not in the mood to play games." Gary's gaze swung around the mall's atrium. "Where are you so that we can get this over with?"

"I'm close enough that I can see you and how, if you're not careful, you're the one who will be arrested, not me."

Gary turned in a full circle. That late Tuesday afternoon, several people crowded one of Raleigh's largest malls. More began filling the massive hall as people got off from work. He picked out a gaggle of college girls strolling with shopping bags on their arms, then some businessmen in their suits and ties as well as other men wearing more casual clothing.

All of them seemed to have cell phones to their ears.

Gary swore under his breath. "Okay. What do you want me to do?"

"Go to Macy's. Buy four rugby shirts there. One red and white. One navy and gold. One navy and white. One dark green and gold. All in a large."

"I'm not your personal shopper."

"I'm not saying you are. Request a paper bag and put the package all the way at the bottom. Then go to the food court and buy a meal. I'll find you."

"How long should I wait?"

Silence.

Gary shoved the phone deep into the inner pocket of his leather jacket. For a moment, he stood there as if in total shock at the mess he'd created. He once more peered around the mall.

No one cared about him.

Whatever.

Before he lost his courage, he began implementing Makmoud's plan by heading to Macy's. He found the rugby shirts easily enough, even in the colors and size his handler had requested.

When he presented his purchase to the clerk, she smiled. "Will plastic be okay?"

"Um, do you have paper? I like to be green, you know." He offered a sick one of his own.

"Of course. I understand." She finished his purchase and handed him the large paper shopping bag.

Gary took it. He forced himself to maintain a purposeful walk rather than the run he wanted. A ride up the escalator took him toward the food court.

People milled around him, oblivious to the turncoat in their midst. He could stop this now, could use his work phone to call his buddies in DC and tell them he had a pretty high-ranking *Quds* agent in the mall and to bring all of the firepower they had to bear upon him.

He couldn't.

Not when Makmoud's operative stalked his family. He had no doubt as to what would happen if he disobeyed.

As if to scold him for even having such a thought, the buzzing in his head returned.

Gary swallowed hard and slipped into one of the bathrooms off the atrium. Inside, he closeted himself in the handicapped stall and slid the manila envelope containing the files he'd surreptitiously printed the day before from his leather jacket. His hands shook as he pulled out the stack.

Victor stared sightlessly at him from the government ID photo.

I'm sorry, bro. Really, I am. But Mary and the kids are depending on me to deliver this.

Gary braced his hands against the tile and hung his head. His chest heaved. He forced himself to take deep, even breaths. Before he lost his courage, he re-secured the sheets and shoved the package into the bottom of the bag.

Gary returned to the throng, which seemed to have grown in the five or so minutes he'd been gone. After buying a meal and finding a seat, he set the bag by his chair and sampled a taco. His stomach almost rebelled at the greasy meat hitting it. *Not tonight. Please, not tonight.*

Where was Makmoud?

Of course, he wouldn't see him in the chaos of mothers with children, teenagers together for a night of hanging out, and families meeting up after a long day. The man had been clever to use this crowd as cover.

Someone sat down beside him, a college kid from what he could tell, all the way from the baggy plaid flannel shirt to mess of long blond hair. He too had a couple of tacos and some of those cinnamon thingies. He crunched loudly on the sweet treats, and even over that noise and the hum of the mall, Gary heard the heavy metal through the earbuds he wore.

The buzzing increased. Gary shoved his tray aside and gripped his head in his hands. He stared at the phone in the vain hope that people would think he focused on something on the Internet. A byproduct of the buzzing, the headache pulsed in time with his heart. Already, it gathered in intensity.

I want this to end. That's all. To end.

Finally, after close to half an hour of sitting there, the nausea increased to the point where he needed to leave. Gary dialed Makmoud's number.

Nothing. Not even voicemail.

He rose, snatching up the shopping bag. To heck with this. He was done with Makmoud and his shenanigans. All he wanted to do was to get back to the hotel so he could throw up in private.

When he got to his room, he tossed the bag onto the bed, then popped some pain meds for the headache. After a few minutes of lying curled up in a ball with his eyes tightly shut, the nausea receded enough that he could sit up and check his phone. He didn't have any messages from Makmoud threatening him with harm to his family.

Gary tugged the shopping bag to himself. At least he'd gained some decent shirts, ones he knew he'd wear when the weather turned cool again. He dumped them out, fully prepared to remove the price tags.

An envelope fell out, this one smaller than the one he'd prepared.

His fingers shook as he undid the clasp.

He pulled a note from the package.

You did well, my friend. One last assignment until further notice. Tomorrow when you arrive in Nashville, you are to call the Low Country CrimeStoppers in the Charleston metro area and tell them that you know about a safe house in North Charleston at the information below. Do so anonymously, of course. If you refuse? Remember that you have a very lovely wife. And your children? Iman will have no problem taking care of them.

Gary's eyes widened. Makmoud had even been generous enough to include more pictures, this time of Mary dining out with her parents, of the kids as they greeted his folks at the door.

The man had been within feet of him and made the switch without his realizing it.

Some agent he'd been.

At least his call tomorrow would be the last of it.

The buzzing receded to silence as if to praise him for a job well done. Like some satisfied mythical dragon, the headache began returning to its lair.

Gary swallowed hard. He'd succeeded, but it would cost Vic and his team their lives.

He found his cell phone on the bed and punched in a number.

When the woman answered, relief made him sag to the mattress. "Mary, hey. It's me. The case wrapped sooner than I expected. I'm headed your way and will be in Nashville by four or so tomorrow."

24

"Red alert! We've been blown!" Victor's shout rang out across the backyard of Last Chance Ranch. From his place next to the back door, he slammed his hand on the red button Shelly had installed in all of the buildings.

The klaxon blared overhead.

He clicked his stopwatch.

Butch and DJ bolted from the Tool Barn.

Victor darted inside. "Breaking glass!"

He hesitated the approximate time it would take to break the glass of the gun cabinet and grab the MP-5s.

Footsteps thundered on the pine stairs. Deborah and Anna raced downward. All three of them burst into the bright, chilly morning. Marie reached her arms toward Victor, and he snatched her up. Deborah did the same with Gracie. Everyone ran as hard as they could toward the barn and the back of the box canyon.

The other Shadow Box members whipped around as if covering their retreat.

The grate Butch had placed over the massive hole they'd dug months ago shook with the pounding of their feet. They hit solid ground. At the base of the canyon wall, Sana and Suleiman heaved open the lid to the chest they'd hidden the autumn before.

Butch mimicked pressing the button on a detonator. "Grate blown! Smoke grenades and covering fire."

Victor set Marie down. "Go! Go! Go!"

Sana scrambled to the top.

The Fields family began their ascent, then the remainder of the team.

Victor clicked onto the line. He pulled himself up by using the hand-holds Sana and Suleiman had dug. The ascender attached to his harness helped.

He rolled onto the ground. With shaking fingers, he detached himself. He climbed to his knees as Butch hauled himself over the edge.

Together, they dashed the quarter mile to the outbuilding where they'd stashed the getaway SUV. He checked the stopwatch. "Ten minutes."

Deborah leaned against the wall. She braced her hands on her knees. Chest heaving, she undid her ponytail. Her hair fanned out along the side of her face. "Is…that…better?"

"Better. I'd like to get it to five."

"I don't know if that's possible." Sana squinted in the bright sunlight. "Maybe if we were all professional rock climbers, it might be."

"It's a goal to shoot for. That's why we blow the grate. Butch, let's make sure the detonators remain in place and are still functioning. Also, let's get that camouflage on it a little better."

"Roger, boss."

"The important thing is that this becomes second nature." Victor focused on Anna.

Though the drill had flushed her cheeks, her eyes remained bright as she gazed at him.

DJ, standing next to her, looked ready for the next round.

Victor wiped the sweat from his brow. "If you hear 'red alert' or the klaxon, you get to the back of the canyon. Good work, gang."

They wandered toward the lip of the box canyon. As Marie descended, her giggles brought a smile to his face. At least they thought it was a game.

His mirth faded. He hoped they'd never have to implement it for real.

"Can we have ice cream now, Mr. Victor?" Marie asked once everyone had reached the bottom.

He grinned and ruffled her hair. "Maybe. Or maybe we'll have lunch and then ice cream."

His phone began chiming. He checked the Caller ID.

Gary.

"Go ahead, Marie. I'll be there in a moment," he added when she tugged at his hand. "Gary, hey. What's up?"

"Good news, finally." His best friend's voice blared into his ear over what sounded like road noise. "Liza escaped."

"What?"

"She escaped."

"When?"

"Sometime very early Tuesday morning. She managed to make it to a fire station somewhere in North Charleston. They took her to the hospital, so it took some time to get things sorted out. My man from Miami's already up there. A Special Agent Karl Becker. That's Karl with a 'K.' He hopped a plane as soon as he got the call." Gary cleared his throat.

"Is there something else?" Victor cast a glance toward the Big House.

Deborah had already headed inside with the children and the other Shadow Box members.

He stopped, turned his back, and leaned against the post of the Laundry Building.

"She's beat up pretty good."

Victor closed his eyes. "She's okay, though. Right?"

"As okay as she can be. Listen." Gary muttered something about bad drivers. "I need you to fly there, get her, and take her to wherever you're keeping Deborah."

"Will do. Thanks, man."

"You're welcome. By the way, if you need me, I'm headed to Nashville to see the folks and Mary's folks, but I'm available if needed."

"Will do. Give everyone my love." Victor remained where he was and surveyed the back of the house.

Fiona, Butch, and Suleiman smoked on the patio. Diana and Skylar brought out sandwiches and settled at the wrought iron table.

He swallowed hard at the news Gary had delivered. Should he tell Deborah? Or wait until they returned? He approached the group. "Hey, Fi, Skylar, Diana, I need you three."

Skylar cocked an eyebrow in wordless question.

"I got a call from Gary. Liza escaped, so get your lunch to go."

Fiona's sherry eyes widened. "When?"

"Sometime yesterday morning early. Fi, Skylar, and Diana, I want you guys to go with me to Charleston. Butch, you'll be in charge until I get back."

"Wilco, boss." Butch saluted him with his cigarette.

"Fi, get the plane ready and a flight plan filed."

Fiona stubbed hers out. "You know they're calling for snow later tonight."

"I do. We should be back well before it starts. Diana, I want you to take any medications you deem necessary. The hospital's got her, but she may need some sedatives. I'll need you to liaise with the doc there to sort things out. Skylar, you and I will run interference."

Skylar wrapped his sandwich in his napkin. "Will do."

"Let's meet in ten and head out." Victor and Butch stepped into the Big House.

Gracie and Marie now colored at the big pine table in the kitchen. Anna read a book in the great room, and blips and bloops from the den told him DJ played a video game. Shelly and Sana had already slipped away.

"Deb?" he softly called to where she spread peanut butter on slices of bread. "I need to talk with you."

She followed him onto the terrace where only Butch remained. "What's going on?"

"Liza escaped."

Her eyes widened, and her hands shot to her mouth.

"She's banged up, but she's alive. They have her at the hospital in Charleston."

"Charleston? I—I don't understand."

"I don't have any details. Fi, Skylar, Diana, and I are headed there to get her. We're going to bring her back here."

"Let me go with you."

Victor shook his head. "I'm sorry, but you need to stay concealed. I'm leaving Butch in charge here."

"We've got you covered, Deb." Butch smiled at her.

She nodded, and a tear seeped from the corner of her left eye.

Instinctively, Victor reached up and wiped it away. "I promise this is good news."

"I—I know." A trembling smile of her own crossed her lips. "Go and get her. I'll wait here."

$$\star \quad \star \quad \star$$

Gary turned off the engine to the Cherokee. For a moment, he leaned his head against the seat and rubbed his temples. He yawned and massaged the back of his neck.

Finally, he sat feet away from his family and his parents.

His light mood dampened. The call he'd made to Vic as he'd passed through Knoxville had set something into motion. What was it? Of course, Makmoud hadn't shared that tidbit with him. All he knew was that it would spell the end of Vic and his crew.

He shut and locked the door as a blonde woman stepped onto the Outback Steakhouse's porch. A grin spread across her face. "Gary!"

He rushed into her arms and held her so tightly that she gasped. Gary inhaled that lavender perfume he'd always associated with Mary. The tears stinging his eyes surprised him.

"Long trip?" She pulled back with laughter dancing in her eyes.

"Something like that. Thanks for meeting me here."

"We were all famished. Maybe we can grab the early bird special."

That garnered a laugh from him. "Or happy hour."

"And possibly a nightcap later," she murmured. Her lips tipped upward in a beguiling smile. She stood on tiptoes and kissed him.

How had he been so blessed with her? He slipped his hand into hers. "We'll eat first. Then maybe we can look into escaping for a night by ourselves."

"Deal."

Once seated, Gary found himself lost in conversation with his family. At least until the phone clipped in his pocket vibrated. His secret phone. He jumped.

"Excuse me for a few," he murmured as he rose.

"Is everything okay, son?" Dad asked.

"Fine," Gary lied. He tried to give a sick smile. "A message from work just came in. I've got an active case going, and something popped up."

He weaved his way among the tables until he arrived in the lobby. With a flick of the fingers, he checked the message.

Makmoud might as well have screamed it. *Why haven't you done as I asked?*

The phone vibrated again.

Iman noted your arrival. I suggest you do as I say. I would hate to see your family and parents have an accident on the way home. This time, his handler had attached a picture, one showing his kiss with Mary.

Gary swore under his breath.

He burst outside, his eyes roving the parking lot and side streets for signs of the female *Quds* agent.

Nothing. At least nothing he could see.

Gary ran a hand through his hair. His hands trembled slightly. He swallowed hard and closed his eyes. After a deep breath, he located the number for the Low Country CrimeStoppers. He needed a pay phone. Now.

His gaze darted around the parking lot. Nothing. He had no choice but to call from his personal cell phone.

"Low Country CrimeStoppers. May I help you?"

Gary's eyes shifted from the glass double doors at the entrance to the parking lot before returning to the street.

"May I help you?"

"Uh, yes," he intoned, making his voice nasally with a Yankee accent tossed in for good measure. "I'd like to report suspicious activity. North Charleston, at this townhouse complex."

He added the details Makmoud had included in his letter before hastily ending the call. He refused to divulge his name.

Gary turned.

Mary stared at him through the doors.

Oh, no. Had she heard him?

She couldn't have.

He lowered the phone.

Once he stepped inside, she asked, "Honey, what's wrong?"

"Nothing." Gary took her hand and kissed it. He tightened his grip and added, "Nothing at all."

"I'm Victor Chavez, here to pick up Ms. Liza Murphy and take her into protective custody." Victor leaned against the receptionist's desk at the Emergency Department in Charleston.

The woman stared at him, her long red nails tapping on her desk. "I don't have a Liza Murphy in my system."

His eyes narrowed. "According to the FBI, she's here."

"Really? And who told you that, Mr..."

"Agent Victor Chavez." He pulled out his cred pack, as did Diana and Skylar. "With the FBI. These are my cohorts, Agent Kasem and Agent James."

"How do I know those are real?"

He rolled his eyes and opened his mouth to retort.

The doors leading to the hallway swished open.

"Victor Chavez?" A man in a tan overcoat stood there.

"That's me."

"Special Agent Karl Becker from Miami." The man flashed his badge. "Ms. Workman, I've got him. Thanks for letting him in."

The woman's face lit up with a smile, and she waggled her fingers at him.

"She's a piece of work," Victor muttered as the Shadow Box crew followed Karl down the hall.

"Nah. You just have to know what makes her tick."

"Flirting?"

"What can I say? She likes hot, single, Jewish guys from Miami."

Not sure how to respond, Victor made introductions, then added, "We got here as fast as we could."

"That's what Gary said. This is what we have. Ms. Murphy escaped sometime in the wee hours yesterday morning. She reported a black SUV chasing her, most likely a Tahoe or Suburban. Something large. She didn't get a plate number. She made it to a fire station where they took her in. They brought her here early yesterday. The docs noticed how beat up she was and called the cops. When they realized her description matched the APB we put out, they gave our office here a call. They called me. I got up here as quickly as I could. Anyway, they insisted on keeping her for observation and until a family member showed up."

"Diana, please talk to the docs for us." Victor nodded at Shadow Box's doctor.

Diana strode down the hall as if she'd worked there for years. She tapped a nurse on the shoulder, who nodded and led her away.

Victor returned his attention to Karl. "Anything else?"

"Her captivity seems almost bizarre. She remembered waking up here after being drugged at her house in Key Largo. Some guy named Daoud sexually assaulted her. Then the next day, some other guy showed up and acted almost like her protector."

"Did the guy have a name?"

"No. But she said his voice was deep and lightly accented. His brother is apparently someone named Jibril Kidari." Karl broke off and ran his finger down a small notepad. "Yeah, Jibril Kidari. His brother apparently got angry about the assault. He told her to clean up and fed her. She must have felt really comfortable because she finally managed to get some sleep. He also gave her some of his clothing to wear."

Victor's breath caught in his throat. Kidari? Maybe rhymed with Hidari? Somehow, he managed to say, "That's bizarre."

"The docs reported she was raped. She said three times. Maybe that's why this dude playing rescuer allowed her to get some sleep." His shoulders rose and fell in a shrug. "Forensics is also going over the clothing she was wearing. So far, they've found a couple of black hairs they've sent off for analysis. Maybe we'll get a match with some other evidence we pulled off her. If we find anything, I'll let Gary know."

His phone buzzed. "Hold on."

Victor joined Skylar, who waited in the hallway near the cubicle Diana had just entered. If Jibril Hidari had been present, then most likely Makmoud was the mysterious brother. How? Why?

He'd have to think about it later.

"Sorry about that." Karl joined them. "That was our field office here. North Charleston PD got a tip from the Low Country CrimeStoppers about a townhouse where some suspicious characters were holed up. It's near the fire station Ms. Murphy wound up at. Their SWAT just raided it. My thoughts are it's related to this case, so I'm headed that way."

He pawed his coat. "Sorry. I need a smoke. Anyway, let me go and clear things up with Ms. Workman so Dr. Kasem can get her discharged. Then I'm gone. Details are in here."

Victor took the offered folder and stuck out his hand. "Karl, thanks."

"Take good care of her."

"We will." Victor's eyes narrowed as Karl wandered to the two agents keeping watch.

Their brief discussion had told him all he needed to know. Makmoud Hidari, the man who'd killed Rachel and had nearly killed him, had a large hand in taking down an FBI agent and nearly killing Deborah. Could he be Murdock's handler?

Maybe Gary would have some answers.

Within two hours, Victor slouched in a chair against the bulkhead of the jet. A mug of coffee steamed on the worktable in front of him, and he clamped the plane's sat phone between his shoulder and cheek.

Gary's voice rose and fell as if riding on the same air currents as the plane. "You think Makmoud might be behind this?"

"I'm pretty sure the name Jibril Kidari is a fake. Kidari rhymes with Hidari. And a deep voice with lightly accented English brings back too many memories." Victor closed his eyes.

Once more, Makmoud taunted him as he lay bleeding on the pavement with Rachel's form already still beside him. He winced.

"So what you're saying is…" Gary's drawl faded. "Makmoud might be behind flushing Deborah out."

"Which means he might be behind killing your guy."

"It's worth checking out."

"Will you keep me posted?"

"It's not your job to worry about that." Gary's voice sharpened. "Your job is to keep Deborah safe until I give the all-clear signal. Got that?"

Victor bit back his sigh. "Roger that. Thanks, man."

Gary hung up without replying.

Victor leaned his head against the wall. The hum of the aircraft penetrated his skull, and he thought about what he'd learned from TL's file and recent events. Deborah had worked to lure out a mole code named Murdock. Nasser went in to do the takedown. Someone, most likely Murdock, murdered Nasser. The dead agent knew his attacker. Three months later, after Deborah rattled cages, she got flushed into the open. Then Makmoud entered the picture.

Why?

He couldn't figure it out. Exhaustion tugged him toward sleep, and his eyes drooped closed.

He found himself running. Deborah's hand gripped his so tightly that it hurt. He didn't dare let go as they dashed through the ponderosa pine forest near Last Chance Ranch. Dusk fell, and fog pressed around them. Footsteps whispered along the pine needles coating the forest floor. His pulse hammered in his ears as he realized their pursuers were of the canine variety. Wolves.

Deborah's foot caught on a root. She tumbled to her knees and cried out.

"Deb!" Victor tugged her to her feet.

"I—I'm hurt." She limped.

Howls broke out. The wolves gained, loping with ease around trees and leaping over downed trunks. Six pairs of red eyes glowed like drops of blood in the deepening darkness.

"C'mon. I've got you." Victor grabbed her hand, urging her along farther.

"Vic!" Rachel's voice made him slow. His fiancée joined them.

"Rach?" Stunned, Victor stared. "Where…"

"We've got to move." Rachel touched him on the small of the back before taking Deborah's other arm. A yank severed his hold on Deborah. Rachel drew her service weapon. "You're too late."

Growling, the wolves encircled them.

He reached toward Deborah.

Rachel jabbed the muzzle of the Sig Sauer against Deborah's skull. "Stay right where you are."

The wolves chasing them stood on their hind legs. Like some sort of weird werewolf movie, they morphed into human forms. Makmoud and his men.

"You shouldn't have been so trusting." With that, Rachel smiled as her finger tightened on the trigger.

"No!" Victor jolted awake. His chest heaved. He trembled.

"Vic?" Diana now sat across from him, concern etched on her face. "You were having a bad dream."

He swallowed hard. "Something like that."

He cast a glance backward. The door to the bedroom was shut, as was the door to the cockpit, where Skylar kept Fiona company.

"Are you okay?" he asked when he noticed how she scrubbed a hand across her face.

"I don't know." Diana bit her lip. "He raped her."

Victor swallowed hard. "I know."

"She fought, but she didn't stand a chance." Diana leaned forward and put her head in her hands. Her shoulders trembled. Finally, she lowered her hands to reveal eyes red from emotion. "She's distraught."

"I can imagine."

Anger flared in those gray-green eyes. "Can you?"

Taken aback by her cutting tone, Victor blinked. "Uh…"

"I'm sorry." Diana twisted a cocktail napkin until it wound into a tight, paper rope. "I know what she's going through."

"I know."

"How can—"

"I read your file, remember? I know what happened in Afghanistan, how your reward for trying to save a boy's life was rape." Victor paused, desperately searching for words that wouldn't hurt or insult. As he chose them with care, he reached out and took her hands. "Deborah's resilient, able to overcome. Liza's cut from the same tough cloth. You are too. Otherwise, you wouldn't have withstood the war or accepted this assignment."

A brief, watery smile appeared. "Sometimes I wonder."

"I've seen your strength. You and Butch were the glue that held us together those first few weeks. You've got compassion in spades where the rest of us have struggled, especially when it comes to Deborah and her family. You've got a lot to offer. Remember that, okay?"

Diana shrugged. Without another word, she rose and retreated toward the couch, where she curled up with a book in her hands.

Victor stared after her for a moment. He meant every word he'd said about Diana. He only wished she could see that in herself. As he rose to reheat his coffee in the galley's small microwave, his mood swung downward. If Diana struggled with something that had happened years before, who was he to say Liza wouldn't either?

Time would tell on that.

25

Exhaustion and hunger nipped at Makmoud Wednesday evening as he strolled along the crowded sidewalks of King Street. The warm evening air tickled his skin. Music assaulted his ears, that of an electric guitar and a man attempting to sing an Eagles's tune he remembered from his time in the States during graduate school. He winced. A glass broke, and a woman giggled, then shrieked. The stale smell of beer turned his already empty stomach.

Makmoud adjusted the straps of his backpack and shambled down the sidewalk like a college student out for a stroll. What with the disguise of messy blond hair, blue contacts, and a fake nose, the same costume he'd used to meet Gary, he knew no one would recognize him.

He crossed Market Street. The noises of the nightclubs faded as he arrived in the more residential part of Charleston. Now, scents of jasmine, magnolia, and gardenia teased his nose. The bark of a small dog penetrated the faint hum of insects singing in the bushes and trees.

The frontage of the houses had narrowed. He found the one he wanted and palmed the key Jibril had given him before he'd headed to Raleigh. After one last look around, he slid it into the lock. With a click, the bolt turned back and admitted him onto the wide veranda.

"Welcome, brother." Jibril's voice reached him. His shadowy form stood in the rectangle of light spilling across the wood.

"So sorry I'm late. I wanted to survey the area for a bit." Makmoud stepped past him and pulled the wig from his head one last time as he entered the kitchen. He tossed it into the garbage bag hanging from one of the drawer knobs and removed the fake nose. "We are hidden?"

"Very. No visibility from the street. And none from any of the other houses if you're on the veranda."

"Good. I heard from an asset who works at the hospital here. A woman matching Liza's description was admitted very early yesterday morning. Not three hours ago, someone checked her out."

"Oh?" From where he leaned against the kitchen counter, Jibril raised an eyebrow.

"Someone who matches the description of Rachel's former lover."

His brother straightened. "Victor Chavez?"

"Exactly." Makmoud hefted the backpack that held a change of clothing as well as his computer. "We give it some time. I'll clean up, and then we can check to see if our device worked."

He tossed his keys to his brother. "Meanwhile, have someone go and pick up my car. I left it at the parking garage on Market Street."

Makmoud took his time after that. The hot shower relaxed him. The supper of lamb, couscous, and grilled vegetables satisfied his hunger. Hot tea would slake his thirst. With his mug and the envelope he'd received from Gary in his hands, he drifted onto the veranda. The warm night completely chased away any remaining tension. He inhaled deeply, smiled, and closed his eyes.

With no sight, his other senses sharpened. The magnolia smell he'd noticed earlier hit him full force now. The warm, humid breeze teased the hairs on on his arms. A cat yowled, most likely the one he'd noticed sitting on the wall that separated the yard from the house next door. More growling followed, as did the cacophony as the cat fought to defend its territory.

The noise brought back a memory. He was six and huddled in the back corner of the courtyard of his childhood home in Tehran. Above him, two cats yowled and screeched as they settled a dispute. At the house, a light glowed behind filmy curtains in an upstairs window. Two adult forms, one the feminine outline of his mother and the other a masculine outline of his father, gestured as if in the throes of an argument. Angry voices filtered through the open window and rose and fell on the breeze as much as the heady scent of the nearby pomegranate tree. The man pushed the woman. Then he raised his hand and slapped her. Its sound echoed across the courtyard. Young Makmoud cringed.

"Makmoud." Jibril's bass voice reached him. "Brother, wake up."

"Huh?" Makmoud blinked as he slowly returned to present-day reality.

His brother stood across the table from him, a laptop tucked under his arm.

Makmoud shifted and picked up his tea mug. It was still warm, indicating he'd not been asleep for too long. He tried not to notice the way his hand shook slightly. "What do you have?"

"Access to a router." Jibril pulled out his chair, turned it around, and straddled it. After opening the laptop, a few clicks of the mouse he'd attached yielded a satisfied grunt. "Your tracking program worked perfectly."

"Let me see it." Makmoud turned the computer so he could see the screen.

A map revealed a flashing icon in the Southwest.

"Arizona?" Jibril leaned in closer.

"It certainly seems to be so." Makmoud zoomed in. "Northern Arizona. Perhaps Flagstaff."

"Go farther." Jibril leaned forward. "As far as you can."

"A ranch." Makmoud rubbed his clean-shaven chin as he stared at the aerial photo.

"This is too easy." Jibril's brow furrowed as he crossed his arms and rested them on the back of the chair.

"Too good to be true, eh? You're right. We may know their location, but we have much to consider before we strike."

"Agreed."

"Victor Chavez leads them. I had Gary print all of the profiles of this Shadow Box team he put together since they're the ones guarding Deborah and her family." Makmoud slid the sheets of paper from the envelope. In the light emanating from inside, he studied them. He already knew about Victor, more than he ever dreamed, thanks to Rachel.

A hiss from Jibril reached him.

"What?"

"Look." Jibril tossed the sheet onto the table.

Makmoud's eyes widened as he stared at the picture of their half-brother. "So Ibrahim thought he could get away with it. Suleiman al-Ibrahim. The fool changed his name."

"And who is this?" Jibril's lips curled. "Sana Jain. Former cat burglar." He handed off the profile. "A pretty girl. And Fiona Mercedes. Former Army pilot. Can fly almost anything, according to her profile."

He drummed his fingers on the table and leaned his chair back on two legs. "And then there is this woman. Shelly Wise."

Makmoud chuckled as he scanned her information. A plan began forming. "The others?"

"Butch Addison, former US Army Special Forces. Interesting. Diana Qasem. An Afghan half-breed, it seems. Former Army as well. And Skylar James. Former CIA."

"Very interesting." Makmoud's eyes narrowed as he considered their options. If he could pull off his idea, Iran could benefit in many ways. "We take them."

"What?"

"We take them all and eliminate Deborah and her children. The team would go to South America with us. There, we would break them."

Jibril shook his head. "This isn't one man to break, like we did Gary. This is a well-trained team."

"And not all with the special kind of training Gary had. Oh, Victor and Butch have that kind of training and perhaps Skylar. But any man breaks. You know that. We eliminated Gary's team because we only needed one at the time."

"What are your thoughts?"

"We will plan well and take our time in doing so. Tomorrow morning, we leave for Phoenix. In the meantime, I'll send these names to my contacts. Perhaps they will have more information we can use to make our case for taking this team. Well, almost everyone on the team."

"And that is because?"

Makmoud's lips curled. "Ibrahim must die for his betrayal."

Deborah leaned against the doorframe on the other side of Liza's door. The house remained quiet save for the soft tears and sniffles of her sister that reached her through the wood of the door. Thanks to the nightmares that even Ambien couldn't diminish, Liza cried in her sleep.

Deborah leaned her head against the wood. What could she do?

Nothing.

Thoughts of sleep completely fled. After grabbing the book she'd been reading from her room, she crept down the steps and into the den. She curled up in the easy chair she'd come to love and turned on the reading light. Her mind focused on Liza instead of the plot.

Tears blurred her vision.

Deborah swiped at them.

She bit her lip.

Hard.

God...

Her plea remained locked in her mind.

Focus. You know how reading can make you sleepy.

Not this time.

A wet spot splashed onto the page.

"Deb?" Vic's voice made her jump.

"Vic, hey." She tried a casual, light tone. "I couldn't sleep, so I decided to read for a bit."

"Let's talk." He held up two steaming mugs. "I even brought hot chocolate for the occasion."

"About what?"

"I watched you for a few minutes, then made us some hot chocolate. I don't think you turned the page the entire time."

Deborah burst into tears.

Victor set the mugs down.

She sobbed so hard that she barely noticed how he closed the french doors to make their conversation private. He shut off the lamp. "Come here."

He tugged her out of her chair and seated her beside him on the couch. Something warm draped over her shoulders, that Navajo blanket she'd noticed and used a few times herself.

Never had she been so out of control.

Warm arms encircled her. She leaned into Victor's firm build and held on for dear life as the tears wracked her soul. Finally, she wound down as he shoved a handkerchief into her hands. She hunched forward, her shoulders still shaking. "I'm sorry."

"For what?"

"For bawling my eyes out. You must think all I do is cry."

He rubbed her back. "No, I don't think that at all. I've seen you laugh. Smile. You have a very pretty smile."

Normally, she would have chuckled at the compliment. Tonight? She couldn't. "What brought you here?"

"Probably the same as you. I couldn't sleep and figured I'd get some hot chocolate and read for a bit. It turned out someone had already grabbed the last packet in our building."

"That man brutalized Liza in the worst way possible." She threaded the handkerchief through her fingers as her thoughts remained in a tangle in her mind. "She's hurting in more than physical ways. I mean, her physical scars will heal. But the ones on her soul… I feel so powerless. And guilty."

"Because she got hurt?"

Deborah turned her head to gaze at him. "How could I not?"

Victor reached up. He took some of her hair between his fingers. Suddenly seeming to catch his gesture, he dropped his hand and took hers. "Look. I'm no psychologist or genius. I'm just a guy trying to process this from a guy's point of view, so don't get mad at me." He hesitated, then continued, "She knew about your job, right?"

"Yeah. We talked about it. Not much, but enough for her to understand what I was doing. I guess…I guess I never dreamed it would come to this."

"I told my handler about the discrepancy in the paperwork. He said he'd look into it." Victor leaned forward so their shoulders touched. "If it makes you feel any better, I'm angry too. But I want you to understand that this sort of thing could have happened anywhere, any time."

"But it happened because of what I did." Deborah threw the blanket to the floor. She jumped up and paced. "They obviously wanted to use her to get to me."

She stopped and stared out the window. Another round of tears forced its way upward. She raised her chin and pressed her lips together. Her shoulders shook once more.

"Come here." Victor drew her close.

Her fingers clenched the flannel of his shirt.

"I think you underestimate the strength of the human spirit," he said after a few minutes of her sniffles and quiet sobs. "I promise you she'll heal."

"But as her sister, I'm too close to her to give her emotional counseling."

"I know. That's why I suggested to Diana that she approach her."

"Why?"

"Let's just say Diana knows how it feels and leave it be."

Mystified, she pulled back and stared at him. Slowly, it dawned on her. Weariness overtook her, and she laid her head against his shoulder. "I'm sorry for burdening you with this."

"Don't be." Victor's arms tightened the slightest bit around her.

His build was so firm, his arms warm and comforting. Her pulse began settling toward normal. At last her nose cleared enough for her to inhale the faint scent of aftershave mixed in with soap. Suddenly, she didn't want him to let her go. "I...I guess we're going to be here for a while."

"You're right. At least until they find Murdock."

As if her emotions had overloaded and shut down to avoid a meltdown, her mind drifted toward other, safer topics. "I have a question."

"Which is?"

"I don't want the kids to fall behind in school. Is there any way I could get their assignments from their teachers? And, I don't have enough clothing for anyone." She shook her head at her lack of preparedness. "Fool me, for thinking five days of light clothing would be enough."

Victor finally released her. In the faint glow of the streetlight from outside, his smile flashed dimly. "Let's do this. Give Shelly the e-mail addresses of your kids' teachers if you have them. She'll see what we need to get and can help school the kids. And give your sizes to Diana. She's the fashion bug of the group and can get clothes for all of you."

"Thank you for taking good care of us."

"Just doing my job." Humor echoed in his voice.

That brought a wan smile to her face.

His own turned tender. "And it's an honor and pleasure to do so."

Suddenly, Deborah found she could barely keep her eyes open. She scrubbed her face with her hands. "I'm so tired."

"Let me walk you to your room." Victor brushed some hair out of her face.

His touch was gentle. Tender.

It set her nerves on fire.

Victor turned to pick up the now-cold mugs. He straightened. "Look!"

She faced the window.

Outside in the glow of the streetlight, snowflakes drifted downward as if delivered by angels. Before her eyes, the snowfall thickened.

As they climbed the stairs to the second floor, peace draped over her heart. It was almost as if God had sent the snow as a sign to her, a sign that He'd heard her pleas no matter how strangled they'd seemed to her own heart and soul. He had them in the palm of His hand, even those who claimed not to know Him.

Like Victor.

Sadness pinched her heart.

Until he briefly touched her cheek in farewell at the door to her room.

She watched him tiptoe down the stairs. As the alarm beeped the signal that he'd armed the system, she stayed there, her heart at once uplifted and burdened at the same time.

26

Two weeks later, anger simmered deep within Victor's heart as he pushed through the door leading to the ranch's workout facility. Except for Fiona, who manned the monitors, the rest of the team worked out. He wandered toward one of the benches where Butch's gym bag rested. As he did so, both Skylar and Shelly, who ran on the treadmills, panted out a greeting. He tossed his water bottle and towel onto the blond wood and noticed how Diana rose up out of the saddle of one of the spin bikes. Sweat poured down her face, which was red from the effort.

"Sana, you totally rock." Butch's voice made him turn. At the other end of the gym from the cardio area, Sana used a springboard to jump onto the uneven bars she'd insisted that Victor purchase. She spun in a series of graceful moves and releases, which reminded him that the former gymnast had once been part of Team USA.

Butch stepped in and spotted her on a particularly tricky release.

In the free weight area that separated the cardio machines from the mat and gymnastics equipment, Suleiman sat on a weight bench and pretended to work his biceps. In reality, his gaze focused on Sana.

That would have made Victor smile under normal circumstances.

Now?

He couldn't. Not with the knowledge he harbored in his brain.

Victor edged to the mirrored wall and threw his leg onto the barre to stretch. Maybe the gentle tug as his muscles lengthened would take his mind off of what he'd read.

It didn't work.

The words from Rachel's journal taunted him as they transformed into pictures in his mind.

On a blustery February morning in 2007, Rachel had her normal Saturday-morning coffee at the shop around the corner from her townhouse in the DC suburbs. A familiar voice distracted her, one she hadn't heard in over eight years. Makmoud. Shock rooted her to the spot. She tried to resist, but the questions burned in her mind. Why had he left her and broken their engagement? He told her he could answer only if she joined him in Miami for some badly needed R&R. At first, she resisted—until curiosity got the better of her.

Victor grabbed a jump rope and began warming up his cardiovascular system. The rope beat faster and faster on the shiny floor in front of the mirrors until his feet caught in it. He staggered and regained his balance. With a jerk of his wrist, he tossed it aside and stepped onto a treadmill. The heavy metal blaring in his ears did little to soothe him. The repetitive motion of running only heightened his angst as another scene came to him.

In Miami, Rachel did her best to resist Makmoud. Gradually, he wore down her defenses, especially when he took her hand. Her sensibilities fought with her emotions. She'd missed him and terribly so. Finally, she caved and headed to his room. They didn't leave it the next day. It was almost like the eight years they'd been apart had never happened. She wanted more and more of him. He gave it to her.

Victor jabbed his finger on one of the console buttons. The belt increased until he ran at a full-out sprint. His heart hammered at his ears. His vision began tunneling. The heart rate monitor on his wrist told him what he didn't want to acknowledge.

He was about to pass out. At least that would end his torment.

Victor slammed his hand on the Stop button. Mercifully, the treadmill slowed. Chest heaving, he hopped off and walked around as he struggled to regain his breath.

Laughter distracted him. Sana now stood on the balance beam. She hesitated, then did a series of back handsprings and a layout as she dismounted.

Butch whistled and applauded.

Victor stomped to the weights and snatched a set of dumbbells from the rack. He began pumping them in a shoulder press.

Rachel's words now taunted him.

She found herself wanting more and more of Makmoud. He promised her quarterly meetings. The first time? The North Carolina mountains. That winter? Costa Rica. Rachel yearned for those times with him, since he fulfilled her physical desires.

Victor returned the dumbbells to the rack with a loud clank. He yanked some weight plates off the stand and added them to a bar sitting on its rack on one of the benches. The music shifted to a country tune about betrayal in love. He began a series of bench presses. Though he meant to focus on the motion and his form, Rachel flashed before him.

In the glowing candlelight of their hotel room in Nairobi, Makmoud took Rachel in his arms. He kissed her before sliding the strap of her sundress off her shoulder. She held him close.

Pain brought Victor out of his private hell. His pecs began screaming in agony. In a brief, panic-filled moment, he realized he'd placed too much weight on the bar.

"Easy there, boss. I've got you." Pressure released as Butch took it from him and set it on the rack.

For a moment, Victor lay there to let his muscles recover. Finally he sat up. "Thanks."

"No problem. C'mon. Let's spar." Butch undid the laces of his gym shoes and pulled off his socks.

"Ewwww! Butch!" Sana giggled from where she stood by the beam. She put her hands on it and hopped up, her legs in a horizontal V before she pressed herself into a handstand.

Butch laughed. "I have to keep you guessing, Sana."

"Yes, you do." She did a back flip and landed off balance. At first, she flailed a little as she tried to stick her landing. Then her arms windmilled before she hopped from the beam. "Thanks Butch."

"I try." Butch nudged Victor again. "Let's do it."

Victor couldn't help but think how Sana had looked the way he felt. Out of control. Scrambling for some semblance of how he remembered Rachel. Finally, he kicked off his shoes and socks and stepped onto the mat. He began bouncing on his toes and circling with Butch, who sent a punch his way.

Victor blocked it.

If he could only do so with what he'd read. Rachel's journals had poisoned his mind.

Another scene popped into his head, this time where Rachel and Makmoud had a lover's quarrel. Rachel's hand flashed toward her lover. Makmoud pushed her onto the hotel's bed and held her wrists down as he explained himself. He kissed her. That ended the argument.

Hot anger crashed over Victor. He struck out in a roundhouse kick.

Butch ducked and tried to sweep Victor's feet from under him.

Victor leapt over his leg. He rolled, coming upright and aiming a side kick in Butch's direction.

The images now attacked him as surely as Butch did.

Makmoud holding her.

Kissing her.

Between the sheets with her.

Loving her.

In a hot rage, Victor punched at Butch, this time shifting his momentum with his hips for maximum effect. The sound of fist on face echoed loudly.

His heart caught. He'd hit with more force than intended.

Butch groaned. His hands shot to his face.

Someone gasped.

Victor whipped around.

Deborah stood at the entrance, one hand holding a cup, the other covering her mouth.

"Butch!" Victor turned to his friend.

"Oh, man, oh, man, oh, man, that hurt." Blood poured between his fingers.

Regret slammed into Victor with the intensity of the punch that had hit Butch. "I'm sorry. I didn't mean to hit that hard."

"Hey, it happens." Butch offered a smile through the scarlet running down his hands.

"Here." Victor grabbed his towel and pressed it over his deputy's nose.

Suddenly, he realized everyone had ceased their exercise. Diana leaned on the handlebars of the spin bike. Sana now stood with Suleiman and gawked. Skylar and Shelly had ceased their running on the treadmills. His cheeks heated. Shame followed closely on the heels of embarrassment when he added Deborah to the mix.

"What was that about?" Diana demanded. She led Butch to a bench and gently pulled the towel away. "Oh, boy. Vic!"

"It's okay." Butch remained cheerful. "Trust me, I've taken worse during sparring."

Indignation slithered through Victor. "I didn't mean it!"

"Whatever," she muttered. She gently replaced the towel. "C'mon, Butch. Let me look at that in my office."

With her hand on his back, Diana escorted him from the gym.

Everyone's gazes weighed on Victor. Embarrassment blossomed into irritation. "I didn't mean to do that, okay?"

He tried to ignore the way his voice had risen.

Without a word, the remaining four Shadow Box members filed from the gym and into the warm afternoon, leaving only Deborah behind.

More than ever, Victor wanted to slink away. He settled for collapsing onto the bench next to his water bottle. He took a pull, all the while avoiding her gaze.

"You want to talk about it?" she finally asked.

"We were sparring. It was an accident."

"I know that. You looked like you wanted to pulverize him."

"What?" Victor blinked.

"I saw your expression. Quite frankly, it worried me."

His hands clenched around the bottle.

"Talk to me. I won't bite. And I won't judge."

Victor closed his eyes as a burning began in them. "I read some more in Rach's journals."

"How far?"

"Up to the end of 2008." He swallowed hard. "I couldn't go any farther."

Deborah remained silent and sipped from the plastic cup she held.

"She reconnected with Makmoud."

There.

He'd said it.

Confessed the awful truth he'd learned.

"When?"

"The beginning of 2007. He approached her in a coffee shop one Saturday morning and asked her to meet him in Miami on vacation."

"She did?"

"Yeah. They wound up in bed together." He lowered his head and muttered under his breath as he rubbed the back of his neck. "Matter of fact, they starting having trysts every quarter. It's like…it's like she was hooked on him or something. Like she got this high from being with him."

"Did you know her then?"

"No." He drained the rest of his bottle. "She was with the Service but was investigating financial crimes. Didn't she know who he was?"

Deborah slid closer so their shoulders touched. "How much detail did she put in her journals?"

"Too much. But she never said who he worked for."

"Maybe she didn't ask."

"How could she not?"

"I can't answer that." Deborah rubbed his forearm.

"When I was with the Service, we figured he'd been working with the *Quds* Force for several years by 2007."

"*Quds?* As in Iran?"

"Yeah." Victor's fists tightened. "She was literally sleeping with the enemy." He muttered under his breath and jumped to his feet. "I don't understand. How could she have been so blind? Of course he was working for the enemy. Why else would he have avoided contact?"

Deborah gazed at him for a long moment. "Maybe her addiction blinded her."

"Addiction?" Victor ceased his pacing and stared.

Deborah remained seated, her face open, her slate-blue eyes focused on him. "There's all kinds of addictions out there. Alcohol. Drug. Porn. Sex. Video games. Facebook. Have you thought about that?"

He hated that she was right, hated it with a passion. A low burn began in his neck. "I thought I knew her. Honestly, I thought I did. Now...I don't feel like I knew her at all. It's almost like she lived two different lives."

Deborah remained silent. Outside, a horse whinnied from the corral in front of the barn.

Victor returned to sit beside her. A dull headache began in his temples.

Finally, she spoke. "I think sometimes, we can get blinded."

"I'm not sure where you're going with this."

"May I ask you a very personal question?"

He felt his guard going up. "Uh, sure."

"Were you two sleeping together?"

The flush exploded in his cheeks. He kept his gaze on the glossy wood at his feet. "I'm not sure what that has to do with anything."

"When two people start dating, what do they usually do? Or what did you and Rachel do?"

"She helped me look for a house in Raleigh. No kidding," he added when she chuckled.

"And you talked."

"Sure. We talked. Went out to dinner. Worked out together."

"When did you kiss?"

"What is this?" Angst sharpened his words as he turned his head to look at her. "Kiss and tell?"

"No." A smile quirked her lips upward.

"Okay. We kissed in December 2009. Her birthday if you want to know the truth. And I gave her a sweater."

"I'm impressed."

"What does that have to do with Makmoud?"

"Maybe nothing, but most likely, something. When did you start wanting to sleep with her?"

Victor rolled his eyes. "When does every guy want to sleep with a girl? When he first meets her."

"Vic."

"Okay. Okay. About six or so months after we started dating, I began sleeping with her. I let her set the pace since I knew about what had happened to her in college." The headache increased. "I still don't see what this has to do with anything."

"What I'm trying to say is that when we date, we're getting to know one another. Kissing is a natural progression. When it goes beyond that, to messing around, and especially to sleeping together, then suddenly, that becomes the main focus. That's how much power the sex drive has. It can blind people to other tics in a person's character that they might otherwise have seen."

He jumped up and spun around to face her. "Are you saying it was wrong to sleep with her?"

"I'm not passing judgment on anything." Deborah rose. She stepped toward him and stopped close enough for him to see the faint lines at the corners of her eyes. "I'm trying to give you a view of how I would see it if you walked into my office with this issue."

"I'm not a client of yours."

"Didn't you want some help? Correct me if I'm wrong, but less than a month ago, you wanted my assistance to help you process what you couldn't do on your own. Right or wrong is not mine to determine. What I'm trying to say is that maybe you got so wrapped up in the physical side of your relationship with her that you missed signs that she was being less than honest with you about her past. Or maybe that she was even continuing her relationship with Makmoud while you were dating her."

Pain shot through him at that notion.

Rachel wouldn't have done that.

Would she?

"Don't you *dare* besmirch her character! Rachel would have never betrayed me," he growled with such ferocity that she took a step back. "You don't know the first thing about me. About my relationship with Rachel. She *loved* me. So take your counseling ways to someone else."

"You asked for my help. I'm sorry, but sometimes, the truth hurts when we face it."

Anger made the heat rise. "I'm done with this conversation."

"You know something? I am too." Tears pooled in those eyes he was fast beginning to love. "I think it's best that we not talk until you've cooled down some. And done some soul-searching in the process."

With that, she turned and strode toward the door. He noted the way her hand shot to her face.

Victor eased onto the bench again and stared at the ground.

He was right.

Rachel would have never betrayed him by sleeping with Makmoud at the same time.

Never.

Doubt nibbled at his heart.

He knew of only one way to vindicate her. He had to finish the journals.

27

"How does it look?"

"Out of focus."

"Wait a moment."

The image in the camera jiggled before sharpening. A large house of stone and wood sitting on the crest of a hill at the end of a long driveway came into view. High canyon walls began rising on either side of the house and beyond it soared above its three-story height.

In the upstairs office at the warehouse in Phoenix, Makmoud opened a mapping program on the other monitor.

"How about now?" Jibril's voice rang clearly through the cell phone.

Makmoud nodded as he verified that what he saw on the street view of the mapping program matched the image from the camera. "Good. Perfect, if you would. I can focus closer?"

"Hit the Up Arrow key."

Makmoud zoomed in toward the yard behind the house. Once more, the technology had been worth the money.

"The good news is that the cameras will record constantly and upload to the Cloud every six hours, which will enable us to have continuous files. The images should be good enough to focus even after they're recorded."

"And the sound?" Makmoud turned up the speakers. It sounded as if an argument was happening somewhere.

"It captures both inside and outside." The wind battered Jibril's voice from his position at the top of the telephone pole. "I tested those when we installed them. The hardest part was finding angles we could use. Fortunately, the telephone poles were appropriately spaced. Now we can only hope they don't call out the real telephone company for any repairs."

"Excellent work." Makmoud lowered the sound. "Your task is finished, and it seems as if Victor Chavez and his team are none the more aware of us. I'll see you in a few hours."

He laid his phone on the table, leaned back in his chair, and laced his fingers behind his head. Voices murmured over the speakers as the conversation intensified. He cocked his head when he heard his name. Makmoud dialed up the volume.

A smile curled his lips when he overheard Victor talking with a woman about him. About his trysts with Rachel. Venom flowed through the man's words. Betrayal too. Makmoud shrugged. So what if Victor had played the fool?

He stared at the cameras. Both showed the house from angles to the right and left of it with good views to the backyard too. On the screen for the right-hand camera, he noticed a figure stepping into the doorway of a building.

Makmoud straightened and zoomed in.

A woman.

A blonde woman.

His gaze shot to the photos he'd pinned to the bulletin board next to the monitor.

Deborah Fields.

Their target.

Perfect.

His computer chimed. He had an e-mail, an encrypted one from the embassy in Caracas.

With growing excitement, he read the message. His contacts had come through. People knew of Skylar James. He'd handed over several of Makmoud's brothers-in-arms for interrogation and imprisonment—or death. And Butch Addison? The man had served with Gary and Victor and wreaked havoc wherever he went. His gaze devoured the information about Fiona Mercedes. She too had served. His comrades in Chad had almost gotten their hooks into her before Gary had sprung her from prison. She could be useful just like all of the others.

Makmoud rose and approached the worktable. Aerial mapping of the ranch lay scattered across the top. He shuffled through the pictures Jibril had taken during his tenure as a bogus telephone repairman. He selected one and also located a close-up aerial shot of the ranch. He ran his finger down it, tracing the outline of a canyon that boxed in the house and backyard. His brother had determined that the walls were too high to climb free form in an escape attempt.

An idea began gelling.

With renewed vigor at the potential payoff, Makmoud began drawing up a plan.

28

She couldn't do it.

Nerves made Deborah's feet stick to the ground as if she'd coated the bottoms of her cowboy boots with glue. She remained frozen steps away from the porch of the Men's Building.

"Deb?" Liza cast a glance at her.

"Mommy, I'm getting cold." Marie tugged at her arm. The Easter basket looped around her elbow bumped against Deborah's leg.

"And I want to go and play with Miss Sana's and Miss Shelly's cats," Gracie added from where she stood with her own basket swinging from her arms.

Deborah closed her eyes as Victor's angry words from earlier that day rang in her ears like out-of-control bells. "She *loved* me. So take your counseling ways to someone else."

"Mommy!" The plaintive tone in Marie's voice finally broke through her hesitation.

Deborah took a deep breath. "All right. Let's go. Gracie, knock on their door."

With her chin held high, Deborah stepped onto the wooden porch with her children.

Gracie tapped on the wooden frame of the screened door.

Butch, who slouched on the couch with Skylar and watched something on television, grinned. He rose. "Well, howdy. What brings you ladies out here tonight?"

"May we come in, Uncle Butch?" Gracie asked.

He opened the door for them. "Of course. Wow. What do you have for us?"

"An Easter basket," Marie told him. Then she thrust it out and piped at the top of her lungs, "He is risen!"

Butch laughed as he carried the basket to the table. "He is risen indeed. My, my, my, what's in here? Chocolate bunny. Hey, Suleiman! Get your rear in here."

Suleiman emerged from his bedroom. "What is it?"

"Here. Have your first chocolate Easter bunny." Butch tossed it to him.

Suleiman carefully began peeling away the foil as he drifted to the couch.

"I call the Peeps," Skylar announced. He grabbed the cellophane package and tore into it.

"You would. Hah. I'll make sure those eggs go into the fridge. They're mighty pretty." Butch set the basket on the table. "Who dyed them?"

"Mom, Aunt Liza, and Anna helped us this afternoon," Gracie told him. She clambered onto a chair to watch as he went through the rest of the basket.

"Chocolate eggs galore. Oh, wow. You guys are awesome." Butch grinned.

Deborah glanced toward Victor's room. He hadn't joined them like Suleiman had. Was he even at the ranch? "Um, is Vic around?"

"He said he was going to get some down time. I think he feels bad about what happened." Butch unwrapped a chocolate egg.

"You are okay, right?"

"No sweat. I promise I've been hit harder during sparring." Butch smiled, which made his swollen nose and cheek contort. He popped the egg into his mouth, chewed, and swallowed. "I remember when we were in SF together. Me, Vic, and Gary."

"Who's he?"

"Our handler. The guy who recruited all of us. Gary and I were sparring once, and he got me good. Broke my nose, to be honest. So this ain't nothing new. And if Vic apologizes one more time, I'm going to clock him."

He glanced at where Skylar now explained the rules of baseball to Suleiman. Liza perched on the arm of the couch. Gracie and Marie had wormed their way between the two men. In a low voice, Butch asked, "You doing okay?"

She shrugged. "I—we—had a disagreement after you left."

"He's probably in the studio." His smile turned tender. "I'll be in prayer for you both."

That garnered a weak smile from her.

"Girls, we need to get going." Liza pulled back. "The ladies still need their basket."

"Mommy, can we play with the cats too?" Marie scrambled from the couch and gazed at her with pleading hazel eyes.

"I'll hang out there for a bit." Liza took Marie's hand. "That way, Diana and I can talk before I tuck these munchkins into bed."

Deborah nodded, thankful that her sister had begun confiding in the team's doctor. "Of course."

"Y'all take care." Butch saw them to the door.

Deborah stepped into the chilly night. "All right, then. Let's go, you two."

It banged softly shut behind them.

"I'll be there in a little while to say good night," Deborah told them.

"C'mon, Marie." Gracie took her sister's hand, and they ran across the yard with the two women as well as Edgar and the Colonel trailing them.

"Say a prayer for me," Deborah murmured. "I'm going to talk to Vic."

Liza only hugged her in return before following her nieces.

Deborah took a deep, cleansing breath of air and made her way between the Laundry Building and the Men's Building. Sweat built on her palms as she thought about Victor. Her breath kicked up a couple of notches.

Would he turn her away?

The rapidly approaching night swallowed her.

She stopped when she noticed him slumped on the couch, unmoving as he stared at the coffee table. Even from that distance, she noticed the lines creasing his forehead.

Oh, Vic, did you read farther?

The Colonel nudged her.

"No dogs allowed, huh?" She tousled his ears. "C'mon. Maybe Mr. Vic will let you inside."

She lightly tapped on the frame of the screened door.

Victor rose and opened it. "Hey."

He didn't smile.

Deborah swallowed hard. "Um, may I come in?"

Without another word, he returned to the conversation area.

Nothing sat on the coffee table in front of the couch except for two lit candles. No journals anywhere in sight, for that matter.

"Sorry I missed supper tonight." Victor faced the fire he must have lit earlier that evening.

"No harm, no foul. You didn't miss much, since Skylar's not the best cook."

"Even Butch cooks better than he does, and that's not saying much."

"Hot dogs all the way." Deborah forced a smile. It faded as she struggled for something to say.

"You look nice." That went toward the flames.

Deborah wanted to laugh, since jeans, cowboy boots, a fleece over her T-shirt, and no makeup didn't constitute "nice" in her book. His solemnity told her not to make light of his remark. "Thanks. You do too."

He did.

Deborah's cheeks warmed a little as she noticed the way he'd pulled on a pair of black jeans and a white shirt with the sleeves rolled up to just below his elbows. Firelight glimmered off the silver trim of his belt.

Victor faced her. "I was going to apologize to you for acting like a jerk today. I figured I might as well dress up to do it, since I have no pride left. You beat me to it."

Deborah turned her gaze to the area near the worktable. Photos of Rachel graced the window sills. Something squeezed her heart. Jealousy? "No apology needed. I know it's—"

"You were right."

Her head jerked around. "What?"

"After I cleaned up, I grabbed a bowl of cereal and came out here to read. All of 2009, 2010, and the first part of 2011."

A chill settled over Deborah as it dawned on her. She joined him and settled onto the couch.

Victor eased down beside her. His focus remained on the candles. "She kept seeing him, like clockwork, once a quarter. Even when we started dating."

"Oh, wow."

He stared at the floor near the hearth where the Colonel now lay and gazed at them with soulful eyes. "Even when we started sleeping together."

"Oh, Vic."

He put his head in his hands. "I thought about what you said. About how I got so focused on the sex that I missed the signs."

A spark popped.

Victor shifted his gaze toward her. "May I speak frankly with you?"

She nodded.

"And none of this gets out to my team?"

"Of course."

His finger traced a crease on his jeans. Then, without looking at her, he said, "I have to say that, yes, sex with her was great. I came to focus on that a lot. Whenever we had time off together, like a few days, we'd spend the night with each other. I craved it, to be honest. I hope this isn't too much information."

"I've heard worse."

That brought a quick smile to his face. "I hope not."

"I think I could surprise you."

He shook his head. "That got me to thinking. I started dissociating myself from that, started looking at everything else in our relationship. I remember how she'd never journal when I was around."

His shoulders rose and fell in a shrug. "I trusted her. I figured it wasn't my business. Was I ever wrong!"

"What other signs did you see?"

"She got scared, worried when Makmoud and Hezbollah started turning up the heat. I remember how in 2010, Maggie did a trip to the Middle East and challenged the mullahs. Makmoud showed up and taunted her. It scared Rach. I mean, that's the first time I saw her confidence crack. Then in the fall of 2011, someone sent a video to Maggie. It showed a woman with a masked man behind her. He gave this speech, then slit her throat."

Deborah gasped.

"The man pulled off his mask, and it was Makmoud. He pointed the bloody knife at the camera and directly told Maggie that she would take the woman's place."

Her hand flew to her mouth.

"That freaked out Rach more than I ever thought possible. I expected to have to reassure Maggie. What I didn't expect was the way Rachel seemed to panic." He shook his head. "It makes sense now. I think she worried that she'd get caught because maybe she'd been handing information to Makmoud. Most likely, he pulled it out of her with ease. Then there were her long weekends away."

Deborah raised an eyebrow.

"Sometimes, we'd work opposite shifts. Either she had a weekend off, or I did. Usually, I did something with the guys like golfing or fishing or going to a ballgame. She sometimes went out of town with some girl-friends from college or DC or to see her parents. Or she said she did. When I asked about her weekends, she'd shrug and say it was fun. I figured she just wasn't talkative."

"Oh, Vic."

He lowered his head. "I feel like a fool, like a patsy. She played me. She said she loved me, but now I wonder."

"Maybe she did. It's entirely possible that she did." Deborah touched his shoulder. "I think...I think that perhaps she was indeed addicted to sex, yet she loved you too. It's possible. Only, most people aren't a good enough liar to fool you like she did. I think…I think she couldn't give up her trysts with him."

"The Service said they found a bank account where deposits of fifty thousand were made quarterly, like a payoff."

She swallowed hard. "So…she was passing secrets."

"Possibly. It's the only conclusion I can make." He sighed. "I'm beginning to wonder if she kept it up after we got engaged."

Victor leaned against the cushions.

"Have you read farther?" Deborah did the same and faced him.

"I'm too scared to."

She nodded. "That has to be when you're ready."

"Enough about me." Victor straightened. "Do you want something to drink?"

"Uh, sure."

"Wine?"

"You have some out here?"

"At first, I thought about having the whole thing to myself. You know, drink myself silly. Now, at least I can share it with someone. It's Merlot."

"That's fine."

Deborah turned over his revelations in her mind. "Not to speak ill of the dead, but I knew girls like Rachel."

"What do you mean?" The refrigerator door sucked open, then closed.

"Stunningly beautiful. Usually blonde. Perfect figure. Smart. Good at everything they did. All of the guys in high school would lust after them and see them as conquests. If they didn't score, they'd lie about it in the locker room after football practice."

"You weren't one of them?" A cork popped, and wine swished into a glass.

"Hah! Hardly." Deborah smiled and accepted one from him. "No. I was probably called a prude behind my back. Not that I cared. I was too busy creating the life I wanted after I graduated high school."

The room dimmed further, meaning he'd turned off all of the lamps so the fire and candles provided the only light.

Her palms moistened.

Victor resumed his seat, but this time, he faced her and handed her a glass. "What were you doing?"

"I didn't go to college when I graduated. I didn't know what I wanted to do as a career, but I knew I wanted to work. I worked on a dive boat and waitressed in the off season. I also enjoyed living with three friends." She smiled as she remembered those heady times when she thought she had the world at her feet. "I went on dates, but most of the guys in Key Largo were interested only in sex. That's it. And then there were these creepy older men who were around for sport fishing or diving. Ick."

"Not your type."

She chuckled. "Hardly. Especially since most of them were married." She sipped her wine.

"How did you and your husband meet?"

"It was 1991. May, to be exact. He and his buds were home from Gulf One with lots of money and time to burn. They all bought Harleys and did a road trip. They intended to go to Key West, but they stopped in Key Largo."

"Where did they meet you?"

"They did a dive on my boat. I guess I caught Derek's eye, because he approached me that afternoon to ask me to join him and his pals for supper." A smile lifted the corners of her mouth.

"What?"

She shook her head.

"Deb…" He touched her on the arm.

"I was remembering how intense those feelings that I had for him were. I was so young back then. Not hot-headed but eager to begin life. I'd always envisioned meeting a handsome guy as part of it. Then it happened. They wound up spending the rest of their time in the Keys with my friends and me. We kept in contact. He came down every chance he got. I was…" She broke off.

"You can tell me. It's not like I haven't bared all." Victor wrapped a strand of her hair around his finger.

She giggled, the wine making her feel a little giddy, as did his touch. "I wanted him to kiss me. I remember how I asked him when he visited at

Thanksgiving if he'd seen his family at all since May. I mean, Derek came down every chance he got. He said no, that they knew he was courting me."

"Courting?" A grin finally crossed his face.

She nodded as she took another sip. "I told him it sounded archaic, almost like some term from the Middle Ages. That's when I realized he was serious. He kissed me that night. Finally, I realized why he'd waited."

"That was?"

"Because he knew we were long distance. He wanted to get to know me as a person without the physical sensations. It took a kiss from him to get that through my thick head." She shifted, edging closer to him.

Victor placed his empty glass on the coffee table. "Did you know what he did?"

"I knew he was Army, but that was it. To me, he was this gorgeous, mature, Christian guy in his late twenties. He fascinated me. His whole family came down at Christmas and got to know mine. When they left, he stayed behind. On New Year's Eve, he suggested that we take a boat out for a sunset cruise. That's when he fully read me into what he did."

"But you had no idea what it meant."

"No. After he proposed to me that evening, it was so hard to wait until marriage." Deborah placed her glass next to his. "You know, it's funny."

"What?" Victor ran his thumb across her cheek.

His touch set off an unexpected tide of sensations. She reached up and took his hand.

"If Anna, Marie, or Gracie found a guy like that, I'd be wringing my hands with worry."

"Why?" The leather cushion shifted as he inched closer to her and stretched his arm out along the back.

"I was still new to the world." She leaned her head against his arm. Her breath quickened at the faint scent of aftershave and soap she'd come to associate with him. "Mom told me years later that she got really worried when I started gushing about this good-looking guy who I'd gone to Key West with. And for good reason, I guess. I was so green, but I didn't realize it."

"That's quite a story."

"And I'm sticking to it." She closed her eyes as contentment washed over her. The wood shifted in the fireplace. The Colonel's low, rumbling snore reached her ears. Every sense came on alert at the feel of his shirt against her cheek.

"I think you're turning into a pumpkin." Victor tousled her hair.

"It's good to spend time with you." Disappointment uncurled inside of her. For the fewest of minutes, she'd been able to forget she was a mother, that she had the responsibility of four children, that she was in hiding. "You're right, though. I need to make sure Gracie and Marie are in bed. I know they're technically not in school, but I want them on some semblance of a schedule."

"I'll walk you to the house." He rose, took her hands, and tugged her to her feet.

The move caught her by surprise. Off balance, Deborah almost fell against him. Her hands spread against his chest. She found she had to tip her chin to gaze at him. Her heart began hammering.

His arms tightened around her.

Something glittered in his dark eyes. Compassion? Desire?

He curled his hand behind her neck.

Heat flooded her face.

Before she realized it, Victor brushed his lips across hers.

Oh, my. Every nerve went on edge.

"I'm sorry. I—I shouldn't have." He pulled away slightly.

A shiver coursed up and down her spine. She nuzzled closer. "Don't be."

"What?"

"Don't be sorry." Before he could answer, she kissed him.

Abruptly, she broke it off. "Now it's my turn to say I shouldn't have. I guess I stink at this dating thing."

He chuckled, a rich sound that made her smile. He pulled her into another, longer kiss.

When he broke it off, Deborah trembled.

Victor skimmed his finger across her cheek. "We'll just have to take it one day at a time."

"That, we will."

Hand in hand, they made their way into the chilly night air and toward the Big House.

29

Early May 2014

Black clouds roiled above the edge of the box canyon. A distant lightning strike briefly lit the bottoms, which seemed to drop even lower. Thunder stalked the land with a guttural growl. The breeze puffed, bringing with it the dampness of imminent rain as it whispered across the bare skin on Victor's arms.

One look at the sky told him all he needed to know. The predicted thunderstorm would pounce upon Last Chance Ranch within the next several minutes.

He dumped the last of the manure and hustled into the barn. Once he left the wheelbarrow in its place, he darted to the small building containing the hay and pulled out a few bales. He distributed bales into each of the eight stalls.

"Mr. Victor?" Anna's voice made him turn around after he tossed the last one onto the stall's floor.

"Anna, hi." He paused, lifted his baseball cap, and raked a hand through his hair. His fingers came away wet. "What's up?"

He shoved the hat onto his head with the bill backwards.

She drifted farther inside. "Um, I, like, have something to tell you."

He cocked an eyebrow as he leaned down to clip the string holding a bale together. "What's that?"

"Mom's birthday is coming up." She wrapped a strand of hair around her finger and lowered her gaze.

"It is?" He picked up his pitchfork and leaned on it.

"Yeah. Like, it's on Mother's Day this year."

He smiled. "How about that? What do you normally do for her?"

A faint pink tinged her cheeks. Her fingers skittered along the wood of one of the stalls. "If it's on a weekend, we fix her breakfast in bed. Miss Wanda bakes her a cake, and we get her presents, and—"

She broke off, her countenance falling.

Victor's heart caught. He knew what she was thinking. They weren't at home in North Carolina. They were in a strange place surrounded by virtual strangers who didn't understand their rituals and traditions. "How about this? We'll have a party for her as part of lunch next Sunday. I'll bet Miss Diana can make a cake, and you're more than free to take her breakfast. Matter of fact, I'm sure she'd appreciate that."

"Can we go into town and get her presents?"

"Um, no."

"What?" Anna's blue eyes, so much like her mother's, widened.

"I can't allow that. You're in hiding, remember?" he added when she opened her mouth to protest. "How about this? Tell Miss Diana what you want to buy her. She and some of the other ladies will get what you want, and you all can help her wrap them. Can you do that?"

Slowly, she nodded.

"Okay. Go and talk to your sisters, and we'll see what we can do."

Anna turned and ran from the barn.

Victor watched her go. His heart picked up when she noticed how Deborah caught her daughter by the arm. They talked briefly. Anna continued toward the house.

Another, louder rumble of thunder snaked through the canyon.

"Do you need some help?" Deborah asked.

"Yeah. All eight horses have to come in."

"I'll get started." Deborah snatched the lead ropes from their pegs by the stalls and hustled into the darkening day.

Victor spread the last of the hay into the stalls, then headed toward the pasture gate where all eight horses waited. The pines on the other side of the riding ring rocked in the wind. The sky darkened so much that the light between the barn and the ring snapped on.

"Take these." Deborah handed two horses to him.

As they escorted the last round to their stalls, a huge drop of rain hit Victor on the arm, then another one. He ducked inside and shut his charges into their stalls.

A loud boom cracked overhead.

Deborah yelped and practically jumped into his arms.

Victor grinned. "Hate thunderstorms?"

"Something like that." She blushed and pulled back. "It reminds me of the day I got the e-mail that set everything into motion."

His eyes traced her figure that the T-shirt and jeans she wore subtly highlighted. Suddenly, he wanted to be completely alone with her. He reached out and took her hand. "I'm not following."

She chuckled. "Sorry. I'd forgotten you weren't in on this on day one. It was last August. The kids were with Derek's folks in Georgia for a week. It stormed really badly, and the wind blew a tree into the house."

She cringed at another crack of thunder. "I guess we're stuck here."

A gust of wind blew wet into the barn. He pulled the doors closed until only a sliver of rain remained.

"Not that I mind." He tugged her to him and wrapped his arms around her. "That means I have more time with you."

He kissed her slowly, deeply.

"Alone," he whispered against her hair.

"Hard to do when I have four children." She released him and smiled over her shoulder as she walked toward another hay bale against a wall between the aisle and one of the stalls. She sat down and leaned back on her hands. "I have a question for you."

"And I might have an answer."

"I want to help you."

"Help me? How?" He joined her.

She giggled and snatched his hat from his head. "Has wearing that ball cap backwards lowered your IQ?"

"Huh?"

She laughed. Just as quickly, she sobered. "Sorry. I forgot you can't read my mind. From what I understand, the FBI isn't any closer to finding out who Murdock is."

"Not that I know of." Victor shrugged. "My handler's been running that down, but he says there's been no progress."

"Who's got the case?"

"I have no idea. I would assume him or TL."

"Maybe Gary's not giving you all of the information."

Victor's head shot around. "How did you know his name?"

Deborah smiled and ran the material of the cap through her fingers. "Butch told me. Look. I know we're stuck here until they find him. Not that I mind." She leaned over and pecked him on the lips. "But it might be good for someone totally out of the FBI picture to take a look at it. Would that be okay with you?"

"Uh, sure. Let's see what we can do to make that happen. I'll get Shelly to set you up with a phone and laptop." Victor paused and listened to the rain hammering down on the metal roof. He rested his elbows on his knees and closed his eyes for a moment.

Like a naughty child, his mind wandered to a little over two years before when he and Rachel had traveled to Hawaii to check out wedding venues. A late-night rain had poured onto the tin roof of their bungalow so loudly that they'd barely slept. Not that they minded. He could almost feel the feathery brush of Rachel's hair against his cheeks.

"This is nice," Deborah murmured. She laced her fingers through his.

His eyes snapped open. Guilt swept over him for thinking about Rachel when he was with Deborah. His mood swung downward as he remembered the anguish that had coursed through him as he'd finished the last of Rachel's journals the day before. Desperate to distract himself, he asked, "How so?"

"Just…being. And doing that with you. It's hard to do with four kids running all over the place. That's why I always craved the times when Derek's folks would take them."

A gust of wind rattled a loose piece of roofing. One of the horses snorted and stomped. Another whinnied softly.

Victor took a deep breath. "Can we talk?"

"About Rachel?" Her compassion radiated through her fingers as they tightened around his.

He ran his other hand along the roughness of the hay. "I finished the journals last night."

"All of them?"

"Yeah. When we got engaged, Rachel moved in with me." He sighed. "I don't know. Maybe she wanted to make a clean start because she told Makmoud she couldn't do the tryst thing anymore. That angered him."

"I'm sure it would."

"She did seem somewhat lighter, freer. I marked it up to being engaged, but maybe…maybe it had something to do with the fact that she'd cut things off with him."

"Was that it?"

"No." Victor swallowed hard. "Have you ever looked back at things that didn't make sense at the time? Then you started putting the pieces together, and it did make sense?"

"I'm not sure I follow."

"In January, we'd gone to check out places in Hawaii for the wedding later that year. When we got back, Rach got a call. Her sister, who was a freelance wildlife photographer on the Kalahari, had been attacked and killed by lions. I guess she got too close to them. Rach went up to stay with her mom." Victor rubbed the back of his neck as he remembered reading those heartrending entries in her journal. "You know, even though she lied to me and betrayed me, it still hurts to read about how much she suffered while she and her mom waited to hear from her dad. He'd gone to Africa to help with the search. They finally declared Susanna dead. Rach took bereavement leave. I offered to stay with her in Manassas after the memorial service, but she told me to go back to Raleigh. When I picked her up at the airport…"

"That bad, huh?"

Victor turned his head and gazed at her. "She was pale. Thinner too, as if she'd hardly eaten. I could tell she was barely holding it together." A lump filled his throat. "I think she cried more in the span of the three days we were together after her return than she had the entire time I'd known her. She was still on leave, and I stayed with her as much as I could. Then I had to go with the detail when Maggie and her husband took some R&R over her spring break. I got home late that Saturday. Rach was already in bed asleep, so I didn't see the shiner on her eye until we woke up the next day."

Deborah reached up and rubbed his back. "She had a black eye?"

"Oh, yeah. A good one. I asked her about it. She told me how she'd been reaching into the cabinet where she kept the flour in a container. It fell out and hit her on the eye. That's when she called herself stupid and started crying. I felt completely and utterly helpless."

"I gather that's not what happened."

He shook his head and leaned forward. Rachel's tear-stained face and defeated posture tugged at his heart even then. "No. Makmoud surprised her, apparently. I guess he knew I was gone for the week, so he ambushed her when she got back from a run the Saturday I returned. He gave her the black eye, then tied her up and raped her. He showed her pictures of her sister and told her he'd had her kidnapped from Africa."

"Oh, Vic."

"Ironic, isn't it? Her journals started and ended with a rape." Victor worked a piece of hay loose from the bale and ran it between his fingers. "Her last entry was dated the day I returned. My guess is she put everything in those hibachi pots after he left."

He threw it down and put his head in his hands. "I feel like someone who's reading a good book where the last chapter is ripped out."

"Why?"

"She died a month later. I mean, I don't know if she was truly loyal and a woman without choices or if she still had loyalty to Makmoud."

"What did the investigation yield?"

"How should I know?" He jumped up and braced himself against one of the stall doors. "They cut me out when they started suspecting me."

"You?" Deborah joined him and leaned her hip against the rough wood. The Appaloosa inside nuzzled her. She reached up and rubbed his nose. "Why you?"

"Because we were lovers." He scowled. "Oh, they quickly realized I was the dupe, but that didn't save my career. I had to resign."

She stared. "Didn't they tell you anything?"

"A little. They told me about the accounts." Victor ran his hand along the horse's face. "They said Rachel used my name to change the egress point. Apparently, when I thought she touched my back to calm me, she actually cut off my comms unit. And the rest? Honestly, I can't remember."

"Oh, Vic. I'm sorry." Deborah wrapped her arm around his waist and laid her head against his shoulder.

He turned and crushed her to him as his chest heaved. He buried his face in her silky hair and took a shaky breath as he willed himself to calm down, to be able to talk again. "I'll never know the total truth."

"What?"

"The Service cut me out. When I resigned, I lost my clearances." He fell silent.

Then he remembered.

When he'd last talked to Miles the August before, he'd had no clearances. But now?

Victor pulled back. "I need to call Miles."

"Who?"

"Miles Norton. He's the agent in charge of Maggie's detail now, and he was the one who ran the investigation. I've got the needed clearances. Surely, he could tell me."

"But would that really get you the truth?"

Victor blinked. "Huh?"

"Would that bring you the truth?"

"I'm not sure I follow."

Deborah wrapped her arms around herself as she wandered to the hay bale again. She kicked at it. "Look. I know you're a truth seeker. I understand that. But sometimes…"

She met his gaze. "Sometimes it's hard to get the entire truth."

"Are you saying I should stop?" He put his hands on his hips.

"No, I'm saying to be aware that you might not get what you want."

"It has to be there. Miles could tell me."

"Would he?"

"Whose side are you on?" That came out a little louder than he intended.

She turned away and stuffed her hands in the back pockets of her jeans. Finally, she faced him. Tears pooling in her eyes made them glimmer in the dim overhead light. "I'm on yours. Always. But sometimes…sometimes we can't know the total truth, at least on this side of heaven's gates. Sometimes, God is the only one who knows the total truth."

"I'll find it. I promise you, I will."

"But at what cost?" A sad smile turned Deborah's lips upward. She glanced outside. The rain had lessened to a drizzle. "It looks like the rain's just about stopped. It's getting late, and I promised I'd help Diana with supper. Think about what I said, okay?"

He jerked his head in a nod.

With that, she pecked him on the lips and wandered into the brightening afternoon.

Victor remained where he was as he considered their discussion.

He pulled back into the shadows and unclipped the phone from his belt. It took him only a moment to locate the number he wanted. As it rang, he lifted it to his ear.

When the man answered, he said, "Miles? Victor Chavez, here. I was wondering about the incident a couple of years ago. Is there any way we could talk about that?"

30

Along with the delicious scent of hamburgers and hot dogs, the sounds of "Happy Birthday" rose from the terrace of the Big House as the Shadow Box Team and Fields clan sang to Deborah a week later on Mother's Day. The discordant sound degenerated into the noise of cats yowling into the night.

The birthday girl leaned forward, closed her eyes briefly, and blew out the candles.

"I think that's the most memorable singing ever." Deborah laughed and brushed a tear from the corner of her eye. Her gaze slid to Victor.

From his position at the head of the table, he rested his elbows on the metal and his chin on his hands. A smile meant only for her curled his lips.

The way a light shade of pink coated her cheeks pleased him. She cleared her throat. "So whose idea was this?"

"Thank your daughter. Anna let me know it was your birthday today." Victor leaned back. "Diana?"

"Time for presents." Diana hopped up and placed a gaily decorated shopping bag on Deborah's lap. "From the guys, sans Victor since all they did was give me money."

"Hey, we're not frequent shoppers like you are." Skylar grinned as he ducked a playful jab from Fiona.

Deborah pulled out a lightweight jacket. "Oooh. I like it. For the chilly nights here."

"And from the girls." Diana added another gift.

"Y'all are too sweet." Deborah smiled as she pulled out a broomstick skirt and top along with a silver and turquoise belt. "A whole new outfit."

"Diana's doing, not mine." Fiona rose and collected the wrapping paper. "She's our fashionista."

"You're good too. You helped with the outfit." Diana set some more presents on the table. "From the children and Liza."

Deborah tore through the wrapping paper. Her mouth formed an "O" as she stared at the silver and turquoise jewelry. "These are beautiful!"

"And it's all handcrafted by the Navajo who live around here. Vic's the one who clued me in." Diana smiled at him and picked up the last gift. "And from the boss man himself."

Victor stilled.

Deborah tore into the package. "A frame."

"Flip it over," he urged her. He rested his chin on his hands.

She did. "This is beautiful!"

Victor smiled. He'd taken pictures of each child and placed them in the black, hand-crafted frame he'd found at one of the photography stores in town. It'd been a risk, but the gratitude in her eyes made it all the more with it.

"Wow, boss. Score one for you." Butch whistled as he examined it with a practiced eye. "I'd forgotten how good you are at photography."

Deborah rose. "Guys, thank you. Normally, I don't make a big deal over my birthday, but this year...it feels good to do so. To celebrate life."

"Hear, hear," Skylar softly said.

With that, the party broke up. As Victor began pulling down the streamers and balloons that had festooned the terrace, he felt a gaze resting on him. He turned.

Anna. She looked away.

He concentrated on stuffing the streamers in a garbage bag. He cast a look at her.

Anna again deflected.

Suddenly, he remembered the way she'd started focusing on him with glances here and there, especially when she thought he wasn't looking.

Now, he realized how her actions the week before had taken the form of flirtation. Discomfort rippled through him. He didn't know what to do but to retreat to his room for the afternoon to escape it.

That night, Victor had one more gift to give Deborah. As the tans and reds of the sun glowing on the walls of the box canyon faded, he headed to the studio to wrap it. The glow from the work lights above the table provided the only illumination inside the studio. He opened one of the drawers in the table. In a small tray at the front sat the jeweler's box he'd picked up when he'd bought the picture frame earlier that week.

He was about to flip it open when the phone rang.

Miles Norton.

"Hey." Victor forced a smile into his voice, something that was especially hard to do since the man had turned him down flat the week before regarding the investigation. His hand gripped the table.

"I'm glad you picked up."

"Oh?"

"Yeah. Listen. I've been giving your request a lot of thought over the past week. Let's put it this way. Maybe you do have a point. You might have something to offer. But, I don't want to talk about it over the phone."

"I understand."

"If you can be here next week sometime, we'll talk. If not, all bets are off the table because Maggie's heading to Oxford on a summer residency program, and she leaves on Saturday."

Victor's gaze flew to the calendar he'd set in one of the sills. It would be tight but definitely doable. "What about Tuesday?"

"You're sure you can be here?"

"Yeah. It may cost me, but that's how important this is to me right now."

"Okay." The doubt rang in Miles's voice. "Text me when you've gotten your reservations made. You're welcome to stay with Allison and me, or I'm sure Maggie would say the same thing. She always keeps a bed made up."

"Will do. Thanks, man." Victor wiped his moist palms on his jeans. At last he'd have his answers.

A tap on the screened door made him glance up. "Butch, hey. Come on in."

"Doing some thinking, boss?"

"Something like that. Sorry I blew off the Uno game."

"Nah. We decided to wait until Friday since Deb wanted the kids to finish their homework tonight. Hey, what's that?"

He nodded at the jeweler's box.

The heat began in Victor's neck and rapidly spread upward. "Um, well, uh…"

Butch grinned. "Cat got your tongue?"

"Uh, yeah. I, um, wanted to get Deb a little something extra." Victor flipped open the lid to reveal an emerald with a border of small diamonds around it.

His comrade whistled. "My, oh, my, that's pretty. She must mean a lot to you."

"She's the world to me now." A dull shock rippled through him. He shook his head. "I can't believe I said that."

"She's a good woman."

Victor eased onto the lab chair. For a moment, the lonely wail of a coyote sifted through the screens of the door and open windows. Slowly, he asked, "Do you think we've compromised ourselves?"

"I'm not following." Butch folded his arms across his broad chest and leaned his hip against the worktable.

"I mean, when I worked with the Service or with Fortran Security Service, we'd literally go to work and guard our principal. Then leave. No deep emotional involvement. This…this felt different. We're hosts as well as protectors. I guess it suddenly hit me how we may have gotten too close to them."

"How can we not?" Butch's shoulders rose and fell in a shrug. "It's hard not to when you have kids involved. And the Fields kids are extra special."

"I know." Victor turned and picked up a picture of Gracie and Marie, both hugging the Colonel, Maddie, and Marvin, Victor's Blue Heelers. "Deb may have my heart, but Marie's a close second."

"I hear ya."

"What brought you out here?"

"Just checking about next week. And to see if you'd heard anything from Gary."

"*Nada.* But, speaking of next week, I'm probably headed to North Carolina for a couple of nights."

Butch raised his eyebrows in silent question.

"I wouldn't go, but this is..." He hesitated, uncertain of how much to reveal to his deputy. "It's necessary. Hopefully out tomorrow and then back on Wednesday. Can you handle things here?"

"Sure. No worries on this end. I'll make sure everyone's taken care of."

"That'd be great. Thanks, man."

"Any time. Well, I guess that seals it. We're still in full security mode next week. But, do you think it'd be okay if the kids did some horseback riding on the ranch trails? I think they're getting a bit restless."

Victor thought about that one for a moment. They'd been in hiding for almost two months with no time away from the immediate confines of the ranch. Since there'd been no sign of danger, he didn't see any risk. "Sure, but I want at least one armed team member per person with them at all times they're out of the canyon."

"That works for me. Thanks, boss. Well, have fun giving that trinket to Deb. I'm sure she'll like it. And..." He winked. "Good catch. I'll be in prayer for both of you."

With that, he shambled out the door.

Victor remained where he was. Slowly, as his mind churned through his upcoming trip, he wrapped the jewelry box before turning his attention to the airline websites. It'd cost him a small fortune, but he could fly out early the following morning and be back mid-afternoon on Wednesday. He cringed as he entered his credit card information.

It would be worth it, well worth it, to get the truth about Rachel once and for all.

The printer spit out his boarding passes and ticket information.

As he reached to pick it up, a feminine figure strolling toward the studio distracted him.

Deborah.

His mouth went dry as the broomstick skirt from the ladies emphasized the sway of her hips. Even from that distance, the silver of her earrings, belt, and other jewelry glimmered in the studio's lights. He greeted her at the door. A dull shock rippled through him when he realized how the makeup she must have borrowed highlighted her eyes and lips. "Hey, come on in. I'm sorry I ducked out on everyone."

Deborah shrugged. "All you're missing is Anna moaning about having to do algebra. Shelly's been so kind to help her. DJ's whining about English. At least Gracie was happy to do her addition and subtraction before I put Marie and her to bed. Oh, and Skylar's on the videos in the study. So there you have it. An almost normal night for the Fields clan."

Victor smiled. He reached up and ran some of her hair through his fingers. "You're too funny."

"I try. What's this?" She cocked her head as she picked up one of the boarding passes from the printer tray.

Victor froze. His cheeks began heating.

"Raleigh? Tomorrow? But...but why?"

"Miles called." He took the sheet from her, gathered the rest into a neat stack, and shifted it into a folder. "He said he was willing to talk to me but only in person. And it had to be this week because Maggie's heading to Oxford for a summer gig."

"But..." Her gaze shot to his. "What about...here?"

"Butch is my deputy, and he's cool with it." Victor rose from the chair and took her hands. "Look. I'm flying out tomorrow morning and will be back Wednesday around mid-afternoon. A hair over forty-eight hours. He's good, and I'm not worried."

"I know." Something in her voice caught. She looked toward the Big House.

"What's on your mind?"

"I'm scared."

"Of Makmoud coming after you? Like I said—"

"It's not that." She lowered her gaze to where their fingers intertwined. "It's not that at all. I'm scared because I realize how much I love you—"

She broke off and clapped a hand over her mouth. "I so stink at this dating thing. I think that was your line."

Victor ran his hand down her hair. "You're silly. Here. I wanted you to have this."

Before he lost his nerve, he reached over and handed her the gift.

"Oooh. Brown paper packages tied up with string. Literally." She grinned. Then her mouth formed an "O" when she tore through the package and opened the box. "Vic, this is…this is…"

"I love you." The dull shock of his admission rippled down his spine. "I knew that the emerald was May's birthstone, and I wanted to get you something to show how much I love you. Here. Turn around."

She did and lifted her hair.

Victor secured the gold chain. Before he released her, he kissed her fair skin at the base of her neck.

When she faced him again, the clear light of the work light made the small diamond border sparkle against her fair skin. The emerald almost glowed.

If only her face did.

"What's troubling you?"

"Do you think Miles can give you the answers you want?"

"I'm sure he can."

She gripped his hands. "But what if he can't?"

"Deb…"

"What if he can't?" The urgent tone surprised him, as did the way her grasp tightened. "What if all you're left with are more questions?"

"Then I'll keep going."

"Until what? You ask Makmoud himself before he kills you?"

"Deb…"

She drifted toward fireplace and stared at the pictures on the mantel. He'd placed many of the team and the Fields family on the dark wood. Only a few of Rachel remained in that position of prominence.

"This is like an idol to you." She reached up and ran a finger down a picture of Rachel he'd taken while they were in Hawaii.

Confusion washed over him. "I'm not sure I follow."

"I think you do. You're so focused on this. So focused and convinced you'll get the entire story and put Rachel to rest in your mind."

"I will."

"And what if you don't?" She sighed and faced him in the dimness on the other side of the room. "Look. One thing I've noticed about you is that you can get so fixated, so focused on something that you ignore what else is going on."

Hurt welled at the accurate observation. "I don't appreciate that remark."

"I'm sorry. I guess I'm too honest." Deborah remained where she was, but her fingers ran along the leather of the chair near where she stood. "I saw it when you were talking about your relationship with Rachel. You were so focused on the physical side that you ignored other signals that things might not have been as you thought. And now? You're so focused on vindicating or convicting her that you'll stop at nothing until you do. That scares me."

"Why?"

"Nothing else matters to you."

His gut tightened. "You matter to me. The kids matter. My team matters."

Anger pushed an edge into his words.

"You're enslaved to this. Even beyond the grave, Rachel has enslaved you. That's what scares me." She eased onto the chair in front of her.

Her words slammed into Victor, hammering him over and over. He stepped to the couch and stood there.

Deborah wrapped her arms around her middle and leaned forward as if her stomach pained her. She kept her gaze on the coffee table. "One thing I've learned over the years in my walk with the Lord is that we humans are created beings. We were made by our heavenly Father to worship Him. In other words, we're wired to worship. Only a lot of us have slid off that path. We have to worship something, so we substitute other things in place of God. Like other gods. Money. Even people."

Victor winced as the truth of her words slapped him across the face.

"From our first conversation, I sensed that you worshiped Rachel. She was the golden girl. Perfect in every way. And even as you've realized she's not, she's still the center of your life. That told me that Christ was not at your center, not like He is for Butch, Diana, Sana, and Shelly." Deborah remained still. "I tried to tell myself, as we started talking and as you walked with me through the whole trauma with Liza, that you were a good friend, that you were there to comfort me as I cried. But then I realized something."

Now she gazed at him, and tears pooled in her eyes. "You surprised me. I fell in love with you, and I feel like the schoolgirl with the unreciprocated crush."

"Rachel's dead, in case you forgot that." His words came across as a growl.

"I know she is. But she's still controlling you. You'll stop at nothing to find out the total truth. I'm worried it's going to tear us apart—among other things." She lowered her head.

"Oh, Deb. Come here." Victor drew her into his arms. "I'm sorry."

She held on tightly. Her chest heaved, and her fingers clenched the fabric of his sailcloth shirt. She trembled slightly.

"I promise that when I get back, I'll put this behind me."

She gazed at him, a tear glistening on her lashes, almost like she doubted his words. "Promise?"

"I do." He brushed away that tear and kissed her.

She melted into him as they sank onto the couch. Half an hour later, he nuzzled her hair and held her close. He ran his hand down her back, thankful that she'd finally relaxed. "I guess I should let you get to bed."

"And you need to pack."

"All I'm taking can fit into my briefcase." Victor kissed her on the forehead.

"Guys." She shook her head and giggled. "I don't understand how all you need to take is a change of underwear and a toothbrush."

Victor laughed. "We do have our ways. C'mon."

He took her hand and tugged her to her feet. They stepped to the worktable, and he reached to turn out the light.

"Oh, my." She touched his shoulder.

"What?"

"I, um, think I got mascara and foundation on your shirt."

He grinned. "It'll come out on the wash."

Hand in hand, they made their way past the Men's Building, which had fallen silent. Not a light was on in the Big House either save for a dim glow from the right side where the study resided.

Victor disarmed the alarm system before opening the door.

Deborah moved to step inside.

He caught her arm and murmured, "A kiss from the lady, if you would."

She obliged.

Not releasing her hand, he slipped inside ahead of her. Once she'd closed the door, he turned, this time drawing her into a deeper kiss.

"Keep that up, and I'll never get to my room," she murmured.

"Maybe that's my intent."

She giggled. "Lead on, kind sir."

He escorted her across the silent great room and up the stairs. Once in front of her door, he stopped and drew her close. "To keep you until I get back."

"Hmmm. I'll take more of that, please." Deborah snuggled closer.

Light suddenly spilled across the walkway.

"It's just like I thought." A strident female voice slammed into Victor.

He whipped around.

Deborah gasped.

Clad in a T-shirt and pajama pants, her blond hair askew, Anna glared at them from where she stood on the walkway. "You just wanted to get in with Mom, that's all."

"Anna, it's not—"

"You said you wanted to protect us. All you care about is Mom! We're...we're just obstacles to you!"

"Anna Leigh, get back into your room." Deborah's voice cracked like a whip across the stillness.

Anna slammed her door.

On the console table between her room and the bathroom, a Navajo vase began teetering. Victor dove for it but missed.

It fell to the floor and shattered.

Across the way, either Gracie or Marie began crying.

From her bedroom at the front of the house, Liza stepped onto the walkway. "Deb? Vic? What happened?"

Victor's cheeks flamed at the implied accusation from Deborah's oldest.

He faced his love.

Her cheeks red, Deborah stared at the floor. "I'm sorry about the vase. I'll make sure we replace it."

"You can't. It was an heirloom."

"Is everything okay up there?" Skylar called.

"Peachy," Victor growled.

"Vic…" Deborah reached toward him.

"I'll see you in the morning." He pecked her on the lips. With that, he stomped down the stairs, any semblance of peace he'd felt now just as destroyed as the vase.

31

Tuesday's midday sun in Phoenix burned onto the roof of the warehouse where Makmoud and his crew holed up. In the upstairs office, the air conditioning units kept the temperature comfortable enough for Makmoud to focus on his work of eavesdropping on the lives of the strange little community beyond the Flagstaff city limits.

"What has gotten into you?" Deborah's voice rang clearly over the computer's speakers.

"You don't understand!" Something banged as if to emphasize Anna's angst.

"Understand what? I thought I raised you to respect adults. And one who's trying to protect—"

"All he cares about is you!"

"You know that's not true."

A door closed.

"All he wants is to get into—"

"Enough!"

Even Makmoud jumped at the ferocity in Deborah's voice.

"Go to your room, and don't come out until you can apologize to me for your disrespect and to Mr. Victor when he gets back tomorrow for your disrespect of him. Don't say another word. Go!" A muttered word bleeped across the miles.

"This is too good." Makmoud's lips curled in a sneer as he leaned the desk chair back on two legs. He folded his arms across his chest and continued to eavesdrop on the unfolding soap opera.

"Deb, what's going on?" Liza Murphy's voice reached him.

"Anna has yet to apologize for Sunday night." Deborah's sniffle reached Makmoud. "I don't know what's gotten into her. She's always been respectful. Helpful. Kind. And now? It's like she's morphed into another person overnight."

"Hormones. Like it or not, she's a full-blown teenager. There's going to be moments like that."

"I know. But saying what she did to Vic..." More sniffles.

"You love him, don't you?"

Makmoud scowled at the caring tone in Liza's voice.

"I do. I just...I just don't know what to do!"

"Praying would be a good start."

A chair shoved back, and metal clinked against ceramic. "But what about with Anna? I don't know how to break this stalemate we're in."

"How about let me go riding with her tomorrow afternoon? Butch said we could go out on the ranch trails so long as we have some of his team with us. I'll talk to her. See if I can't get to the bottom of this. And let's worry about you and Vic and everything later. Like when he gets back."

Water ran into a sink. Then Deborah spoke again. "Thanks, sis."

"I'm glad I can be of help."

The chair legs slammed onto the floor. Makmoud switched off the speakers. He pushed to his feet, yanked open the door, and thundered down the metal steps. They shook beneath him. "Jibril!"

He hit concrete and circled the three vans, all of which had been painted to look like vans of the local telephone company in Flagstaff.

"Here." Jibril, who'd been leaning into the rear of one of them, faced his brother. "What is it?"

"We need to move out at dusk."

His brother cocked his head. "Why is that?"

Makmoud smirked. "Opportunity. Victor is out of town until early tomorrow afternoon. And tomorrow afternoon, Liza will be riding with her oldest niece, which will divide the team since they must guard them on the trails. We strike then. And to make it clean, we must grab Victor before he gets to the ranch."

"But how?" Jibril frowned. "We don't have enough men to split up into three squads."

"We don't have to. Who does Victor know and trust?"

His brother nodded. He chuckled. "Of course. Gary."

"Exactly. Are we ready to leave here?"

"Almost. We will be so by dusk."

Makmoud peered into the back of the van where an instrument that looked like a futuristic ray gun filled almost the entire interior. "You say this will work?"

"Senthil!" Jibril called.

The bespectacled young man who crouched next to a control panel and tinkered with it stood, rapping his head against the roof. He winced. "Yes, sir?"

"Tell him about the weapon."

"It emits an electromagnetic pulse and will neutralize all electrical equipment within a half-mile range." He began spouting off technical details in his sing-song voice. As he jabbered, his hands gestured as if his words weren't enough.

Makmoud tuned him out, then cut him off. "Enough. We leave at dusk for Flagstaff."

He took his brother's arm and led him away from the van. At the base of the stairs, he stopped. "Where did you find him?"

"One of our Phoenix cell knew him. He is in the States from India on a doctoral research assistantship. The promise of extra money to send to his family was enough to lure him."

"Then ensure that his family is paid and that he does not return to Phoenix. Both him and the device."

Jibril nodded.

"When you're done, come see me so we can plan the ambush." Makmoud clapped him on the shoulder and returned to the office. His eyes shot to the clock on the wall. Close to four, therefore close to seven on the

East Coast. Meaning that Gary would be at home or at least with his family.

When Makmoud called, Gary had to answer.

He picked up his phone and dialed the number for Gary's personal phone.

"Gary Walton." The FBI agent's voice came in sharp and clear.

"The desert is beautiful this time of year." Makmoud leaned against the desk as he used the code phrase that would let Gary know another assignment had come.

"What do you want?" That came as a hiss from his mole.

Cheers and clapping reached him.

"To chat. And where are you?"

"My son's baseball game."

"I suggest you get to somewhere private where we can talk. Now."

Murmuring ensued, followed by a chuckle that sounded strained, even to Makmoud's ears. Then Gary expelled a breath. "Dang it, I told you I'm done."

Makmoud began pacing. "Oh, you're never done, Murdock. Never. I have another task for you."

"What do you want me to do?"

The forlornness in his voice made Makmoud chuckle. "Don't sound so worried. It's easy. I want you to fly to Phoenix in the morning. You see, Victor arrives on the 3:30 flight to Flagstaff from Phoenix. You are to meet him there and intercept him. Then bring him to us at his ranch. I'll text you the address. How you do so is up to you. Am I clear? I'll expect you in Phoenix first thing in the morning so that you can make it to Flagstaff with time to spare."

"Makmoud—"

"Remember that you have a lovely family. I would hate for anything to happen to them."

"I'll be there." Gary ground out those words.

"Text me when you have your reservations." With that, Makmoud ended the conversation. He once more leaned against the worktable for a few moments as he considered this mission. It carried its own risks, for sure.

He braced his hands against it as he gazed at the aerial photos of the Chavez land. His eyes wandered to the ones pinned to the wall that showed the riding trails along the property. He began nodding. It would take some skill and plain luck on his part, but it would work because Jibril would engineer it to perfection.

His phone chirped. Makmoud grinned as he noted the flight number for Gary from Dulles to Phoenix.

He dialed another number.

When a husky female voice answered, he said, "Iman, I need you to be on a flight from Dulles to Phoenix to follow Murdock. I'll text you with additional instructions."

32

"What can you tell me?" Victor asked Tuesday evening as the waitress walked away after delivering two burgers and foaming mugs of beer to their bar table.

Miles Norton's lips twitched upward in a quick smile. "You do know how not to mince words, don't you?"

"I came here to get answers about Rachel." Victor blew on the foam of his beer.

"I'm not sure how much help I can be."

"I want to know what your conclusions were."

"It's—"

"And please don't tell me I'm not cleared for this." Victor set his mug down with a thump. "You know I am. I'm sure you checked up on me before you called on Sunday."

"Don't cut me off." Miles's green eyes narrowed. "You know better than that."

Victor swallowed hard.

"What I was going to say before you interrupted me is that it's not a sure thing I can get you the answers you seem to need so badly."

"Try me."

For a moment, Miles stared at the cars passing by the open-air restaurant at the northern edge of Raleigh's downtown. He took a bite of his hamburger and chewed slowly, almost like he wanted to make Victor wait as punishment for his outburst.

Victor popped a fry into his mouth to avoid forcing the issue.

Miles swallowed. "Okay. So you want to know what we found out. What do you remember about that day?"

"Everything that night is really fuzzy."

"Which is expected. But what about that entire day?"

Victor picked up another fry and took a bite. "Rachel wasn't the same. She hadn't been since she'd gotten back the memorial service." He closed his eyes as he remembered the way she didn't ask questions like she normally did during the final briefing before they headed to Raleigh. "She was quiet. Withdrawn."

"Then?"

"When we left late that afternoon, she was texting a lot. She said her dad wasn't doing well. It gets blurry from there."

"Do you know how many texts we found on her phone that day?"

"No."

"Dozens." Miles set his burger down. "And they weren't to her parents. They were to a burner phone we think was with the kidnap team, maybe even with Makmoud Hidari himself."

Victor closed his eyes. Thanks to what he'd read in the journals, no shock rippled through him. "When you thought I was a suspect, you accused me of turning off my comms unit."

"Whoa. Stop." Miles held up his hand. "I want to get one thing clear here, son. My investigation of the incident followed protocol. We had to look at everyone on the detail, especially those on duty that night, and most especially the whip agent. Understand? Honestly, I never considered you a suspect."

"Then why did your so-called team come into my house when I was barely home from the hospital, take me away for interrogation, threaten to arrest my sister when she protested, and finally lock her in the bathroom so they could knock holes in the walls all over my house?"

"Greg overstepped his duties and now resides in our Anchorage office. I heard it gets cold and dark up there in the winter." Miles sipped his beer and stared down his former agent. "When we found out that Rachel and not you called in that egress point change, I began to suspect her more than anyone else. Why? I knew you'd never break protocol by having her make that call. We also found her prints on your comms unit."

A dart of betrayal stabbed Victor's heart. What he'd thought was a comforting touch had sealed their fates. He took a deep breath to force away the pain of that confirmation. "Maggie told me later that Rachel suggested going toward the amphitheater."

"We suspect she was leading all of you into a trap. If it hadn't been for that shot you fired and keeping Maggie calm, neither of you would be alive today."

That didn't comfort Victor at all. He stared at his hamburger and tried to process that bit of news. After a deep, shaky breath, he took a bite as he thought about his next question. "What else did you find?"

"We began focusing on Rachel. Look." Miles leaned forward. "I've known Daniel Marina since we were both young bucks coming up through the ranks. I knew Rachel since she was a little girl. Or at least I thought I knew her. She had what we'd call the typical all-American childhood. Good at sports. Smart. Popular, thanks to her looks. That rape that happened after her freshman year in college nearly tore her family apart."

He paused. "You don't look surprised."

"I know all about that."

"Yeah, that's right. You should since you two were so involved. Boy, when she got engaged to you, there were a lot of sad guys out there. She had a rep in the Service. Most of the guys out there, even some of the old fogies, lusted after her."

Deborah's words about high school golden girls rushed back to Victor.

"We discovered how she got intimate with Makmoud Hidari when they were both in graduate school together. She'd already received her security clearances by that point, so that didn't raise any red flags. It wouldn't have anyway because he was a mere graduate student back then who swore no allegiance to Iran. Nothing abnormal turned up until spring of 2007. It took some doing, but we found an offshore bank account linked to her.

Like clockwork, on a quarterly basis, we found deposits of fifty thousand dollars."

"After she saw Makmoud," Victor muttered.

Miles cocked his head. "How do you know that?"

"I'll tell you later." Victor waved away his question. "This is more important."

"She never made any withdrawals."

"A frame job."

"You do have my curiosity up. Why don't—"

"Let's finish what you're saying first."

Miles hesitated as if he wanted to argue. Then he sighed. "Okay. We started looking at her finances more closely and found charges associated with travel at times shortly before those payments showed up. Places like the North Carolina mountains. Costa Rica. Nairobi. Myrtle Beach. That's when we began asking questions and digging deeper. It was hard because a few years had passed since everything started. After that long, hotel staff turns over. People's memories get foggy. We pieced together enough information to conclude that she was meeting Makmoud on a regular basis. Those meetings seemed to stop the fall of 2012."

"When we got engaged," Victor muttered.

"I guess that's correct." Miles nodded. He signaled the waitress for another beer. "Then nothing between them save for a few illicit texts we found as Makmoud instructed her in preparing for the kidnap attempt. We found those on a phone she'd kept hidden in the house."

Victor hung his head.

"Look. I know this is hard on you. It's been hard on me too. Like I told you, I'd known Rachel all her life. All I know is that the rape did more damage to her than anyone realized."

"Don't I know it." Victor swallowed hard. It was confession time. Slowly, over the course of another beer for the both of them, he explained everything, from how he'd found her journals to what he'd discovered about the woman everyone thought they'd known but hadn't really. Finally, he wound down.

Miles remained silent as if processing and linking up missing pieces of data.

Victor focused on the pedestrians strolling along the sidewalk on the other side of the railing from them. Their lives were so…normal, nothing like the way his now lay shattered like broken glass on the ground.

"Things start to make sense now." Miles's voice reached him as if from a distance.

"How so?"

"It's as you say. She was addicted to him. I could see where time with him was her reward. Maybe those deposits of fifty grand were there like you said, to frame her in case she decided to come clean."

The question now clawed at Victor as if it wanted to break free. He wasn't sure he was ready for the answer.

"Here's a question for you." He took a deep breath. "Where…where do you think her loyalties lay?"

"That's a tough one." Miles blotted his lips and laid his napkin on his plate. "From what you told me and how that jives with what I know, Rachel was an addict. I think she knew it, but she never did anything about it. Why? Well, we'll never know. The thing is, she was addicted to the one person who was most dangerous to her. It's clear from what we know about Makmoud Hidari—his past with Rachel and his current role—that he played upon her weaknesses to obtain information. When she got engaged to you, she cut things off with him. Wrong move."

Victor nodded and raised his hand for the check.

The waitress placed it in front him.

Miles waited until the she'd left them alone again. "We knew Susanna was alive."

Stunned at the revelation, Victor stared at him. "But…how?"

"One of Makmoud's guys walked away from the Hezbollah compound in Venezuela almost two years ago. He cited his reasons as being that he'd come to his senses when he saw the way Makmoud broke Susanna and turned her into his mistress. The CIA briefed the president on that. He ordered that everything possible be done to take out the compound."

The very thought of that made the bile rise in Victor's throat. He tossed his credit card onto the bill and clamped his jaw shut.

"We staged a raid to rescue her and take them down, but we were too late. They were gone, and we have no idea if Susanna is dead or alive. We only suspect they're somewhere deeper in the jungle. No way can we get to her because the Venezuelans raised a stink about the raid and claimed we invaded their sovereign territory."

"But...Rachel...and—"

"Her loyalties? I don't know. I honestly don't. She could have come to us when he kidnapped Susanna, could have told us everything. We'd have kept it on the down-low and for sure bagged Makmoud. Thing is, we probably could have saved Susanna as well. Sure, Rachel would have lost her career and most likely spent time in prison, but at least she'd be alive and her sister would be back with her family."

"I know." Victor's words were a mere whisper. Anguish filled him.

Miles sighed and checked his watch. "Look. It's getting late, and I don't know what else I can share. Sorry, but I'm on duty again at seven tomorrow morning."

"No, no. It's been enough. Thanks, Miles." Victor scribbled his signature on the bill, pocketed his wallet, and followed the Secret Service agent through the low gate and onto the sidewalk.

They paused at a black BMW sedan. "Hey, Vic, one more thing."

Victor met his gaze.

"Regarding having to ask for your resignation, I didn't want to do it. I really didn't, because I knew what a good agent you were and how you nearly died to save Maggie. She spoke up for you as well. But I had no choice. With Martin, I knew I had to since he supervised Rachel. But, well, the director asked for the resignation of everyone involved on the detail that night, especially you. His assumption was guilt before innocence. I had no choice."

"I understand. When everything happened, I pretty much realized I'd be resigning."

"It was good to see you." Miles held out his hand. "You want a ride back?"

Automatically, Victor shook it. "I think I'm going to walk. Lots to think about."

"Again, I'm sorry. I don't think I answered your questions. Keep in touch, okay? We'll be back at the end of July."

Victor nodded.

The walk to Maggie's house in one of the older sections in Raleigh passed in a blur with Victor lost in his thoughts. It was almost like his own reality had swung wildly on its axis, and now, he stood on the outside looking in at everyone else's normal, problem-free lives. Finally, he greeted the agents on duty at the end of Maggie's street. Within minutes, he stood inside the kitchen.

Maggie and Rod had gone out for the evening, so he left a note on their kitchen table stating that he'd headed to bed early because he wasn't feeling well.

That wasn't too far from the truth. His heart ached as Deborah's words came back to him.

"This is like an idol to you. You're so focused on this. So focused and convinced you'll get the entire story and put Rachel to rest in your mind."

Victor turned on the water in the shower as hot as he could stand it.

His mind wandered through his talks with Deborah, which became entangled with everything he'd learned from Rachel's journals and his talk with Miles. Rachel, the woman everyone had thought perfect, had more tarnish than many people her age, most of it by her own hand. Far from the loyal agent with the stellar career, she was an addict, a turncoat, and a liar. At least to him, she was. She'd played him to be the fool. And he'd gone right along with it. After all, anyone as perfect as Rachel wasn't capable of nefarious activities, right?

Wrong.

She'd used that trust, that understanding, to continue passing secrets to the enemy as a way to feed her addiction, which she in turn passed to Victor.

His chest heaved, and he braced himself against the wall and hung his head.

Again, Deborah's accurate observations stung.

"I saw it when you were talking about your relationship with Rachel. You were so focused on the physical side that you ignored other signals that things might not have been as you thought."

Now, as he remembered those nights together with Rachel, only grief echoed, not those brief moments of ecstasy.

"God, where did I go wrong?" Those whispered words surprised him. His fingers clawed the slick tile as water sluiced over him.

His conversation with Deborah on her birthday came flying back to him.

"You're enslaved to this. Even beyond the grave, Rachel has enslaved you. That's what scares me."

Now he saw it so clearly.

He'd made Rachel an idol, one that shattered in the light of the information he now had as surely as if he'd taken a bat to a porcelain statue.

Finally, Victor turned off the taps, dried, and dressed. He dragged himself into the bedroom and stretched out on his back with his hands laced behind his head.

"Who were you really, Rach? Who were you?" A tear trickled down his cheek and into his ear. "Were you really loyal to the Service and your country, or to Makmoud?"

Suddenly, it dawned on him with clarity what Deborah had seen when they'd talked.

He'd never know the truth.

Never.

The grief nearly drowned him.

"Oh, God!" He rolled onto his stomach as his tears wet the pillow.

Let it go.

The voice echoed in his soul, quiet but demanding attention over his agony.

I love you, My child. Let this go to Me. Let Me fill your heart.

"I can't. I need to know."

Once more, Deborah's worries resounded in his ears.

"What if all you're left with are more questions? Until what? You ask Makmoud himself before he kills you?"

He'd promised her he'd let it go no matter what he found on his trip. Deborah had seen through his little lie.

Suddenly, he knew what she'd seen, that his focus on Rachel had consumed him to the point where others entrapped by his flaming desire would get burned—including the woman who he now realized he wanted to marry.

Unless...

"Can You take this from me?" Anguish laced his words as he asked them into sheets damp with tears. "God, can You take this from me and throw it away? I want to be there for Deb and the kids and the team. All the way there. Can You?"

That still, quiet voice didn't answer, but a peace began seeping through him.

Victor drew in a shaky breath.

Slowly, he slid out of bed and onto his knees.

"God, I see now how Deb was right." His words remained low, trembling. "I see now what she so clearly saw, how this thing with Rachel consumed me over You. And how, through my life, I let my focus reside on other things rather than You. Forgive me. Fill me, Jesus, because I feel so empty now."

The peace remained, and a profound weariness arrived, so much so that he barely had the strength to climb into bed. Maybe God had heard his plea.

33

"Lord, I don't know what to do," Deborah murmured as she closed her Bible. "About Anna. About Vic. I'm plain out of answers, and I need Your wisdom on this."

For a moment, she absentmindedly traced the gold lettering on the cover with her index finger. Deborah rose and carried her coffee mug to the sink. Through the window overlooking the terrace, she noted how Liza had seated all four children at the table for that morning's homeschooling session.

At the head of the table, Anna slouched with the novel she was supposed to read for a book report propped open in front of her. She turned a page, but Deborah noticed the way her gaze flicked toward her sisters. At the other end of the wrought iron table, DJ had a textbook open and scribbled notes. Liza sat between Gracie and Marie with another book. She turned a page and read something to her two youngest nieces. In front of them, five jars sat on the table, each containing a roach, a spider, a centipede, a scorpion, or a beetle.

Deborah shuddered.

Marie climbed onto her knees and leaned forward as she asked a question. She reached for the jar with the scorpion.

Her mother cringed.

"Looking at my handiwork?" Butch's voice made Deborah whirl around.

"You scared me!"

"Sorry." He grinned and hooked his thumbs over his belt. "It's not like I was in stealth mode. Matter of fact, I've been watching you for a few minutes."

Heat rushed to her cheeks. Had he heard her prayer?

"Hey, no problem with the bugs. The outdoors is full of them. And I'm glad your girls aren't afraid of them." He opened the shiny stainless steel refrigerator door.

"Gracie and Marie aren't. Anna takes more after me. You helped them with that?"

"Liza and me. I don't mind creepy crawlies, and neither does she, it seems."

"She's the biologist, not me."

He chuckled and pulled out a milk carton.

She groaned as he drank directly from it. "What is it with you guys?"

"Huh? It's got my name on it. See?" He held it up so she could see his name scrawled in black permanent marker. "Milk carton rights. If the name's on it, then the owner gets to drink straight from it."

A smile finally crossed her lips. "Derek would do that, especially when I'd go out of town."

Then the joy of the early morning phone call she'd received from Victor came flooding back to her. "Oh, I've got some news."

"You and Vic are engaged?" He cocked an eyebrow.

"No. I talked to him really early this morning. He…" The tears that sprang to her eyes surprised her. "He accepted Jesus as his Savior last night."

"Well, I'll be." Butch's eyes crinkled at the corners when he smiled. "It's about time he did. I've been in prayer for him for years."

"And he asked a favor of me. Can you take a box into town and FedEx it for me?"

"Sure. I'm headed that way in a few to pick up an old tractor Victor bought at a good price."

"When?"

"'Bout twenty minutes or so. As soon as I can get the trailer hooked up."

"That'd be perfect. Swing by the studio, and I'll have it ready."

"That works." Butch stepped toward the mudroom. He turned. "And Deb?"

"Yeah?"

"Hang in there with Anna." He leaned against the archway. "She's had a lot of changes lately. And probably a lot of new feelings to deal with. Not to mention hormones."

"Butch…"

"Hey, I had a sister. I know it can be hard. She'll come around. Just keep that in mind."

Stunned, she nodded. Deborah followed him into the chilly morning air. The sun's gentle rays warmed her face and the bare skin on her arms. She paused at the table. "How's everyone doing?"

Anna met her gaze for a moment, then focused on her book. She didn't say anything.

Gracie hopped up. "Mommy! Uncle Butch helped us catch a spider and a scorpion!"

"And I got the beetle," Marie chimed in.

"Guess who got stuck with the roach and centipede." Liza grinned. A small glimmer had returned to her sister's eyes.

Deborah smiled. "What are you talking about today?"

"Bugs!" Gracie piped up.

Liza laughed. "The difference between arachnids, insects, and other creepy crawlies."

"Mom, can I go with Uncle Butch to get the tractor?" DJ gazed at where Butch pulled his pickup truck to the trailer parked beside the Tool Barn.

Shadow Box's mechanic leaned down and secured the ball on the hitch.

"How about finish your history? When he gets back and after lunch, maybe he'll let you work on it with him." Deborah cast a glance at Anna.

Her daughter scowled and seemed to focus all of her effort on avoiding eye contact. Her hands gripped the edges of the book so tightly that her knuckles turned white.

Deborah bit back her sigh. "Well, everyone have fun. I'll be back in a few minutes."

With that, she turned and resumed her path toward the studio. When she arrived at the door, only stillness greeted her. She stepped inside. Nothing moved. She missed seeing Victor sitting at the worktable with the furrow in his brow that she'd come to associate with his concentration. Yearning to see him and hold him suddenly filled her.

Deborah surveyed the worktable. It had drawers beneath the flat surface that held only a computer monitor and docking station for his laptop. Below those were open bookshelves where he stored what seemed to be manuals associated with his time in the Army and the Secret Service. Beside those were books on photography. Her gaze landed on the metal coils of composition books.

Deborah crouched and pulled out the one on the far end. 2012.

She'd found Rachel's journals.

She ran her fingers down the front cover as she realized she held in her hands the very intimate writing of someone who even from the grave had held sway over the man Deborah loved.

But no longer, it seemed. No longer.

"Thank You, Lord, for saving Vic," she whispered into the quiet air. Any temptation she had to read them for herself disappeared.

She rose. Using the information she'd found on her phone when she'd risen that morning, she located the box and needed supplies to send the package to Victor's Secret Service contact. Scrawling Miles's contact information on the shipping label she found in a drawer gave her a great amount of satisfaction.

A knock on the door made her glance up.

Butch stood there, his sunglasses propped on his bald head, keys dangling from his hand. "Hey. You got it ready?"

She tapped it with her foot. "Right here. Be careful, it's...heavy," she added when he picked it up like it was a box of tissues and put it on his shoulder.

"Thanks. I'll be back in about an hour and a half. I've got Shelly on the cameras. Skylar's my deputy if you need anything. He's in the Men's Building on the computer."

"All right." Deborah watched as he strolled toward his pickup truck. She turned back to put away the tape and scissors. As she shut the drawer, her eye fell on a vertical file holder beside the monitor. She froze as she stared at the names on the tabs. Deborah Fields. Liza Murphy.

After the briefest of hesitations, Deborah reached for them. When she opened the one with her name, she realized it was the information TL must have sent to Victor when he'd been dispatched to rescue her and the kids. Once more, the "None" typed for siblings bothered her. Was it indeed a typo? If not, who could have changed that? She shut that one and turned to the other.

Liza's folder contained the information Gary had sent Victor during the frantic search for her sister.

For a moment, she considered her options. In her e-mail account, she also had the file TL had sent her about Murdock, but she hadn't looked at it yet due to her fight with Anna. Maybe the file, combined with what she now held, would yield some answers. With folders in hand, she headed toward the house.

Once she'd retrieved a laptop from Shelly, she took it into the den and kicked off her cowboy boots before settling on a chair at the game table. As she waited for it to power up, she surveyed the information in her folder once more.

The "None" almost mocked her, like she was missing something critical in that one word.

Anger tightened her gut.

No matter what, she'd get to the bottom of this mystery before the end of the day.

Makmoud rested against a rock adjacent to the exit to the slot canyon through which his prey had to ride on their return to the ranch. He fingered the tiny firecrackers that would begin the afternoon's festivities. As he did so, his gaze slid toward two piles of brush farther toward the entrance.

Only the piles weren't natural.

They lived and breathed since they contained two of his comrades who he'd selected for this part of the takedown. Neither moved.

Perfect.

Makmoud adjusted the boom microphone in front of his lips. In a low voice barely audible over the stream burbling on the other side of the path, he murmured, "Any sign of them?"

"Nothing," replied the observer he'd posted just outside the canyon's entrance.

"Keep me—"

"Wait!" His word blared through the earpiece. "I hear voices." A sharp intake of breath followed. "I see them. Perhaps thirty seconds until they reach the entrance."

He went silent.

Makmoud withdrew so he crouched completely hidden behind the rocks. Using a periscope, he monitored the entrance.

The voices and snort of horses reached him before he saw them.

Fiona laughed. Then came a girl's giggle.

The group came into view.

Fiona led, her rifle slung over her shoulder. Anna was next.

Three taps from the observer indicated that someone else had entered. Then came four taps.

Makmoud flicked the lighter until a small flame appeared. He waited a few more dangerous seconds.

Fiona came closer.

He touched flame to wick. With an easy lob, he tossed the firecrackers so they landed at the feet of Fiona's horse.

They popped and crackled in small puffs of light and smoke.

Fiona's horse whinnied and reared up on its hind legs.

Fiona tumbled from the saddle. She landed almost head first on the ground. The sound of a bone snapping reached him.

Anna screamed. She jerked the reins.

Makmoud's two comrades jumped up.

Her horse reared, its front legs windmilling as it panicked. She clung to the saddle and struggled to keep the horse under control.

One of his men snagged Liza's arm and dragged her from the saddle. She cried out. He jerked to the side, and they rolled into the stream. The horse's hooves landed where they'd crashed to the ground.

"Red Alert! Red Alert! Argh!" From his saddle, Skylar spasmed. He fell headlong from his mount, the wires from the Taser Makmoud's observer held still impaled in his clothing.

Makmoud dashed toward Anna. He grabbed the bridle of her horse. In one swift motion, he yanked the teenager from the saddle.

Anna fell to her knees.

Before she could react, he aimed his pistol at her head. "No one move. Rasheed, take their guns and radios. Put them against that wall."

He jerked his head toward the wall of the narrow canyon across from the stream.

Rasheed, who held Liza, shoved her to the ground.

Makmoud pulled Anna to her feet. She stumbled as he pushed her against the red rock. "Stay there. Rasheed, guard them."

"Wha—what hit me?" Skylar moaned and climbed onto his hands and knees. He shook his head as if trying to clear it.

Musa shoved him with his foot.

He collapsed, and Musa dragged him to the other two.

Makmoud approached Fiona.

She lay curled on her side and cradled her broken arm. A whimper escaped her.

"Get up." Makmoud lightly kicked her.

"Hey!" She cussed at him.

"Pity you never learned to fall from a horse." Makmoud bent and removed her headset, rifle, and pistol. He tossed them into the stream. "Now get up and sit over there with the others."

He dragged her to the group. "Ali, tie them up and hood them all except for Anna."

Ali went to work. Using cable ties, he lashed their wrists together. Rasheed pulled hoods over them.

Makmoud nodded in satisfaction as Ali shoved Skylar onto the back of his horse.

Rasheed knelt in front of Fiona and grabbed her injured arm.

"Don't touch me!" Fiona kicked him.

He slapped her.

She spat on him.

"Bind her wrists loosely," Makmoud instructed. He grabbed Anna and secured her hands.

She yelped and pulled away with such force that she fell onto her side. Eyes wide with fear, she tried to crawl away.

Makmoud easily snagged her and hauled her to her feet.

She trembled beneath his hand.

"I will not hurt you, Anna." He brushed the strands of blond hair that had fallen from her ponytail away from her face.

She shook her head. Her chest heaved with panicked sobs.

"I will not so long as you obey me. Now come with me." He lifted her to her feet.

Anna stumbled with him to where Ali held her horse. She stopped. "I—I can't."

"Can't what?"

"Mount with my hands tied." Her voice trembled.

"I think you can." Makmoud helped her into the saddle. With almost effortless grace, he swung up behind her. He took the reins and steadied the uneasy animal. One glance behind him assured him that his men had done the same, with their hostages laid out across the saddles.

With a satisfied smile, he faced forward. Into Anna's ear, he murmured, "I will not hurt you, but do not think that you can throw me. I have many more years of experience on a horse than you, and if you even try, you will regret it. Am I clear?"

"Y—yes." The girl shook from fear.

"Good." He nudged the horse, and it moved forward at a walk. As they began the trek to the ranch, he changed frequencies on his radio. "Jibril."

"I am here, brother."

"I have the packages. Move out."

"Will do."

Satisfaction filled him. Makmoud took a deep breath and relaxed. The next step of the takedown began.

The key lay in her profile form. That and the way the mysterious man she assumed to be Makmoud Hidari had treated Liza with unnecessary kindness.

As the afternoon burned on, Deborah surveyed the files spread on the top of the game table. She sat cross-legged and rubbed her hands across the denim of her jeans.

If only she could have accessed Makmoud's file.

TL had told her she wasn't cleared for it. Period.

Why would Makmoud have looked out for her sister? From her conversations with Victor and the information she'd found in Liza's file, it didn't seem like he was the kind of guy who protected those who couldn't protect themselves. Unless…

Unless what?

Deborah sighed.

I'm so close! I can feel it.

Maybe a break would help. She rose and stretched. As she did so, her gaze drifted to the french doors opening onto the patio and the backyard beyond. Outside, Gracie and Marie played freeze tag with Sana, Diana, and Suleiman. In the open bay of the Tool Barn, DJ leaned over the open hood of the decrepit tractor Butch had brought to the ranch on the trailer. His mentor pointed to something related to the engine.

Deborah fixed herself some hot tea and resumed her cross-legged position. She set her file on her lap and closed her eyes. As she rubbed her temples, that terrible night almost two months before came rushing back to her. She remembered shivering as she headed to the studio for the first time. Her concern for Liza echoed in her ears. Then came Victor's reply. While she didn't remember the exact words he spoke, she recalled something else.

His confusion.

Victor had truly not known she had a sister.

Deborah's eyes flew open.

"That has got to be the key," she muttered as she flipped to her contact form again. Maybe TL could help. She reached for the phone and dialed his number.

"TL Jones."

"TL, it's Deborah."

"Hey there! I was just getting ready to head home. How's it going? Did that file I sent you help?"

"I'm not sure. Um, I do have a question."

"Fire away."

"I'm looking at the profile form Victor Chavez has about me. For siblings, the box says 'None.'"

"Huh?"

Her hand tightened on the phone. "Nothing. It doesn't have Liza's name in it."

"Let me pull up my copy." Tapping reached her, followed by an audible intake of breath. "Mine has her name there. That's strange."

"I don't understand." For a brief, insane moment, she wondered if TL were Murdock. No. He'd been on the other end of the radio when Nasser had breathed his last. All too well she remembered his anguish when he'd called her the December before.

"You're not the only one. I personally vetted that form. I would have never changed it."

"I know. But didn't you check it before you sent it to Vic?"

"I didn't send it directly to him."

"What?" Deborah's free hand balled into a fist.

"I sent it to his handler."

"Gary, right?" Deborah shifted.

"Yeah. Gary Walton. He's our go-to guy when it comes to counterterrorism. I sent it to him."

Suddenly, it dawned on her. She shivered. "TL, do you think..."

Her e-mail pinged.

TL said, "I just sent you what I sent him."

She opened the file, verifying his claim. A shiver coursed down her spine. "Do you think he could've changed it?"

"Possibly. Very possibly." Tension clipped his words. "Let me do some checking. Stay at this number, okay?"

"I will." Deborah hung up and laid the phone next to her computer. The minutes ticked by as she waited for his call. When it finally rang, she snatched it up. "What did you find?"

"No one knows where Gary is."

"What do you mean?" Her voice rose slightly.

"I talked with his admin assistant, and she said Gary called in about having to leave town suddenly for a case. Except he didn't get her to make his flight reservations like he normally does. And when I called his wife, she reported that Gary told her he had to go away on a case. Neither knows where he went."

"I think he was the one who changed the file." There. She'd said it. Aired her suspicions regarding the man Victor trusted and viewed as his best friend.

"It at least warrants some questioning. I've called him and left a message. Told him to call me ASAP. Is Victor there?"

"No. He's...he's flying back from North Carolina and should be getting in about..." Her eyes flew to the clock on the computer. "About now."

"Call him and leave a message, okay? Tell him to call me ASAP when he gets it. Even before he calls you. Does Gary know where you guys are?"

"No. Vic said something about compartmentalization."

"Good. Victor definitely needs to call me. If you're right, we've finally busted the Murdock case wide open. Summarize what you found and send it to me. I'll take this to my boss, and we might just have enough to drag Gary's butt in for questioning."

"Will do." Deborah closed her eyes. She swallowed hard and dialed Victor's number. As she expected, it went straight to voice mail. "Vic, it's Deb. You need to call TL Jones even before me, okay? It's about the Murdock case. We had a break in it. Here's his number."

She recited the number she'd committed to memory long ago. "Call him even before you call me. And...I love you. See you soon."

She set the phone aside and began typing her summary.

Her screen went black.

The light over the table flickered and died.

"Huh?"

The klaxon bleeped and went silent.

Deborah jumped to her feet as the back door banged open.

"Red Alert!" Butch's voice bellowed over the shriek of the alarm.

"What?" Deborah spun around as he appeared in the doorway.

"We've been blown!"

"EMP!" Shelly's cry reached her.

Deborah yanked on her cowboy boots. "I—I don't understand."

Glass shattered.

She bolted into the great room just in time to see Butch yanking out several MP-5 guns.

He slammed magazines into them. "Shelly, here."

"Electromagnetic pulse." Shelly caught the gun Butch tossed her way. "It took down the cameras, alarm, anything electrical."

"Deb, go." Butch slung two over his shoulders and cradled the other one.

She hesitated.

"Go! Get Gracie."

She fled out the door into the warm afternoon.

Sana darted ahead of them. Diana had a crying Marie in her arms. Deborah snatched Gracie off her feet and tore after her with all of her might.

From somewhere behind her, van doors screeched.

Run, she told herself. *Don't be like Lot's wife. Run!*

Pops echoed.

Gracie's cries screamed in her ear.

Run!

More gunfire, this from closer behind her, sounded like firecrackers.

Her arms began aching as her feet stumbled onto the grate. She angled toward the back of the box canyon.

Sana had already scrambled the fifty feet upward to the lip of the canyon. DJ was on his way up with Marie close behind. Diana held at the ready position the sidearm Victor had required all team members to carry.

Gracie thrashed, catching her mother on the knee with her foot.

Deborah moaned and let her go as she tumbled to the ground. Pain slashed through her right knee as it came into hard contact with a rock. "Go, Gracie. I'm right behind you."

She climbed to her feet and tried to take a step. Her knee gave way.

Something cracked over her head.

A bullet.

Her heart caught.

A loud rumble shook the ground beneath her.

"Deb?" Mighty arms grabbed her and lifted her to her feet.

Butch.

"I'm good." Deborah winced as the pain surged in her knee.

"Get going. We've got your six. Go!"

Deborah staggered to where Suleiman held a harness for her. She jumped into it. She ducked as bullets chipped rock near her head. Shards sprayed her face. She flinched.

"Get going," Suleiman urged her.

She found her first handhold. Her knee protested and threatened to give way.

Focus. Handhold. Foothold. Ascender. Go! Go!

She worked her way upward as if in automated motion. Her knee screamed.

Strong hands grasped her.

Pulled.

She rolled onto firm ground.

Sana unhooked her from the rope. "Good job. Get going."

317

Deborah pushed herself to her feet. She limped the quarter mile to the shed where they kept the escape Suburban. By the time she reached it, she could barely stand. She leaned against the wall with all of her weight on her good leg. Marie ran over and clung to her.

Anna. Liza. The realization of their absence slammed into her.

"Anna…"

"They got them. The Red Alert was from Skylar." Diana clipped her words. "Shelly, help me get these doors open."

Deborah's heart dropped. Her daughter and sister had—

"Everyone in!" Butch's command jolted Deborah. Face dusty and gun in his hands, he skidded to a halt with Suleiman next to him. "We may have slowed them down, but that doesn't mean we've stopped them. Get in!"

Suleiman, Sana, and DJ scrambled into the very back. Deborah, Shelly, Gracie, and Marie piled into the backseat.

Butch jumped into the driver's seat and cranked the engine. He turned to Diana, who now rode shotgun with a rifle across her knees. "Diana, get that phone on and call Vic. Now."

34

Gary paced the sidewalk outside of the terminal at the Flagstaff Pulliam Airport. A chilly breeze blew from the nearby mountains and made him stuff the fedora on his head down a little tighter. He stopped and peered at the front entrance.

"Where are you?" he muttered so low that no one could hear him.

A security guard approached him. Her hand rested on the butt of her pistol. "Sir, may I help you?"

Gary pulled out his cred pack and flashed it. "I'm waiting on a contact to arrive."

The guard's gaze flicked downward to where Gary's sidearm rested. She studied the credentials, then Gary's face. "Official business?"

"You got it, ma'am."

Liar.

"Carry on, then." She walked away.

Gary released a slow breath. That was close. He turned away from the guard as he unzipped his leather jacket enough to slip his hand inside. His fingers brushed the tools of his trade for that day: a Taser, cable ties, a gag, and a rolled-up burlap bag. If the guard had asked to search him…He tried not to think of the consequences.

The work phone on his hip buzzed. So did his personal phone.

Gary jumped as if stung by a cattle prod.

He checked the numbers.

TL Jones.

Mary too.

He let both roll to voicemail. For good measure, he powered them down so no one could track him to Flagstaff.

A tall, slender man strolled from the terminal lobby.

Vic.

As if confirming his target, the buzzing began low in his head.

Vic lifted his cell phone to his ear. His yawn shifted to a frown as he listened to something, most likely voice mail.

"Vic," Gary called.

His best friend lowered it. "Gary, hey. What brings you here?"

Gary joined him. "Important stuff. Walk with me to your car?"

"Of course. I need to get back anyway. Got in later than I thought, you know?"

"I do. C'mon." Gary took his arm and led him across the street and toward the parking lot where he'd found Vic's Commander earlier that afternoon.

"What's the big deal?"

"A break in Liza's case."

"Really?" Vic glanced at him. "What happened? Did they find out who phoned in that tip?"

"They found the identities of the guys who stayed at the safe house." Gary slowed as they approached the Commander. He unzipped his jacket a little. "Dang, it's getting warm out here."

"Wait. What's really going on?"

"I'm not following."

Vic's eyes narrowed. "I never told you where we were."

"I know. TL told me."

Vic lowered his gaze as he pulled out his keys.

Gary's hand snaked into his jacket and grabbed the Taser.

"And I never told—"

Gary jabbed the Taser into his friend's side.

Vic's body stiffened as thousands of volts surged through it.

Gary released the trigger.

With a low moan, Vic began collapsing.

Gary crowded him against the driver's door as if they were having a heart-to-heart conversation. He lifted the keys from his paralyzed hand. "Sorry, bro. I had to do it."

He released the locks and fumbled for the handle. Once he had the back door open, he heaved Vic onto the floor. "I had to do it."

Noises came from his friend.

Gary secured his hands behind him, gagged him, and yanked the burlap bag over his head. "You may not understand, but I had to."

Once he shut the door, he climbed into the Commander and started it. On the secret phone, Gary pulled up the text containing the address that Makmoud had sent him.

Perfect.

With the SUV in gear, he eased through the parking lot and onto the access road. He picked up speed and headed toward the ranch.

"Get them inside." Makmoud slid from the horse.

His comrades dumped Liza, Skylar, and Fiona onto the ground. Once they cut the ties on their ankles, they hauled them upright, pushed them onto the terrace, and shoved them into the house.

"Anna, come." Makmoud helped the teenager from the saddle. With his hand gripping her arm, he walked her inside.

In the great room, his comrades had secured Skylar and Liza to chairs.

Fiona squirmed against Ali's grasp. "Stop! Can't you tell I'm hurt?"

"And you'll only hurt yourself further if you keep resisting," Makmoud dragged over a captain's chair. "Secure her to that. Bind her broken arm loosely."

Rasheed wound rope around Fiona's uninjured wrist, ankles, and chest, thoroughly securing her to the wood. He looped a length around her injured arm near the elbow.

She spat at him.

He laughed before slapping her hard across the face.

Anna cringed and backed against Makmoud as if he could protect her from Fiona's angst. Beneath his fingers, she began trembling.

"Sit there." Makmoud shoved her toward Ali, who forced her onto a chair next to Fiona.

"Makmoud." Jibril's voice made him turn. His brother stood in the open doorway leading onto the terrace. In Farsi, he continued, "I need to speak with you."

Makmoud stepped into the fading afternoon light. "What is it?"

Jibril scrubbed his face with a wet rag to remove some of the dust coating it. When he lowered his hands, tears streamed from his eyes as they flushed the particles away. "They got away."

He coughed and cleared his throat. His deep voice had a gravelly scratch to it as he continued, "They had a trench dug. A big one with a grate over it that was camouflaged. They blew it with charges and almost took us down. We couldn't cross it in time, and they escaped up the wall."

"How?"

"They probably had footholds and handholds dug out." Jibril grimaced as he brushed his clothing. Dust rose from it in a fine cloud.

"Interesting." Makmoud rubbed his chin.

"We were so close!"

"It's of no matter."

"But—"

"It's of no matter, my brother." Makmoud gestured toward the great room. "We have enough hostages to have an advantage. Come with me."

Jibril followed him through the mudroom and into the great room.

"I see." The tautness in his shoulders relaxed.

Makmoud surveyed the semicircle of four hostages.

Liza and Anna kept their gazes to the floor.

Skylar focused on him. His expression conveyed boredom, as if he were relaxing in a lounge rather than tied to a chair.

Makmoud wouldn't get anything from the former CIA agent, not without a lot of work, which would take too much time.

"It seems as if your friends had the foresight to escape." Makmoud chuckled and paced in front of them. "Yet they left the four of you behind."

"At least they're gone." Fiona's voice reached him.

Makmoud approached her. "Yes, they are. Pity for you. Where did they go, Fiona?"

She looked away.

"I'd like to know where they went. I know you had a contingency plan in place." He stopped in front of her. "Now where did they go?"

She clamped her jaw shut.

Makmoud grabbed her forearm—right at the break.

Fiona screamed.

Beneath his fingers, the broken bones scraped against one another. "Stop!"

"Where did they go?" He tightened his grip.

"I. Don't. Know." Tears ran down her face as she bit off those words. Tension riddled her body.

"Tell me." He shifted his hand.

"No!" Another howl emanated from her. She cussed at him, a round of Italian, Spanish, Arabic, and English so vile that even his men looked embarrassed.

They'd get nothing from her.

He released her.

Fiona moaned, and her head hung forward. Her whole body shook, making her chair scrape against the hardwood.

The sound of an engine reached them through the open windows and doors.

"A Jeep comes. A white Commander," one of the guards reported.

"Gary. Wave him to the back." Makmoud strode through the mudroom and onto the terrace.

Gary climbed from the SUV, the yellowing rays of the sun hitting his graying blond hair. He opened the back door and hauled Victor to his feet.

The Shadow Box leader struggled. Sounds emanated from him.

Gary pushed him against the side of the vehicle. "Stop struggling, bro. Things will go much better if you do."

Victor ignored him.

Gary kicked the back of his knees.

With a groan, Victor collapsed.

"Excellent work, Gary. Jibril, take him inside." He nodded to his brother, who grabbed Victor's arm.

"I'm done with this." Gary remained by the driver's door. "I took a huge risk in coming here."

"I know you did. And now you get to see the fruits of your labor." Makmoud smiled and gestured toward the house. "Come with us."

"I can't. I've got to get back, and—"

"You will come with us, Murdock." The smile dropped away. Makmoud focused on him and took a step closer.

He wilted under his intense gaze. "I…"

"You have no choice. Come with me, if you will." Makmoud stepped aside and gestured for his mole to precede him up the steps, onto the terrace, and into the house.

His demeanor strangely calm, Victor now stood in front of the group with the hood still on his head. On either side, Rasheed and Musa kept their rifles trained on him. Jibril stood slightly behind him.

Makmoud ripped the hood from the man's head and pulled off his gag.

"Vic!" Liza's gasp said it all.

Makmoud smirked. "Yes, I have Shadow Box's fearless leader now. Jibril, search him."

His brother patted him down. "He has only this."

He handed him a cell phone.

"Tie him to the chair, if you will." Makmoud toggled it on.

Jibril cut the ties holding his hands.

Victor whipped around and jumped him. He landed a punch that made Jibril grunt.

Musa leaped forward. He grabbed him in a half nelson choke hold and forced him to his knees. Victor bucked, throwing him off balance. Rasheed joined the fray. He popped him across the face with the butt of his rifle.

Stunned, Victor collapsed to the floor.

Musa grabbed him again. He hauled him to his knees and twisted his arm behind his back so that any movement made Victor moan in pain. The leader's chest heaved. Blood streaked his cheek from the cut the rifle had opened.

Makmoud studied the keypad that had appeared. "What kind of wealth hides behind the code? What is it, Victor?"

Victor clamped his mouth shut.

"I see that you will be less than cooperative. That Special Forces training kicks in, no? You see, Victor, with enough time, I can break anyone." Makmoud stared down Gary.

The FBI agent lowered his gaze.

"But I have only minutes, not weeks like I did with your *best* friend. And that means I must take more radical measures."

"I'm not going to tell you anything." Victor growled those words between groans of pain.

"Oh, I know you won't. And neither will your comrades. Even Fiona with her broken arm." He chuckled as Fiona lifted her tear-stained face. "Liza and Anna? They know nothing. But..."

He stepped to Anna and rested his hand on her head. "That doesn't mean they can't help persuade you."

His gaze remained on Shadow Box's leader.

Anna whimpered.

Victor tensed against Musa, who jerked on his arm. Victor sank lower to ease the pain.

Perfect.

Makmoud sifted some strands of her hair through his fingers. "She is a beautiful girl, is she not? She looks very much like her mother."

He lifted her chin.

A tear seeped from the corner of her eye and tricked down her dusty cheek.

"Anna, did you know that in some cultures, you would already be married with a child or perhaps two?"

Her mouth opened, but no sound came out.

"What's not to stop me or one of my men from doing taking you as a wife?" He skimmed his fingers down her cheek, then her neck. "Unless you tell me the code, Victor."

A strangled cry escaped Anna.

With one deft motion of his wrist, Makmoud grabbed the neck of her T-shirt and ripped it.

Anna began sobbing.

"No!" That one word thundered from Victor.

"No? Why should I stop?" Makmoud snagged the torn fabric.

"Don't hurt her." Victor's words came out low, threatening.

"Then tell me the code."

Musa twisted Victor's arm again. He grunted.

"Four. One. Eight. Four." He panted out each word.

Makmoud keyed it in, and the home screen popped up. He chuckled. "I knew you had a soft spot for her. You love her like a daughter, yes?" He scrolled through the contacts. "I see Gary's name and those of your team. Ah, and one that says Emergency SUV. I imagine that is the vehicle the rest of your team used to escape."

He pulled up the number, then dialed. He smiled. "We'll see now, won't we?"

★ ★ ★

Deborah grabbed Gracie and Marie to keep them from getting thrown into the air as the Suburban jounced over the unpaved road on the northern part of the Chavez land.

"He doesn't answer," Diana reported. Her voice quavered a little. She clutched the handhold above her as the SUV dove into a huge rut.

Butch muttered as he yanked the steering wheel to avoid a pothole. "This isn't good."

Marie clung to her mother and sobbed. Gracie too. Deborah risked a glance in the rear view mirror.

His face tinged red from the dry soil, DJ huddled against Sana as she held on to him to keep him from flying into the cargo area.

Shelly finally hooked her belt. "Slow down, will you?"

"Sorry, Shelly. No can do." Butch bit off his words.

With a final bounce that rattled Deborah's teeth, they slid onto State Road 64 and sped away.

"Where are we going?"

"The rez. Vic's daddy's family has—"

The phone in Diana's hand began chiming the theme from "Raiders of Lost Ark."

"Speak of the devil…" Butch grabbed it from her and pulled to the shoulder of the road. "Vic, hey— Oh? All right."

He thumbed it and set it on the console.

"I assume this is the rest of Shadow Box, yes?" A man's voice filled the small space. "With Deborah Fields and her children nonetheless."

Goose bumps popped up along Deborah's arms. She shivered and shrank down as if the man stood outside the vehicle.

"With whom am I speaking?" The man's lightly accented English blared from the speaker.

"Call me Death," Butch growled.

"Ah, Butch Addison, eh? Your voice cannot be that of my turncoat brother, and I have the other two Shadow Box men with me. You listen to me. I have Fiona, Victor, Skylar, Anna, and Liza as hostages."

"I want to hear from them."

"Perhaps you will. My demand is simple. You are to be at the ranch by four in the morning tomorrow. All of you. And if not?"

Suddenly, the sound of Anna's tears echoed in the quiet space.

Deborah's heart hammered. "No, please—"

Butch stuck out his hand and shook his head.

"So Deborah Fields is indeed there." The smirk radiated from Makmoud's voice. "Anna almost found out what it is like to know a man."

Deborah's hand shot to her mouth in a desperate bid to tamp down her moan. She squeezed her eyes closed.

"If you want to keep your daughter safe, Deborah Fields, then you and your other children will be here along with Shadow Box. Good day now."

The line went dead.

Butch pulled onto the road. The engine roared as they tore down the highway.

Tears poured down Deborah's face. Her breath came in short gasps.

Before her eyes, images of Anna sprang up. Terrible images of—

"Oh, God, no…"

Her grip tightened on her two youngest daughters.

She trembled. She couldn't get enough air. Lightheadedness made her world spin.

Gracie's and Marie's cries echoed in her ears. Did she hear Anna's mixed among them?

The SUV slowed.

Outside the windows, the shacks and trailers of a small town appeared amidst sagebrush and tumbleweeds.

Butch turned in to a gas station. "Shelly, Diana, you two take the girls to the restroom. DJ, you and Suleiman go and grab us something for the road and top us off. Okay?"

His words echoed in Deborah's ears as if she'd fallen into a well.

Slowly, the team climbed from the Suburban. Diana took Gracie's hand, and Shelly took Marie's. DJ scrambled after Sana and Suleiman, who snagged the credit card Butch tossed in his direction.

Deborah wept. She leaned forward and put her arms on her knees as sobs wracked her.

"Hey, Deb." A strong hand rested on her shoulder.

She raised her face. "Butch, we…we have to go back. Let me go—"

"Not going to happen, all right?"

"But Makmoud—"

"Just…listen, okay? Can you take a deep breath?"

"I—I—"

"Deb, please."

She sucked in a deep breath, held it, and did another one. Her heart slowed from its rocket pace.

Butch fixed her in his dark gaze. "Listen to me. When we received the mission, we were charged with keeping you and your family safe. You were our primary objective. And that's what we're going to do. We're taking you to a house Vic's extended family has on the Navajo reservation that's like a getaway place for them. It's secure enough until we can get the FBI in to take you to safety."

"But Anna and Liza—"

"Right now, your safety and that of the three children with you are our primary objectives."

Her heart broke, and more tears began streaming down her face. Nausea rose inside of her, and she tasted bile. She clamped her hands over her mouth.

His grip on her shoulder tightened. "We're not going to leave this alone. I can promise you on that. Not only do they have your oldest and your sister, but they've got comrades of ours. And we leave no man behind." A wicked grin crossed his face and faded. "We're going to go in and get them, but we need to regroup and get some protection on you so we can. So no more talk about giving yourself up."

"I—"

"It's not going to happen." Butch peered through the windshield.

Deborah followed his gaze. Diana had come outside from the restrooms with Marie's hand in hers.

Marie's wails reached her even over the murmur of the air conditioning. The child raised her arms toward Diana.

The team's doctor picked her up and held her tightly as she rocked her.

Butch returned his somber gaze to Deborah. "Remember that your kids are feeding off your emotions. If you panic, they'll panic. Got it?"

She nodded.

"Let's get you to relative safety and call the feds. Then Suleiman, Diana, Sana, Shelly, and I have some planning to do."

She sniffled and took several more deep breaths in an effort to reign in her emotions. "O—Okay."

He smiled and gently chucked her under the chin. "That's my girl. And remember one thing."

"What...what's that?"

"God's got this under control. This didn't surprise Him, even if it did us. Got it?"

"I—I think so."

He reached out, took her hand, and briefly squeezed it. He glanced up as the others returned.

"We'll get them back." Butch's voice rang with steely determination. "That much, I can promise."

35

"I've got to go." His gaze never leaving Vic, Gary edged toward the wide hall of the mud room that led to the outside—and freedom.

Makmoud once more turned his penetrating gaze to him. "I want you to take Victor to the room on the third floor."

"I need to—" Gary quelled under his intense scrutiny. He swallowed hard as those dark eyes burned into his and once more seared his soul like they had years before.

"You will take him upstairs." The leader's eyes narrowed. He took a step toward the FBI agent. "Musa, I want you to tie the other hostages together on the floor against the hearth."

The man Makmoud had called Musa wasted no time in securing Vic's hands behind his back. He hauled him upright and shoved him to Gary, who escorted him up the first set of stairs.

"Why'd you do it?" Vic's question cut into Gary's heart, his soul.

Gary marched him around the walkway to the stairway leading upward. "Do what?"

"Betray me."

They reached the top. Keeping one hand around Vic's arm, Gary pushed open the door to what appeared to be a master suite. He pushed his friend inside.

Vic stumbled. He swung around to face him. "Why'd you do it?"

Gary dragged over a stool to the middle of the room and pointed to it. "Sit."

"Not until you answer my question."

"You wouldn't understand."

"You're right. I don't. I trusted you, and you did the worst thing possible."

"I had no choice, all right?"

"He broke you, didn't he?"

Gary flinched. The buzzing flared as if to reprimand him for thinking about his captivity.

Vic eased onto the stool. "Don't think I missed what he said about breaking people. Or your reaction."

"You remember ten years ago?" Gary glowered at him. "How my team drew the short straw on that mission? It was Makmoud and his gang who ambushed us. Him and that brother of his. We all got shot up. They killed our comms guys."

"I remember."

"I took two bullets, one to the shoulder and one to the leg. When they nursed us back to health, the fun began." More images flashed across his mind.

His lying on the floor of the torture chamber.

The last shots he fired before he passed out.

Mary's farewell kiss before they deployed.

Makmoud kneeling beside him and showing him a photo of Mary's painting they'd hung above the fireplace in their house.

They sped up into a blur that faded. On the heels of that came the headache that always joined the buzzing.

"Makmoud set to work breaking us. The torture was awful. One by one, the other guys broke. I guess he thought they were weak because he executed each of them. I lasted eight weeks."

"Everyone breaks. We all know that."

"And then..." The headache strengthened. He winced and rubbed his temples. "I don't remember what happened. Or I can't remember."

He paced and clenched his head between his hands. "There's this…buzzing, like a swarm of bees. It shows up each time I try to remember or when…when he wants me to do something. And…this headache."

He wagged his head as if the motion would disperse it. "For a while I couldn't even remember who Makmoud was. And I can only remember the name of my handler when I'm—"

He flinched as the buzzing nearly deafened him.

Vic's low voice finally broke through the noise. "You didn't have to do this. People could die you know. Deborah could. And her—"

"*Deborah* was the one who started this mess."

"Don't you blame her—"

"For what? For this unfortunate position I'm in?" Gary stopped and bent, his hands on his knees, their noses inches apart. "If she'd backed off, laid off her mission, then you and I wouldn't be sitting here now. But no. She had to keep looking, didn't she? Had to keep pressing the issue—"

"Because you're Murdock." Vic's eyes widened. "You're the one who killed Nasser al-Saad. And several others."

Gary straightened. His hands clenched. "I had to."

Vic quirked an eyebrow at him.

"Don't you get it? One thing you don't know about Makmoud is that he is very, very good at what he does. They'd call me with a phrase." As if to agree, the buzzing rose to a crescendo. He grasped his head with his hands. "I hate this! That…that phrase triggered a name and a number I was to call to get my assignment. I'd carry that out. Then that information would disappear. Poof!"

Gary moved his hands to simulate a small explosion. He shook his head. As if thrown into a corner, the buzzing receded. "Then I'd get fifty grand. You know my little gambling addiction? He fed that. At least those payments got Mary off my back."

Vic glared at him. His jaw flexed. "I—I can't believe you. You sold out completely, didn't you?"

"I told you I didn't have a choice."

"Don't you realize what you've done? You've sentenced a woman and her four children to death. And what about this team you put together?

You betrayed us in the deepest way possible. Betrayed *me*, your best friend. I trusted you completely."

Gary's face flushed with anger. His hands balled into fists. "Yeah? Well, trust is highly overrated my friend. Like I said, I had no choice."

"You always have a choice. What is Mary going to think when all of this comes to light?"

His fist flashed out and caught Vic across the face.

His former best friend tumbled from the stool. He landed heavily on his side. A groan escaped him. He struggled to sit up.

"You'd like to think that. You weren't in my shoes. You never were. You didn't suffer like I did and still do!" He jabbed his toe into Vic's solar plexus.

His friend moaned and crumpled to the ground.

"You didn't hear three comrades slowly die. Their screams, their pleas for mercy. You didn't suffer from malnutrition and lack of hygiene and sleep. And they knew everything about me. They were even in my house!" He kicked him in the side.

The air whooshed out of Vic's lungs.

"And you didn't get pictures from your handler showing scenes of your family, didn't get the messages like I did threatening to kill them if I didn't obey. Don't you *dare* preach to me like I had a choice in the matter!" He reared back for a final, punishing kick.

"Enough." Makmoud's voice cut into Gary's rant like a samurai sword.

Gary whipped around. His handler stood in the doorway, his hands hooked in his belt, a smirk on his face as he observed the meltdown of a friendship. Something in his dark eyes made Gary swallow hard. Chest heaving, he backed away from Vic.

The accusation in his friend's eyes said it all.

Their friendship of fifteen years had crumbled in the span of an hour.

"What time is your flight, Gary?"

He broke eye contact at Makmoud's question.

"Red eye. Ten o'clock." Pain in his hand made him glance downward. His knuckles swelled from where he'd hit Vic.

"Then I suggest that you be on your way to Phoenix. Have yourself a nice supper at the airport and relax before you return to your family. Shadow Box and Deborah? We'll take care of them."

Gary cast another glance at Vic, who remained on the floor, his struggles now weaker.

"Go on," Makmoud urged. "No one will be any the wiser."

Finally, Gary turned away.

Vic was right.

He'd betrayed his best friend in the worst way More than that. He'd sentenced his friend to die alongside the comrades who'd also trusted him.

Anguish filled his heart and bled into his soul.

Gary fled downstairs, out the back door, and to the Commander. He'd take it to the airport and retrieve his own car.

Then he'd set about rearranging his life in an attempt to forget the treachery he'd committed.

"Get up, Victor Chavez."

Makmoud's low voice breached the pain blazing through Victor.

Finally, he regained his wind enough to push himself to a sitting position. His abs protested. He got a foot under himself. A wince coursed through him as he stretched his jaw and rotated his shoulder. The pain receded in both, and he eased onto the stool.

In front of him, Makmoud eyed him and chattered into his phone in Farsi.

Victor thought he heard Gary's name mixed into the foreign language, but he couldn't be sure.

Makmoud lowered his phone and slid it into an outside pocket of his desert camouflage fatigue pants.

"Now that my little conversation is finished, my apologies." He shut the door, sealing Victor from any chance at escape. "You had quite a setup here, didn't you? You thought you were safe. But you forgot about what the Greeks called the Trojan horse, yes?"

"I'm not sure I follow."

Jennifer Haynie

Hands behind his back, Makmoud began circling Victor like a professor lecturing his class. "Tell me something. Did you ever wonder how Liza Murphy escaped so easily?"

"I figured she outsmarted your dimwitted minions."

The blow across his head startled more than hurt him.

"Hey!"

"Fool." Makmoud's voice lowered. "You see, Gary had no idea of where you were based. Absolutely none. I must applaud you for keeping him from finding out. I knew I needed other methods. Other, better methods. Jibril and his comrade kidnapped Liza and took her to our safe house."

"North Charleston."

"Correct." Makmoud stopped in front of him and folded his arms across his chest. "Believe it or not, I did not give permission for her mistreatment, but it played right into my hands." He lifted his chin and smiled. "She got raped and beat up, and I played her savior. I fed her, protected her, and let her sleep. With the help of a heavy sedative, that is. And once she did? Then it was simply a matter of injecting a tracking device into her. You'll find it in her right calf muscle if you look."

He resumed his walk. "Of course, that won't matter soon, now will it? And once I'd completed that task? I let her go. I let her go because I knew your first instinct would be to reunite her with her sister."

Victor bit back his groan. He'd played exactly into Makmoud's hands.

"It's so very interesting that Gary chose you to lead this team. You, a washed-up former Secret Service agent. One who had been played for a fool for years, yes? By none other than the woman you loved."

Hot, boiling anger that would get him into trouble if he weren't careful rose in Victor's chest and worked its way to his neck. His hands balled into fists. "I loved her."

Makmoud paused behind him. "Oh, I know you did. Just as I loved Rachel long ago. You know, Victor, I taught her everything she knew. I learned about this little weakness she had. And then when we reconnected? I fed that addiction. It was never about love between us in those later years. She wanted something. I gave it to her in exchange for information. Until you proposed to spend the rest of your life with her."

Agony exploded in his kidney from Makmoud's fist. Victor moaned and sagged forward onto the floor. He gritted his teeth and panted to alleviate the pain. Slowly, he drew his leg up and climbed to one knee.

Makmoud stood near him, his feet shoulder width apart, his arms still folded across his chest.

The strength began rushing back to Victor.

The sneer crossed his foe's face. "You left me with no choice. I was going to have Maggie McCall one way or the other. So I took Rachel's sister to force her to do my will. And now? Susanna is my concubine."

"You..." Victor pushed off and charged him.

Makmoud batted him away with an open palm.

Off balance, Victor stumbled.

With one move, Makmoud swept his feet out from under him.

Victor hit the ground hard. Pain exploded in his skull as he rapped his head on the stool.

"Get up, you fool."

Gritting his teeth against the agony, Victor rose to his knees.

He collapsed onto his side.

"Yes, Gary was right in his tale that I broke him. I have to admire his tenacity since he was indeed the last one standing. Then, with him pliable, I rebuilt his psychological profile into someone I could use. Just as I'll do with all of you." Makmoud nudged him. "You see, when Deborah and her children arrive with the rest of your team, we'll execute her and leave her body. Your team and her children will disappear. Gary will claim he had no idea that you'd gone rogue."

He grabbed him by the collar of his shirt and his belt loop and dumped him onto the stool. "And when we reach our destination? We'll see exactly how tough everyone is as I break all of you, including Deborah's son. Jibril also said something about wanting Sana as his own. And Anna?"

Makmoud stepped to the door. "Perhaps I'll make her mine. Something to think about, yes? Enjoy your last few hours of freedom, Victor Chavez."

With that, he shut the door.

Victor groaned and hung his head. They were trapped with no way out. He could only watch time ran out for them.

36

Gary sped down I-17 toward Phoenix as if evil spirits pursued him. His head pounded. The buzzing had grown so loud that even the hard rock blaring from the Fusion's speakers didn't cover it. Images of Makmoud ripping Anna's T-shirt attacked him. Her tear-stained face morphed into Morgan's. Mary's voice from one night shortly after his rescue echoed in his ears before the buzzing drowned it out.

Then came a picture of Vic as he'd lain on the floor only an hour before. The look in his friend's eyes stung him over and over. Vic had trusted him with his career, his teammates, and his life.

And what had he done? Handed him over to the one man who'd already tried to kill him. Now, Makmoud would most likely finish the job he'd started over two years before.

I'm sorry, Vic. I had no choice.

Those words mocked him. He'd had a choice.

He could have ended it.

At the cost of his own life and that of his family.

Gary tasted bile at the thought.

The buzzing screamed at him.

"Go away! Leave me alone! I said I'm done."

Then, almost like a pop, it vanished, as did the experiences of the past couple of days. Only the headache remained, a nauseous reminder of...something.

Why was he speeding away from Flagstaff? He couldn't remember.

He needed a Coke to settle his stomach. That and some aspirin. Then he could head to Phoenix, check in for his flight, and return to Washington.

A sign for a rest area came into view.

Gary put on his blinker and slowed to take the exit. He pulled into a slot several feet from the main building. Three spaces closer, a brunette in a white suit and deep green top climbed from her car and slung her purse over her shoulder. He followed.

Once he arrived at the drink machines, he fished six quarters from his pocket.

One by one, he let them drop into the slot. They tinkled downward.

Suddenly, like a brick falling from a wall, a name came to him unbidden.

Ahmad Hidari, Makmoud's youngest brother and his primary handler all these years.

Gary froze.

He now knew something that could strike a blow at Makmoud. He had to call TL.

It was the best he could do to assuage his guilt.

Coke forgotten, Gary pushed through the doors and headed to his car to retrieve his phone.

Heels tapped on the sidewalk behind him as the woman hurried toward her vehicle. He slid over a little to let her pass.

"Special Agent Walton?" Her husky voice startled him.

Automatically, he slowed.

"A word with you, please." She wrapped her arm around his waist.

Something in her left hand poked him in his side.

A gun.

The nausea from his headache worsened.

Her right hand slid under his jacket and deftly removed his sidearm. In low, accented English, she murmured, "Continue to your car."

Suddenly, he realized the identity of his kidnapper. "Iman."

"You're rather bright. Makmoud said you would be. Unlock your car and put your hands on the roof." She jabbed the muzzle of her gun into his side. "Now."

Gary swallowed hard. He used his fob to open the doors.

She yanked his handcuffs from their holder. "Get in. Hands on the wheel."

Gary obeyed.

Iman secured his left wrist to it.

"Now open the trunk."

He did. His heart sank as he realized how she disabled the car's GPS unit. And forget his phones. He'd powered them down when he'd first arrived in Flagstaff.

Iman slipped into the passenger's seat. She kept her weapon pointed at him. "Drive."

"To where?"

"I will tell you. Get onto the interstate heading south. Take the next exit and turn right."

"Makmoud put you up to this, didn't he?"

"Shut up." Iman snatched his cell phones from where he'd placed them in the slot beneath the radio. She tossed them onto the backseat along with his gun.

Gary clamped his jaw shut.

Ten more minutes passed. An exit sign whizzed by. Two miles.

Suddenly, he realized her intentions. "I'm not going to say anything. Why would I?"

"Are we to believe that? Take this exit."

"Iman—"

"Do it!"

Gary hesitated, then turned on his blinker. His mind raced as he assessed ways to get out of his predicament. He could speed up, maybe catch the attention of a cop. No, he'd be dead. If he could get free of the cuffs, maybe he could fight her. He eased onto the ramp and stopped at the top.

"To the right." She gestured with her gun.

"Okay," he drawled.

Mary's face floated before his eyes. He could almost smell her lavender perfume. Suddenly, the urge to survive thrummed through his veins. The plan came to him with lightning speed.

He had to do it.

He had no choice.

The road led them into the desert.

"Turn left here," she ordered.

Gary did so, and they followed it for a minute.

He cranked the steering wheel hard to the right.

They careened from the blacktop onto the rough desert soil.

"What are you doing?" Iman's shout of surprise gave him a small amount of satisfaction.

"Saving my skin." He jerked the wheel to the left.

The car tipped onto its two right wheels as it began a slow skid. Gary pulled harder.

It flipped.

Pain exploded in his head, and he blacked out.

A whining sound reached him, followed by moans. Was that the wind? Or his own voice? Agony surged through his left arm. He opened his eyes. During the wreck, he must have gotten tossed around. Only having his left wrist cuffed to the wheel had kept him from getting thrown clear—at the cost of his arm. Sickness swelled within him when he noticed how his arm just above the wrist was bent almost at a right angle.

Gary tried to move it. The cuff popped open, meaning Iman hadn't secured it as well as she'd thought. His arm fell, sending shards of pain up to his shoulder. His vision darkened. He took a deep breath as it returned.

Where was Iman?

Cradling his injured arm against his chest, he turned onto his left side and peered out the shattered windshield.

She lay on the hard ground several feet from the car, one of her legs bent at an odd angle. Moans came from her as well.

Gary did a quick catalog of his body. His head hurt, but that wasn't surprising. He could wiggle the fingers on his right hand. And his legs seemed good too. If he could find one of his phones, he could call for help. Relief surged through him—until he saw her roll onto her side.

His blood froze as she used her elbows to crawl toward a black spot that he now realized was her gun.

"Where is it?" His gaze roamed around the interior of the car as he frantically searched for his own service weapon.

He peered through the shattered windshield. There it was, laying maybe twenty feet from the car. Adrenaline surged through his veins. With his injured arm tucked to his chest, he pulled himself to a crouch. He stumbled to his feet, only to fall to his knees.

Iman seemed to realize what he was doing. Her grunts reached him as she struggled toward her prize.

"C'mon, c'mon, c'mon!" he muttered. He sprang forward again, this time landing against his mangled arm. The pain surged through him as he reached for his weapon with his good hand. His fingers brushed the gun. They tightened around the grip, and he rolled to his knees.

He refocused on Iman.

She reached toward hers.

Gary thumbed off the safety.

A loud report echoed through the desert.

A red spot appeared between her eyes.

Something slammed into Gary's chest.

Oh, no. They'd fired simultaneously at each other.

Pain radiated outward as fast as the blood spreading across his white shirt. The gun dropped from his fingers.

He groaned and toppled onto his side.

The strength began draining from him as surely as his lifeblood did.

"Mary, I'm…" He began coughing. Something dribbled down his chin. "I'm…sorry."

The coughing turned to gasping. He rolled onto his back.

"I love you." Mary's sweet voice filled his ears.

He opened his eyes. She leaned over him and touched his forehead.

"I…I love you too." His heart pounded. It slowed. He raised his arms and reached for her.

They flopped to the ground as blackness descended.

The world swam before Deborah's eyes, thanks to the painkillers Diana had administered from the FBI medic's bag. Shadow Box's doctor had wrapped cold packs around her right knee to ease the swelling. From where she sat on the porch of the small adobe house, the sun bathed her in its golden light as it rapidly set. Within half an hour, darkness would enfold the land.

It already threatened to envelop her heart.

Somewhere to the southwest, Anna, Liza, Victor, and part of his team remained in chains.

As for her, being surrounded by members of the FBI's elite Hostage Rescue Team, as well as TL and the remaining members of Shadow Box, did nothing to comfort her.

She leaned her head against the warm adobe and listened through the open door and windows as Butch debated their strategy with TL.

"At least let us help you," her handler said.

"Sir, with all due respect, no can do. We know Last Chance Ranch the best. We know its strengths and weaknesses." Butch cleared his throat. "And we know how to get in there without being discovered."

Something thumped onto a table. "If you guys go in there, you'll be dead before you even get close to the house. We saw at least eight tangos during our escape, but I wouldn't be surprised if there's more since Fi and Skylar got ambushed out on the trails."

Deborah glanced over to where Shelly sat on top of a barrel, her legs aimlessly thumping against the wood as she stared at the laptop the FBI had brought. Her fingers tapped on the keyboard.

Sana curled up on the porch's thick wall and leaned against a post.

From inside came a plaintive question from Marie and Diana's calm response.

She was sure Suleiman remained prone on the roof, his eye pressed to the scope of the FBI's sniper rifle he'd grabbed as soon as the HRT had arrived.

Paper rattled as Butch said, "Now, I've got a plan, but if we don't get a move on it, we have a snowball's chance in Hades of accomplishing it."

"All right, all right. I hear you."

"Good." Butch strode onto the porch. "Sana, Shelly, I need you two. Diana's waiting on us. Hey, Suleiman, let the HRT guy take over. Meet us at the Suburban."

The three Shadow Box women followed Butch to the SUV.

Scrabbling emanated from on top of the roof. A moment later, Suleiman swung down from where he'd taken up his observational position. The rifle hung from his shoulder. With a faint nod in Deborah's direction, he joined his comrades at the hood of the Suburban.

Deborah tried to rise. Her knee protested the action, so she settled for crawling to the porch steps.

At the SUV, Butch scribbled something on his notepad. Suleiman pointed at it. They talked some more.

Deborah rested her head against the railing and closed her eyes. The world spun. She clung to the wood.

Lord, I'm scared. I need peace. Please.

"Deb." Butch's voice reached her.

How much time had passed?

A goodly amount since barely any light remained.

She struggled to rise. "What is it?"

"Don't get up." He nudged her back to a sitting position. "We're headed out. The feds have given us the ammo we need. And the camo too."

He nodded toward where all of his team now wore camouflage of blacks, grays, and whites. They helped each other darken their faces. Camo paint and a black do-rag covered his head. "I promise we're going to get them back."

Swallowing hard, she nodded. She knew it was pointless to tell them to be careful. "What can I do to help?"

"Pray for us." A tight smile crossed his face and disappeared.

She nodded.

"Uncle Butch! Don't go!" DJ tore from the house and ran to Butch. He flung his arms around his waist.

"Hey, hey, easy there, little brother." Butch crouched and put his hands on the boy's shoulders. "Listen to me, okay? I need your help too. Help Mr. TL look after your mom and sisters, okay?"

Tears streamed down DJ's face.

Butch tightened his grip. "Can you do that for me? That way, I can get your sister and aunt and my team back."

Sobs heaved at her son's shoulders.

"Can I count on you? Then, when I return, we can get that tractor running. How about that?"

Finally, DJ nodded.

"Good man."

Finally, Deborah grasped the rough wood of the railing hauled herself to her feet. She pulled her son to him.

He trembled.

Deborah tightened her grip on his arms. "Godspeed, Butch."

"Thanks." Butch tipped an imaginary hat. "We'll give the all clear by six tomorrow morning. If not, TL knows what to do."

Deborah refused to dwell on the "if not." She bit her lip as she watched them pile into the Suburban. The big engine cranked, and it rumbled down the road in a cloud of dust. She stood there and watched until she couldn't see it anymore.

With a great cry, DJ tore from her arms and bolted inside.

A door slammed.

TL joined her on the porch. "You want me to talk with him?"

Deborah shook her head. "Leave him be."

She limped inside and found Marie and Gracie curled up asleep on the couch like two lost puppies. Someone had draped a blanket over them. "Could you...could you take care of the girls for a bit? I need to be alone."

"Will do. I'll keep an eye on DJ as well."

Deborah smiled her thanks and retreated to a bedroom. Once inside, she slowly knelt by the bed and winced as her injured knee protested. She rested her elbows on the mattress. Her breath jerked a little as her spirit calmed.

Then she waded into war and prayed.

37

As night darkened the master bedroom, Victor's spirits sank. The latest set of cable ties had long since drained sensation from his hands. His stomach rumbled. His mouth felt dry with a thirst no desperate sips of water from the bathroom faucet could slake.

Time was running out for him and the others.

But maybe not for Deborah.

As his deputy, Butch had understood the mission. Protect Deborah at all costs, even that of losing his teammates and her children. He knew Butch would carry out those orders. And their own fates? It didn't take a genius to figure out that Makmoud would break him, Fiona, and Skylar. His ex-best friend was right. Anyone would cave given the right conditions and amount of time. And Anna and Liza? They would suffer too as the playthings for Makmoud's merry band of men.

Unless...

Lord, I know You and I have just started talking. Is there any way You could pull out a miracle?

He nearly laughed at that.

Night continued its onward march.

His periodic glances at the clock as well as the checks by the guard told him so. Finally, two turned over to three. In the distance, low whumps reached him that gradually increased until they pounded at the house.

Victor risked rising and stepping to the window.

Three darkened shapes landed in front of the house.

Blackhawk helicopters, if his ears were correct.

Their ride to bondage had arrived.

He hung his head, wincing as muscles, stiff from sitting so long, stretched.

Faint scratching from the balcony reached him.

A shadowy form crested the railing and dropped onto the floor. It raised hands toward the lock of the sliding glass door. Within seconds, it slipped through and pulled away a scarf.

"Sana!" Victor's whisper bled with relief. "Am I ever glad to see you!"

"Ditto on that." She scrambled over to him. "Are you okay?"

She reached behind him and clipped the cable tie.

"Now that you're here." He sighed when his hands came free.

Footsteps approached the door. The guard.

"Hide!" he hissed.

She darted into the shadows in the corner behind the door.

Victor sat on the stool and crossed his wrists behind him like he remained tied.

The guard glared at him for a moment before shutting the door.

"That was close," Sana murmured when she returned to his side. "I've got a comms unit for you."

By now, the pins and needles surged through his hands as blood flow returned. "You'll have to put it on. My hands are useless right now."

She looped it around his head and adjusted the boom so the microphone hung in front of his mouth. The small unit went into his pocket.

"Butch?" he murmured as he stood to stretch.

"Right here, boss. Man, it's good to hear your voice."

"We've got more company."

"Yeah, I saw them. Looks like just the pilots because they're staying put. Sana knows what to do."

"Tell me, Sana."

She leaned into him and whispered their plan into his ear.

Victor nodded. They had no choice but to go with it.

He resumed his seat and waited a few more precious minutes for his hands to regain feeling.

Sana slipped into the bathroom to hide.

Softly, he called, "Guard!"

The door flew open, and the man glared at him. "What do you need?"

"To use the restroom. Please." Victor squirmed. "It's urgent."

The guard stared at him as if considering his words. Then he muttered in Arabic, "Little men with little bladders."

He came all the way inside and approached Victor to undo his bonds. Victor tensed.

When the guard came within striking range, he bolted upward and slammed his forehead into the man's nose.

The guard moaned and fell backward.

Sana rushed forward. She caught his inert form and staggered under his weight.

"Get that door closed," Victor whispered as he searched him.

A rifle, pistol, and knife gave him great comfort at the moment.

"Amir?" Another guard must have heard the noise.

Victor muttered under his breath.

"Amir, are you all right?" The voice in Arabic drifted upward from the second floor landing.

"Fine, fine," Victor called, desperately hoping his Arabic matched that of his guard.

A shout answered him.

Victor shot onto the landing and unleashed a volley of bullets. "Get this party started. Sana! Assist!"

Wood splintered around him as automatic weapons chirred.

Sana crouched as she reached into her pocket. She popped up and hurled a throwing star in the direction of the gunfire.

Someone cried out, and it ceased.

Victor bolted down the steps. He slammed into the wall of the music room and hit the smooth wood of the walkway's floor.

Bullets flew overhead.

Glass shattered.

Victor covered his head as shards fell. Two large pieces impaled themselves in his back. He groaned.

More screams reached him as Sana unleashed several more shurikens. Outside, gunfire began.

"I've got you." Sana pulled out the glass spikes. She tossed them away.

"Get down there. I've got you covered." Victor crawled to the railing.

A female voice cried out.

Victor peered into the great room.

A tall, male silhouette dragged a shorter shape with long hair away from the den.

"Sana!"

"I see them. Cover me."

Sana leaped onto the railing. With a war cry, she jumped into the empty space of the great room. She snagged the chandelier, rode it outward, and disappeared somewhere toward the kitchen.

Shouts to pursue her followed.

At a crouch, Victor ran around the walkway. He dove onto his stomach. When no bullets followed, he darted down the stairs. He threw the deadbolt on the front door to prevent reinforcements.

Anna screamed and struggled against a man who had to be Makmoud.

"Anna!" Victor drew his sidearm. "Let her go, Makmoud. It's over."

"Is it?"

Victor registered the shape of a gun against Anna's head. He froze.

"You put down your weapon now, Victor. Or she dies."

Anna's sobs reached him.

Victor wavered.

"Do it!"

Out of the corner of his eye, Victor noticed a dark form scuttling toward the den. Sana. She pointed toward Makmoud.

"Okay." Victor lowered his gun.

That made his foe relax in the slightest. "Excellent. Put it on the floor."

Victor did so and raised his hands.

Makmoud pulled the muzzle away from Anna's head.

Like a spring, Sana shot forward and slammed into him.

Off balance, Makmoud staggered.

Anna yanked away.

Victor wasted no time. He grabbed her and rolled with her.

She shrieked.

"It's me. C'mon." He hauled her to her feet and pulled her down the short hallway that led toward the study and laundry room. They huddled together against the washer and dryer.

Victor swallowed hard. They had so way to defend themselves since his gun rested on the floor in the great room. "Butch, sit rep. I'm in the laundry room with Anna."

"Right outside. Send her through the window."

Victor leaped up. He yanked open the window across from the dryer. "Anna, go."

She hesitated.

"Go!" He shoved her through the opening and wormed his way into the great room.

Sana screeched.

"I have one of your ladies, Victor. Give it up."

In the dim light, Victor noticed how Makmoud had wrapped his arm around Sana's chest and lifted her.

She wheezed and struggled against him. "Let...me...go."

Makmoud laughed.

"Let her go, Makmoud." Suleiman's angry voice reached Victor from above.

He craned his head and noticed the muzzle of a sniper rifle peeking through the banisters. The laser formed a dot on Makmoud's head.

The leader yanked on Sana, bringing her effectively into the line of fire. She moaned.

"Ibrahim, my brother, I heard you'd joined this team. You are a fool!"

"Let her go, Makmoud! Or I'll kill you."

"Suleiman, you don't have a clear shot," Victor murmured into the comms unit.

Only the sniper's heavy breathing answered.

"Don't. It's not worth risking killing Sana." Victor turned his gaze toward where the petite gymnast struggled.

Her hand snaked into a cargo pocket. She withdrew another shuriken. She slammed it into Makmoud's shoulder.

The man moaned.

As she fell away, Makmoud dove into the den.

The sniper bullet slammed into the stone of the fireplace and embedded itself in the wood floor.

Victor scrambled toward Sana as another window shattered at the front.

Suddenly, the roar of the helicopters filled the air. Bullets raked the front of the house.

Victor huddled with Sana and rolled with her until they rested against the hearth. He shoved her underneath him.

Silence fell.

A grunt reached him, someone sounding like Skylar.

Victor sat up.

In front of him, three sooty forms tied together emerged from the dormant fireplace.

"Skylar?" Victor blinked. "Fi?"

"We're here." A groan from Fiona reached him. "When they started shooting, Skylar made us get into the fireplace to minimize the angles of fire."

A smile tugged at Victor's lips. Then laughter emerged as if a relief valve had been triggered.

Slowly, he gathered them into a hug and held on for the longest time.

38

"Here. Drink this." Victor eased down onto the wooden porch of the Women's Building and leaned against the stone wall.

Anna huddled under a blanket against it.

He placed a steaming mug of hot chocolate in her hands.

She offered a weak smile and took a sip. The liquid trembled.

"You did great in there."

"I was so scared." She laid her head on his shoulder.

"I know. I was too."

"You were?" Anna pulled back and looked at him.

"Spitless."

A grin appeared, then a small giggle.

Liza stepped through door. "It looks like a fraternity party gone wild in the Big House."

"With bullet holes even." Victor rose and winced as his injuries protested.

"Diana said Fiona's resting. She also said to see her about those gashes on your back and everything else."

"I will. As soon as I check on Sana," he added. "Speaking of which, where is she?"

Liza shrugged as she settled next to her niece.

Victor wandered toward the Men's Building.

In front of the terrace, Butch and Skylar guarded the four surviving prisoners. Another four were dead inside, and the remaining eight had escaped, including Makmoud and Jibril. The Colonel stood nearby, his tail erect and his gaze intent on the four men as if he recalled his days as a military working dog. Edgar sat beside him.

Victor bit back his sigh at having missed his chance to bag Makmoud. He cast a look at the Women's Building. Another smile crossed Anna's face as Liza talked to her. His frustration eased. Liza and Anna were safe, as were Skylar and Fiona. That was all that mattered now.

Victor turned his gaze toward the Men's Building.

Sana leaned against a post of the front porch with her legs stretched out. She cradled one of her cats in her arms. Suleiman leaned against the other post as he talked to her. Then he nudged her foot with his before rising.

Victor approached the front steps. "How's the lip?"

"I feel like I've been to the dentist." She tried a smile and failed.

Victor settled beside her and let his legs dangle off the front. "You did great, you know."

"I did?"

"I had my heart in my throat for a while. When you leaped off the railing…" He shuddered as he remembered waiting to her thud onto the floor of the great room before getting speared by the chandelier.

"I knew it'd hold me. I don't weigh that much."

"That, it did. Good thinking. Now I know why Gary chose you for the team." His mood turned downward at the mention of his friend.

"What happened to him?"

"I don't know."

"I have a question."

"Shoot."

"Why did Makmoud call Suleiman 'brother'?"

He considered that for a moment. "Lots of times, when people are of common faith, they can call each other 'brother' or 'sister,' right?"

"Yeah. I guess so." Doubt still clouded her voice. "It's weird that he called him Ibrahim too, but I know sometimes guys call each other by their last names. How do you think he knew us?"

"Gary." Again, his friend's betrayal stung him.

Engine noises reached them.

Victor raised his gaze when he noticed a caravan of black SUVs pulling to a stop behind the house. "Looks like we have company."

The doors flew open on all of the vehicles.

Victor searched for Deborah.

"Anna!" Her cry shot through the clear morning air.

"Mom!" Heedless of the blanket falling from her shoulders, the teenager rushed down the steps of the Women's Building and into her mother's arms.

Deborah held on tightly. Her gaze met Victor's.

The heat rushed to his cheeks. Mindful of the tenderness from his injuries, he climbed to his feet. Almost timidly, he approached the group.

The remaining three children swarmed around Liza and Anna.

Deborah turned to Victor.

Slowly, he drew her into a tight hug and held on for dear life. The rush of emotion stunned him, and he kissed her hair.

"Deb, we've got to get going." TL's voice reached him.

"No." Deborah stepped back but clung to Victor's hand. "We stay."

"We don't know where Gary is, and if he's—"

"I'm tired of running, TL." She didn't move. "We're staying here until you guys find him."

"What do you mean you can't find him?" Victor demanded.

"He never showed for his flight to Dulles." TL stared at the house. "We've got men searching for him and an APB out, but that's about it. I can't let you stay—"

"I'm staying. *We're* staying," Deborah added as the children gathered around her. "Vic and his team protected us. Please. I don't want to uproot anyone anymore."

Her handler sighed. "You're as stubborn as they come. Well, all right. But where would you sleep?"

"She can stay with us," Diana replied from where she stood on the porch of the Women's Building.

"Can we have a slumber party?" Marie asked.

That did it. Victor began chuckling. Then, as if to release the tension, everyone laughed.

Later that night, Victor stood in front of the studio's hearth. The low fire he'd built to chase away the evening chill glowed in the fireplace. He gazed at the mantel. At that point, no pictures save for one of Rachel sat on the dark wood. The remainder rested in a box, ready to ship to her parents as soon as he could make it into town.

With a smile, he bent and picked up a picture of Deborah and the kids. He placed it on the mantel. Other ones of the Shadow Box team and their charges joined it.

"Swapping out?" Deborah's soft voice reached him.

Without a word, he crossed the studio and drew her into his arms. Tears pricked his eyes when he realized how close he'd come to losing her. "I figured it was time."

She hugged him tightly.

He winced as her hands brushed the stitches Diana had put into his back that morning. "What's going on inside of you?"

"Too many thoughts."

"Try me."

She pulled back. Tears pooled in her eyes. "The Marshals just showed up."

Victor sucked in a breath. "What?"

"TL called the president, who then called the Marshals. They're..." She cast a look toward the Big House.

Now, in the gaps between the Laundry Building and the Women's Building, he noticed the sleek black shape of an SUV. His heart tightened. "But you said—"

"It doesn't matter what I said. Or what TL does. They took over. We have to leave." She wrapped her arms around him. Her voice trembled. "I...I don't want to go. I'm afraid—"

"Deb!" TL's voice reached her.

"Please. Hold me," she whispered.

He did until TL finally knocked on the door.

"Deb, I'm sorry. They're ready for you."

Finally, Deborah stepped back. With tears in her eyes, she touched his lips. "I love you, Victor. I truly do."

Then she slipped out the door and out of his life.

EPILOGUE

Early October 2014

Quiet filled the box canyon surrounding Last Chance Ranch, broken only by the sound of hammering coming from the horse barn as Victor drove in a nail of the new frame for the barn door. As he stepped back and surveyed his work, his breath escaped in a vapor. He shivered.

The predicted cold front had arrived, bringing with it the possibility of the first snowfall in the long-range forecast. Skiers in the area rejoiced.

He didn't.

It only signaled the changes that had turned his life on its head over the past several months.

Shadow Box? Disbanded.

Deborah? Gone.

His pride? Tattered.

He shrugged into a fleece and picked up another nail. He tapped it in and began hammering. The blows echoed into the stillness as surely as the words from the president had destroyed his livelihood and team.

"Victor, I'm sorry," President Badin had told him that blistering hot July afternoon when he'd visited the White House. "I'm under enough fire regarding appointing a traitor to put together the team. I've got no choice but to disband it."

At least Victor had negotiated pay and benefits until the end of September.

The unity the Shadow Box team had worked so hard to build crumbled over the summer. It started with minor squabbling.

Fiona complained about Shelly's and Sana's messiness, not to mention their cats. Skylar whined when Victor wouldn't let him run any scams in town. Then Suleiman approached Victor and confessed that he'd heard embarrassing noises coming from Skylar's room at night. It'd taken only a little connecting of the dots for Victor to realize that Fiona and Skylar had become romantically involved. Victor tried to call them on it. That ended with Skylar and Fiona seeking the greener, glitzier pastures of Las Vegas. They'd left the day before with scarcely a goodbye.

Maybe that was for the best.

Peace and quiet reigned at the ranch, almost too much so.

Victor paused, savoring the breeze as it whispered through the needles of the ponderosa pines between the outbuildings and the riding ring.

"I've received an offer to practice in Phoenix," Diana had confessed the morning before. She barely met his gaze. "I can feel the depression coming back, and maybe all of that sun will help me. I start after the first of the year."

Shelly had news of her own that night. "I got a job in Phoenix with a defense contractor. I'm sorry, Vic, but I hate the way the profs here are treating me."

He couldn't argue with her, but in his mind, it marked his failure as a leader.

"What's happening to us?" Sana's sad voice from later that evening echoed in his mind.

Only Suleiman and Butch remained unruffled by the events of the preceding months.

Suleiman had enrolled as a full-time student at the community college as he began seeking his GED. He waited tables to earn money.

Butch seemed to have borne the changes with an ease Victor envied.

"Hey, boss, I'm headed to Phoenix today," he'd said that morning as he finished a breakfast of bacon and eggs. "Got to pick up some stuff for the grand opening on Wednesday, you know."

"How are we going to make it, Butch?" Victor asked as the two men walked outside.

Butch stopped at his pickup truck. He smiled as he stuffed his baseball cap with the bill backwards over his bald head. "Don't worry, boss. God always works in base hits."

He hoped so, since he worried about how his twenty hours a week as a sheriff's deputy would cover the bills.

"I'm learning about 'give us this day our daily bread'," he'd told Deborah during a Skype session a few days before.

She'd laughed and drawled, "Honey, I learned about that a long time ago."

Deborah.

Sadness ripped at Victor's heart. The Marshals had become his least favorite government agency thanks to the way they'd ripped her away the day of the rescue. Deborah's too, it'd seemed.

And then? He swallowed hard as he remembered.

"They found Gary's remains in the desert," TL Jones had told him the day Deborah finally returned to North Carolina two weeks after the Marshals had whisked her away. "Someone saw vultures circling overhead and flying down, so they investigated and found two badly decomposed bodies. They called the sheriff. The bodies were a man and a woman. Seems the woman had kidnapped him because Forensics found a handcuff on the steering wheel and with only her prints on it. She was dead from a head shot. She got Gary through the heart. Mary's devastated."

Butch had gently pried the telephone from his paralyzed hand.

Phone calls, texts, e-mail, and Skype kept him connected with Deborah, but he'd found it a poor substitute for having the living, breathing Deborah with him. Now, he missed her so much that he considered starting over for a fourth time, this time back in North Carolina.

"Let's pray about it," Deborah had suggested one night when they'd talked on the phone.

Pray.

Oh, he'd been praying.

A lot.

A whole lot.

For provision.

For peace about Gary's betrayal and losing him.

For peace at the ranch.

For his future with Deborah.

He'd come to realize how needy he was. That drove him to his knees every night. God had grown him so much that he felt like he had growing pains.

Gravel crunched, drawing him back to the present and making him realize he'd been staring at the frame for the past ten minutes and not moving. So much for finishing the doors when he hadn't even installed the tracks for them.

The rumble of the V-8 made him glance up. He caught a flash of silver between the trees.

Butch had returned from Phoenix.

Victor resumed his work.

He eyed the frame. Finished. He'd do the tracks tomorrow.

"Victor." The familiar voice had to be from his mind.

Victor raised his gaze.

Deborah stood there.

The hammer thudded onto his foot. He barely felt the pain as he blinked in surprise. Finally, his voice worked. "Deborah!"

She ran into his arms.

Laughing, crying, he swung her around. "You're...you're here!"

"That's why I went to Phoenix, boss." Butch, his baseball cap still on backwards, grinned.

Victor laughed. "You stinker."

"And I got it all on tape." He held up his phone. "For when you get married. I'll leave you two lovebirds be for a bit. Ma'am."

He tipped an imaginary hat toward Deborah.

"Butch, thanks." Deborah refused to release her hold on Victor.

"Always my pleasure." With that, he strolled whistling toward the Men's Building.

Victor turned back to Deborah. Suddenly, he realized she wore the very same outfit she'd received for her birthday, except that she wore the emerald instead of the silver and turquoise necklace. He skimmed his fingers down her face. "I feel like I'm living a dream."

"I'm no dream." Deborah took his arm and drew him into the barn. "I'm no dream, beloved."

He wrapped her in his arms and kissed her. Yep, he held the living, breathing Deborah in his arms. "What made you come?"

He settled with her on a hay bale.

"I couldn't stay away." A smile crossed her face. "You can thank Butch. Do you remember when he went to North Carolina to finish the sale of his shop?"

"I do."

"He spent Labor Day weekend with us. Honestly, at that point, I'd been struggling so much about what to do. I missed you terribly. So did the kids. Well, you know that."

"Anna hates high school."

She sighed. "Still. But that's another story for later. Marie kept asking when she could go and ride your horses at the ranch. So did Gracie. And DJ said he missed hanging out with Uncle Butch."

Victor smiled.

She ran her fingers along the top of his hand.

Rational thought began disintegrating.

"Butch told me to call a spade a spade. He reminded me that God had both you and me in the palm of His hand and that it was high time I stopped dancing around the subject of whether or not I could commit to you."

Victor smiled. He brushed back a strand of hair that had fallen from her braid. He kissed her forehead. "There were times when I wondered if I should break it off."

"I know." She leaned into him. "I couldn't, and I felt so selfish. It's almost like I was refusing to give myself permission to be someone other than a mom. Butch called me on that."

"Yeah, he's been good at keeping me honest too."

"That's when he offered to pick me up in Phoenix and surprise you."

"I'm very glad he did." Victor enfolded her in his embrace.

"I don't know where this is going to lead, but I know I want to marry you, and—" Her hand shot to her mouth.

"What?"

"I so stink at this dating thing. I think that was your line."

He laughed. "You keep stealing my lines."

"I do. I love you, Victor Chavez, and I want to spend the rest of my life with you."

"I think you did it again." He kissed her. "But, if you're willing to take it one day at a time, then I'm willing."

She smiled. "Me too. One day at a time. That's all I can ask for."

Acknowledgements

Putting together a novel is never a solitary effort, and Operation Shadow Box was no exception. I struggled with this concept for the longest time. A big thank you first goes out to God for the gift of writing he gave me. Thanks go to my husband, Steve Haynie, as well for his encouragement as I wrestled with the concept for the Shadow Box team. Thanks to for my cover designer, Dafeenah Jameel, of Indie Designz. Her artwork has now graced the covers of three of my books, and I hope to make that many more. Also, I thank the ladies of my writers critique group who offered many comments as I brought excerpts forward: Katharine Parrish, Kim Smith, Catherine Painter, and Alice Wisler all heart bits and pieces years ago as I was drafting it. Finally, many thanks to my beta readers who helped shape the novel to what it is: Cathy Berger, Melba Hanson, Carey Shook, and Marion York. In addition to my husband, all of you have made my work the best it can be.

Made in the USA
Columbia, SC
19 December 2017